I0650278

Penumbra

A Journal of Weird Fiction and Criticism

No. 3 ☾ 2022

Edited by S. T. Joshi

"Slowly the penumbra, the shadow of a shadow, crept on over the bright surface . . ."--H. Rider Haggard, *King Solomon's Mines*

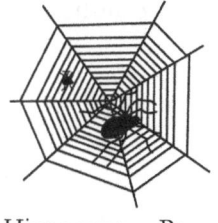

Hippocampus Press

New York

Published by Hippocampus Press
P.O. Box 641
New York, NY 10156
www.hippocampuspress.com

Cover art by George Cotronis.
Cover design by Daniel V. Sauer, dansauerdesign.com.
Hippocampus Press logo designed by Anastasia Damianakos.

PENUMBRA is published once a year, in Summer. Articles and letters should be sent to the editor, S. T. Joshi, % Hippocampus Press. Literary rights for articles will reside with PENUMBRA for one year after publication, whereupon they will revert to their respective authors.

ISBN 978-1-61498-389-7 (paperback)
ISBN 978-1-61498-390-3 (ebook)

Contents

Poetry

Notes on Contributors

אמת

Stephen Woodworth

By the time I got to Wenceslas Square, there was nothing left of the suicide but an oblong scorch mark, its charcoal corona outlining a vaguely human silhouette on the pavement in front of the National Museum.

Beside it stood Lieutenant Volopich of the StB—the *Státní bezpečnost* or State Security of the Czechoslovak Socialist Republic. Like most members of the local secret police, he dressed in plain-clothes, bundled in a fraying wool coat, scarf, and hat against the February chill. He was conferring with one of the Warsaw Pact soldiers charged with guarding the Square, who handed him what appeared to be a small 8mm movie camera. Volopich nodded as the young soldier murmured in his ear, then waved him off as he saw me approach.

"Good morning, Major Bykov!" He smiled his equivocal Czech grin, which could be either ingratiating or insolent.

"I see nothing good about it." I indicated the blackened area at our feet. Flecks of ash and spatters of carbonized fat, like the scrapings from a frying pan, still dotted the brickwork. "Where is the body?"

"It has been removed." Volopich knew I hadn't mastered his prickly Slavic tongue, and I suspected he disdained to speak Russian and thus feigned ignorance of it, so we conversed in German, a language for which we shared equal contempt.

"It must be cremated at once."

"Well! Lucky for us, the job's half done." Another smile dimpled his broad, flattish cheeks, but the gray-blue eyes remained sly, wary. I neither liked nor trusted him.

"Who was the man?" I demanded.

"A student by the name of Svoboda. Jakub." He indicated a large rectangular gray plastic container that had been cast off to one side, its cap off, its contents drained. "He poured gasoline on himself and flicked a cigarette lighter."

"Why?"

"Perhaps he was cold." He regarded me with maddening nonchalance. "After such a warm spring, a Prague winter can be very harsh."

If he'd meant the remark as a joke, I did not find it funny. My troops had been sent to this recalcitrant country because its president, Alexander Dubček, had allowed enemies of the revolution to undermine the authority of the communist state during his "Prague Spring" of 1968. We needed to suppress the insurgency before it infected every nation in the Warsaw Pact.

"We don't want any more Palachs," I reminded Volopich. "One martyr is already too many. And what the devil is *that?*"

I pointed past the burnt mark on the pavement to the wall beyond. It supported the stairs that ascended to the entrance of the National Museum, a palatial neo-Renaissance structure ornamented with the gaudy excess of a Greco-Roman portico and surmounted by gilded cupolas and statues of angels about to take flight. The stolid nineteenth-century brickwork had already been pocked and chipped by bullets when we'd fired upon the demonstrators last year, but now the wall bore a deliberate defacement. Snaking lines of what appeared to be black spray paint formed three strange glyphs on the stone:

אמת

"Is it the mark of some counter-revolutionary group?" I demanded.

"I don't know." For the first time, Volopich grew pensive. "It's Hebrew."

"What does it say?"

"I can't tell you. Hebrew is a language I never learned. Like Russian." He gave another infuriating smile, but I'd seen the disquiet of recognition in his expression.

"Did Svoboda paint this? Or did he have an accomplice?"

"No one we've interrogated knows. They were too busy watching him burn. But perhaps this can tell us." Volopich proffered the camera the soldier had given him. "We confiscated it from a tourist who happened to film the incident."

"Don't let it out of your sight." I indicated the graffito. "Who can tell us what this means?"

"Good question. After Hitler and Stalin, Jews in Prague are hard to come by."

I pulled a pen and notebook from my coat and carefully copied the Hebrew characters. "Get rid of it," I commanded. "Sandblast it, paint over it—do whatever you have to do. And don't let anyone photograph it."

Volopich nodded. "Of course, Major."

"Now let's get Svoboda's body before someone enshrines it."

Volopich barked orders at the nearby soldiers, then hastened to accompany me as I stalked back to my waiting staff car.

On 16 January of this year, at four o'clock in the afternoon and in the heart of Wenceslas Square, Jan Palach, a twenty-year-old Czech history student, doused his body with gasoline and immolated himself. Aflame, he ran across the plaza until he collapsed at the foot of the National Museum, an antemortem funeral pyre. Although several people rushed to tamp out the fire with their own coats, Palach died of his burns in a hospital a few days later.

The spectacle of his suicide made him a hero to the counter-revolutionaries mourning the collapse of the Prague Spring. Nearly three-quarters of a million people swarmed his funeral, filing past his coffin in the Old Town Square and demonstrating with banners in the streets, and so many protests erupted around the country that it would have been dangerous to suppress them all.

In a suicide note, copies of which he sent to several sympathizers and to the Union of Czechoslovak Writers, Palach demanded an end to censorship and to the publication of *Zprávy,* the official newspaper of the occupying Warsaw Pact armies. He entitled the letter "Torch No. 1" and intimated that an entire underground resistance movement of individuals was ready to immolate themselves in rebellion against communist and Soviet control. The threat of this clandestine organization seemed to be confirmed when, a month later, Jan Zajic, a fellow student who dubbed himself "Torch No.2," set fire to himself in the exact spot in Wenceslas Square where Palach had fallen.

And now Svoboda. Torch No.3.

The following morning Volopich and I scrutinized the 8mm film of the self-immolation, which we'd had developed the previous afternoon.

Moving in silent pantomime on the blank white wall of my office, Svoboda was nothing more than a nondescript blur of long-sleeved white shirt and black trousers. Although the 8mm film was in color, only the washed-out sepia of the faces in the crowd enlivened the dreary monochrome of the scene. Yet Svoboda stood out from the other pedestrians in the square, for despite the January cold, he was not wearing his coat.

He knew he would be far warmer soon enough.

Unaware of the coming spectacle, the photographer had not centered the image on Svoboda, who at one point walked out of the frame entirely. He did not come back into view until the photographer panned across the front of the National Museum while shooting a panoramic view of the square.

Unlike those who passed him with heads bent and eyes downcast, Svoboda glanced from side to side rapidly as he advanced to the approximate spot where Palach and Zajic had martyred themselves. He had a black coat draped over his arm that he cast aside, unveiling the gray plastic container he carried.

At this point he caught the attention of surrounding spectators.

As Svoboda uncapped the container and showered himself in fuel, the 8mm photographer trained the camera directly on him. Svoboda dropped the container and pulled a cigarette lighter from his pocket.

Realizing what he was about to do, a few spectators rushed forward to stop him, but instantly recoiled as a yellow-orange aura bloomed around him. The camera's poor focus turned Svoboda into a hazy firebird fluttering wings of light as he ran a few steps with arms outstretched, and for a moment it seemed as if he might actually take flight. But the halo of flame could not obscure the great dark yawn of his mouth as he screamed.

Svoboda was brave, but he still felt pain.

All we could hear now, however, was the clicking of the film's sprockets and the whir of the projector's fan. The smoke from Volopich's cigarette, billowing in the light of the projector's beam, added a ghastly third dimension to the image of the fire.

On the wall before us Svoboda pitched forward onto the cobblestones, floundering in agony. Two businessmen and a day laborer all took off their coats and tossed them over the body in order to smother the flames. The crowd closed around the dying man, obscuring the camera's view, and a moment later the Warsaw Pact soldier who'd given Volopich the camera stepped in front of the photographer and raised his hand to cover the lens.

The wall went white as the end of the celluloid spooled off the upper reel and slapped against the projector.

Volopich plumed more cigarette smoke as he shut off the machine. "You didn't see it, did you?"

"Run it again," I snapped.

"You didn't see it because it *wasn't there*."

"Run it again, damn you!"

Volopich shrugged, rewound the film, and threaded it back though the projector.

The scene played out again on the bare patch of office wall, but this time I kept my gaze trained not on Svoboda but on the wall of the National Museum in the background behind him.

It was bare. No cryptic Jewish runes.

To emphasize the point, Volopich risked melting the film by stopping the projector on a single frame.

"You see? Svoboda has already torched himself." He indicated the pyre of the man's body in the foreground, then pointed to the museum. "But no graffiti yet. That means Svoboda couldn't have painted it. Someone else must have taken advantage of the distraction to do it later, when no one was watching."

He flicked off the projector and turned on the office's overhead light.

I groaned and grabbed my olive-and-red cap and jacket off the coat rack. "It's worse than I feared. If Svoboda was not acting alone, then there really is a counter-revolutionary insurgency at work. If we do not stop it now, we could have Torch Numbers Four, Five—a hundred, a thousand."

"I wouldn't worry, Major. I'm sure this rebellion will burn itself out." Volopich was not smiling but had his lips pressed together, as if trying not to laugh.

I glared at him. "I hope you don't think that was funny."

"Not in the least." He stubbed his cigarette out in the ashtray on my desk. "I presume you'll want to go to the morgue now?"

"At once. We must make sure Svoboda's henchmen do not get their hands on his corpse." I straightened my uniform as we strode out the office door.

The Czechoslovak Communist Party made a grave error in handling the matter of Palach—Torch No. 1—and Moscow had sent me to correct it. Eager to maintain peace after the Warsaw Pact troops had quelled the Prague Spring and fearing further unrest, the weakling Dubček allowed the people to celebrate the suicidal student as a hero, and he inspired hunger strikes and other protests across the country.

Klement Gottwald, first president of the Czechoslovak Socialist Republic, would not have made such a blunder. He famously hanged his foreign minister Vlado Clementis, then had Clementis's image airbrushed out of official Communist Party historical photos.

Gottwald knew: you don't enshrine your enemies; you erase them.

Thanks to Dubček's incompetence, Jan Palach had become far more dangerous dead than alive, and we needed to eradicate his influence as quickly as possible. His grave in the Olšany Cemetery had become a pilgrimage site for would-be dissidents, so we'd already exhumed his ashes and removed the grave marker. But someone had foolishly permitted the sculptor Olbram Zoubek to make a death mask of Palach before the man's body was cremated, and we had yet to retrieve and destroy it. Such a potent symbol could incite further insurrection.

I was determined not to make the same mistake with Jakub Svoboda's body. We would cremate him and dispose of the remains before anyone could make a reliquary of them.

Volopich and I loitered for more than half an hour outside a small, low, nearly windowless building with a tile roof on the shore of the Vlatava River near the Charles Bridge. The door was still locked and pounding on it received no answer.

I glanced at my watch. "Where is he?"

Volopich gazed out over the river as if enjoying the view. "Maybe he is still at the office."

"I thought *this* was the office."

Volopich chuckled. "You obviously don't know the ways of the Czech. The 'office' is a café downtown."

"Lunch should have been over an hour ago!"

"Czechs feel no hurry to rush back to work, particularly when they think they're working for Russians." His eyes flicked toward someone behind me on the right. "But not to worry! Here he is now."

"Good, because I intend to give him a lesson in punctuality."

"A pity he speaks neither Russian nor German." Volopich raised his hands to calm me. "I shall make your displeasure known."

A squat little man with a thick mustache and a crown of frizzy brown hair waddled up to us. Far from berating the man, Volopich smiled broadly and shook his hand, and they exchanged pleasantries in incomprehensible Czech as though they were long-lost friends. Grinning, the coroner unlocked the morgue and motioned us inside with Slavic hospitality.

My first thought was that not many people must die in Prague, for the place only had a couple dozen storage compartments for the cadavers along two of the four walls in the main room. A single ceramic-topped autopsy table occupied the center of the room, traces of blood still in the gutters that ran around the edge of the tabletop.

Volopich made some sort of joke that caused both him and the coroner to laugh heartily. Perhaps I only imagined that their mirth was at my expense. Then Volopich asked a question, of which the only words I understood were "Jakub Svoboda."

The coroner nodded vigorously and opened a drawer. A stench of rotting meat assailed my nostrils. The coroner shook his head, closed the first drawer, and opened another. Perplexed, he closed that one as well and consulted some documents on a clipboard.

"Well?" I demanded.

Volopich queried the coroner, who babbled in evident annoyance, tapped the clipboard, and threw up his hands.

"He says he never got the body," Volopich summarized, no doubt leaving out much of the man's tirade.

I was livid. "I *ordered* you to keep possession of the body."

"And I conveyed your order to the troops who carried it away. Rest assured, I shall investigate the matter thoroughly and reprimand them for their carelessness. But do not fret: if corpses could revolt, the entire Eastern Bloc would have collapsed by now."

I opened my mouth to denounce his mockery but was interrupted by the clangor of a massive black telephone mounted on the wall. The coroner answered and exchanged unintelligible questions with the caller, then offered the receiver to Volopich.

Obviously surprised that the call should be for him, Volopich conferred rapidly with the unheard interlocutor on the line, his expression darkening. The only word he spoke that I recognized was *Zprávy*.

"I'm afraid your fears of an underground conspiracy were well founded, Major." He hung up the phone. "There's been an attack on the newspaper office—"

"I knew it!" I regarded Volopich and the Czech coroner with disgust. "Again you've allowed the counter-revolutionaries to wreak their havoc. I want you to find that body and get it back, no matter where it is or who has it. Do I make myself clear?"

For once Volopich looked chastened. "Yes, sir."

"Now I have to go and see what mess they've made of *Zprávy*."

The two Czechs murmured conspiratorially in their infernal gibberish as I stalked out of the morgue. I did not give them the satisfaction of a response.

The choice of *Zprávy* as a target for counter-revolutionary anarchy was not lost on me. In his "Torch No. 1" suicide letter, Jan Palach himself had demanded the cessation of the newspaper, which disseminated propaganda for the occupying Soviet forces after the suppression of the Prague Spring. Clearly, some of Palach's co-conspirators had realized their dead leader's objective.

The newsrooms of *Zprávy* had been established in offices adjacent to those of *Rudé právo*, the daily Prague paper of the KSČ, the Czechoslovak Communist Party. They were located in a block of brick buildings on Na Prikopi, one of Prague's main thoroughfares, and faced the Communist Party headquarters. The reporters for *Zprávy* could look out their square office windows at an enormous, billowing banner affixed to the façade of the opposite edifice, urging voters to *"Volte Komunisty 1,"* with a marquee below in Czech that avowed "Together We Build a Strong and Happy Republic."

The chaos outside the newspaper building as I arrived suggested the republic was neither strong nor happy. Red Army troops had cordoned off the street, pushing back the throng of Czech citizens who still massed outside the barricades to gawk in curiosity. Soldiers stood sentry outside the structure's entrance, their Kalashnikov rifles aimed at the door as if enemy forces might burst from inside at any moment.

Their commanding officer had to shout at them to hold their fire as army medics emerged bearing a stretcher. The victim they carried to a waiting ambulance was covered in a white sheet marred with a wet red stain on the right side.

The officer, a sergeant named Alexeyev, saluted me as I approached. "Who did this?" I demanded.

"We are still trying to determine that, sir." The question obviously discomfited him. "The accounts of witnesses are . . . conflicting. But they seem to agree there was only one assailant."

I flailed a hand toward the building in disbelief. "One man did *this?* Where is he now?"

Alexeyev swallowed hard. "We have troops combing the building, floor by floor. If he's still here, we'll get him."

"If?"

The sergeant averted his eyes. "Perhaps you should inspect the damage yourself, sir."

He barked orders at the sentries, who shouldered their rifles and saluted as we passed through into the vestibule. Other soldiers were positioned in the central hallway and side corridors of the ground floor, and Alexeyev alerted them to our presence to prevent the possibility of friendly fire. Although the building had a functioning elevator, Alexeyev thought it safer to take the stairs to avoid the possibility of an ambush.

The *Zprávy* offices occupied the whole of the fourth floor, yet as soon as we stepped out of the stairwell I could see that the entire place was a shambles. Glass partitions separated several large newsrooms, and all these interior windows had either fractured into spiderwebs of shards or shattered altogether. The cramped desks, each one barely big enough for a schoolboy, had all been overturned. Typewriters and Teletype machines had been hurled against the walls, and the heavy cathode ray tubes of televisions and computer monitors had splintered as if smashed by a giant fist. Pages of type-script and fanfold snakes of printout paper, crumpled and torn to shreds, blanketed the floor like new-fallen snow.

The black-and-white litter made the random splotches of crimson on the paper stand out in even starker contrast. For the vandal had demolished the *Zprávy* staff with the same ferocity with which he'd destroyed their equipment. Many of the victims had already been removed by the medics, their places marked by soggy red sheets of sodden paper.

But at least one still sprawled amidst the wreckage, the cuffs of his dress shirt rolled neatly to the elbow, his tie knotted and clipped, his collar buttoned. There was nothing above the collar, however, but a wrenched tangle of severed veins, tendons, and skin. A head with spiky, crewcut hair lay several feet distant, the jowly face open-mouthed and aghast, the eyes bulging.

I glared at Sergeant Alexeyev. "*One man* did this?"

His lips whitened as he pressed them together, reluctant to re-ply. "You'd best talk to her."

He pointed me toward a woman seated on a rolling swivel chair beside the door to a glassed-in alcove that jutted into the newsroom proper. It contained the office's massive facsimile machines, each one the size of a player piano and comprised of a metal control board with knobs and meters and a central metal cylinder to print the reproductions. Dressed in a knit sweater blouse and knee-length pencil skirt, the woman wept with her face in hands, her bouffant bob in disarray, a pair of horn-rim glasses swinging from a chain around her neck as she blotted her eyes with a handkerchief.

"Major Bykov, this is Hedvika Červenka, one of the reporters for *Zprávy*. She survived by hiding in the facsimile room here, but she witnessed the assault." Fortunately, Alexeyev spoke the local tongue, if somewhat haltingly, and he was able to interrogate Čer-venka on my behalf. He had difficulty translating, however, when she began sobbing out her story.

"She says the attacker was already here when she and the other staff members arrived for work this morning." He paused, straining to comprehend her rapid, anguished babble. "They saw the newsroom in disarray—and heard crashing from around there." He indicated the outside corner of the facsimile room. "Through the glass . . . they could see the vandal. Moving about . . . smashing things . . ."

"What did the man look like?" I asked.

Alexeyev relayed the question but appeared puzzled by her answer. "She couldn't tell. The man—he wore . . . some kind of suit." Alexeyev groped for words. "Like . . . armor. All a gray color. But he was big—nearly seven feet tall, with an enormous chest and thick arms and legs."

"Why didn't they report this intruder to the authorities?"

Alexeyev posed the query to the woman, which sent her into another bout of hysterics, gesticulating wildly as she described the scene.

"They tried." The sergeant stared at her intently, as if trying to read her lips. "She went to a phone . . . but before she could reach the police, the intruder began killing the men who'd come in with her. Ripped them apart. That's when she ran to hide in the facsimile room. Someone downstairs heard the screams and called for help." Alexeyev squinted as if unsure he'd understood her correctly, and evidently asked her to repeat what she'd told him. "Through the glass she watched as the attacker tore off one man's arm . . . and used it as a paint brush. To do this."

Alexeyev led me around the corner of the facsimile room toward the far wall of the newsroom. What I at first took to be an abstract mural before us was actually a hieroglyph drawn on the wall in swaths of smeared blood. Despite the crude rendering, I instantly recognized the characters:

$$\text{אמת}$$

Drips of crimson streaked down from each vertex of the unfamiliar letters. Below the graffito the arm of a man, wrenched free from its body, lay on the floor, still wrapped in a shroud of sleeve. A discarded stylus, it oozed its scarlet ink into a puddle on the shabby carpet.

I peered at the writing on the wall and seethed.

"Do you know what it means?" Alexeyev asked.

"No. But I will." I wheeled to face him. "Where did the attacker go? How did he escape?"

"A service entrance for the commissary in the rear. The door had been torn from its hinges. We think that may be how he first got into the building, in the early morning hours before dawn."

"And *no one* saw him?"

Alexeyev pressed his lips together again, as if debating whether to speak. "I was one of the first troops to arrive," he admitted. "We did a sweep of the ground floor, and I discovered the destroyed service door. Stepping out into the street beyond, I could see this . . . hulking gray figure lumbering away, like a giant gorilla made of cement. His feet scraped against the cobbles with the sound of mill-stones grinding.

"At that point I hadn't even heard a description of the attacker, yet I raised my rifle and shot at him anyway." He shook his head, eyes gazing into the distance. "I swear I hit him, too. I even saw the bullets blow puffs of dust from the shell of that . . . armor he wore. Whatever it was made him impervious: he kept moving as if the bullets were nothing but raindrops. I ran after him, but he turned onto an adjoining street and I lost sight of him before I could catch up."

"This 'armor,' as you call it. Was it military? Did it have insignia?"

Alexeyev shook his head. "I only saw it from behind. It was all gray, just as Hedvika Červenka said."

"This is an even greater threat than I imagined. Perhaps a new secret weapon from the West." I peered at the three enigmatic runes swabbed in red upon the wall. "Question the woman again. Find out if she can remember any more details about the attacker, no matter how small. And see if she knows anything about *this*." I indicated the graffito.

"Yes, sir."

Alexeyev saluted as I strode out of the *Zprávy* newsroom.

As I exited the building, whom should I find waiting for me on the street out front but Volopich, grinning as smugly as ever?

"Do you find something amusing about this slaughter, Lieutenant?" I bellowed.

"Not at all, Major." He tipped his hat in mock deference. "I merely thought you might be pleased to hear that I have found someone who can help translate those Hebrew symbols we discovered near Svoboda's corpse."

My heart quickened. "You have?"

"Indeed. And I think you'll be even more interested to learn who that person is." His smile widened. "Svoboda's grandmother."

Vladěna Svobodová, paternal grandmother of Jakub, resided in Josefov, the former Jewish ghetto of the city. At the heart of the Jewish quarter sat the absurdly named New Old Synagogue, so called because other "new" synagogues rose around it following its completion in A.D. 1270. From the outside, the two-story, dual-nave structure resembled a Spanish mission, with plain walls of brick and plaster punctuated by the arched eyes of Gothic windows, yet with a steep, peaked roof like that of a Swiss chalet. By some miracle it had survived centuries of pogroms against the Jews of Prague, to say nothing of the Nazi occupation, which was almost enough to make one believe in the divine intervention of a Semitic deity.

Volopich and I entered a town house on the street corner opposite the synagogue, its façade frilled with sculpted Art Nouveau flowers. We climbed three flights of narrow wooden stairs to reach the top floor where Vladěna Svobodová had her flat. A damp, earthy smell as of wet plaster wrinkled our noses as we ascended, and I wondered if melted snow had leaked through the roof.

Having reached the highest garret, we knocked on a lacquered wood door ornamented with a florid number 9. A small, stout woman with gauzy white hair and sagging cheeks opened the door. She wore a dark, shapeless dress akin to an artist's smock, with white buttons and baggy sleeves.

"Frau Svobodová?" I asked in German. As was the custom among Czech wives, she had added the feminine suffix "-ová" to her husband's surname "Svoboda" when she married.

"*Paní* Svobodová," she replied, substituting the Czech title for a woman. "Yes?"

Ever ingratiating with his countrymen, Volopich removed his hat for her, but continued the conversation in German for my benefit. "Pardon the intrusion, paní Svobodová. This is Major Bykov, and I am Lieutenant Volopich of the StB. We are investigating a murder and have need of your academic expertise. May we consult you?"

His unctuous sycophancy nauseated me, but it had the desired effect. Vladěna Svobodová smiled and opened the door wide for our entry. "Of course, gentlemen. Please, come in."

The old woman gave me a wry, top-to-toe look as I crossed the threshold, as if she shared the same secret joke that Volopich and all their Czech brethren smirked about.

We entered a rather cramped living room made even more claustrophobic by the crush of clutter and ornate Art Nouveau embellishments. Mismatched bookcases crammed with crumbling leather-bound volumes lined two sides of the chamber. Framed prints of the works of Czech artist Alphonse Mucha claimed what little wall space remained: luminous, pale women enshrined in bowers of stylized flowers, as if they were illustrations taken from the illuminated manuscript of some unknown, matriarchal version of the Bible.

The unpleasant mineral odor of silt grew stronger.

"Murder, you say!" Vladěna Svobodová shook her head. "I can't imagine how *I* can help you with that."

"We understand you are proficient in Hebrew," Volopich said.

"Yes. Goodness! Has someone been killing Jews again?"

I cut in before Volopich could make more idle chitchat. "On the contrary—this time it appears the Jews may have done the killing. Are you Jewish, paní Svoboda?"

She gave me a shrewd look. "I survived the war because I am either not a Jew or am too clever to admit that I am. In either case, I shall answer 'No.'"

"Then how is it you know the Hebrew tongue?"

Svobodová abruptly answered me in flawless Russian. "The same way I know *yours*, Major Bykov."

She bowed slightly and reverted to German. "The truth is, I had the dubious distinction of being appointed to help curate Herr Hitler's 'Museum of an Extinct Race.' He wanted us to preserve all the artifacts of Jewish culture here in Prague for the derision of future generations of Aryans, long after the Semitic extermination had been accomplished." She chuckled. "Now it seems it's his Master Race that needs the museum, no?"

Volopich pulled a piece of paper from the breast pocket of his coat and unfolded it. "We hoped you might translate these symbols for us."

She took the paper from him and regarded the writing—how shall I say?—*fondly*. "That is easy enough. It is the Hebrew word *emet:* truth. Or, as you might know it . . . *pravda*."

Svobodová passed the paper to me with an arch smile. She knew perfectly well that *Pravda* was also the name of the Communist Party's newspaper in the Soviet Union.

I wagged the paper at her like a shaming finger. "Do these symbols mean anything else to you?"

She shrugged. "Should they?"

"They were written near the spot where your grandson immolated himself," Volopich said.

Svobodová sighed. "Poor Jakub."

"*And* at a later murder scene."

"Really?" The old woman cocked her head. "How extraordinary!"

"We think these symbols are the emblem of a group of dangerous counter-revolutionaries. It would be better for you to tell us everything you know." I showed her the paper again. "Again I ask you—do they have any other meaning for you? Have you seen them before?"

She paused to consider. "There is one thing … but I'm sure you'd think it silly."

"Anything you could tell us may be helpful," Volopich urged.

Svobodová eyed me. "Are you familiar with the Golem of Prague?" When I registered no recognition, she turned and waddled over to one of her overladen bookshelves. "No, I don't imagine they trouble Russian children with such bogey stories."

Rising on her tiptoes, she pulled a thick tome from one of the upper shelves and took it to a small writing desk in front of the dormer window that overlooked the street. As she opened the volume on the desk, I noted that she did not have to flip pages to find her desired selection; the place had been marked with an old milk bill. The text on the left-hand page appeared to be all in Hebrew, justified at the right-hand margin but of varying lengths at the left, as though it were a mirror image of ordinary writing.

On the facing page was an engraving of a monster coming to life.

In the manner of a medieval sorcerer, a bearded man in a robe and ceremonial headdress stood before an archaic grimoire, his hand raised to enact some forbidden spell. On the wall behind him hung the six-pointed Star of David. Out of the mists of his conjuration a half-formed stone giant arose, its gargantuan arms, torso, and head barely shaped into the semblance of a man. Its face consisted of nothing more than two black sockets for eyes. The only truly distinguishing features on the figure were the three unmistakable marks chiseled into its forehead:

$$\text{אמת}$$

Vladěna Svobodová touched her withered finger to the robed man on the page. "In the sixteenth century, Rabbi Loew used ancient Jewish mysticism to craft a man out of clay. Right there, in the attic of that very synagogue." She nodded to the peak-roofed temple across the street, which was visible through the window. "But to imbue the statue with life, he needed to inscribe it with a Hebrew *shem*—a name of power. In this case, the greatest power of all: *emet*. Truth.

"Rabbi Loew intended for the Golem to protect the Jews of Prague from those who oppressed them. But such a great, unnatural force is difficult to control, and the Golem turned its power and fury against the Jews themselves. Rabbi Loew then had to take away the life he had granted by effacing one of the letters of its *shem*—"

"This one?" Volopich indicated the first of the three characters on the monster's forehead.

Svobodová smiled indulgently and pointed out the window to the old Jewish Town Hall, which stood adjacent to the New Old Synagogue. "You see the clock there? Not the one on the tower with the Roman numerals—the one below it with the Hebrew letters. It runs counterclockwise. In the same way, the Hebrew language runs right-to-left, the reverse of what the Gentiles do."

I huffed. "Backward!"

"Only if you are used to reading left-to-right. To the Jews, *you* are backward." She touched the rightmost symbol on the Golem's brow and moved her finger leftward as she named each of the letters. "Aleph . . . mem . . . tav . . . spells *'emet.'*

"But if I take away the aleph . . ." She covered the right-hand letter with her fingertip, leaving the first two symbols, like so:

$$מת$$

"Mem . . . tav . . . spells *'met':* dead. And so the Golem becomes inert. Because without truth, there is death." The old woman peered at me keenly then cackled, eyes twinkling. "These Jews, they are clever, no?"

I frowned. "Tell me, paní Svobodová, did you ever share this 'bogey story' with your grandson?"

Her glow of amusement dimmed. "I might have told it to Jakub when he was a boy."

"And what about his friends? Say, Jan Palach or Jan Zajic. Did you tell them about your Golem?"

Her gaze hardened. "They already knew truth, Major Bykov."

Sensing our conversation was about to conclude, Volopich donned his hat. "We regret to report that your grandson's remains have gone missing. Would you have any idea who might have taken them?"

She shrugged. "The communists would not let his body be in life. Why should they in death?"

"Enough. We shall be in touch if we have any further questions." I gave Vladěna Svobodová a curt nod and led Volopich out of the apartment.

He waited until we were out on the landing and the old lady had shut the door behind us before commenting. "Well, Major Bykov, do I need to issue an arrest warrant for a walking statue?"

"Nonsense!" I waved off his sarcasm. "It's obvious Jakub Svoboda's counter-revolutionary group adopted this Jewish fairy tale as its creed. And the old lady clearly knows more than she's telling—keep her under surveillance. But she did reveal the group's goal: to destroy the Communist Party's propaganda apparatus. I'll wager, if we stage an ambush in every news outlet in Prague, we'll soon catch our 'Golem.'"

That calciferous odor, as of stalactite drippings in a cavern, assaulted my nostrils again, and the misshapen man-thing from the engraving flashed in my mind. I finally recognized what the smell was.

Wet clay.

We immediately set about planting Warsaw Pact troops in every conceivable location of Prague that the counter-revolutionaries might target, from the newspaper delivery warehouses to the groundwave transmitters that jammed Radio Free Europe broadcasts from the West. I myself led the detachment that occupied the insurgency's most likely quarry: the local studios of *Československá televize* or ČST, the nation's sole television network.

ČST operated out of a complex located in the hills of Kavčí along the Vltava River southwest of central Prague. The main studios were located in a high-rise office tower of glass and steel surmounted by an antenna. During the Prague Spring, Dubček's government had carelessly permitted the station to feature inflammatory news coverage of the insurrection, but since the Czechoslovak Communist Party had instituted its normalization of the media, the network had largely reverted to innocuous musical performances and documentaries extolling the virtues of the agrarian economy and the hard-working proletariat.

Although I wanted this to be a strictly military operation, Lieutenant Volopich insisted on accompanying me as the regional officer for the investigation of counter-revolutionaries. "If you catch your Golem, I get to interrogate him." He smirked. "We make even the stone talk, eh?"

I grunted. "Just stay out of our way."

We occupied the building first thing in the morning, as ČST was preparing to begin its broadcasting day. Everywhere in the foyer we were greeted by the network's logo, an oval formed by a stylized C and T with a snaking S in the center: on the glass doors of the entrance, on the front of the reception desk, on the whitewashed wall facing the entryway.

The station manager, a sweaty little man in a dark suit named Pokorný, awaited us. He had a spiky widow's peak that resembled a shoeshine brush and fidgeted as if he were late for another appointment.

"Major, are you sure the madman will strike here next?" From a previous conversation on the phone, Pokorný knew to speak German in my presence. "Wouldn't it be better for us to cease operation and evacuate?"

"We cannot allow the counter-revolutionaries to intimidate us," I retorted. "The station must broadcast as usual. The Warsaw Pact will defend you."

I signaled to the troops behind me to file toward the stairwells in order to patrol every level of the building as we'd planned. I instructed Volopich to remain on the ground floor, while I led Sergeant Alexeyev and his men up to the fifth floor to what I believed was the most likely place for the insurgents to strike: the studio where the network televised its daily, Party-approved news programs.

The studio's set was simple, with one male and one female news anchor seated at a desk in front of a backdrop that displayed a map of the Czechoslovak Republic. Two crew members photographed the reporters with video cameras the size of anti-aircraft guns, while a director and technical crew monitored and edited the live broadcast from a soundproofed booth behind the cameras.

Alexeyev and I observed from the control booth while four infantrymen stood sentry at the perimeter of the studio, outside the cameras' view. Viewers of that day's program must have been curious as to why the news anchors kept glancing anxiously off-screen while reciting their reports.

The day passed without incident, as I expected. I felt certain the cowardly counter-revolutionaries would wait until the network closed its broadcasting hours with an on-air test pattern and the studio went dark and vacant before commencing their vandalism.

We would be ready for them.

After giving the men a final break for food and cigarettes, I had them turn off the studio lights and hide themselves as best they could—one in each of the studio's far corners, while Alexeyev and I crouched in the dark control booth. Through the two-way field radio I carried I ordered the troops on each floor of the ČST building to take their positions as well, so we might ambush intruders wherever they appeared.

The hours dragged. Alexeyev and I could barely see each other as we leaned against the back wall of the booth. I could tell that he was agitated, however, by the way he would take the white stick of his unlit cigarette from his mouth, twiddle it in his fingers, then put it back between his lips. I'd forbidden the men from smoking while we were on alert, but he clearly wanted something to calm his nerves.

"Do you really think that thing will come here?" he whispered.

"I think the anarchist who attacked *Zprávy* will try again, yes," I answered, although I began to wonder if I'd selected the correct target after all.

Alexeyev's cigarette danced fretfully in the shadows. "Are you sure we have enough men? That creature—my bullets did nothing to it . . ."

"That thing was a man." I pictured the giant of stone rising from the mist in Vladěna Svobodová's engraving, but quickly brushed the image aside. "And we can capture or kill it like any other man."

"Yes, sir." Alexeyev sucked at his cigarette as if an infant with a pacifier.

Around three in the morning, my field radio crackled. I held the receiver to my ear and heard the fuzzy, panicked voice of Private Kovalenko, one of the men guarding the ground floor. "Major Bykov! The building has been breached."

I spoke into the headset's mouthpiece. "Report."

"We heard a crash. One of the plate-glass windows—"

The tinny spitting of gunfire sounded in the background.

"It's not stopping! It's got Peshkov."

I heard a hollowed-out scream in my ear, as though it hissed forth from a conch shell.

"Stand your ground!" I urged. "Surround the enemy."

"It's no good! It swats us like flies. We can't— A final yell dissolved into static.

"Kovalenko! Report!" Only white noise replied, and I set down the radio's headset.

Alexeyev grabbed his rifle, his voice quavering. "It's coming, isn't it?"

I answered him by drawing the pistol from my side holster and taking the hand lamp from my belt. Through the control booth's window I flashed the lamp one—two—three times to signal the men in the studio that an attack was imminent. I could not be sure if the intruder were headed to this particular area, and I still had hope that the troops on the lower floors might stop him.

That hope was soon dashed.

Despite the control booth's soundproofing, Alexeyev and I could hear the leaden tread of the figure that thumped into the newsroom, a sound like cinderblocks dragged over pavement. We could see only its vague, hulking shadow, for the studio beyond the thick glass remained as murky as a polluted aquarium. With trepidation the silhouettes of the four soldiers advanced on the looming entity, which stood at least a foot higher than the tallest of them. Muffled staccato bursts of machine-gun fire followed, and the glass shuddered as one of the soldiers' bodies was flung against it.

I motioned for Alexeyev to follow me out the control booth door. Before we could open it, one of the massive video cameras, complete with its rolling dolly—easily two hundred pounds in total—smashed through the glass partition to land where we'd stood an instant before.

As soon as the soundproof barrier burst into fragments, the volume of the pantomime battle before us crescendoed with the panicked cries of the three soldiers still standing. They fired their Kalashnikovs until they emptied their magazines, yet each crack of a gunshot was echoed by the *ping* of a ricochet as the giant's skin deflected the projectiles.

Alexeyev and I charged out of the control booth, guns at the ready. I switched on my hand lamp and trained the beam on the assailant to illuminate our target. Fear petrified both of us as the lamp spotlighted a monstrosity.

The figure, indeed, had the shape of a man but magnified to enormity. Its gray surface appeared ill-formed and blank, as if the sculptor had abandoned its creation before adding detail. I assumed it must be some kind of body armor, yet I could see no joints or hinges to permit the limbs to flex nor any seams that revealed how the occupant might get in or out of the outfit. As the giant moved, its silicate arms and legs seemed both solid and fluid at the same time, the musculature rippling beneath the crust as if molten magma.

One of the soldiers fumbled to change his magazine and reload. The monster clamped the man's head between its crude, three-fingered hands and crushed it like a grape. The wine of his blood speckled the nearby wall while the headless corpse dropped from the creature's grasp.

The thing pivoted to corner the second remaining soldier, who fired the last of his ammunition at it. Even as the rifle hailed it with bullets at point-blank range, the giant snatched the weapon in its pincer-like grip, flipped it around, and impaled the infantryman with the gun's barrel.

The entire mêlée had lasted less than a minute.

The only surviving enlisted man blubbered like a schoolboy and backed away.

"Attack!" I bellowed, but he bolted from the studio.

The giant turned to face us for the first time. Jolted out of his paralysis, Alexeyev let out a hysterical war cry and peppered the giant with machine-gun fire as it advanced. It did no good, but to his credit, Alexeyev didn't run, even as the titan reached for him.

With the thing so close, the smell hit me, more strongly than it had in Vladěna Svobodová's flat. Lurking beneath the sulfurous haze of gunpowder . . . a mineral tang, as of freshly poured concrete. As it leaned into the beam of my hand lamp, I at last saw the monster's face.

The gray lump of its head was almost featureless, with no mouth, nose, or ears to humanize it. Two sockets, deeper and wider than a skull's and so filled with shadows as to be opaque, served for eyes. The implacable visage offered no hope of mercy.

And on its forehead it bore the *shem*—the Hebrew name of power:

אמת

Aleph . . . mem . . . tav . . . spells 'emet' . . .

I cast aside my pistol, for I sensed it was useless.

Alexeyev screamed as the monstrosity took hold of his arms and pulled him apart as if dismembering a rag doll.

As it bent over him, I leapt upon its back, hugging it around the neck with my right arm while brandishing the hand lamp as a club with my left. I strained to remember Vladěna Svobodová's words.

But if I take away the aleph . . .

Reaching over its head, I swung the hand lamp at the aleph on the left side of its brow. The first blow nicked the inscribed sigil, and a hairline crack split the clay above its left eye.

The creature jerked bolt upright. It had no voice to express alarm, but it thrashed from side to side to shake me loose. It pawed behind its head, but I dodged its hand and tightened my chokehold on its throat.

I struck the aleph again. With a loud crunch, a large chip broke off the forehead. The lamp's lens and bulb shattered.

The giant grabbed the forearm I'd curled around its neck and snapped it like a twig.

Though I howled in agony, I wrapped my legs around its torso and kept the crook of my broken arm clamped around its head to hang on. The lamp nearly slipped out of my left hand.

Plunged into darkness, I clubbed at the thing's head blindly, in desperation. There was a whisper of crumbling masonry, and then the thunderous crash of an avalanche as the titan toppled, carrying me with it.

Pain flared in my bruised torso as the giant landed on top of me. I felt its hard clay carapace fracture. I lay stunned for I don't know how long, but the instant I regained my senses I crawled out from under it and groped in the dark to retrieve the hand lamp that I'd let fall to the floor beside me. Although it hadn't moved since it collapsed, I straddled the beast and frantically clubbed it with the lamp, aiming in the dark for where I thought the aleph would be.

"Major Bykov?"

Panting like a cornered animal, I whipped my head around, my wide eyes blinded by the beam of another hand lamp. As he lowered the light from my face, I saw Lieutenant Volopich peering at me with a mixture of puzzlement and concern. A couple of Warsaw Pact soldiers flanked him, their rifles raised.

"Stand back!" I shouted. "Your weapons are useless. The others—it tore them apart."

His expression skeptical, Volopich swept the beam of his lamp over the sprawled figure beneath me. Pockmarks riddled the torso where the soldiers' bullets had impacted it, and a web of fissures now threaded over the length of its gray ceramic body. Blood spatters spotted the surface with dots of a muddy-looking burgundy color. A large wedge had fallen away from the left side of the creature's face. The cleft exposed the eye socket of a blackened human skull, to which a few bits of charred flesh still clung.

The aleph on the forehead had disintegrated. Only two of the three Hebrew letters remained intact.

Mem . . . tav . . . spells 'met' . . .

Dead.

I rolled off the broken icon to quiver on the floor beside it, for I already knew whose skeleton had been entombed in that sarcophagus of clay skin.

I did not have my suspicions confirmed until three days later, when I finally convinced the doctors at the hospital to let me return to work at my office. Lieutenant Volopich welcomed my return with his usual flippancy.

"As you might imagine, the body was in pretty bad shape by the time they chiseled the clay off it. Apparently, the sculptor disjointed the embedded skeleton to make the figure as big as it was." He thumbed through the pages of the autopsy report on his clipboard. "However, based upon the charring of the bones and a comparison of the skull with dental records, the coroner gave his considered opinion that the corpse is Jakub Svoboda."

I downed a shot of vodka from the glass in my hand and poured another from the bottle on my desk. "Did he come back from his 'office' at the café to tell you that?"

Volopich cheerfully ignored me. "So . . . you foiled the counter-revolutionary insurgency and recovered Svoboda's remains. Moscow should be pleased, no?"

Every ounce of my body ached as I sagged in my office chair.

With each breath I took, my cracked ribs throbbed beneath the brace around my midsection. The cast on my right arm prevented me from putting on anything more than a loose undershirt, so I'd draped the jacket of my uniform around my shoulders. This hardly felt like victory.

"You know I can't let this go." I coughed on another swig of liquor. "That Svobodová witch—she used her Jewish magic to create that . . ." I couldn't bring myself to name the creature. "She must have put her grandson's body inside the monster so he could accomplish in death what he couldn't in life: to seek vengeance against the Communist Party for its lies."

Volopich shook his head. "I did not put any of that superstitious nonsense in my report. Our official conclusion is that the clay figure was merely a means to hide the corpse from the authorities. The real insurgents left it behind as a calling-card when they fled after the attack on the television studio. Unless, of course, *you* wish to explain to Moscow about walking statues and such."

I hung my head, gazing morosely at the faded photo of my wife Margosha and my six-year-old son Ony that I kept in a frame on my desk. I hadn't seen them in nearly a year, and if Moscow kept sending me to put down rebellions in the farthest reaches of the Eastern Bloc, I might not see my boy again before he realized his dream of being the first cosmonaut on the moon.

"No," I sighed, "I think your report is . . . accurate."

The Czech police lieutenant grinned. "Splendid! This is *pravda*, after all, is it not?" He bowed in mock salute. "Congratulations, Major Bykov! You are a hero of the Revolution."

Volopich whistled as he left my office to file his fictitious report, leaving me alone, in dread of deferred punishment yet to come.

Yesterday I again saw commotion in the thoroughfare of Na Prikopi. A large crowd milled about the Communist Party headquarters, murmuring in astonishment as they gazed up at the building's façade.

The billowing campaign banner had been torn down and now

lay in a deflated heap on the pavement, like a collapsed parachute that has failed to deploy. In its place, a black graffito four stories high branded the building:

אמת

I peered up at the letters and quaked. They might have been painted by Vladěna Svobodová and her fellow insurgents, I told myself. But the dread in my heart told me a force more than human was responsible.

The concrete structure resembled an enormous head of clay, its windows like eyelids about to open to reveal two black pits of glaring judgment. I imagined the entire stone city of Prague as a dormant colossus ready to awake and tear free of its foundations, to rend and trample us all for our propaganda and prevarications.

One day soon, I fear, Truth shall have the final word, and none of us will be spared its wrath.

Sisterhood of Shadows

Wade German

We'll return to the ruins long before the eventual solar horror
while all the blood upon us
still looks black in the melancholy rivers of moonlight
I hear a moth very far away
the soft thrumming of nocturnal wings
It reminds me it reminds me
my dear
I still remember that night
we had traced the Sodality of the Oracle
to its medieval source

the crumbling pile sequestered in sylvan splendour
in the fragrant evergreen solitudes
of remote mountains
the time-shattered walls and ramparts
the semi-intact towers arches
these owl-infested and cobwebbed remains
in remote mountains
far from villages down below
these fragrant and splendidly depopulated evergreen solitudes

Back then ages ago your thoughts and theories
glowed like lamplight
your dreams were oceans of pink plasma
streaked with red currents
flowing inevitably towards the castle ruins
you said everything revolves around the phenomenon of blood
the arcane system of circulation
those mysterious channels withholding mysteries
and you said to me
somewhere between the wisdom of Chaldean sorcerers
regarding piss and pus
and the archaic medical belief
regarding melancholic humours and ichor
was a key to the everlasting
and now our naked feet tread through the dust of epochs of eons
were we puppets or corpses or persons
when we passed over and beyond the pit of oblivion
to land again
on this phantasmal planet

There was no struggle in our climb
there was only a sense of forgiving and communion
as your fingernails clattered
like glass vials of anointing oils on the stones

amid the faint scent
of slightly rotted carrion and feral life
as we climbed the stones into the house of the oracle mother
in the ruins
in the ruins of the castle she raised herself
many hundreds of years ago
as we climbed
the everlasting oracle the sublime witch mother
waited with ever-evolving vision
in the vast black chapel of her disembodied heart
she saw us coming
through the darkness of dark ages
and we were received
even before she raised this haunted house all by herself

Now gliding lovely so lovely from the open mouth of the crypt
from the smooth void of the mausoleum
In the underworld of our loves
you come to me with hair floating as if alive in the air
with beautiful smiles febrile beyond the pale
those perfectly elegant teeth gleaming white gates to hell
amid sighs and whispers of ghosts
where the invisible footfalls of creeping things
are amplified in our ears
and shadowy truths
sprout from mouldering decay
like so many very delicate blueish-green mushrooms
you come to me bearing gifts
mewling gifts to share
to share and very gladly feed upon

As the solar god nears the horizon in his abominable chariot
let us lie in the vaulted chamber
in cerements of black fur

in bedsheets of black soil
in our deliciously cool black beds
and breathless as the love bites of incubi and succubi
let us embrace
come to me with the cemetery of your touch
in your gelid lips
in the white worm of your tongue
I have received solace at the outer limits of extreme unction
and in the crucifix of embrace
in the inverted crucifix of embrace
in the black sabbath that is our true embrace
the things I bring to sleep
rise out from ancient abyssal layers
to dream with until twilight
beneath my mossy marble slab until crepuscular murmurs
hint at the emergence of stars
and the opening of night's portal way
when we rise again
to hold hands
to revisit familiar haunts of our familiars
and again tread through the immemorial dust of epochs of eons
and all the worlds
we have brought to death
enlivening my meditations on evil

You say there is no warmth only horror
what is cold is beautiful like the most elegant logic
And I weep for the beauty
I weep translucent spiders that crawl down my gladdened cheeks
from the teeming nest of my nighted mind

It's beautiful here
it's so very beautiful here
the ceremonious phantoms howl in ecstasy

The Many Lives of Carmilla Karnstein

Manuel Arenas

At some point in my life I became fascinated with the Victorian vampire tale and sought out every extant instance of it that I could find. I haunted my local bookstores and purchased from mail order catalogues specializing in dark fantasy and horror (obviously this was in the days before the Internet), but after a while I began to see the same stories and, after having read them, there were only a select few which I ever felt compelled to return to. Such a one is "Carmilla," the celebrated novella by Joseph Sheridan Le Fanu. It is largely known nowadays as the story that spawned the genre of sexually ambiguous vampires, but it is much more than that and deserves to be acknowledged as one of the greatest Gothic horror stories ever written.

It was originally serialized in the short-lived literary magazine, the *Dark Blue*, from September 1871 to March 1872, with illustrations by Michael Fitzgerald and David Henry Friston, respectively. It is presented as an account written by the protagonist, Laura, ten years after her encounter with the eponymous vampire.

Carmilla is an aristocratic teenage vampire who plays on social etiquette to wheedle her way into the homes of the gentry, where she woos and feeds on the young women of the household. To keep herself fit during her protracted courtships she creeps out at night and drains the village daughters. It is this emphasis on same-sex seduction that has given the tale its notoriety. Hammer Studios exploited this in their 1970 film, *Vampire Lovers*, which alternately boosted and doomed the career of the curvaceous Polish-born actress Ingrid Pitt. Although in her thirties at the time, her mesmerizing portrayal of the predatory countess is so iconic that it guaranteed her an esteemed place through posterity in the horror film annals alongside her male counterparts, such as Christopher Lee.

The movie was basically Hammer's attempt to spice up its brand with a saucy new franchise, which came to be known as the Karnstein Trilogy, named after the family of vampires of which Carmilla was one of the lone survivors. Surprisingly, the film follows Le Fanu's story fairly closely, although it does play up the erotic aspects of the tale and even has Ms. Pitt frolicking naked with co-star Madeline Smith (who plays Emma, the film's equivalent to Laura) and seducing anyone and everyone (male or female) who has the arguable misfortune to come within her path. She is very charismatic and has a sensual allure that is very like her literary counterpart; like her, when it comes time to vamp out, she is genuinely terrifying.

The film did well enough to spawn two sequels, but Ms. Pitt declined to renew her role for fear of being typecast, and the follow-up film, *Lust for a Vampire* (1971), was a weak link in the series. The story had some good plot ideas but was marred by the cardboard acting of Danish model-turned-actress Yutte Stensgaard and an emphasis on lurid, puerile softcore scenes. The third installment, *Twins of Evil* (also 1971), had a better script, the delectable Collinson twins, and a grave performance by the recently widowed Peter Cushing, to recommend it.

Oddly enough, in the featurette on the Blu-ray release of *Vampire Lovers*, from Shout Factory, the director, Roy Ward Baker, as well as many of the others involved with the movie claimed they never saw the Sapphic subtext in the Le Fanu story. I find that hard to believe; either they're being coy or they are willfully ignoring the obvious. That said, I don't think Le Fanu intended for his tale to be salacious, as he never stoops to tawdry titillations in his descriptions of Carmilla's heated declarations and osculatory embraces. A modern reader must understand that in the Victorian mind, homosexuality was considered an unnatural transgression and a damning affront to godliness; this can be seen in Laura's adverse reaction to Carmilla's advances, which she initially tries to dismiss as "mysterious moods." They trouble her greatly, but Carmilla's glamour of preternatural beauty and persuasive powers have a way of softening her aversion.

There is great Gothic atmosphere in the story as well as some genuinely creepy moments that are brilliantly written, as when Laura describes her spectral visitations; the first visit from Carmilla as a young child is particularly vivid and disturbing:

> The first occurrence in my existence, which produced a terrible impression upon my mind, which, in fact, never has been effaced, was one of the very earliest incidents of my life which I can recollect. Some people will think it so trifling that it should not be recorded here. You will see, however, by-and-bye, why I mention it. The nursery, as it was called, though I had it all to myself, was a large room in the upper story of the castle, with a steep oak roof. I can't have been more than six years old, when one night I awoke, and looking round the room from my bed, failed to see the nursery-maid. Neither was my nurse there; and I thought myself alone. I was not frightened, for I was one of those happy children who are studiously kept in ignorance of ghost stories, of fairy tales, and of all such lore as makes us cover up our heads when the door creaks suddenly, or the flicker of an expiring candle makes the shadow of a bed-post dance upon the wall, nearer to our faces. I was vexed and insulted at finding myself, as I conceived, neglected, and I began to whimper, preparatory to a hearty bout of roaring; when to my surprise, I saw a solemn, but very pretty face looking at me from the side of the bed. It was that of a young lady who was kneeling, with her hands under the coverlet. I looked at her with a kind of pleased wonder, and ceased whimpering. She caressed me with her hands, and lay down beside me on the bed, and drew me towards her, smiling; I felt immediately delightfully soothed, and fell asleep again. I was wakened by a sensation as if two needles ran into my breast very deep at the same moment, and I cried loudly. The lady started back, with her eyes fixed on me, and then slipped down upon the floor, and, as I thought, hid herself under the bed. (276–77)

I was also blindsided by the implication, through the restored portrait of a maternal ancestor, that Laura may be distantly related to the Karnsteins. It made me wonder: is Carmilla trying to bring another family member into the depleted Karnstein family vampire coven? Laura's mother died young, and I believe she may have been taken, or at least an attempt was made to abduct her, although this isn't fully explored in the tale. Carmilla alludes as much, and more, in this telling passage from chapter 4, wherein I believe she hints at her vampiric nature, which she claims even she cannot control, and that, once initiated, Laura will bring others into the fold as well:

> She used to place her pretty arms about my neck, draw me to her, and laying her cheek to mine, murmur with her lips near my ear, "Dearest, your little heart is wounded; think me not cruel because I obey the irresistible law of my strength and weakness; if your dear heart is wounded, my wild heart bleeds with yours. In the rapture of my enormous humiliation I live in your warm life, and you shall die—die, sweetly die—into mine. I cannot help it; as I draw near to you, you, in your turn, will draw near to others, and learn the rapture of that cruelty, which yet is love; so, for a while, seek to know no more of me and mine, but trust me with all your loving spirit." (291)

Although not the first literary vampire, "Carmilla" did help establish many of the tropes we expect nowadays from our vampires, such as returning to their place of burial each night, their mesmeric power, pointy teeth, the ability to shapeshift (Carmilla turns into a great shadowy cat), and even the ability to breach locked doors without effort.

Bram Stoker appears to have been familiar with the story, as there are some analogous scenes and details in *Dracula* (1897). In fact, before he discovered Emily Gerard's treasure trove travel essay *Transylvanian Superstitions* (1885), Stoker was going to have the novel take place in Styria, the Austrian state where Le Fanu's tale takes place. I also suspect that perhaps the Baron Vordenburg (Baron Hartog in *Vampire Lovers*), who is the vampire authority in the tale, could have been an inspiration for Stoker's Abraham Van Helsing.

I wonder as well whether the tomes Le Fanu mentions as coming from his library—which, after an unfruitful cursory search, I assume are fictitious—might not also be considered precursors to the imaginary grimoires of the Lovecraft mythos, predating even Robert W. Chambers's *The King in Yellow*.

Nowadays, any time someone writes an erotic vampire tale, especially if it hints at lesbianism, the character of Carmilla is bound the make an appearance at some point. The Karnstein name has been bandied about in many horror and exploitation films over the years, and Carmilla has appeared in countless comic books, cartoons, video games, webisodes, rock songs, etc.—there's even an opera! In fact, despite never having quite become a household name, she is probably the most famous literary vampire, after Dracula.

Both stories are heavily plundered in the 1977 exploitation film *Alucarda,* by Mexican director Juan López Moctezuma. A few scenes are taken directly from "Carmilla," such as the one in which the hunchback tries to sell the girls charms, and the bit where they enter the crypt and find Alucarda's friend Justine reposing in a coffin overbrimming in blood—an allusion to the sanguinary ablutions of the Countess Bathory? According to some online sources, among the books Le Fanu referenced when writing "Carmilla" were the *Treatise on the Apparitions of Spirits and on Vampires or Revenants of Hungary, Moravia, et al.* (1751) by Dom Augustine de Calmet and *The Book of Were-wolves* (1863) by Sabine Baring-Gould, both of which treat of Erzsébet Báthory, the Bloody Countess, and other historical vampire cases.

Lastly, I have been smitten with Carmilla for decades; her story has had an indisputable influence on the development of my own vampire women, Thalía and Morbidezza, and I imagine I'll continue to be in her thrall until the day I stretch out for a *dolce far niente* in my own narrow house, to dream of bats, blood, and fair fey women amidst the crumbling tombs of the Karnstein family crypt.

Works Cited

Le Fanu, J. S. "Carmilla." In *Best Ghost Stories of J. S. Le Fanu.* Ed. E. F. Bleiler. New York: Dover, 1964. 274–339.

A Glint amid the Corn

Geoffrey Reiter

"I can't believe Adam isn't texting me back."

Sofia watched as Chrisleigh sighed in exasperation and stared into her phone. Matt tried one more time to start the car, again to no avail. Sofia pulled out her own phone and checked the time: 4:45. Practice would start in fifteen minutes.

Dante put his arm around Chrisleigh. "Come on, babe," he said, "he's probably already at the field."

Chrisleigh finally tore her metal-gray eyes from the screen. "God, Dante, how are we going to get to there in time? I don't want to be late again."

Sofia glanced at the profusion of green maple and oak trees around them, shading the gravel parking lot where Matt's black-sheened car now rested, angled awkwardly beside a row of SUVs. He had just managed to get it off the road before its final sputtering fume-fueled lurches. Sofia clenched her teeth to keep from castigating her boyfriend, who had passed two gas stations en route to the school practice field. She could see that he was panicked enough as it was.

"Who else might give us a ride?" she asked. "Maybe Ava . . ."

"Hell no," Chrisleigh shot back. "We're *not* asking her."

"We're so close . . ." Dante trailed off, peering toward the woods. They were at the edge of the park, next to a green-and-tan plastic playscape from which they could hear children crying out excitedly. Nearby, a scarlet smear marked the trailhead that meandered west. Sofia could see the park sign, plastered with the ubiquitous warning that displayed the speckled and garish red form of a spotted lanternfly, declaring unsubtly, "STOP THIS INVADER!"

But the trail would not help them; they needed to get north, not west. Dante was right: they were achingly near their destination.

"Let's cut across the Fisher farm," Matt interjected suddenly. He took Sofia's free hand and began leading her across the lot toward the north end of the park.

"Matt, we can't do that," Sofia objected, holding back. He released her hand and looked back at her, his hazel eyes squinting quizzically.

Ahead of them, past the playground, the park property ended. The high school was only a couple thousand feet beyond. But between the park and the school lay the wide cornfield of the Fisher farm. Zephaniah Fisher had inherited the land when his father passed away, and the Fishers grew all manner of crops on their 75 acres, which ran adjacent to the school. The other plantings stretched north of the park border, however; only the late-summer corn separated the four young athletes from the garish green turf of the football field.

"Sofia, it'll be like ten minutes if we hurry," Matt replied to her. "The corn's so tall, they won't even see us passing through it."

"Man, I'm with Sofia," Dante piped in.

This time it was Chrisleigh's turn to insist. She grabbed Dante's hand and began tugging. "Matt's right, babe. If Adam won't answer, this is our best chance."

Dante kissed her gold-sheened hair but then arched an eyebrow. "Are you serious? Sure, let's have the huge black man trespassing on an Amish farm. What could possibly go wrong with that?"

"We'll all be with you," Chrisleigh groaned, the impatience near panic in her voice now. "We'll all be together. Sofia, you're friends with them anyway, right? If somebody sees us, you can just put in a good word."

"I can't do that," Sofia maintained, pulling Matt closer to her and away from the park border. "I know Joelle a little, but I don't want to walk through her family's land."

Chrisleigh released Dante's hand and moved to Sofia, looking directly at her. Through a break in the tree shadows, the lowering sun's light made her eyes look more blue than gray for an instant. Sofia realized that in three years of doing cheerleading together she'd never really seen Chrisleigh's eyes before. They were always either cast down at her phone or out toward an audience. Now they rippled, through glare and incipient tears.

"You don't understand," Chrisleigh said in a raw, sob-choked voice. "You get A's in your classes; you've got your music and your family. Cheerleading . . . this is all I've got. I can't get in any more trouble with Coach."

"We've got to do something soon," Matt prompted. "Look, we can keep trying to text people, or we can walk the long way around, or—"

"Fine," Sofia sighed. She looked out at the park boundary as though it were a perilous realm, though she usually loved the sight of crops. They made her think back to visiting her *abuelo*'s plantain farm outside Ponce before he had been forced to sell. This was an illusion, perhaps: the great frondy leaves of plantain trees only resembled cornrows from a distance. Still, Sofia felt more kinship with the agriculture than many of her classmates, whose preferences pulled them toward downtown Lancaster. "But Matt's right. Let's just make it quick. And try not to be seen."

She desperately didn't want the Fishers to know she was trespassing. The quiet reserve of Amish famers could scarcely be more different from the voluble, gregarious life of her grandparents in Puerto Rico, let alone the boisterous existence her parents had carved out for their family in Pennsylvania. But Sofia saw Joelle at their family's stand week after week in the farmer's market, and one shy sentence at a time, they had grown to be something like friends.

Dante rolled his eyes and sighed resignedly, though he still looked nervous. Chrisleigh pulled his head down far enough to kiss his cheek, and then they began to jog to the back of the park. In moments they were at the chain-link fence that separated the properties. Matt didn't hesitate, scrambling up and over the perfunctory obstacle and beckoning for the others to join him. Dante, inhaling deeply, looked back at the dark wood of the park, then climbed over. Chrisleigh followed suit, waving off Dante's chivalrous attempt to help her. So now it was only Sofia, and she wanted so much to run the other way, to kick Matt's car once more and hope it started, or to follow the road around the farm's perimeter, or even just to skip cheerleading practice for one damned day. But of course, she did none of these things. Instead, she leapt the fence nimbly and landed gracefully on the far south boundary of the Fishers' land.

Across that boundary, directly ahead, the corn stretched out before them. To the east on her right, it was planted as far as the road, across which lay a larger industrial soybean farm. To her left, the west side sloped upward, disappearing from view, though if Sofia squinted, she could see the Fishers' house and barn up on the rise. She thought she even saw a small iota of human movement, but she turned away quickly from it; if someone was nearby, she'd rather not know.

They tried to run through the cornstalks, but it was difficult. They were tightly spaced and mature, and the thick green stalks gave little room for her feet toward the ground. Her head was submerged beneath the stalks' tasseling tops, and she could just barely see Matt ahead of her, though he was less than a yard away. In the light late-summer breeze, she could hear the rustling whisper of their leaf blades rubbing up against one another. There seemed to be another sound beneath that riffling, however, a curious hum, like the steady whirring of a machine, though Sofia couldn't trace its source.

But she wasn't paying much attention to the noises anyway; she was simply trying to stay calm. Matt was still visible nearby, but she had lost Chrisleigh and Dante entirely. She couldn't see anything around her but the stalks' towering green, and with even the sun occluded from sight she wasn't certain they were moving in the right direction.

"Sofia, Matt?"

She heard Chrisleigh's voice above the wind to her left, and she fought through the crowding corn, but still all she could see were rows of green and the red sliver of Matt's T-shirt between them.

"Chrisleigh, where are you?" Sofia inquired.

"We're right here," came the reply, but Sofia saw nothing.

"There's an open spot in the cornfield this way," Dante added. "Let's just keep talking, and we'll meet each other there."

"Sounds good," Matt replied.

"Here we are," Chrisleigh said. "You can find us now, right?"

Sofia kept tracking them, and she knew she was getting closer. Yet something was complicating her task; the once-ambient hum around them seemed to be getting louder, so loud that it threatened to eclipse her friends' words. And as she walked on, she felt a strange prickling against her skin, a different sensation from the slightly coarse ticklish rubbing of the leaf blades. This was sharp, even a little painful, and so surprising that it caused a surge of fright to gather inside her. She looked frantically around, and as she did so, Matt took her hand in his, and the two hastened on until finally they burst out into in the clearing that they sought.

It was a little open patch in the waves of corn, close to seven feet by seven feet, Sofia thought, though it wasn't quite square. The ground was lower here, with some grimy, pooled-up water in a declivity near the center, and she guessed that a heavy rain at planting had washed out the seeds in this spot months earlier. Dante and Chrisleigh were already there. When they arrived, Dante pointed to Sofia.

"What's that on your shirt?"

She hadn't noticed anything, but at his words she looked down at the Eagles jersey she was wearing. There were tiny holes in several places, and she now saw blood beading up in those spots. It occurred to her that she was bleeding in exactly the places where she had felt a prickling moments earlier. Almost by reflex, she dropped her duffel bag and began batting at the tiny rents in her fabric and her flesh. She heard again the peculiar hum and saw strange flashes of movement shimmer past her, zipping out toward the cornstalks.

Even as she was doing this, she noticed in her periphery her friends making similar motions. When she was afforded a moment, she saw that each of them had similar tears in their shirts. Now the air was alive with a preternatural humming, and she caught bright glints amid the corn as the lowering sun struck its dazzling upon the bizarre dots that skittered around them.

"Okay, what the *hell* was that?" Matt demanded as he continued to check his red shirt.

Chrisleigh knelt down to the barren spot of earth at her feet and took something between her thumb and index finger. "Look," she said, rising.

They gathered around her to see what she held. It was a dead bug of some kind, but though Sofia thought of herself as pretty good at biology, she certainly couldn't identify this species. It was an insect, six legs and segmented body, perhaps just shy of an inch in length. Its carapace was black like night in the countryside, so shiny it might have been made of chrome. But it was also covered in a profusion of sharp spikes, even on its wings, extending all the way to its head. That head made up over half its length, dominated by a wide jaw that ended with a pair of serrated mandibles.

"I've never seen anything like that before," Matt said.

"I've never even heard of anything like this," Sofia mused, taking the bug from Chrisleigh. "Could it be some kind of endangered species?"

"If it's endangered, it's doing pretty well for itself here," Dante said. He nodded toward the field, and they followed his gaze.

All around them, they could now see that the cornstalks were teeming with the insects. The daylight washed across their lustered shells, making them look like a shower of sparks from a welding torch. Most crawled across leaf blades or used their pincers to burrow into the corn ears, but many flitted and flew around.

"That's some weird shit," Matt acknowledged. "But whatever. We've just got to go, man. We must be almost to the practice field by now."

"I can see the sun over there," Dante pointed. "That's west, so north must be that way," he added, sweeping his arm in a 90-degree arc.

"It's easy enough to say that here," Chrisleigh retorted. "But we could get lost again as soon as we step back into the corn. I'm not taking any chances. Follow me."

She pulled out her phone to use as a compass and purposefully strode up to the north perimeter of the clearing. But even as her phone's screen lit up, the insects' hum transmogrified into a roar like thunder, and a cloud of thick darkness descended upon her. The creatures swarmed over Chrisleigh, and she screamed as they did so, and Sofia wanted to run to her friend and claim her from them, but trembling wracked her frame and the terror subdued and paralyzed her, and she stood as still as a grave. She glanced at the boys; Matt stood helpless, mouth stupidly agape, while Dante shuffled forward tentatively and uselessly, trapped between desire to act and vexation at the horrid deathliness of it all.

And so it was that they all stood and observed while Chrisleigh died. She thrashed and swiped at the things as they congregated over her, and she tried to run, but their jaws stripped the muscle and sinew from her legs, and she collapsed to the earth. Still she flailed, and still she screamed and screamed and screamed, senselessly and horribly at the shock and the betrayal and the pain. The insects gathered and gorged themselves on her skin and on her blood, and farther into the deepest regions of her body, though Sofia only caught glimpses of this in little bursts of fluid spurting from the ground. Mostly, what she could see was a vaguely human form, shrouded by a shadow of an army, thousands upon thousands, cutting and swarming and hopping and destroying.

Chrisleigh's cries turned to whimpers before they were silenced, but all this occurred in seconds. Sofia quietly, slowly edged backward, terrified that they would move on to her, but when they had eaten their fill the insects turned back to the corn rows, though not out of her sight. Their mouths, fresh from the flesh of her friend, returned to the crisp crops as though there were no difference between a girl and a grain. Beside Chrisleigh's bag and phone and flayed clothes, they left behind them only jaw-notched bone with splinters of nail and strands of golden hair—and, beneath it all, a small damp piece of soil.

"Oh, God," groaned Matt. He doubled over and vomited, a lumpy pink mass of soda and pizza, though even then he kept his eyes up toward the field.

Dante was crying as he stared at Chrisleigh's remains—Dante, whom Sofia had never seen in sorrow before, weeping, the tears dribbling down his face.

"This doesn't happen," he muttered. "She was just here, talking to us, doing her thing. My baby girl is dead." Then, wet eyes glaring, he looked down at Matt. "This was your idea, damn it. This was your *goddamned* idea!" He reached down and took Matt by the shirt, then struck his puke-stained face, splitting his lip. "Chrisleigh's dead because of you, you stupid bastard."

Matt's frame hung limp in Dante's grasp, his head nodding vigorously, and the tears were in his eyes now too. "You're right, you're right, this is all my fault."

Dante brough his fist back for another blow, but at this point Sofia jumped in and grabbed his arm. He hesitated, looking over at her.

"That's enough, Dante," she said. "Please just stop. It was a stupid idea, and you're right . . . Chrisleigh's dead. But we—I mean, we've got to find a way out of here. Beating the hell out of each other isn't going to help." She inhaled a great breath, then exhaled solemnly. "We just have to . . . think."

Dante released Matt, who crumpled to the ground like a half-empty sack.

"Yeah. Yeah, sure, right. We've got to think."

Matt looked north again, the direction marked out by Chrisleigh's bones. "We're so close. Maybe we should just make a run for it."

Dante looked back down and squinted. "Man, are you serious? I can run a 4.6 40, but not with those cornstalks, and not with those . . . things."

"Why did they kill her so quickly?" Sofia wondered. "We were walking together for a while, and only a few of them attacked us. What was different?"

She hated to talk so clinically, to act as though her friend's death were simply an event to be analyzed and not a grief to be mourned. But she knew the time for her mourning had not yet come; they needed their minds in these moments.

"There might be more of them on that side of the clearing," Matt suggested.

"I don't know about that," Dante replied. He motioned south, from which they'd come, and they could see countless dark specks wriggling about the fibrous green.

"What, then?" Matt asked.

Dante looked back at fragments of his girlfriend and abruptly closed his eyes. "Her phone."

"We've all got our phones with us," Matt reminded him.

"Yeah, but none of us were using them. That's seriously the only difference."

"They didn't eat her phone."

Dante glowered at Matt, and Sofia jumped in, "Yeah, but he's right. Who knows, maybe the power it was using set them off, or the light from the screen. Somehow it agitated them."

"So we might be safe to try running if we keep our phones off."

"Matt," Sofia interjected, "do you really want to risk that? They may not be going after us now, but they don't exactly look like they've calmed down to me."

Dante's brow creased. "Why *aren't* they going after us? Why is this spot clear?"

Sofia wondered that too. A few intrepid scouts were ambling at the perimeter of the clearing, but most of the swarm remained amid the corn.

"There's no corn here for them to eat," she said. "But we're here now. Why didn't they come after us once they'd finished . . . ?" She trailed off, not wanting to trace her thought back to its origin.

"What about the water?" Matt asked, pointing to the puddle beside him. "I toss stinkbugs and June bugs into the water all the time because they can't deal with it."

"You might be right," Dante acknowledged. "But I don't know how that helps us. This is just a puddle, and I don't think I've got enough Gatorade to chase off a million of them."

Sofia paced the small bare patch of dirt, eyes up into the blazing blue of the summer sky, trying to keep her gaze from the death and the danger that lay feet from her, though those dangers prowled about in her thoughts. This day was not the first fear of her life, yet the alienage of the enemy, the sheer eldritch horror of their situation, rippled through her gut and her soul.

"Who's down there?"

She heard the new voice descend, like a plumb line plunging to the infernal abyss in which she lay sunk. It startled all three of them, so unexpected was it to hear someone else speak within their desolation. The voice was a shout from some distance, female, with the throatiness of a slight Pennsylvania Dutch intonation. The boys looked baffled, but Sofia knew in an instant who it was.

"Joelle!" she shouted back.

Joelle Fisher stood upon the crest of the rise to their west, beyond her house and near the edge of the cornfield. The light of the sun behind her cascaded across her plain lavender dress and even danced a little on the brown hairs that strayed from beneath her white bonnet. The light fell like flame upon the dark glasses that concealed her eyes as she peered down at them intently.

"Yes," she replied. "I am Joelle. Who are . . . ?"

"It's me, Sofia Morales, from the market."

"Sofia?" Joelle sounded surprised, yet less so than one might have expected. "What are you doing in our field?"

"My friends and I—we're trapped," she called back, and she explained what had happened as concisely as she could. While she spoke, she could feel the seeming outlandishness of their situation weighing upon her, the implausibility catching on her tongue like an acrid and bitter flavor. And she was no less aware of the awkwardness, of having to shout every syllable to the diminutive Amish girl who stood demurely so far away.

But when Sofia was threatened with thoughts on the absurdity of their condition, she needed only to glance once more to jumble of white bone in the right corner of her vision. She could imagine Chrisleigh's mother and sister and stepfather waiting in vain for her to return from cheerleading and her night shift at the diner. She could know that the two of them would never again stand outside school on a cold winter afternoon debating the relative merits of reggaeton music while waiting for their boyfriends to arrive. She knew that every breath of her friend, the irritated sighs and the caustic laughs and the sudden, unexpected tendernesses and tears, had all been abruptly swallowed up by the earth and these interlopers. One by one, she could see those minuscule soldiers growing braver and creeping past the threshold of the field. Thinking on these things, Sofia raised her voice free from reticence so that Joelle might hear it, clear and loud above the buzz that surrounded them.

"Can you get help?" she concluded, desperately looking from Joelle back to the insects. They were encroaching in greater numbers now, staying on the ground, still avoiding the water, but massing even as she spoke. She and Matt and Dante all gathered as close to the puddle as they could get.

"My family are all away," Joelle answered. "It is only me and my little brothers, until tonight."

Sofia's stomach tightened at those words. Matt took her hand in his, tenderly, not as he had when he pulled her out toward the field just a few minutes earlier. She squeezed it back in return as she cast her sight back toward Joelle, the purple cotton of the girl's dress framed in the burnishing of the sinking sun.

Then an abrupt change fell upon Joelle's demeanor, a kind of stateliness Sofia hadn't seen before. She appeared to rise, though she had always been standing, and she shouted down to them, "I know what to do. Be ready!"

A new fear gripped Sofia. She wanted to live, voraciously and desperately, not to be ribboned in agony like Chrisleigh. But even now, even with bile swelling in her throat, she couldn't bear to imagine Joelle dying for her. The Amish girl must have been Sofia's age, yet she felt somehow years younger, and so there seemed a particular sacrilege in the thought of that shy, slender body being sacrificed to the swarm.

"Don't come after us!" Sofia cried out. Matt and Dante looked sharply at her as she spoke, and Joelle held her gaze.

"Don't worry!" Joelle called back. "Just be ready to move. When the time comes, it will be quick."

She turned away, skirt flaring from breeze and from motion, and she ran back toward the house and the barn, her bare feet kicking up dust.

"What the hell's she talking about?" Matt asked.

"I don't know," Dante replied, "but she said to be ready, so let's do it."

"What does that even mean?" Matt demanded.

Sofia looked around her, saw the rim of their small haven growing dark with a tightening ring of carapaces. Set against the spiky shells that encased the bugs' inner parts, the skin uncovered by her summer shorts and jersey felt appallingly exposed.

"Quick," she enjoined the boys, "pull out whatever clothes we have. Let's put something between us and their teeth."

"It won't make much difference," Dante responded, though he was unzipping his own bag. "Our practice uniforms are short too."

Sofia removed every fabric item in her own bag; fortunately, she had stuffed it full of clean outfits that morning. Instead of putting the clothes on, however, she began wrapping them around her limbs.

"It's not much," she said. "But I don't know . . . we need to do something."

Matt nodded. "Okay, but if we're doing this, let's really do it." He pulled in a deep breath, then knelt down into the puddle. "I don't know if they're really avoiding the water, but it's worth a try."

"Sure." Sofia kissed Matt on his damp, muddy hair as he got up before crouching down to do the same herself. It seemed humiliating, yet the touch of the cool water on her clothes felt oddly comforting. Dante briefly hesitated, but after one more glance at Chrisleigh's bones, he too immersed himself. Were the insects slowing their ghastly progress as the three splashed water about them? Sofia thought they might be, though she didn't trust her own perception. Slow or not, they certainly weren't stopping: an army of dark arthropods writhed nearer and nearer.

"Is there anything else?" Sofia asked. "Anything else we can do?"

"What about our phones?" Dante suggested.

"Dude, you're smarter than that," Matt castigated. "That's what got Chrisleigh . . ."

He trailed off when he saw the tempests in Dante's glare. For a terrible instant Sofia thought he would attack Matt again, would spatter his blood in the soil and leave him there for the bugs. And Dante clenched a fist—but then dropped his arm to his side.

"I don't mean keep them with us," he said. "When the time comes, we turn them on and toss them as far as possible. They didn't eat the phone—but they were drawn to it. It could be a distraction."

Matt hung his head. "Yeah, let's do it." Then he looked up. Wiping the blood from his mouth, he met Dante's gaze without flinching for the first time since Chrisleigh's death. "I am so sorry." He glanced at the bones, then turned to Sofia. "I'm sorry for all of it."

Sofia embraced him, her head on his shoulder, and she could hear his heart rustling through his damp shirt. Dante sighed, rolled his eyes, and looked away.

"It's okay, man. I mean, it's not, but . . . It's all right. We've just got to stay alive now."

Sofia glanced at the Fisher homestead, then back to Matt and Dante. Even knowing their proximity to death, she almost laughed. Under other circumstances they would appear comical, most of their bodies wrapped like bargain-basement mummies in sopping athletic wear, their exposed faces dripping in mud and sweat. She did not feel like any kind of hero or soldier—she felt like a scared, silly girl, and not far beneath the bravado Matt and Dante looked like frightened boys.

She heard it before she saw it, but not long before, because it came in so quickly. There was a sound like flood or flame, rolling down from above on the hillside, emerging from beneath the rays of the westering sun. The source of the sound was a harvest wagon, a simple assemblage of gray boards on metal wheels hitched up to four bay Percherons. Their massive forms had been doused in water, and the late-day light frolicked across their taut muscles as they galloped. And standing at the front of the wagon, her slim hands firmly gripping the reins, was Joelle Fisher.

Dropping down from the crest of the westward hillside, the wagon accelerated on the descent as the horses tore through the yielding green cornstalks. At the rate they were traveling, the horses would draw the harvester toward their clearing in seconds.

"Our phones!" Dante yelled, and Sofia and Matt needed no prodding. With all the skill of long use, they snapped on their devices—then hurled them southeastward. A plume of roused black beetles followed the arc of the phones, and their buzzing increased to a noise that rivaled the great reverberance of horse hooves in the farm soil. Yet many of the insects remained behind, closing warily but steadily toward the center of the clearing.

Joelle slowed the horses slightly as she approached them, but Sofia could see the swarm moving toward the wagon. It was clear that the wagon wouldn't stop when it got to them. With the boys to her left, Sofia braced herself for its arrival, knowing she might get no other chance. She saw a couple of intrepid bugs dart toward her face, and she flicked them frantically away. Then the curtain of corn was torn free, and she could see the brute, beautiful pectorals of the four charging draft horses.

The three friends shuffled parallel to the horses for a moment, but they couldn't keep alongside very long before the dense field started up again. The wagon was narrow, but Sofia was able to jump onto its side, with Matt right beside her. The two reached out and steadied Dante as he leapt with all his force onto the back. Sofia could feel him in her grip, his muscles straining as he sought not to fall backward; Joelle kept her focus straight ahead, and Sofia knew she would not be pausing. Quite the contrary, as soon as the horses passed the threshold of the clearing they accelerated into a gallop that seemed even faster than their speed when they came down the hill.

Matt and Sofia helped Dante pull himself fully onto the well-worn boards, but now they could hear around them the great rattle of myriad wings. The insects were in Matt's hair and on his face, and smeared across Dante's back, and she could feel them burrowing into the bare flesh of her cheeks. Each of the three rolled on the moving wagon, thrashing and flailing as Chrisleigh had done, and Sofia despaired at the thought that it was too late, that the army had besieged her body and would consume it, that all she knew of life would now cease in a few scattered seconds of torment.

But whether by the rate of their movement or the efficacy of their precautions or some outworking of fortune and providence, their tiny assailants had not gathered in the same multitude by which they had devoured Chrisleigh. Sofia's actions sent them fluttering off her face and scattering away from her clothes. In the rush of towering stalks that now engulfed them, she could still see their chrome-like bodies looping and whirling, and some approached her again. She persisted in waving her arms, looking like an idiot no doubt, yet her seeming foolishness warded them off. Matt and Dante were similarly abasing themselves, shedding their vanity for the sake of their lives.

Then, like a chariot in victory, the harvester burst free from the field, and they were suddenly on the road east of the Fisher property. Joelle silently directed the horses to follow the road north, and though they slackened their pace slightly, their gait retained a dread urgency. To the south, Sofia saw the great horde of insects, whose interest had returned to the crops. There, a few yards behind them, a great column of shadow occulted the road at one point. Sofia realized then that the bugs hadn't started on Zeph Fisher's land. They were pouring into it from the massive farm across the street, where the once-flourishing rows of soybeans had been stripped bare. Now the great galvanized steel grain bins in the distance towered, glinting, over acres of ravaged plantings.

Joelle brought the wagon back onto her property once they were clearly beyond the margin of the cornfield, and the swarm had not reached this place yet. She brought them back up to her house at the top of the hill before finally releasing the reins and allowing the Percherons to rest, their huge brown chests heaving. Her bonnet and her lavender cape dress had been torn in several places, with blood welled up around her shoulders and neck. Quietly, she stepped down from the wagon to stand behind a spigot, planting the sturdy black shoes she now wore onto her ancestral soil.

Sofia stepped down too, beholding the same sight. Her body ached in a thousand sites from tension and adrenaline, but she gave thanks for the ache: the pain meant she was still alive.

"What are they?" she asked as she watched the pall spreading over the green corn rows.

Sofia hadn't really expected a response, so she turned with a start when Joelle answered her.

"I saw them somehow, in a dream," she declared in a soft, otherworldly voice that wafted like flame on the wind. She took the glasses from her face, and for the first time that day, Sofia saw her eyes, blue like the heavens, as they surveyed her family's ancient lands, lands upon which generations of Fishers had toiled. "I saw them, and I saw you. I dreamed the other night that you would come like this, and so would they, and you would be here."

Sofia had never heard Joelle talk like that before—cryptic, oracular, quite unlike the reserved, practical Amish girl she met on weekends. She spoke so earnestly that they all—Sofia, Matt, Dante—turned away from the field to look at her.

"What do you mean?" asked Dante, and in the reddening sun his earthy eyes seemed to sparkle like stars.

"It's the judgment upon the land," Joelle replied intently, as though the words were being poured into her.

She said nothing more. Sofia glanced at Matt; his customary crafty grin had been effaced, supplanted by a bedrock-deep solemnity. She took his hand, felt the tackiness of the blood that had been drawn from it. Then she felt a pressure on her right palm; Joelle was clasping it, even as she now held Dante's hand on the other side. The four of them gazed across the countryside beneath the crest of the hill.

"Good Lord," she breathed.

Below them was a vision like blood and fire, the swarm pluming like a column of smoke as, one by one, a thousand thousand minute mandibles devoured their way through the growth. They stood there, the four of them, in the arterial glow of the sun, shocked and sorrowing in their rent garments, beholding the reckoning of a mighty scourge over the earth.

Trauma, Possession, and Witnessing in the Noir Supernatural Cityscapes of Joel Lane

James Goho

In the noir supernatural cities of Joel Lane (1963–2013), it is always "bad at home" for children (*LD* 2). In "The Lost District" (2001), they seem to have been born into a violent prison. Shadows look "like the bars of a giant cage," trees seem "like huge railings," and "spiked railings" surround buildings (*LD* 5, 6, 7). Everyone is trapped. Nicola knows nobody gets away. Everyone is under surveillance, not for their protection but for a voyeuristic spectacle. Many of Lane's weird stories expose that surveillance. In his imagined cities, "[t]he night has a thousand cameras" (*ES* 37), which abound in *Where Furnaces Burn* (2012) with the pervasive presence of CCTVs. Lane's fiction critiques that modern sense of sadistic spectacle by emphasizing the emotional states of his characters, who suffer under those unescapable urban eyes. Nicola and Simon feel observed, so she takes him inside an abandoned, decaying school where her memories bring only tears. She leads Simon to a storeroom to show him a collection of preserved babies or fetuses in glass jars where "they shivered" from cold and loneliness (*LD* 9). Simon steps away until the darkness wraps around him. He thinks of lost lives, failures, and bodies distorted by violent trauma. This setting typifies Lane's ability to capture pivotal moments in uncanny scenes that fuse realism with the supernatural. Why are those deformed fetuses preserved in an abandoned school? Lane created a startling image of how violence at an early age disfigures the life of children. "The Lost District" illustrates a pervasive theme in Lane's fiction. Decay and ruins form the dark urban setting in Clayheath (a place that eventually disappears). Many of his stories depict the corrosive effects of the modern, desolate city. That desolation especially affects the young.

Joel Lane was a brilliant British author and literary critic. He was born in 1963 in Exeter in the southwest of England. When he was young his family moved to Birmingham, where he lived much of his life and which appears as a dark setting in his short fiction. He graduated from the University of Cambridge. In his too-short life, Lane published two mainstream novels, many short stories, several collections of stories and poems, and perceptive nonfiction and editorial works. Much of Lane's astute analysis of the history and nature of weird fiction appears in *This Spectacular Darkness* (2016). Peers recognized his writing excellence with awards. Lane won an Eric Gregory Award in 1993 for his early poetry. *The Earth Wire and Other Stories* (1994) won a British Fantasy Award for Best Anthology/Collection in 1995. "My Stone Desire" (2007) won the British Fantasy Award for the best short story in 2008. Shortly before he died, *Where Furnaces Burn* won the World Fantasy Award for Best Collection in 2013. Lane was a modern master of the noir urban supernatural.

In this essay, I will explore a sample of his stories that focus on the experiences of the young in the nightmare city. Violence arises from the nature of the modern city with its uncountable waste grounds, vast ruins, and structures of surveillance. That violence expresses the malignancy of the modern city. In Lane's fiction, the modern city is an eerie environment: not a mere location for malignancy and chaos, it is a malignant chaos: "[t]he place of desolation" (*WFB* 122). It is a nightmarish urban environment that expresses a deeper metaphysical enmity.

Many of his stories explore the nature of violence and its lingering traumatic effects. This violence produces ongoing trauma, which Lane transformed into supernatural possession. This possession manifests itself in a multiplicity of spectral images of terror. Lane's stories witness this legacy of violence on children and young people in a non-voyeuristic manner, which shows the anguish of victims, not the horrific spectacle. These victims often are abused and abandoned kids, lost young people, refugee women, the poor, and the non-binary. Lane depicted a violent urban environment at "the edge of the unknown" (*WFB* 168), where the homeless end up as a "heap of blankets [. . .] frozen to an empty cast" (*WFB* 30). It is a hostile cityscape that spreads violence.

Lane's stories also work as a form of witnessing, giving a voice to those who have suffered. Many of his stories have a socially critical edge, revealing the ideological foundation of modern urban violence and its resulting traumatic impacts on people. Lane's stories—for example, "Wake Up in Moloch" (2012)—fit into the tradition of Gothic supernatural literature critiquing the abuses of societal power structures. His modern devastated cityscape represents those structures of violence that erode communal compassion. That desolate cityscape appears in stories found in each of his major collections, including *Where Furnaces Burn* (2012). There, the unnamed narrator experienced violence as a child and continues to do so as a police detective. *Where Furnaces Burn* is a supernatural case study of the effects of violence and trauma experienced in the modern Gothicized city.

The stories I will concentrate on in this essay reflect Lane's sensitivity to the hurt inflicted on children. In addition, his stories explore the moral problem of depicting such traumatic violence. He overcame this by expressing the importance of witnessing violence from the perspective of the victim; that is, the voices in his stories are the voices of victims to show their suffering. From her clinical experience, Annie G. Rogers tells of the inability of victims to speak about their devastating traumas. It is a horror from which they seem unable to escape because it is, for them, unsayable. And it is often hidden from them. That initial trauma now controls their unconscious, which traps the victims in silence and recurring suffering. Lane's stories work to expose that possessive element of trauma.

The Urban Gothic and Noir Traditions

In his depiction of the modern post-industrial city, Lane refashioned original Gothic images from dangerous castles to ruined council blocks, toxic waste grounds, decaying factories, and closed schools; from perverse aristocrats, monks, and priests to corrupt officials, rent-hoarding elites, and crime families; and from underground cellars and torture chambers to labyrinthine streets and confined basements. He wrote stories within the long tradition of Gothic and supernatural fiction criticizing existing power structures, as Mario Praz argued the original Gothic did. It critiqued an inequitable society. The abyss between the rich and poor was unbridgeable. The original Gothic showed the corrupt social edifice for what it was: violent in enforcing a rigid social order and full of depravity against the poor, women, and outsiders.

Lane's urban noir horror also reflects the tradition of urban horror that started with the American Gothic novels of Charles Brockden Brown. Alan Lloyd-Smith concludes that "Brown invented the American urban Gothic" (30). Brown's *Ormond* (1799) and *Arthur Mervyn* (1799, 1800) depict Philadelphia as a nightmare city. In *Ormond,* Philadelphia becomes a decimated city of decay, disease, and death. It is a space of deception and deceit among the inhabitants. The diseased city becomes a malignant thing devastating the populace and changing the city from rationality to madness, from community to lawlessness. This malignancy appears in many of Lane's stories, where the city, often Birmingham, is itself the origin of a disease of violence that spreads like a fungus. In *Ormond,* Philadelphia is infested by yellow fever. Similar to Brown's Philadelphia, Lane's Birmingham is dangerous to its inhabitants. In Brown's *Arthur Mervyn,* the city becomes chaotic, almost barbaric. The "malady was malignant, and unsparing" and "terror had exterminated all sentiments" among residents (346). The wealthy flee while the poor try to survive not only the disease, but also hunger and the growing hostility of all against all. Many of Lane's stories emphasize the effects on young people of our dark age of communal collapse.

The sense of the city as a place of darkness became the theme for more recent urban writers such as Fritz Leiber (1910–1992) and Ramsey Campbell (b. 1946), about whom Lane wrote insightful essays in *This Spectacular Darkness.* In Leiber's stories, ghosts seem to arise from the urban environment itself. It is a dangerous space of grime, waste, and soot that fouls the hearts and minds of people. In such stories as "A Bit of the Dark World" (1962) and "Black Glass" (1978), Leiber unearths a deep unease, a fear beyond the technological, a fear of the ultimate nothingness. Ramsey Campbell is the master of modern urban Gothic. He deploys urban spaces, objects, technology, and structures to expose the darkness of the city, which injects its darkness into human hearts. In Campbell's short fiction, living darkness materializes in ordinary urban spaces and objects to infect the minds of characters. His modern city is chaotic and inchoate; it is immense and inescapable. Despair and dread are the nature of existence in Campbell's cities, where horrors flourish in rubbish and ruins, for example in "Mackintosh Willy" (1979), where urban litter and debris come to life to kill. But in these stories, Campbell also articulates social anxieties and highlights the disparities in cities, which Lane did in many of his fictions.

Another major influence on Lane's work arises from the American noir fiction and movies of the 1930s and 1940s. According to Jeffrey Andrew Weinstock, the American noir had a significant influence on much of modern urban supernatural horror. Dashiell Hammett and Cornell Woolrich set their fatalistic tales of crime in gritty urban settings. The films adapted from these stories depict the city as sinister and riddled with crime, corruption, and deprivation. The characters seem caught in a dreadful march toward doom. Lane's violent city reflects the fiction of American noir authors. It is a nightmare city of violence. Such a city manifests the social and moral breakdown in the modern city, where everyone is a stranger and the streets are dangerous.

In "Forbidden Questions: The Politics of Noir Fiction" (2009), Lane examined the genre. He argued that Hammett made the noir detective story a mode of social analysis, focusing on deceit and corruption across a community. Lane's prime example was "Nightmare Town" (1924), which depicts a town controlled by crime, money, and power, where criminals rule and the innocent are in prison. Urban places in Lane's stories have "a vibe of imprisonment" (*WFB* 199). Commenting on Cornell Woolrich's *Deadline at Dawn* (1944) in "Forbidden Questions," Lane said the key idea is the city as a malevolent presence, which gets inside and manipulates the characters. In *This Spectacular Darkness,* Lane argued that Woolrich's works were not crime mysteries; they explored mortality, terror, and loss. The sense of loss and death pervades Lane's fiction of the malevolent city. Malignancy rules everything in Woolrich. His stories and novels are set in cities that seem to have suffered from metaphysical devastation. Many of Lane's bleak Birmingham stories exhibit a similar tone, although his are fashioned from melancholy and rage.

Violence and Trauma in Lane's Dark City

Lane built on this long tradition and shaped a more sinister and violent city: a city that compels violence, a city that enforces isolation and loneliness. The structures, streets, and design of the city breed crime. Greed rules. There is no feeling of community. Rather, the inhabitants are akin to inmates in separate cells, where they languish in isolation and loneliness.

In Lane's "Quarantine" (2012), lodgers in a hostel keep on killing themselves behind locked doors and barred windows. As the detective says, it would have made more sense to "take the building itself in for questioning" (*WFB* 77). The hostel is a so-called refuge for the vulnerable: "transients, DSS misfits, immigrants looking for work, mental patients looking for a foothold" (*WFB* 77). It does not save them; nothing in Lane's modern city does. In the story, the detective passes through a black arch of decay on a wall in one of the hostel's rooms and sees the city's diseased malignancy. That is why the detective is so concerned about infection. He sees woodlice, slugs, and creeping vermin. He sees "hungry life teeming in rain pools, [headless] bodies floating in the water [. . .] tissue cultures on the walls [. . .] diseased pigeons" (*WFB* 83). These are images of a diseased city, a city with an infection of violence. The detective feels that infection on his skin and tries to scrub it off, as he struggles to keep the police station sterilized. This infection of violence drives the detective to threaten his daughter. I suspect Lane called this story "Quarantine" as a dark jest.

Urban malignancy manifests itself as violence and trauma in Lane's fiction. Children and young people are abused and forsaken, bullied and battered, molested and wasted. Broken by their trauma, they strive to survive or die on derelict streets. Many turn to crime, alcohol, drugs, or violence to break from their families, their schools, their city, and their memories. In Lane's fictional cities, the young become possessed by their trauma. The detective narrator in *Where Furnaces Burn* hears "the cry of a child" (*WFB* 37) in every siren and the whine of warplanes. It expresses the fear children experience in modern cities and a world of endless wars. Fear is their world. They die quickly at birth, as in "Without a Mind" (2012). They are abandoned by fathers, for example, Ian and Lorraine in "The Death of the Witness" (1991), and as the detective does to his child with Kath in "My Stone Desire" (2007). Children seem born to die in "Making Babies" (1997), where they have short, dreadful lives and keep returning for another horrid life as if trapped in perpetual supernatural reincarnations of horror.

The violence inflicted on the young haunts them forever. Some react to that violence by hurting themselves. In "The Last Gallery" (2009), Sean cuts himself with a razor and Carol burns herself with cigarettes. But Lane creatively transformed self-harmers into pain artists whose skin becomes canvases, expressing their trauma to the world. In "The Death of the Witness," Sarah bites her wrists into a tapestry of scars reflecting her parents' bloody fights. But not everyone survives in these stories. Sarah witnesses a fourteen-year-old girl diving from a parapet into the ground seven floors down. But this could be Sarah's exterior action caused by her internal trauma. Sarah knows life "is solitary confinement," because she is possessed by her suffering. It is her sentence for the "years of blacking out her mind" trying to repress her trauma specter (*EW* 107). She witnesses her own death.

Children and young people in Lane's stories struggle to exist in desolate cities and towns. They end up homeless, like Stephen in "Common Land" (1991) or Tony in "The Pain Barrier" (1994). Or they try to survive in hostels such as the prison-like one in "Quarantine." They are trafficked across international lines, for example, Tania in "Even the Pawn" (2012). They are sacrificed as Elizabeth Kindling (a deliberately ill-fated surname for the victim) is in "Beth's Law" (2009). There is no childhood in the city. Children find no solace. In "Prison Ships" (1998), a child begs another character named Sarah for help. She leads Sarah to a garage full of children under the age of ten. One brandishes a knife and pleads with Sarah to give her comfort. The modern diseased city is a place of shattering.

It fragments the lives of the young. Lane's stories creatively tell the traumatic pathology of the young in the city of violence. The stories explode with experiences of violence. And that violence often returns in the form of the supernatural possession of a character. Many traumatized people compulsively expose themselves to situations reminiscent of their original trauma. This illustrates the continuing effects of that initial violence. Lane crafted imaginative sensory portraits of the hyperintense agony of returning trauma. The title of the story "Wave Scars" (1993) expresses the ever-returning trauma of Steve. "Imprisoned by his childhood" (*EW* 97), he must repeatedly return home to witness the supernatural wreckage of his past. That possession appears as harrowing images of bodies washing up on a Fishguard, Wales, shoreline and bleeding away into the sand.

Such stories depict the recurrence of childhood trauma in nearly clinical terms. Pierre Janet (1859–1947) pioneered the study of trauma and its long-lasting effects. He argued that harrowing memories of traumatic events persist in the psyches of the damaged. Such memories may return as the recurrence of the physical pain, dreadful images, horrific nightmares, and behavioral repetitions of the initial violence. In "Waiting for a Train" (1992), Jason appears doomed to repeat his attempts to escape his pain indefinitely. Possessed by his trauma, he compulsively lays his head on a rail, waiting for the long time it takes for the train to arrive. Similarly to Janet, but creatively,

Lane showed how traumatized individuals become trapped by and fixated on their trauma. They become possessed by that trauma. According to Bessel van der Kolk ("The Compulsion to Repeat the Trauma"), children seem especially vulnerable to the compulsive repetition of trauma. Because the phantom of their trauma controls their lives, they are unable to grow from later experiences.

That phantom possesses Matthew in "Branded" (1994). In her bedroom, Lisa traces the scars ("at least ten years old" [*EW* 81]) on Matthew's body. These scars appear to be cigarette burns or worse. Lane used this physical image to reflect the everlasting effects of trauma on children. Violence brands his body and his mind. Cornered by his trauma, he will find freedom off a canal bridge. Akin to many in Lane's stories, Matthew had been abused, brutally it appears. He is now in foster care, which seems to provide little real care. After a night out that he will not reveal, Matthew flees to Lisa. Matthew's silence does not actualize his experience of trauma, because it is unsayable. Victims frequently remain silent because the violence is beyond comprehension. Matthew struggles to understand a world with such violence against children. His knuckles bleed, and his sleeve smells of petrol. His responses to childhood abuse may be manifested in violence against others, things, and himself.

That's because violence "is the only thing one knows how to do" (Morrison 261) when one is possessed by trauma in Lane's noir urban environments. In his work, the modern city becomes a nightmare maze trapping people in a perpetual state of violence wherein the only response is more violence against themselves and others. Lane's city incises dark possession into the human heart. For example, the character, Sean, in "Branded" knew that "violence was a part of life, you couldn't rise above it" ever since he was a child (*LD* 36). Once harmed, that specter will return to haunt again and again. The past horrors inflicted on children revisit as a form of spectral presence perpetuating hurt. In the morning, Lisa and Matthew walk together. Halfway across a canal bridge, he lifts a fist in salute. Lisa responds in kind, but he has vanished. This is Joel Lane's literary act of solidarity with those abused and his resistance to sensationalizing that abuse by telling their pain.

The Importance of Witnessing

In "The Pain Barrier" (1994), Tony suffered repeated beatings from his father, as did his mother. The white scars running over his body appear industrial, as if caused by an organized program of terror and pain. Tony thinks that perhaps as a victim he could be saved. But violence against the young never relents, the trauma always returns. And the modern city kills any community that would protect them. As with most of Lane's stories, "The Pain Barrier" is a complex, layered story. The characters may be one character with two personalities, each produced through violence and trauma—one of whom may be dead.

"The Pain Barrier" illustrates the importance of witnessing, but also the dangers of doing so, because authorities build "a special graveyard for witnesses" (*LD* 15). Lane's stories often show a witness. In "Branded," Lisa witnesses the traumatic possession of another young person. Indeed, in *Where Furnaces Burn*, the detective embodies the importance of witnessing. That is the reason for his chronicling the violence in the city.

Roland Barthes wrote: "Death, real death, is when the witness dies" (36). Furthermore, Barthes argued that writing what one had witnessed stored it in people's memories so the crime and horror were not forgotten. Others must speak for those silenced. Genuine witnessing insists on the facts in the face of oppression. In a dream sequence, Lee, a character in "The Pain Barrier," circles a death camp. The prisoners are starving. Their "eyes were gaps," and their "mouths were scars" (*LD* 20), indicating the horrors the prisoners experienced. Lane stressed the importance of continuing to tell the truth about violent authoritarianism, which inflicts despair, pain, terror, and death. Yet he stayed silent on unthinkable horrors. That's because, as Jean-François Lyotard argued, recording the full horror of the Holocaust is impossible. There is no idiom in which it can be represented as it happened. Lane stressed the experiences of victims, not the brutalizing crimes.

There are no witness protection plans in these stories. Lane expressed this fragility of witnessing in his noir "The Last Witness" (2010), where fourteen witnesses of a violent crime never get to testify. But Lane's short stories work as a form of witnessing the violence that harms the vulnerable. Nathan in "All the Shadows" (2011) is another young person who has "a bitter, terrified child locked somewhere inside" (*AN* 27). For him, "the future is missing" (*AN* 30), which rings true for many young people in Lane's modern violent city. "All the Shadows" seems to be the unnamed young narrator's despairing message from the afterlife, which is the ever-recurring march of the traumatized dead into the tired, black waves of the night ocean where they die alone endlessly, longing for the ones they love.

The unnamed detective who narrates *Where Furnaces Burn* represents the victim's point of view, not that of the perpetrators, not the agents of harm. He is the witness of violence and trauma in "Beth's Law." It is a distressing tale in the desolate modern city of a cruelly murdered child and the detective linked by violence and driven by fate to encounter each other in the supernatural.

Ten-year-old Elizabeth Kindling disappears from her home. Beth's abduction spreads like an infection through all the newspapers and news outlets, which sensationalize it with associations with alleged pagan rituals performed by outsiders. This culminates in the killings of Romanies. The story ends with the detective and fellow officers on a stakeout in a stinking, dark basement, where they find a rip in the screen between their world and the unknown. In that darkness, Beth screams from her newspaper self about pain and suffering. Readers see Beth come to life as newspaper shreds to tell of her abuse and molestation. These verbal images disorient a reader. That is because they transform the suffering of one child into a supernatural outrage at the ongoing torment that children endure in the tower apartments, houses, waste grounds, basements, and cellars of the nightmare city. The images also illustrate how violence fragments the bodies and minds of children. Bessel van der Kolk ("Post-traumatic Stress Disorder") contends that most trauma is pre-verbal. That is, people keep trauma as fragments or bits of experience rather than in a traditional narrative memory. The brain cannot process what has taken place. Lane described Beth's anguish in fragments to render that anguish to the reader. His stories make us feel the hurt of the victim, suffering a "sense of deadness" (*WFB* 41), which describes the feeling of trauma.

Deadness is what the detective feels in "Even the Pawn." A sex-trafficked young woman, Tania, suffers brutal attacks. The detective—along with a reader—feels the terror, pain, and anguish of Tania. But there is no spectacle of her being attacked. Lane depicted her trauma in one fractured tormented paragraph. That paragraph of fragments cries out her voice, which exorcizes any sadistic voyeurism over Tania's abuse. Tania has a double in "Winter Journey" (2008). Irena is the sex-trafficked young woman in a story the police detective says is not easy to tell. Many of Lane's stories are challenging to read because he explored issues of violence against the vulnerable. They express the anguish of those who suffer violence. "Scratch" (1996) is an aptly titled story about sex trafficking. Miki is lured into the sex trade by a man whom she thought would save her from the streets. He brands her with a bloody cut on her cheek. In "A Faraway City" (2012), Lane described the despair and anguish of yet another young woman forced into prostitution, as she loses her identity and name, and falls farther into abuse and degradation by men. Kathy cannot "break free. Not on her own" (*SC* 44) from that power. She ends up alone in an unknowable city, which describes Lane's Gothicized urban environment. She becomes Katrina.

But there may be a kind of transcendence for these characters who have suffered. In Lane's poem "The Refugee," we may see the teenaged, sex-trafficked Tania, Irena, or Miki finding a joyful ending. Her skull "you noticed when holding up / its yellowed cheekbones to the rain, was how it smiled"; now that it was "among the rocks and stars" (*AM* 7).

Lane's prose style creates a looming mood of desolation, harm, and melancholy, stirred by an underlying rage. It has a dark power. Many of his stories and poems are abrasive. They leave scars on a reader's mind: traces of the terror experienced by those trapped in the nightmare cityscape. Yet he also crafted images of compassion and beauty. For example, in "My Stone Desire," lovers feel the "warmth of slow decay" as they unite with stone under a railway bridge's iron lattice that appears like a "stained-glass window" (*WFB* 7, 4). The characters slip away from their agony into the supernatural embraces of stone.

Nevertheless, there seems no escape from the city of dread for the young, who dare have such dreams. "Echoland" (2015) dispels that illusion. No magical city lies beyond Birmingham; only darker ruins, patrolled by creeping shadows, with tall towers filled with dark windows, and only the wind in "empty buildings" (*SC* 65).

Lane's complex, impressionistic form of narration and story construction, combined with his use of reanimated memories and dream sequences, transforms readers into witnesses to the violence and trauma of modern city life. And that is part of his purpose, I think. Lane's characters appear in splinters and pieces because real trauma shatters the mindscapes of people. Traumas reappear as hauntings or phantoms in fractured images, arising from the rubble of memories to hurt yet again. Lane wrote hard-edged, eerie, intense visualizations of remembered trauma returning as phantoms. Expressing this is challenging. He showed recurring trauma in startling images of the feelings of those who have suffered.

Lane's Social Conscience

Lane's stories are a form of protest, resistance, and resilience against dominating political and economic forces. The stories speak for the poor, outcasts, the homeless, and especially for children and young people who strive to survive in a time of violence. In "For Crying Out Loud" (2015), Lane creatively twined trauma and the dark supernatural to express his vision of life in the modern city where "there's no community, not any more now" (*AN* 96). In that story, the character, Mike, catches the cries or echoes of anguish from those who died violently in the city, but in the end no one hears the woe of the dead. Lane wants those voices to be heard.

I believe that Lane wrote in the tradition of Thomas Hardy (1840–1928), who chronicled the brutal shift from an agrarian, communal society to an industrial, urban one. Hardy's novel *The Woodlanders* (1887) evokes the hurt, pain, and destruction of the shift. Hardy wrote with a despairing feeling of the horrors inflicted on ordinary people in his fictional Wessex at the end of the nineteenth century. He described the rupture between the natural world and the increasingly industrial one built on technology—a technology that separates humans from nature and each other. That industrial technology and the economic and social conditions it engenders capture many people in prison-like living and working conditions. There, they serve at the will of power structures and the dictates of the machine. Lane chronicled the shift from the industrial age to the technological and information age within an urban environment, especially in his Birmingham. Akin to Hardy, Lane's stories expose the harsh realities of the world with a sensibility attuned to its utmost strangeness.

"Basement Angels" (2013) illustrates this strangeness mixed with a critique of modern technological consumer society. In the story, Max Parry suffers from an unknown trauma that manifests itself in blackout episodes that alienate him from others. The only exception is Colin Harpa, who befriends him and offers to help with his trauma through magic cures, symbolic of the modern disregard of proven remedies. The story illustrates that in consumer society someone will be your friend, only if you buy something from him or her. But all consumer products end in trash heaps as depicted on the floors of the Outsider Arts building, where Max discovers his mental health challenges will sentence him to a living death on a cold basement floor. Two startling images at the end of the story will haunt readers. One depicts Colin slicing up Max Parry's shadow into twitching negatives of his body on the floor, which suggests the thousand deaths that Max will endure in the dark. The second image describes a dead white Max among a dozen others like him, all frozen in fetal positions while their eyes scream silently in the darkness. These images display Lane's ability to combine moments of supernatural dread with social criticism into powerful and disturbing scenes.

Those cold, pale bodies on a cold basement floor are sacrifices akin to Elizabeth Kindling. In "Beth's Law," the detective aches to "learn the name of the dark god to whom the child was sacrificed" (*WFB* 33). That god comes to light in "Wake Up in Moloch," which is Lane's critique of the ideological core behind much of the violence and ensuing trauma experienced in the decaying city. Decaying, in part, because there is no sense of community, no moral center, or concern for one's fellows, which suggests a malevolence embedded in people by the nightmare cityscape.

That cityscape seems akin to the Topheth. Rachelle Gilmour says the Topheth in the Valley of the Son of Hinnom, later Gehenna in Jewish tradition, was thought of as the center of detestable acts, notably child sacrifice. Some traditions say the sacrifices were to the god Moloch (also known as Molech or Molekh). Or the term "Moloch" may have originally referred to the act of child sacrifice. In medieval times, Moloch was depicted as a bull or calf-headed idol. In *Paradise Lost*, John Milton depicted Moloch: "First Moloch, horrid King besmear'd with blood / Of human sacrifice, and parents tears, / Though for the noyse of Drums and Timbrels loud / Their childrens cries unheard that passed through fire / To his grim Idol" (1.392–96). But the prime source of the title of Lane's story comes from Allen Ginsberg's poem *Howl*, which Lane explained in his interview with Michael Gottert. Part II of the poem constantly chants "Moloch" as the embodiment of the suppressive powers of society. During that interview, Lane said, "Ginsberg uses Moloch as a symbol of exploitation and the machine age." It represents "the mechanization of people" (Gottert).

In Lane's story, Moloch is the machine-like, monetized city, where "people are as nothing before their machines" (Berry 105). In Ginsberg's poem, the repeatedly shouted "Moloch" illustrates the pervasiveness of the machine, that is, technology as Jacques Ellul saw it. For him, technology meant efficiency at all costs, including the human cost, which Rajan experiences in "Coming of Age" (2003) when he descends into a basement housing a noisy factory of pain for young people. Ellul contended that technology separates individuals into isolated beings and destroys communities. This is Moloch, identified by Lawrence Ferlinghetti as the "avaricious industrial uncivilization," which seems like a "fanatical religion with its omnivorous consumer machine devouring us" (109).

In "Wake Up in Moloch," Lane crafted a story about the insidious and dangerous allure of technology. The story depicts machines as unnatural destroyers of people, including a kid of seven, a teenage girl, and a man in his fifties, to show the complete range of sacrifices required by the machine. The detective's investigations lead him to a grotesque factory that houses a giant machine made of pistons, wheels, and chains. Naked young people appear to be worshipping that insidious, bloody, mechanical thing, as it strokes and tears them apart. It is a disturbing image of the adoration of machines and technology despite the brutality of its demands for sacrifice. A similar image occurs in "Coming of Age," where young people flay themselves with bits of machinery in a filthy basement. The machine is a metaphor for the demands of modern industry and finance. Moloch means money and greed, which cause inequality and injustice and lead to violence. Lane presented it as a supernatural disease in "The Night Won't Go" (1990), where Peter sees "money breeding in the dark" and "cash that multiplied itself like a sack of worms" (*EW* 51). Lane's stories work to expose the ideological foundations of violence in the modern city and move beyond the pathology of violence.

Commenting on Lane's unpublished novel, *Missing Tracks,* Nina Allan says he deeply felt the "social injustice and stark inequality" of the dominant political culture (*SC* 226). Moreover, in Peter Coleborn and Pauline E. Dungate's *Something Remains: Joel Lane and*

Friends, Nicholas Royle, Mark Valentine, and Ramsey Campbell comment on Lane's acute sense of justice. S. T. Joshi argues that Lane's stories are significant social commentaries on current social and economic inequalities. In this, Joel Lane harkened to Frank O'Connor's call for stories to speak for the "submerged population" (40). Lane's fiction creates a literary space for those who are marginalized, damaged, or afraid to speak.

In Summary

In the first story of *Where Furnaces Burn,* the narrator detective describes his dreadful flat in Coseley, where the "pipes had the ghost of a murdered child" (*WFB* 3). This is not a cleverly wrought image; rather, it expresses the fate of too many children. While searching for Elizabeth in "Beth's Law," the police officer uncovers more than a dozen skeletons of newborn babies in a waste ground—an area that turns out to be a burial site for many of those forgotten, unwanted, trafficked, murdered, or drugged. Lane's nightmare city is a graveyard. His fiction exposes cracks in the modern urban environment through which all the horrors issue. The city's dark streets, scarp yards, derelict factories, wastelands, and shuttered schools dehumanize people, especially young people.

This essay has explored a sample of Lane's fiction as a modern British expression of urban supernatural fiction. His stories renew the urban horror tradition that started with Charles Brockden Brown and was made modern by Fritz Leiber and Ramsey Campbell. His fiction also reflects the influence of American noir authors, such as Dashiell Hammett and Cornell Woolrich, who portrayed grim, crime-infested cities. But Lane's writing is unique with its moods of violence, darkness, and melancholy told through characters who are lost, terrified, and brutalized by the city itself. His urban environment causes violence, either directly, as a supernatural malignancy, or through its effects on its inmates—the inhabitants of cities. Violence is the modern city's dark soul. That violence seems especially targeted at the innocent and vulnerable. In turn, this violence perpetrated on the young causes them to suffer long-term trauma, which Lane transformed into a form of supernatural possession. The possession razes the lives of victims. Lane's stories also act as a form of witnessing. They are non-voyeuristic expressions of the violence and trauma experienced by his characters. These witnessing stories allow victims to voice their hurt. Lane avoided the spectacle of savagery that pervades modern society. Furthermore, many of his stories reflect his social conscience, revealing the ideological underpinnings of modern urban violence and the terrible consequences for many people. His work deepens the Gothic literary tradition of criticizing the abuses of society's power structures.

Works Cited

Allan, Nina. "Socialism or Barbarism: Joel Lane's Blue Trilogy and the Poetry of the Lost." In Mark Valentine and John Howard, ed. *This Spectacular Darkness*. Leyburn, UK: Tartarus Press, 2016. 320–35.

Barthes, Roland. *The Rustle of Language*. Tr. Richard Howard. Berkeley: University of California Press, 1989.

Berry, Wendell. *The Unsettling of America: Culture and Agriculture*. Rev. ed. Berkeley: Counterpoint, 2015.

Coleborn, Peter, and Pauline E. Dungate, ed. *Something Remains: Joel Lane and Friends*. Staffordshire, UK: Alchemy Press, 2016.

Ellul, Jacques. *The Technological Society*. New York: Vintage, 1964.

Ferlinghetti, Lawrence. *Little Boy*. New York: Anchor Books, 2020.

Gilmour, Rachelle. "Remembering the Future: The *Topheth* as Dystopia in Jeremiah 7 and 19." *Journal for the Study of the Old Testament* 44, No. 1 (2019): 64–78.

Ginsberg, Allen. *Howl and Other Poems*. San Francisco, City Light Books, 1956.

Gottert, Michael. "An Interview with Joel Lane." *African Paper* (March 2013), africanpaper.com/2013/03/16/personal-loss-is-an-important-literary-theme-and-one-that-i-return-to-quite-often-interview-with-joel-lane/. Accessed 10 September 2021.

Janet Pierre. *The Major Symptoms of Hysteria*. London: Macmillan, 1907.

Joshi, S. T. *Unutterable Horror: A History of Supernatural Fiction*. 2012. New York: Hippocampus Press, 2014. 2 vols.

Lane, Joel. *The Anniversary of Never*. Dublin: Swan River Press, 2015. [Abbreviated in the text as *AN*.]

———. *The Autumn Myth*. Todmorden, UK: Arc Publications, 2010. [Abbreviated in the text as *AM*.]

———. "Basement Angels." In Joseph S. Pulver, Sr., ed. *The Grimscribe's Puppets*. New York: Miskatonic River Press, 2013. 51–57.

———. *The Earth Wire*. 1994. London: Influx Press, 2020. [Abbreviated in text as *EW*.]

———. *The Edge of the Screen*. Todmorden, UK: Arc Publications, 1999. [Abbreviated in the text as *ES*.]

———. "Forbidden Questions: The Politics of Noir Fiction." *Socialism Today* No. 132 (October 2009), socialismtoday.org/archive/132/noir.html. Accessed 10 October 2021.

———. *The Lost District and Other Stories*. San Francisco: Night Shade, 2006. [Abbreviated in the text as *LD*.]

———. *Scar City*. London: Eibonvale Press, 2015. [Abbreviated in the text as *SC*.]

———. *This Spectacular Darkness*. Ed. Mark Valentine and John Howard. Leyburn, UK: Tartarus Press, 2016.

———. *Where Furnaces Burn*. 2013. Hornsea, UK: Drugstore Indian Press, 2014. [Abbreviated in the text as *WFB*.]

Lloyd-Smith, Alan. *American Gothic Fiction: An Introduction*. New York: Continuum, 2004.

Lyotard, Jean-François. *The Differend: Phrases in Dispute*. Tr. Georges Van Den Abbeele. Minneapolis: University of Minnesota Press, 1988.

Morrison, Toni. *The Source of Self-Regard: Selected Essays, Speeches, and Meditations*. New York: Alfred A. Knopf, 2019.

O'Connor, Frank. *The Lonely Voice*. London: Macmillan, 1963.

Praz, Mario. "Introductory Essay." In Peter Fairclough, ed. *Three Gothic Novels.* New York: Penguin, 1986. 7–34.

Rogers, Annie G. *The Unsayable: The Hidden Language of Trauma.* New York: Random House, 2006.

van der Kolk Bessel. "The Compulsion to Repeat the Trauma: Reenactment, Revictimization, and Masochism." *Psychiatric Clinics of North America* 12, No. 2 (1989): 389–411.

———. "Posttraumatic Stress Disorder and the Nature of Trauma." *Dialogues in Clinical Neuroscience* 2, No. 1 (2000): 7–22.

Weinstock, Jeffrey Andrew. *Charles Brockden Brown.* Cardiff: University of Wales Press, 2001.

Nyarlathotep

Ngo Binh Anh Khoa

From out a nameless pit midst sweltering sands
Since aeons long before old Egypt's birth,
He's roved the ancient seas and primal lands
And spread his influence o'er the infant Earth.
A cryptic figure cloaked in sunset's hues
By countless names and faces known, he's trod
Across the ages, moulding mankind's views
To serve the wills of his still slumbering God.
With him come Chaos, ruins, anarchy,
And those by his strange sciences seduced
Drink in his every word fanatically,
Made into puppets to be briefly used.
Like countless Empires toppled in his wake,
All built by Man, beneath his feet, shall break.

In the Graveyard

Scott J. Couturier

I can never express my gratitude. Giving me shelter in this damnable weather, in the pitch of night . . . you do look a bit peaked, though I can understand. My appearance is no doubt alarming. On a night like this, when ghosts must be abroad, and me blanched pale as marble, white as a sheet! The shock of it all has gotten to me, and I admit I am not myself. But you . . . my friend, I know you will listen. Always ready with an attentive ear, though usually as a covert confidant. If nothing else, your instinct for gossip should ensure you hearing me out.

You've caught wind, no doubt, about the desecration in New Hope cemetery, the grave of young Mary Meadley dug up and refilled by unknown hands. It's been in the headlines for over a week, so I won't preamble, but you must be told straightaway it was the four of us who did it. Dudley, Gerncroft, and Croates, and I hatched the whole thing together, out of practical rather than ghoulish impulses. Croates courted the girl last summer, even taking her for a few carriage rides out into the country. On one of these trips she showed it to him—the biggest, yellowest diamond you've ever imagined. "This," she told him, "is Cassilda's Star. Passed down in my family for generations, mother to daughter. If ever the line ends, the family will dictates it be buried with the last female heir." Why she showed Croates I have no notion; maybe she hoped to inflame his passion, or perhaps his envy. Whatever the case, Mary soon tired of him and told him in a frank letter to stop coming by. Of course, we all know Croates can be a tiresome fellow, especially around ladies. I'm surprised she put up with him for so long.

Then came this damnable summer, pestilence and disease hovering over the valley like a fog, slaying sleepers in their beds—and always a fierce battle fought, the sheets of the afflicted soiled and disordered, nightstand toppled and mattress rent by their contortions, jaw fixed wide in an endless scream. You, ever-wise in the wherefores of flight, were fortunate in leaving for the highlands come spring. The Meadley family got hard hit in May, her brother and father getting taken off at once. Last to go before Mary herself was her mother, stern old Mrs. Meadley, who suffered through three nights of torment before her violent end. In a delirium she rose and attacked her caretaker, Ms. Mosley, who was forced to lay her out with a fire iron, later being found dead of the disease herself. After that Mary became the last female Meadley heir, but not for long: malingering for a few weeks, the sickness finally took her in mid-June.

I admit it wasn't long before we started hatching the scheme. Over late-night drinks, all four of us afraid to fall asleep lest the sickness should take us, we talked at length about that yellow diamond. Gerncroft was skeptical, as he always is: "Probably just a piece of costume jewelry, some gewgaw from the opera." Dudley, meanwhile, had heard Croates tell the story before, and was more inclined—whether by greed or familiarity, not to mention his own lewd fixations—toward credulousness. "I say it's worth looking into," he said, rising and going for a trowel in the corner. "Let's get to the cemetery tonight, hop-step!"

For my part, I found myself less suspicious of the tale than Gerncroft, though I doubted whether the diamond had made its way into the young unfortunate's coffin. Restraining Dudley, who anyway was already reeling from drink, I said, "Let Gerncroft make inquiries at his firm about what was placed in her coffin. Surely he can find out what the young lady wore to greet her eternal reward." Then, to Dudley, "And you, old rascal, think for just a moment! She's new-buried, the cemetery besides sown thick with the dead of this plague. Better, I say, for us to wait out death's siege, each risking internment in that ground we propose desecrating till the mortal toll subsides. Surely it would be best to let her body settle before unearthing it; and there are always gravediggers working now, all through the night hours.

Yes, best to wait, and drink to each other's health!"

So wait we did, though it chafed Dudley to distraction, at least until the third toast.

In July and August the reaper was busy indeed. I've no doubt you received some sort of news, even in your mountain seclusion; how else would you know it was safe to return? But word of mouth cannot convey the virulence that stalked both town and countryside, though ironically it can convey the disease itself. Every day a parade of pine boxes, borne to the churchyard in black wagons hung with lace, and the church bells tolling, tolling! How the four of us survived I've no notion, save that the devil often favors his wicked. Dudley did try to flee, driven by that same impetuosity that impelled him toward the trowel, but was held up at the road out of town by a band of regimentals wearing the king's insignia. They leveled rifles when he tried to push his cart through their ranks, and afterward we knew we were truly cut off from the outside, to live or die as nature saw fit.

Gerncroft, with a few subtle inquiries, was able to confirm the presence of a large yellow jewel strung around the dead Mary Meadley's neck. "The coroner said it had a hint of bile in its coloring," he recounted, "set on a silver chain. He inspected her just before the coffin was closed, and asked the lawyer present whether he knew anything about the stone. He said it was just an old family keepsake, nothing of value unless sentiments can be so measured. Clearly a lie, but Higley said nothing further, just nodded and helped hammer down the lid."

John Higley—once coroner of our quiet community, now much quieter since the plague's coming. He was stricken in August, and after that they just started piling the bodies in the chapel of Our Lady of Perpetual Grace.

Confirmation of the diamond's existence excited us, providing welcome distraction from the welter of both heat and disease. Doubling down on our plans, we set aside such supplies as any good graverobber needs: shovels, lanterns, dark clothing, and a good pistol for each man, simultaneously divesting ourselves of any meddlesome pangs of conscience. By August's end the rate of infection slowed to a crawl, that deadly miasma beginning to dissipate upwards and away, brisk northern winds cleansing the atmosphere as a monk might sweep out a dirtied fane. The four of us—Krantz, Dudley, Gerncroft, and Croates—began to breathe a bit easier, thinking perhaps we had dodged the fate shared by a good third of the town. The gravediggers, themselves months interred, had been replaced by others, who at last were able to rest their weary arms.

Finally, as September unwound gray and cool, we determined the time had come for our midnight excavation. The last reported death was over a week before, and that a babbling peddler from the hills, his body dumped in a communal grave dug in the potter's field; so, of no threat to us. Merry indeed was the party that set out under a new moon, shuttered lanterns slashing lances of light over the fog-laden fields, each of us in turn resisting the urge to set up a happy worker's song, or at least a peppy whistle. Croates was attired in a black greatcoat, his 'great-Croat' as he called it with something analogous to wit, shambling along with a broad smile on his dual-scarred features. Then came Gerncroft, tall and thin as a stork, his long shanks swirling the mist into weird specters as he strode. Then Dudley, pudgy and querulous, with a sap's grin to match Croates, though a life of cowardice kept him from boasting the same collection of cicatrixes. We each wore a beaked leather mask over nose and upper face, stuffed with garlic and cloves to hold at bay any lingering contagion—and to hide our identities should it become necessary.

A lonely, lorn night it was. Gerncroft had managed to do some research on Cassilda's Star, consulting the firm's ledgers, and he related it to us in whispers as we slunk through the night toward New Hope. "Supposedly mined somewhere in Siberia, most likely Yakutia, though more than a few accounts claim the diamond, and I quote, 'fell as a star from the heavens.' It was prized by the Russian nobility for a half-century before disappearing, funnily enough, from inside a young woman's grave." He paused and cleared his throat as we digested this ironic revelation. "Her name was Anna Popova, the common lover of an aristocrat. She died from consumption, and he buried the stone with her to prove his grief."

"A noble in deed as well as title," Dudley mumbled sardonically, the attendant pun well beyond his conscious faculties of construction. "Save that he could have fed a whole ghetto by selling off the thing instead. Where did it show up next?"

"It resurfaced in Paris, coming to the Meadley line through what can only be termed a most fortuitous marriage. In time, the family—or at least its fortune—was done in by syphilis and poor habits, and again the diamond vanished from all record, presumably sold off amid their dissipation. Until—well, until she showed it to you, Croates. Who can know what compelled her? For that matter, why keep such an invaluable secret when one could instead live lavishly off its proceeds?"

Dudley snorted. "Beyond that, burying the stone with Mary is simply an affront to common thrift. Why surrender such a precious object to death?"

Croates leered at him. "Most would say Mary Meadley was the precious object surrendered to death," he quipped, guiding the discourse back to crudity with finesse. "I missed my chance to try her charms while she lived; perhaps what's left in the grave will be worth a fondle."

We all recoiled at this, though more from dread of plague than any puritanical aversion. "I've danced with death enough this summer," Gerncroft mumbled, "though, given your temperament, I can understand an attraction to the deceased. They cannot fight you off, get with child, or go and reveal damaging information to powerful fathers." At this we all shared a sickly snicker, and Croates blustered something about it all being a joke anyhow. Well you know how the gang gets on, especially when we've had a few; needless to say, it took more spirits to compel us to the cemetery than we feared encountering there.

The stars glistened overhead, only a few faint clouds smudging the western horizon. We arrived at the graveyard and shone our lamps around hesitantly, listening in the silence for any foreign footfall or voice. The tombstones stood like gleaming white sentries in the darkness, each straight-backed with soldierly austerity, newly erected row upon newly erected row—for the first month or so they still managed the propriety of putting up stones, giving way rapidly to planks and crossed sticks. We knew more or less where to find Mary's grave, and tentatively crossed through the bent iron gate, speaking only in whispers now when we spoke at all, everyone jumping when Dudley's spade clanked against the head of the shovel I shouldered. Nerves got to us quickly, even through the haze of drink, and we all paused once to remove our masks and pass around a flask of bitter, fiery liquor. You can be assured we were oft thankful for Croates's still, those long dry months.

We found her grave beneath a rowan tree near the cemetery's edge, stone already slumped forward toward the now-sunken earth. "Coffin must have caved in," Gerncroft revealed ominously. Looking each at the other, we had our final moment to back out of the affair; all it would have taken was a single vote of Nay. But summer's hardship had strengthened our fortitude to the unwholesome, and greed is a potent driver of action regardless of season or circumstance. With a collective grimace we all began to dig, making short work of the compacted earth, my shovel striking home on wood after scarcely an hour's labor. Setting aside our tools, Gerncroft and Dudley aimed the lantern-beams downward while Croates and I completed the excavation. The lid of the coffin, indeed, was cracked lengthwise, through it hadn't caved in entirely. We were careful not to widen the split as we dug in the wet, wormy soil by hand, only after clearing enough space to open the lid turning our attention toward that ultimate act of violation.

Of course, it was Croates who did the honors. Baring a grimace of stained teeth, he pulled out a hammer and started prying free the nails, already rusty and warped. We all stood back at grave's verge, looking down silently as he set about his grim task with gusto. At last the final nail popped loose, and bereft of a moment's hesitation he gripped the lid's sundered edge and tore it sideways, exposing—in theory, at least—the coffin's mortal contents.

Perhaps I did see Mary Meadley's body, if only for an instant. Pale, distorted, sunken, all her hair fallen out to mound around the corpse's gaping jaw; or this could be an image I've built for myself, a lesser horror to abut the greater. What I *did* see indisputably was an outwards belch of yellow smoke, as if someone had tossed a burning peat-ball into the grave. This blast of fumes rose up so thick and fast it obscured everyone's vision, lanterns highlighting coils of sulfurous stench as they boiled about us. We could all hear Croates gagging as he struggled to climb clear, see the lantern's crazy bob as it swung in his fist. Then a cry and final gurgle, followed by the sound of a heavy body collapsing, accompanied by the crunch and crack of broken wood. I daresay we all winced, having retreated some distance now to open ground rather than helping to extricate him. A column of gas rose into the darkness, staining the starlight yellow, spreading fingers of foul mist through the tombstones. At last, after almost a minute, the flow petered to a choleric jet, then to nothing. Trembling with apprehension, sick with the stink, we at last dared to ease graveside and see what had befallen our presumably erstwhile comrade.

Croates lay there with a foolish grin on his face, looking happier in death than he ever did in life. The coffin had shattered from his weight, but no sign could we see of Mary's body underneath. Instead he lay splayed on the splintered wood as if arranged on a bier, hands crossed over his chest, heels neatly together, eyes closed and covered with stones in the place of coins. Around his neck, gleaming in the lantern-light, was strung a silver chain, from which depended a faceted yellow stone of extraordinary size. As big as a child's fist, with fires dancing in its heart—flashes of deeper yellow amid the yellow! With hardly a moment's hesitation Dudley hopped down and ripped the stone from around the corpse's throat, scattering hither and thither links from its silver chain. We helped him scrabble out, then turned and ran fast as ever our legs would manage, eager to be clear of the lingering stench which now pervaded the graveyard.

Several hours and quite a few nips later, we sat before the fire in my study, examining the stone by holding it this way and that in the hearth's light. At last, one of us—I think myself, who maintain by principal a residuum of cunning tact—suggested that we return to the cemetery and fill in the grave over Croates, so none might be the wiser. Of the yellow smoke we all agreed, by unspoken resolution, to say nothing; how truly forbidden is that topic which goes unremarked upon by a consent likewise silent! We had the stone—and with Croates gone, no need to split the dividend four ways. All that remained was for us to conceal the evidence, despite limbs made wobbly by excess of fear and drink.

Going by black horse and coach, we arrived at New Hope cemetery just as dawn blossomed in the east, a titter of birdsong accompanying the hurried completion of our midnight disinterment. Croates still lay as we left him, though death had begun to tug at and mold his face, that appalling playfulness which results in corpses looking waxy, puffy or sunken, inhuman. I admit we did a very poor job filling in the plot, partly owing to collective inebriation, partly to the horrid implications of oncoming sunrise. There are deeds which must be done by night; done by day, they take on a whole new hideous semblance. At last we stamped down the mound, turned and mounted the coach, horses pawing restlessly at a recently dug grave they'd strayed onto.

Right then—just as Gerncroft took up the switch—we all heard a scratching sound, like a fingernail on stone. It froze us to a man, and slowly in unison we turned, seeking out the noise's source. Had someone witnessed our unholy act? If so . . . my hands gripped tightly on my shovel, forcing me to wonder to what lengths I would go in protecting my possession of Cassilda's Star. I felt not only greed, but a compulsive willingness to commit any atrocity, just to make it away scot-free. . . . One of those perverse human impulses you always go on about, when you're around to go on.

The sound originated from behind Mary's tombstone. It came again, then again, a low and rhythmic scratching, insistent. The sun started its rise, first rays lighting the tops of the tallest trees; just then, something stood up from behind her marker. Pale as death, with a wide lolling mouth full of fangs—a stomach swollen with gluttony, flopping over the stone's top! Mary Meadley stared at us through eyes of piercing yellow, no pupil or white, satiated smile splitting her throat as would a wound, red rilling down over her breasts and stomach like wax from a guttered candle. I swear to you I saw her— we all saw her. Like a moment in some drama, each of us let out a little despairing sound, an exhale of our vital élan, never to return.

A slant of sunlight cut athwart the cemetery, breaking through the forest canopy where a dead tree hung its solemn branches. The thing before us vanished like a mist, a dazzlement, though it left its loathsome outline imprinted on all our retinas. With a collective shiver we leapt into the coach, and Dudley whipped the horses to a frenzy, leading to those pernicious reports of a suspicious black carriage seen hurtling along the byway shortly after dawn.

Our botched exploit made all the papers, a disturbed burial proving sufficiently morbid to intrigue even a plague-worn populace; the police went so far as to excavate the grave, finding it eerily empty. Vying for these headlines were reports of more deaths, the nighttime effluvium returned and rampant, victims now found drained of blood in addition to other nightmarish signs. Gathering over the next few days in my study to gloat over Cassilda's Star, we spent long hours fingering the stone, making fatuous plans for our future fortunes. The town still under armed quarantine, there was nowhere we could safely pawn the thing off; and anyway, its beauty was such that we all wondered if we shouldn't keep it in secret, passing it among ourselves yearly as a sort of talisman against death. "Or a talisman to attract death," Gerncroft noted; I give him credit where credit is due. Of course we groused a bit about poor Croates, and drank more than a few toasts of his own rotgut in dubious honor. No one in town, it seems, noticed his absence enough to warrant remark.

Dudley eventually and unsurprisingly decided he wanted to take the stone home. Like the yellow mist before, none of us dared mention Mary's apparition, or her empty grave; probably the lazy coppers hadn't dug deep enough. We ignored the town crier as he ran by shouting updates, always more dead, drained of blood like butchered cattle. With reluctance I handed Dudley the gem, and he snatched it with a prurient covetousness. "Mary never took to me, wouldn't even let me fetch her eggs," he muttered as he clasped the thing, then opened his hand to regard it anew. "With Croates gone, and this diamond as bait, perhaps she'll come to me at last."

We must pity the prophet by rule of history, especially those who declare their own demise. The next day Dudley was found pale as fresh tallow, mouth gaping and body contorted, not a drop of blood in him, though a few stains dappled the sheets. His bedside window hung open, considered an invitation to disease; had he gone mad, his relations wondered? Or was it something else, something only whispered in hushed rumor, something Father Benjamin at the church had already heard confessed to him as heretical superstition: the dead walking, Mary Meadley risen from her grave to feed on blood by night! I saw Dudley's body, alongside Gerncroft, and can attest the extent of his sufferings. "He was bled quickly, violently," Gerncroft averred, "by no mortal tool." At this I merely nodded, eyeing the yellow diamond, which glinted on Dudley's dressing table. A shiver of horrible anticipation raced through me, impossible to describe; under normal circumstances I would have demanded the diamond for myself. Instead we both lowered our gazes, turned and left Dudley to death's ministration, by unspoken decision agreeing to leave the star as well. Little deprives greed of power like ill-omen; let another unlucky soul take up the curse.

That evening, as a pitched storm raged outside, keeping me from whatever scant sleep I might otherwise have snatched, I swore that I could see shadows circling outside my house. As if something were flying by repeatedly but intangibly, or so fast as to be almost indiscernible. Then, as if created out of the night itself, I saw Gerncroft's bean-thin body appear outside the door to my garden patio, his palms desperately clamoring against the glass. A crazed look shone in his eyes, and I leapt from beneath my sweat-stained coverlet, unlatching the door sans any apprehension beyond worry for his well-being.

Gerncroft stumbled in, body drenched by rain, so pale I thought he must be in the early grip of hypothermia. "My good man," I stammered to him, and manhandled him over fireside, where I clumsily stirred up the coals. "What are you doing out there, on a night like this?" You may be surprised at my solicitude—only Gerncroft, of our lot, deserves such treatment. Had any of the rest of you stumbled to my door in a thunderstorm, I should have laughed myself silly watching you get drenched.

I got no reply at first, though I plied his tongue with good brandy and questions, stoking the fire to a hot blaze that dulled the lightning's jagged, intermittent flashes. Shivering and dripping he sat there, one hand thrust into his pocket, his pupils wide-blown like one in the grip of opium, or the glazed eyes of a corpse. "Gerncroft," I said at last, sternly, taking his shoulder and shaking it until his head bobbled, "speak, damn you, and tell me why you've come here, in the middle of the night, unasked for! Are you ill?"

The shadows again flashed by my window, discernible against the lightning's flare. Just as my head turned to catch them, Gerncroft looked up at me, the hand in his pocket withdrawing, fingers uncurling to reveal the yellow gleam of Cassilda's Star.

"He brought it back to me," he said, in a choked voice.

I stared at the diamond as one regards a poised serpent, hissing through my teeth as I replied, "Who brought it back to you?"

Gerncroft's dark eyes widened into black pools. "Dudley."

I bolted for the door—why? A feeling, prescient, of mortal danger, blood thrumming fiery in every nerve like a drug. Perhaps I realized the shape of the shadows I saw darting past, how one of them had Croates's idiot outline and another Dudley's paunch, the third resembling a woman with burning yellow eyes. Perhaps I noticed the way Gerncroft rocked eagerly forward as he spoke, gaze fixed on the manic pulse at my wrist. Perhaps it was the smell—like a charnel-yard—that stole out from his body, the way he twitched as he spoke, like a marionette with a clumsy puppeteer. Perhaps I just wanted to escape the sight of that diamond.

As I grasped the handle the windows exploded inward, night and storm and shadows rushing inside, hearthfire going out with a roar like the Devil in Hades.

Bartleby sat frozen as his friend finished his story, or at least trailed off into silence. Krantz was pale, too pale to look at, his eyes wide-blown and glazed; one tremulous hand was fixed in his pocket, clutching something with avaricious intent. Outside the half-moon gleamed through a rood-screen of branches, casting crooked shadows over the plush carpeting of Bartleby's bedchamber. Just back, after an interminable summer whiling away his doldrums in the highlands, waiting for Death to conclude his business. A summer of sheep-watching and rude fare, living in a hut rocked by the wind, no good music or conversation or civilization, nothing for a rumor-monger like himself to feed on. His sense of relief at the plague's abatement can be summed up by the reckless expediency of his re-turn, oiled by a hefty bribe to the regimentals; they'd grinned mali-ciously as he proffered the purse, causing Bartleby to wonder. Only after his anonymous homecoming did he realize the plague had re-vived, and more virulent than before.

Krantz, as if catching the drift of Bartleby's thoughts, smiled and spoke up. "Of course, with your resources you knew plague was coming. Burning up the southern trade routes since March, and none of us the wiser. . . . But you, with you connections, your business, you knew. Always the five of us have shared this wretched lot, wringing brotherhood from depredation, each cheering on the others in minor infamies. You should have been with us that night, digging up Mary's grave—but then, none of this would have happened had you told us, warned us. Instead you flitted off and abandoned your brothers, on some trifling pretense of investing in wool as I recall."

Three flickering shadows flashed by the window, followed by a fourth: it wore the mask of a woman's face, pale and cold as snow-fall, lit by eyes of yellow sheen. Bartleby felt the blood turn to slush in his veins. "I—" he said, then choked on his half-formed denial, ashamed for once of his own conduct. "I thought it would be amusing," he admitted at last, in a terrified drawl, "to see which of you made it through."

Krantz gave a slack-jawed grin, and it looked to Bartleby as if his teeth shone yellow, tapering to points. "Surprise surprise," he whispered. "We all made it through. And we are wealthy, a wealth we would share with you."

So saying, his hand tugged loose of his pocket, filthy fingers uncurling to reveal the choleric gleam of a huge diamond, large as a child's fist.

Unlike Krantz, Bartleby made no bolt for the door.

The Instructive Pleasures of Horror Fiction

Carl E. Reed

We know that we will not forever be
strong lords & masters of these failing forms;
the horror tale is black-heart ribaldry:
dark-booming, crackle-lightning'd thunderstorm.
Through the transportive art of weird fiction
the morbid, probing reader, in due course
will silently remouth malediction—
thus place a trembling hand on his own corpse.
The whirlpool void within calls to without;
this world is strange—far stranger than we know.
We grasp at fleeting shadows, gnawing doubt
suffuses & informs short lives of woe.
The end of all endeavor: cold abyss.
Horror plants foreshadowed nihilist kiss.

Dracula: Bram Stoker's Love Letter to the Human Race

Katherine Kerestman

It is ironic that Dracula, creature of the night, is seldom out of plain sight. In fact, it is not often that a week passes without a person encountering some sort of allusion to *The Master*—or to another vampire derived from his myth. Dracula is practically ever-present in our collective psyche. He has fastened his fangs into it. The sharpness of his teeth makes your blood run cold. A glimpse of him standing on a winding stone staircase induces the flow of adrenaline throughout your body. The slight movement of his cape causes you to catch your breath. The *Idea* of Dracula is visceral.

Bram Stoker's novel strikes a primeval nerve. It scratches its sharp nails on the stuff and matter of humanity, raising patches of goosebumps. Its poignancy is universal. Its brilliance lies in Stoker's ability to pack just about every human truth or mystery into his monster story.

These reflections came upon me in a backwards way. I was enjoying several radio plays based more or less upon Stoker's masterpiece. I listened to an Atlanta Radio Theater production of Thomas E. Fuller's *Brides of Dracula* (2007); a BBC radio play adaptation of *Dracula* starring David March as Dracula (1975); and a CBS Mystery Theater version starring Mercedes McCambridge (1974).

Brides of Dracula adds to the story an emphasis on lesbianism, bisexuality, and rampant, unrestrained sex. Mina seems to welcome Dracula's sanguine seduction—and then she turns the table and sucks him dry, not quite killing him. This version features Latinate refrains (repeated "Ave's") and blood-drenched imagery. In the BBC *Dracula,* Lucy is engaged to Dr. *Arthur* Seward; as do so many retellings, this one eliminates two of her suitors, thereby eliminating the rivalry among the three suitors for her hand—as well as the formation of the Band of Heroes when the rivals come together to risk their lives for the women, and for their civilization. In this version, the gypsies stop at an inn, where their gossip reveals the shipment of the Count's coffins. The CBS adaptation includes the new elements of a *single* Mina *Harker,* automobiles, Dracula revealing his vampiric nature by his fear of the Bible, and the concept of the vampire as the unwilling pawn of Satan.

All these additions to the myth bespeak a prodigious amount of creativity and yield a great deal of entertainment value. Still, I tend to regret what these—and many of the countless other radio, film, and print adaptations—have lost.

What is lost by the enlargement of the sexual comfort zone in modern renditions of *Dracula* is not simply the superfluous Victorian prudery, but also one of the chief elements of the profound horror of Stoker's work. In *Dracula,* sexual selfishness, depravity, and loss of self-control are more horrific than jugular bloodletting. The horror is that of human beings reducing one another to objects for their personal gratification: we become monsters. In that kind of world, you are very much alone.

On the other hand, giving of oneself, concern for another's feelings, helping someone save face, and regulation of one's passions to avoid exploitation of another—these are not antithetical to sexual pleasure, nor to any of the other joys of human existence. In fact, respect, compassion, and nurturing serve to enhance the love between Stoker's Jonathan and Mina. Each respects the other's work: she his law practice, and he her legal assistance work.

Each jealously guards the other's self-esteem. Mina hesitates to read Jonathan's diary and then forebears to judge him when she is forced to learn his shame at the hands of Dracula's brides; she reads in order to help him achieve self-forgiveness after his breakdown. Jonathan, although he does not find his Mina as disgusting as she herself does, accepts her self-appraisal as unclean after her blood exchange with Dracula; and he helps her find spiritual healing according to her own standards. Each supports the other in his own spiritual journey: each helps the other shoulder his or her own "emotional baggage." Neither prescribes values or rules for the other. Neither passes judgment. Each restrains the impulse to say, "Get over it." Each is a helpmeet to the other.

Their restraint is emblematic of their ability to postpone selfish pleasure. A premature resolution of the tension must be at the expense of the other's own moral agenda. Although Jonathan and Mina each yearn for a consummation of their love and a happily-ever-after, each waits for the other's readiness. In *Dracula,* self-restraint and sexual governance are profound gifts of one's self to one's beloved. Retellings of *Dracula* usually are anything but restrained.

Another difference between *Dracula* and its literary and film progeny is the theme of temptation. Everyone is tempted in *Dracula.* The good people resist temptation, practicing heroism daily in their lives—even prior to becoming the Band of Heroes. Mina and Jonathan face sexual temptation by seductive vampires. Their experience resembles date rape, which usually occurs after a trusted person administers a drug to an unwitting victim: the vampires have an unfair advantage, their great sexual power receiving supernatural enhancement from their mesmerizing psychic powers. Mina and Jonathan admit to their own arousals by their assailants prior to the assault. Facing their weakness with humility rather than denying it, Mina and Jonathan are full of self-loathing, as are many rape victims.

Beautiful, vivacious—and virtuous, too—Lucy enjoys the attentions of her suitors, eventually favoring Arthur Holmwood with her hand. Lucy's temptation is that of pride, for she fails to discourage two of her suitors, a violation of the social norms of her time. By *fin-de-siècle* social convention, however, she is simultaneously prevented from acknowledging a preference for Arthur until after he first declares his own affection. Trapped by competing conventions, she must bide her time until Arthur makes the first move. In the meantime, Lucy enjoys life as a social being, the belle of the ball. She is, alas, a flirt, a good woman one step from becoming a fallen woman on the slippery slope of virtuous womanhood. Hers is a venial sin. Even so, although she stays the course in life, she succumbs to Dracula in un-death.

Early in the story, friends Arthur Holmwood, Dr. Seward, and Quincy Morris compete to win Lucy Westenra to the bridal bed. Directly upon being denied her hand, the losing contenders adopt a gentlemanly attitude and offer their congratulations to the affianced couple. They do not vent their disappointment and pain; instead, they govern themselves, and they honor their friends, Lucy and Arthur. Sexual energy in *Dracula* is a powerful force. In the hands of Dracula, it can destroy lives and civilizations. Harnessed, it can galvanize Stoker's heroes into a formidable force for battling evil.

It is the rare *reader* who is not titillated by the *ménage à quatre* with the beautiful vampire brides, as is Jonathan; their allure is so powerful they needn't have any psychic powers to reduce most readers to putty. Stoker's skillful sexual stimulation of the reader as the *ménage* scene builds to its crescendo is abruptly halted by Dracula's violent assault upon the women. He throws them off; he then offers them a baby to torture and kill. The orgasm is aborted, as is the child. This sexual encounter is wrong on so many levels. Later the child's mother comes crying for her baby outside the castle walls, only to be torn apart by Dracula's wolves. Unregulated sexual behavior results in horror.

So, too, Mina's chaste mouth on Dracula's chest, lapping up his blood while her husband lies senseless next to her in the bed, is powerful imagery. Mina is horrified at her own sexual response to the murderer of her friend and the usurper of her husband's place. As is the reader. The Band of Heroes bursts in—and the consummation of Mina's "blood wedding" with Dracula is also interrupted—by the entrance of her defenders. They feel compassion for her; she feels shame.

Sexual arousal is a normal human response for both the characters and the reader—and the sex appeal of Dracula is not unlike the power of Milton's Satan, *almost* irresistible. But there is grave danger inherent in giving full sway to our feelings. Good versus evil is played out in *Dracula* in the constant tension of the subplot of Virtue versus Sensuality and Eroticism. The reader engages in the same internal drama when he or she is aroused by Dracula and his wives—who are mass murderers. The reader must also confront his or her own conflicting emotions.

Victorian England had a plethora of social conventions by which people were helped to maintain self-control; the rules for courtship and sexual engagement, although now seen as somewhat stuffy and tainted by a double standard, were conceived for the greater good. Enter Dracula, a suave interloper from the far-off *Land Beyond the Forest,* bringing alluring Old World mannerisms and speech, loads of money, aristocratic forebears—and disease. Along with the rats on the *Demeter,* who carry the plague from port to port, Dracula brings moral taint, spiritual contamination to England—the Other from the Orient carries contagion. *Dracula* is an epic played across the continents by a larger-than-life protagonist, who falls by his hubris at the hands of decent, honorable, technologically advanced, Christian English citizens.

The threat Dracula represents is not merely the loss of blood and the transformation of his victims into blood-sucking Undead beings. The threat is a worldwide pandemic of Evil, the loss not only of life but of Virtue. Without the ability to feel shame, one cannot strive toward virtue. What looms is the prospect of a world destitute of goodness and morality, the earth as a seething mass of corruption. What is at stake is the very concept that we have an eternal soul.

Mina and Jonathan, like Eve and Adam, must seek forgiveness of their God and their fellow men; forgive themselves and each other; and go bravely forth to create a new, post-Edenic world shorn of their innocence. By their strength, ingenuity, and willingness to submit to honest self-examination they carry on the good fight. But they first must conquer their own internal demons. Many of the derivative versions give short shift to the equal moral partnership of Jonathan and Mina.

The Icelandic version of Dracula, *Makt Myrkranna* (*Powers of Darkness*), was published in serial form in 1900 and 1901 in a Reykjavik newspaper and has been recently translated into English. A swirling controversy and literary mystery now revolves around the relative contributions of Bram Stoker and translator/editor Valdimar Ásmundsson. There are many differences between *Dracula* and *Powers of Darkness*—both in characters and plot—and many similarities. It is a different Dracula story, and a good one. It is significant that Harker, imprisoned in Dracula's castle in the Icelandic version also, is concerned that his employer Hawkins would desire to know what kind of man he is bringing into England, and Harker thinks that if he could warn Hawkins, perhaps he would decline to do business with Dracula. In the "Missing Chapter," Harker writes in his journal his reflections on English values as opposed to those of Count Dracula:

> our moral aspirations are supported by decency in speech, written word and behavior . . . Surely the community that is ashamed of its filth is truly healthier than that in which people are shameless enough to throw their rubbish on streets and crossroads as if it does not matter . . . I do not pretend to be very strict with morals myself; still, I cannot condone that the only strings constantly struck are those of uncurbed carnal craving. (173)

Makt Myrkranna also recognizes the epic scope of the struggle between ordinary people trying to be good and the forces of evil which they must confront head-on, lest they be lost to themselves.

Makt Myrkranna, it turns out, is an abridgement of *Morkrets Makter*, the Swedish adaptation of *Dracula*, by A-e, which was serialized from 1899 to 1900 in a Swedish newspaper. Its recent translation into English and publication by Centipede Press have triggered an explosion of literary curiosity; and questions regarding the textual origins of this version (early drafts of *Dracula*, Bram Stoker's notes, the novel itself), the identity of A-e, and the extent of Stoker's knowledge and involvement have mobilized a legion of literary forensics sleuths. In this version, as in *Makt Myrkranna*, a great many characters, scenes, and plot lines have been added to Stoker's original—and many have been left out. The poignant scenes of the mother crying for her babe devoured by Dracula's wives; of Mina's blood wedding to Dracula; and of the race to death of the Band of Heroes in defense of Mina first (and the world at large second), which culminates in the destruction of Dracula (the spawn of devils) in Transylvania, have all been discarded. In their place are the murder of a girl, whose death is part of a frame-up of Harker; hermetic seances and ritual sex at Carfax Abbey; and the apprehension of the leader of a worldwide anarchist plot in his suburban villa. The aforementioned are only a small portion of the significant alterations to the 1897 *Dracula*.

The net result of the deviations is, for better or worse, a series of episodic horror narratives entwined with a detective story, à la Sherlock Holmes versus Professor Moriarty, with a marked de-emphasis on supernatural elements in favor of rational explanations ("some as yet undiscovered law of nature" [611]) for phenomena. Whether the variations are pleasing is a matter of the reader's taste. The upshot of these changes, though, is that, in shifting the focus from the individual suffering and heroism of Lucy, Mina, and Jonathan to a global conspiracy (of which the travails of our heroes are merely collateral damage), *Morkrets Makter* has lost the tragic and epic power of *Dracula*. In the words of Wilma (Mina), who—although worried sick about her missing fiancé Thomas (Jonathan) Harker—is continuously reminded that the detectives have greater fish to fry: "it is difficult for me to refrain from a certain bitterness at the thought of how unimportant the fate of a single human being actually seems to be in the world" (541).

In *Dracula*, the enemy is the vampire, who threatens to destroy Lucy, Jonathan's, and Mina's immortal souls, as well as others', spreading vampirism in the process; in *Morkrets Makter*, the foe is a cabal of anarchists, who may or may not possess supernatural powers ("Villains are villains," declares detective Barrington Jones) and who imperil liberty by planning to establish a new moral and political world order based on "might makes right" (752). In the Swedish version, one's self must be subsumed by either the Interests of Society or by the Powers of Darkness: in either case, a discrete and autonomous soul and selfhood is no longer the thing at stake, as is the case in *Dracula*. Mina understands the tragedy that everyone else fails to recognize: the individual is a pawn in the struggle between competing social orders.

Dracula is an heroic novel on more than one level. It is a worldwide struggle of Good against Evil, godliness versus the demonic. More than that, it is the epic struggle of the human being to be master of his own soul, to own his own thoughts and emotions, to accept accountability, and to attain the spiritual and intellectual heights it can reach. It is *The Pilgrim's Progress* writ with a Gothic quill. It is the hard-won victory of women and men against that which seeks to destroy us—both the creatures of darkness without, and the demons within our own selves. This is the legendary power of *Dracula*— which is discarded by most of its reincarnations. This is the authority that makes it one of the best-known and loved books across the globe. Imitations tend to abandon the majesty and beauty of Stoker's novel—and even to defang Count Dracula—by denying the struggles within and among the Band of Heroes to retain their sovereignty of their own selves in the midst of the forces of evil.

Works Cited

Fuller, Thomas E. *Brides of Dracula*. Atlanta Radio Theater Company, 2007.

Lowthar, George. *Dracula*. CBS Mystery Theater Radio Drama, 1974.

McDonald, Eric. *Dracula*. BBC Radio Play, 1975.

Stoker, Bram. *Dracula*. 1897. Garden City, NY: International Collectors Library, 2003.

———, and A-e. *Powers of Darkness: The First Dracula*. Tr. Rickard Berghorn. Ed. S. T. Joshi and Martin Andersson. Lakewood, CO: Centipede Press, 2022.

———, and Valdimar Ásmundsson. *Powers of Darkness: The Lost Version of Dracula*. Tr. Hans Corneel de Roos. New York: Peter Mayer, 2016.

Hands Up

Harley Carnell

I walked down the high street, past corrugated shutters decorated with graffiti palimpsests, and turned the corner into the housing estate. The part of it I lived on was dark, even though it was early in the night. This was mostly because the streetlights had either been smashed, their bulbs spray-painted over, or they had simply extinguished and not been replaced by the local council.

It was not so dark, though, that I couldn't see The Teenagers. I had always called them The Teenagers, even though their ages varied. Some were so young they were not teenagers yet; some so old they hadn't been for some time; for some, it was hard to imagine them ever having been teenagers. How many literal teenagers The Teenagers contained, I wasn't sure. There was just something about them that evoked the idea of teenagers, even if that thing wasn't their ages.

A combination of the dark, and the fact that each of The Teenagers was encased in a hoodie, meant that I could see none of their faces. Yet it was unmistakably them.

As always, I felt fear when seeing them. And also as always, I tried to diffuse that fear with reason. Nothing was going to happen. Nothing had ever happened. In thirty, forty seconds I'd be in my flat.

I walked forward. I had nothing to worry about. I was just being silly. I was being paranoid. I passed them. See, it was fine.

Then, from behind me, I heard a voice.

"Oi!" it said. I wanted to keep on walking, maybe bolt for my flat, but thought better of it. They knew where I lived, after all.

I turned around. The Teenagers were all still, except for one younger boy who had stepped forward. I could tell he was younger because of his size, and because he was now close enough that I could see his face through his hood. I would have been shocked if he was thirteen.

"Hands up, mate!" he said. At this, I felt my heart sink. Gun crime was rare in London—stabbings were far more common—but it did happen.

But then, looking at the boy's expression, I could see that he was just taking the piss. He had no gun. He just wanted to frighten me, and my shocked face obviously gave him gratification, because he stopped smirking and started grinning. It was a strange grin—one that seemed to lack any kind of joy or humour and looked more like a baring of the teeth.

I was about to turn around, grateful that I was going to walk away with just a bit of humiliation, when I saw him reach into his pocket. As he did so, his face became serious. He slowly drew his hand out of his pocket. His thumb was bolt upright with his index finger pointed towards me—the universal symbol for a gun.

"Put your hands up, mate, you're gonna get hit. You don't wanna get hit, mate. You don't want that." I waited for the laughter, but there was none. Was I imagining things? Did he actually have a gun and I just couldn't see it? The brain was capable of strange things in moments of trauma. Was this some kind of defence mechanism, an optical illusion conjured by my brain to spare me the true terror of what was actually happening?

Not knowing what else to do, I turned away and began walking to my flat. A few seconds later there was an eruption of laughter from The Teenagers.

"You got hit, mate! You got hit!" said the boy over the laughter. I flinched, anticipating a short delay before the onrush of pain that happens when you have been struck unexpectedly by something.

But I felt nothing. Maybe they had shot me with a pellet gun or a paint gun, and I hadn't been able to feel it through my thick coat. The latter would be more probable, as it would explain the laughter. My dark black coat would now be covered in a Rorschach splatter of yellow paint. I would not be able to afford to get it dry-cleaned, let alone buy a new one.

I went inside my flat, closed the door, and double-locked it behind me. I took my coat off, hesitating for a few seconds before looking at it. Aside from the odd bit of fluff and stray hair, it was completely clean. Nor was there any dent that would suggest a pellet. I had not been hit.

I laughed to myself in relief while, outside, I heard The Teenagers also laughing.

When I left the flat the next morning, I looked out for The Teenagers but couldn't see them. Not that I was surprised. For one thing, they didn't tend to be out this early. Secondly, it was rare to see them in the same place twice in such quick succession. The estate I lived on was so large that you could sometimes go weeks without seeing them.

When I came back from work that night, they were not there either.

"Are you okay?" Mary asked me. I jumped a little. I had been eating lunch, staring at an online news article without really reading it, and her voice had surprised me.

"Sorry?" I said.

"Are you okay?" she repeated. "I hope you don't mind me saying, and I hope I'm not being nosey, but you just seem a bit . . ." Her sentence trailed off as she struggled to find something that bridged the gap of accurately describing how I looked while not sounding rude.

"I'm just a bit tired," I said.

This was an understatement. Because while I had been sleeping normally, I *was* tired. I was exhausted, in fact. If I had just stepped into my body at this moment, I would have thought that I'd been getting two hours sleep a night. Although, having said that, my tiredness was not really physical. Rather, it was a kind of . . . mental tiredness.

I wasn't quite sure how to elaborate on that, even to myself. There was certainly no way I would be able to explain it to anyone else. But, vague or not, "mental tiredness" did essentially convey it.

"Late nights?" Mary asked.

"Yeah," I said. "Something like that. You know me, Mary, I'm out every night, partying."

She laughed, and said: "Yep, that's what we all say about you: party animal."

"But I'll be fine. Just a night's rest and I'll be great."

I'd been feeling this tiredness ever since my encounter with The Teenagers. The morning after, I'd felt it, but had been so preoccupied with worry that they might be outside that I'd ignored it. I'd felt it later, when I was on the bus to work. I'd felt it at work, and in the evening. It had been nearly a week now since I'd run into The Teenagers, and every day since then I'd felt this tiredness.

As usual, I got on the bus after work. As usual, there were no seats. As usual, I was forced to stand in the aisles for thirty minutes, while the laws of physics were broken as more people than should have been able to fit on the bus managed to get on it.

I must have taken this bus journey hundreds of times over the years: first for school, and now for work. In that time I had gotten used to this congestion. Over the past few days, though, my tiredness was making it harder to cope with. The thirty minutes were agonising, congealing into what seemed like hours. With each new person who shoved past me, not even bothering to try and tilt their body but just slithering their way past me, I felt myself twitching. Every time the bus driver stopped the bus to let people on even though it was clearly full, or enjoined us over the PA to "move down inside the bus please!" even though there was no more bus to move down into, I felt my blood pressure rise and my heart sink. And when I got off the bus I was so tired that I could not even savour the relief of being out in the fresh air.

Apart from a few takeaways, everything was closed. As in my estate, none of the streetlights were functioning, so the only illumination came from the neon lights of the shop fronts, giving everything a strange kind of hospital-hallway glow.

Homeless people had begun to take residence in the empty doorways. Some were sleeping after long days. Others were sitting up or kneeling forward, preparing themselves for a night of begging. I ignored the few requests for change, using my headphones as an excuse for not hearing. Usually I'd feel terrible for this. After bills, council tax, and the canned matter that barely qualified as "food" on which I subsisted, I barely had much money myself. But still, I felt guilty. They were, after all, by definition worse off than me.

Over the last few days, though, I had stopped feeling like this. Instead, the kind of reactionary sentiments I read on news sites' comments sections, or heard on radio phone-ins, seeped into my mind. *Get a job! They're just going to use it to buy drugs! They're only homeless by choice! They're all secretly millionaires!*

That I didn't accept any of these thoughts, and that they repulsed me, did not change the fact that I was thinking them in the first place. In the past, I never would have even thought stuff like this. Nor would I have felt, as I did now, a sense of rising disgust as the various requests for "change, change please" penetrated my headphones.

I had forgotten to buy toilet paper.

I swore out loud, not caring that the people next door had almost certainly heard it through the thin, tissue-like walls. I grabbed the grey tube, a sliver of white paper still clinging to it, and flung it against the wall. It was so light, and made such an unsatisfactory impact, that I grabbed a bottle of shower gel. As angry as I was, I managed to stop myself. If I threw it, all that would happen was that the bottle would burst open, leaving me to clear up shower gel for the next few hours. (Which, considering it would lather at the slightest contact with liquid, would be a Sisyphean task.)

Putting the shower gel down, I swore to myself again and headed outside.

Apart from the tiredness and the anger, something else had happened since the night with The Teenagers. It was now ten o'clock, and I was outside my flat. This is something I never would have done before. Unless I was dying of hunger or needed some kind of emergency medical treatment, the idea of going outside past eight or nine o'clock would have been unthinkable.

When I had been in school, even some of the tougher boys had talked about how intimidated they were by the area. I had spent my whole life scared of where I lived. But as I prepared to go out, I realised that I was not scared.

In fact, as I walked out of my front door and into the street, I actually felt buoyed. I say buoyed, because I was not "happy" as such. It was more like a rush of adrenaline, or the kind of energy boost you might get after a strong coffee. I was almost strutting down the street. I felt as if I *wanted* something to happen. Everything I had always feared, from being attacked to getting mugged, seemed somehow appealing now.

But there was no one, either on the street or in the newsagents. The only person inside was the shop owner, the same tired man with the same desultory expression he'd had since we'd all gone to the shop as schoolkids. Our interaction was the same as always: no words exchanged, a brief transfer of cash, and change given back in resentful silence.

As I was leaving the shop, a guy bumped into me. He was on his phone, not looking where he was going. He was in his forties and wearing a suit. Probably one of the middle-class people who had recently been moving into the area because of the cheaper property prices and luxury apartments that bookended and towered over estates like mine.

Instead of apologising for bumping into me, he smirked, muttered something to himself and proceeded to walk into the shop. Without thinking, I put my hand out to block him.

"Wha——" the man begun.

"Say sorry," I said.

"What are you—"

"You bumped into me. Say sorry."

The man was about to protest again when I grabbed him by his suit and pushed him back against the door. I then leaned my face in close to his. The look he'd previously had—a kind of quizzical, uncertain smile—disappeared. It was replaced by discomfort, and then fear. In a quick, stuttering voice he said:

"Okay, I'm sorry. I'm sorry."

"Yeah," I said. "That's what I thought." And then I walked off, not looking behind me.

When I got home, I felt triumphant.

What a rush!

The look on his face; the fear in his eyes; his terrified, pathetic apology.

But it was an odd kind of rush. Like earlier, when I had been buoyed going to the shop, it was not a feeling of happiness. It wasn't even just plain pleasure. Instead, it was a kind of hollow feeling; the mental equivalent of a fake laugh. I could feel my heart beating faster, the adrenaline pumping, and I knew that if I needed to I could step out onto the street again without any problems. But I wasn't happy.

And this was even before the shame began to set in. The guy was a bit of a knobhead, but what I had done had been a complete overreaction.

But the shame was hollow, too. It wasn't that the shame wasn't there; it was just that I couldn't feel it. Like when your mouth is numbed at the dentist: you know that your tooth is being drilled into, you can feel the pressure of the drill tearing away at it, but you feel nothing.

My job was, bluntly, a call centre job that didn't happen to be in a call centre, but rather a small office. I spent the majority of my time cold-calling people, reading from a script, and trying to sell them things they didn't want to buy. There was a lot to get used to in the job—sore throats, backache, the slow erosion of your soul—but the worst was the abuse. Most of the time people would hang up. Occasionally there'd be a polite rejection. Everything else was pure, unfiltered, insults.

I had been doing the job for over a year now and had learned to cope with it. By not taking it personally, by recognising that I'd probably feel the same as the customers if I was in their shoes, I could get through the day.

Recently, though, it had not been so easy. As physical tiredness makes it harder for you to cope with physical strain, so mental tiredness makes it harder for you to cope with mental strain. Each "fuck you," every "I'll come down to where you work and shove that phone up your arse," stung as if I was back on my first week.

This had all been before yesterday, and the man outside the shop. As people abused me over the phone, I replayed that scene over and over in my head. I alternated it with fantasies in which I found these people's addresses and went to their houses. Someone would call me a prick, hang up, and go about his day. Later there'd be a knock at his door. He'd see me, confused, and I'd say "I'm a prick, yeah?" before slamming him against the wall or punching him in the stomach.

I could not do that, of course. My company kept people's addresses private for that exact reason. So after a while, when the fantasies were no longer enough to keep me calm, I did what I *was* able to do. A customer was halfway through telling me that he'd stepped on a piece of dogshit yesterday that wasn't half as repulsive as I was, when I said: "Oh, go fuck yourself." And suddenly the tiredness was gone. The hollowness was gone. I felt actual joy. It was like slipping into a hot bath with a cold beer on a warm day. There was a long silence on the other end, but the guy had not hung up. At the thought of him sitting there, shocked and open-mouthed, I felt even more pleasure. Eventually he said, in a quiet voice:

"What did you say?"

"I said 'Go fuck yourself.'"

"But you . . . you can't talk to me like that?" He worded it like a question.

"Oh yeah? I know where you live. I've got your address on the screen here. I'm from Gritton, you prick. You don't know what you're dealing with. I'll fuck you up. I'll come to your house while you're sleeping and——"

I was cut off. While we were never told the specifics of how and when our calls were monitored, they were. Plus, unlike a call centre, there were not tens or hundreds of us, so the odds of you being the one monitored at any given time were relatively short. When you had a particularly long and unsuccessful call (as I'd had earlier), you were much more likely to have your subsequent calls monitored. Perhaps I was being monitored because of that. Perhaps I was just the one to be monitored at that time, and was unlucky. In any case, I had been being monitored, because my supervisor cut off my call and then stepped out of his office. He didn't even need to say anything. With a massive smile on my face, I headed towards his office.

I passed Mary, who was staring at me. She looked shocked, and also a little scared. I turned away from her. I didn't like seeing that look on her face. Seeing it almost made me feel ashamed. Mary was a nice person, and I liked her. I didn't want her looking at me like that. It threatened to take away the rush, and I had to hold onto that for as long as possible.

It wasn't until I was on the bus that everything properly hit me. The joy of threatening the man was gone. The mental exhaustion was back in full sway.

I was now unemployed. Instead of spending my weekend in front of the television as I'd planned, I'd frantically have to search for jobs, sign up for temping agencies, and research my benefits options. Bad as they'd been in the past, from what I understood they were much harder to claim now. If they had been a maze before, now they were a labyrinth. A friend of mine had told me, "It's almost like they have to give it to you—like legally—but they don't want to. They want to make it so hard to get benefits that as few people get them as possible. It's no coincidence that you see more homeless people now than you used to."

Standing on the bus, with people brushing and shoving past me, the fulness of this hit me. I'd had a good sleep the night before; I'd had only a half day at work; I had eaten a full lunch in the work ca-fé; I had no illnesses; and yet I was thoroughly, utterly exhausted. It was an effort just to stand up straight. I kept my two hands wrapped firmly around the bar behind me, worried that if I didn't I would fall onto my knees. The only thing keeping me awake was the anger, and the hatred of the people brushing past me.

The moment I got off the bus, I felt worse. My head spun as I walked down the street. I rubbed my temples. I was so exhausted, and I knew that it was a tiredness I could not reach, even with sleep.

I thought back to last night, when I had pushed the man in the shop.

When had I ever had that feeling? When was the last time, even, that I had just been happy? Even before The Teenagers, I had not felt this basic, mundane happiness or contentment in so long. Thinking about it, the last time I was happy was probably when I was a child.

I turned onto the high street. I was approaching my flat when I saw a homeless man in one of the doorways staring directly at me. I was home early, because of being sacked. The homeless people didn't usually come out this early, as they waited for the shops to be shut. But there he was, in a doorway surprisingly dark for this time of day, in front of a shop I couldn't recall seeing before, staring at me. He didn't ask for any money, he just stared. But no. He wasn't just staring. He was smirking at me. Laughing at me. It was hu-mourless, but still a laugh.

I ran over to him, furious.

"I don't fucking have anything!" I screamed. "I don't have any money! I have nothing! Get a fucking job!" Without thinking, and as if I had always been destined to do it, I kicked him. Instead of the satisfying crack of bone or the soft whoosh of a deflated stomach, I hit nothing other than a concoction of dirty clothes, rubbish, and an (empty) sleeping bag.

I ran the rest of the way to my flat.

At ten o'clock I left my flat. The Teenagers were not outside, so I turned right and walked into the puzzle that is my housing estate. For the next fifteen minutes I turned into alleyways and walkways, ending up back in courtyards I had started in; I jumped over walls; I climbed stairs; I turned into more walkways that turned out to be dead ends, but when I returned to them a few minutes later seemed to be open; I climbed back downstairs; I got into lifts where vomit, piss, and disinfectant fought for prominence and which took me up to levels that were identical to those below.

Then, eventually, I found them. They were in the distance, standing by some railings. We were so high up that we looked down over the whole of South-East London, the gleaming skyscrapers of Canary Wharf in the near distance.

I walked up to them slowly, knowing they were watching me the whole time. As I got closer, I thought back to the bundle of clothes I had mistaken for a homeless man earlier. What if this group of people, these "Teenagers," were not in fact there? What if it was an urban mirage? Maybe, because these were railings, I was in fact looking at a bunch of floral tributes, cards, balloons for a stabbing victim (there had been another last week), and my tired mind had transmogrified them into the people they were memorialising.

But as I got close to them, it was unmistakable. They were people. I could see their faces (just about, through their hoods).

I got up close to them and then stood in front of them.

"What did you do to me?" I asked. "The other week, last week . . . nothing's been the same since then. What did you do?"

One of them stepped forward. A girl, with long greasy hair.

"You got hit, mate," she said.

"What do you mean?" I asked.

She smiled at me. It was not a mocking smile, or a gloating one. It was . . . understanding. Sympathetic. She shrugged.

"Don't know what to say, innit. Is what it is. You got hit. It can happen to anyone."

I looked behind her, at the other Teenagers. They all removed their hoods, and I could see them properly for the first time. Like the girl, they had the same sympathetic expressions on their faces.

I realised something. These were not people who would judge me. If they heard that I had sworn at the customer, they would have laughed. They would have cheered me for pushing the man in the shop. If the bundle of clothes I'd hit had turned out to be a homeless man, they'd have said nothing. There'd be no condemnation. No disgust. No fear, like how Mary had looked at me. They'd know about the tiredness. They'd know about the rush. They would not judge.

The girl came right up next to me. She put her hand on my shoulder, and I followed her towards the others.

"That one?" I said, indicating a guy in the near distance who was trying to avoid our gaze and walk quickly to his flat while being weighed down with shopping bags from the newsagent—probably all one-pound ready meals and cheap lager. My friends nodded, and I stepped forward.

"Oi, mate," I called out. He turned back, the terror on his face visible in the dark. I tried to hide my smile. Even buried under my hood, he'd be able to see it. I kept my face neutral.

"Mate," I said, reaching into my pocket. "Hands up!"

From Superstitious Fantasy to Scientific Fiction: A Baconian Reading of the Weird Tale from Shelley to Lovecraft

César Guarde-Paz

> The eternal silence of these infinite spaces terrifies me.—*Pascal* (S233/L201, 73)
> . . . infinitum vero malitiae dedecus est.—*Boethius*[1]

The present study seeks to analyze the juncture between scientific discovery and history of literature or, in more concrete terms, the literature of the weird, as essential in understanding the plural structure of the weird tale as a literary melting-pot of revolutionary ideas developed, mainly, during the second half of the nineteenth century and the early twentieth century. In his celebrated and widely re-printed essay, "A Literary Copernicus" (1949), Fritz Leiber, Jr. thoroughly established that H. P. Lovecraft (1890–1937) "shifted the focus of supernatural dread from man and his little world and his gods, to the stars and the black and unplumbed gulfs of intergalactic space" (290). But although Lovecraft's contributions to the weird tale were powerfully innovative and have achieved posthumous recognition—mainly due to the editorial efforts of his friends August W. Derleth (1909–1971) and Donald A. Wandrei (1908–1987)—his pioneering effort of casting aside the conventionalities of the past Victorian genre, with "man and his little world and his gods," was by no means unprecedented. The example of William Hope Hodgson (1877–1918), whose well-known *The House on the Borderland* (1908) undeniably contains all the traits of the Copernican shift as defined in Leiber's essay, is paramount (Weinstein 17),

---

1. Boethius, *De institutione arithmetica* 1.32: "The unlimited is in truth an ignominy of malice" (my translation).

and indeed Leiber himself recognized the role, however ancillary, of Hodgson and other pioneers of the science fiction movement, from Edgar Allan Poe to H. G. Wells (291).

Notwithstanding prominent and significant contributions on the innovative role of these individual writers, the complex and multifaceted evolution of the weird tale, from its classical form in the familiar Jamesian (malevolent) ghost, constrained by "the rules of folklore" (James viii), to the contemporary horrors of cosmic irrelevance and indifferent eldritch entities peopling Lovecraft's fiction, was by no means a singular event, but a plural, continuing journey spaced out over time through a great variety of authors and works, and mostly influenced by the increasingly inescapable revolution in our scientific understanding of the cosmos. The horror emerging from the opening of the boundaries of our known, little universe, first with the geographical discovery of the New World, followed by the confirmation that the Earth was not the center of all creation, as well as the anthropological and psychological nature of mankind and, finally, with our perception of the true immensity of that universe—all these things existed before Lovecraft (Moreland 14).

Whereas the growth of any literature is confined within the limits imposed by the contributions of individual writers, literature per se dwells in present and past worldviews advocated, consciously or not, by the authors who contribute to it. Consequently, the complex interactions between science and literature in the realm of the weird tale demand a decentralization of and an emancipation from the iconoclasm of the significance of individual writers—an authentic Copernican shift of focus from an author-centered approach to the worldviews that, through science and superstition, molded *fin-de-siècle* narratives of the genre. For this purpose, I shall begin with a discrete and episodic digression on the relationship between science (astronomy and cosmicism)[2] and superstition (astrology) during

---

2. The influence of anthropology and evolution in the "genealogies of monstrosity" in Gothic literature has already been studied, for instance, in Corina Wagner.

Modernity, with a special emphasis on the figure of Sir Francis Bacon and his "astrologia sana," to serve as a reflected image of the evolution of the weird tale and its long process of emancipation from the traditional clanking chains of supernatural superstition.

The "Deseschatologization" of Science and the Baconian Reform

The idea of a "Copernican Revolution" in the realm of supernatural literature, personified in the figure of H. P. Lovecraft and his fiction, runs parallel to the commonly held belief, rooted in Thomas Kuhn's homonymous magnum opus, that for the last eighteen centuries what we call today astronomy and astrology had "constituted a single professional pursuit," utterly indivisible and indistinguishable from each other (92). However, the incompatibility of these two branches of inquiry was seldom doubted by many of the most remarkable scientists who embarked in their quest for knowledge. The observation of the movements of the celestial bodies was a science imbued with sureness, whereas the prediction of events thenceforward was seen as dubious in repute, albeit not entirely useless (Geneva 6). Ever since the earliest astronomers, and specially as science started to gain ground on religion following the Renaissance and the Age of Discovery, there was a general consensus that the art of predicting future events through observation of the heavenly bodies needed reform (Ptolemy 1.1–3).[3] Christianity was nevertheless the pervasive element of any philosophical compound, and it was from its deep belief in the literality of biblical narratives that astronomers received a breath of fresh air.

By the sixteenth century, and in the years following the slow acceptance of Copernicus's discoveries and writings, astrology became

---

3. However, it should be noted that, contrary to Geneva's account (6), Ptolemy did call these two branches "astronomy"—his demarcation was methodological rather than nominal (Tetrabiblos 1.1), the latter being only distinguished in our modern use of the terms.

promptly eschatologized[4] due to the interpretations of a number of biblical predictions about the Second Coming in the light of the proliferation of "celestial signs," now easily observable thanks to new scientific developments. These predictions concerned the so-called Elijah prophecy from the Babylonian Talmud, according to which the original duration of the world was six thousand years, and two passages in Matthew's Gospel—one shortening the number of years "for the elect's sake" (24:22) and another announcing "the sign of the Son of man in heaven" (24:30; Westman 119–21). As for the astronomical prodigies, 1572 saw a supernova in the constellation of Cassiopeia—traditionally shaped as a cross, the nova resembled a crown over the head of a crucified Christ—and, just a few years later, the Great Comet of 1577 and the Great Conjunction of all planets in Aries in 1584 confirmed the imminence of the Second Coming before the new century (Tessicini 54). Most astronomers subscribed to this interpretation to a greater or lesser extent, from rather obscure figures such as Cyprián Lvovický (1514–1574), Thaddeus Nemicus (1525 1600), Cornellus Gemma (1535–1578), or Michael Maestlin (1550–1631) to more influential scientists, including Helisaeus Roeslin (1545–1616), Thomas Digges (1546–1595), and Tycho Brahe (1546–1601).

But as the new century opened, it not only became increasingly difficult to maintain faith in those predictions, but new prodigies in the skies, such as the immediate supernova of 1604, demonstrated the futility of astrological prognostications. Tycho Brahe, whose observations made possible the acceptance of Copernicus's theories in the years to follow, had been one of the first to call for a reformation of astrology, repeating the original arguments of Ptolemy (Brahe 33; Thoren 218). His assistant and eventually successor as imperial

---

4. In theological studies, "eschatologization" (opp. "deseschatologization") refers to the process of reinterpreting history from a teleological perspective centered upon the salvation of mankind as a special creature of God. The term was popularized with the publication of Reventlow's "The Eschatologization of the Prophetic Books."

mathematician, Johannes Kepler (1571–1630),[5] still held dear some aspects of astrology with the obstinacy of someone reluctant to give up his inherited beliefs (Caspar 183–85; Field 169), "throwing out the chaff" yet keeping too much of the grain (Simon 440). But it was Giordano Bruno (1548–1600), famously executed for his belief in the plurality of worlds, who laid the first stone toward a scientific reformulation of the cosmos. Bruno not only laughed sarcastically at those literalist chronologists and their biblical calculations prognosticating the end of the world, providing examples from other, more ancient cultures with historical registers thousands of years older than our six millennia (Bruno, *Expulsion* 249–51; Spruit 238–49), but he also "deseschatologized" the universe by declaring Nature boundless and homogeneous, and the Earth just another body in the immensity of a purposeless cosmos filled with infinite solar systems where the stars, and the planets around them, were not God's prophetic signs and meant nothing to the dwellers of this little speck of dust: "for instance the stars themselves," he wrote in 1590, "which neither cause anything, nor meant anything" (Bruno, *Principiis* 3.544, my translation).

This scientific and philosophic efflorescence achieved its apogee with a comparatively neglected figure—the English philosopher and statesman Sir Francis Bacon (1561–1626). Usually eclipsed by his contemporary, René Descartes (1596–1650), Bacon came to occupy a prominent place in the philosophical and scientific tradition, firstly due to his pioneering articulation of the inductive method, which was immediately followed by modern science, bringing together and consolidating the significance of previous discoveries surrounding the so-called "Copernican Revolution"; and secondly because of his development of a new notion of science, understood as the progressive accumulation of knowledge. Bacon had started writing when the intellectual revolution that was giving birth to Modernity was

---

5. It should be pointed out that Kepler authored what some consider the first science-fiction novel, *Somnium,* or "The Dream," as early as 1608 (Lear).

already in motion (Rossi 25; Hill 63), and although he was—like most of his English contemporaries—a firm believer in natural magic and alchemy (Bowden; Thomas, *Religion* 270), his relation to astrology was at best less ambiguous and contradictory than his predecessors. As early as 1605, when the eschatological conceptions of Nature were being shaken by the utter failure of a century of unsuccessful millenarist predictions, Bacon wrote that astrology must rely on reason "to discover that correspondence or concatenation, which is between the superior globe and the inferior" (3.289). A more radical idea, however, was put forward in his *De Dignitate et Augmentis Scientiarum* (1623): "As for Astrology, it is so full of superstition, that scarce anything sound can be discovered in it. Notwithstanding, I would rather have it purified than altogether rejected" (4.349). It is in these two works that Bacon introduced what he called "Astrologia Sana" or "just astrology" (Geneva 77; Bacon 3.4–6, 4.351–55), a purified, healthier science of the stars to be employed for the prediction of non-anthropocentric, natural phenomena, such as weather, comets, floods, heats, or earthquakes (Tester 221–22).[6] This process of purification, once extended to the whole scientific system, allowed Bacon to introduce Giordano Bruno's repudiation of cosmic finalism into science, depersonalizing knowledge and shifting the focus from the trivialities of individual men (terrestrialism) to the uncertain immensity of a vast, boundless universe (cosmicism). Prior to Bacon's scientific reform, philosophers had regarded Nature as a mere object of contemplation and meditation, with a degree of indeterminacy or uncertainty that allowed the supernatural to flourish and thrive. Bacon had been the

---

6. Tester's assertion that Bacon was more dismissive of astrology in his *Novum Organum* (1620), written three years before *De Dignitate et Augmentis Scientiarum*, is incorrect: the original Latin text of the 46th aphorism reads "all superstition, whether in astrology" (omnis superstitionis, ut in astrologicis), as properly translated in James Spedding's edition (Bacon 4.56), and not "all superstition is much the same, whether it be that of astrology."

first to conceive Nature as something to be constrained, harnessed, and molded, a Nature subjected to invariable laws that do not discriminate between humans and animals, or between our planet and the stars (Kennington 50).

This emergent fracture between the supernatural and the material that pervaded the seventeenth century was also the result of a slow process of separation of faith and science, where reason stood somehow in-between. Copernicus had been dazzled by the consequences of his discoveries and the theological problems of a moving Earth, and even Descartes, despite his notoriety as an epitome of materialism and his overshadowing influence, could not but fight against Giordano Bruno's anti-finalism and Bacon's healthification of science when he created the idea of the soulless "animal machine," as opposed to the spiritual nature of human beings whose reason made them the center of creation.[7] And thus, a philosophical debate of the utmost relevance, which still resonates today, was ignited. Pascal reflected on the boundless void of the universe and its significance for human existence:

> I do not know what my body is, or my senses, or my soul, or that part of myself which thinks what I am saying, which reflects about everything and itself, and does not know itself any better than the rest. [. . .] I see the terrifying expanses of the universe which close around me, and I find myself pinned to a corner of this vast space, without knowing why I have been put in this place rather than in another, nor why the short time given to me to live is assigned to

---

7. See Descartes's fifth Discourse, AT 6.56–57: "if there were such machines having the organs and outward shape of a monkey or any other irrational animal, we would have no means of knowing that they were not of exactly the same nature as these animals, whereas, if any such machines resembled us in body and imitated our actions insofar as this was practically possible, we should still have two very certain means of recognizing that they were not, for all that, real human beings" (Descartes 46). Abbreviations for philosophical works follow academic conventions, for which see the referenced edition within brackets.

this moment rather than another in all the eternity which has preceded me and shall come after me.

I see nothing but infinities on all sides, enclosing me like an
atom, or a shadow which lasts only for a moment and does not return. (S681/L427, 160–61)[8]

But this debate was not exclusive of science and philosophy, and it
occupied, consciously or not, most writers of the weird and fantastic,
for whom the increasingly terrible truths behind scientific advance-
ment—the demise of any speck of supernaturalism in Nature, and of
purpose and an afterlife—and the unyielding confirmation of cosmicism entailed the ultimate challenge for their creative spirits. The
efforts to reform science in general, and astrology in particular, to purify and healthify its prerogatives, were also mirrored in the efforts of
reforming the weird tale and purifying it from its hitherto omnipresent supernaturalism, either to ground it on science or in a version of
spiritualism that could live up to the challenges of modernity.

Frankenstein, or a Copernican Revolution in Literature

Although traditional horror stories are customarily subjected to "a
peculiar place between the real and the fictive" (Stewart 35), it is
with the introduction of the Baconian worldview of science and the
desacralization of the world that mankind's previous experience of
the "fictive" is shaken and displaced until almost all possibility of
wonder dissolves. Indeed, after the introduction of scientific realism,
the uncanny, as Freud famously wrote, only "retains its character in

---

8. Philosophy had assumed hitherto the Aristotelian notion of horror vacui
("nature abhors vacuum") for nearly two millennia. The horrors of infinity
disturbed philosophers thereafter: Hegel (1770–1831) condemned "the bad
infinite" ("die schlechte Unendlichkeit," Aesthetics I, II.ii, ch. 1.2C, in
Hegel 1.466) regarding it as damnation, whereas Friedrich Nietzsche
called it "the heaviest weight" ("Das grösste Schwergewicht," FW 341, in
Nietzsche, Gay Science 194), and "a terrible, paralyzing thought" ("eine
furchtbare und betäubende Vorstellung," PHG 5, in Nietzsche, Philosophy
in the Tragic Age of the Greeks 54).

real-life experience and in writings that are grounded in material reality," but it vanishes if "the setting is a fictive reality invented by the writer" (*GW* 12.266; Freud 157). Mankind's conviction in supernatural agency is of course a behavior so ingrained in our species that the use of reason and science are historical and unnatural singularities dependent upon education, repetition, and industriousness (Boyer 321; Clasen 51; *CE* 5.38–44 and 85–95). Hence, weird tales grounded to a greater or lesser degree on scientific reasoning and truths, devoid of the fictive spaces that require the continuous and absolute suspension of natural laws *from the very beginning*, are most likely as restricted in their appeal as science and reason themselves.

As we have seen in the particular case of the convoluted relation between scientific astronomy and prognostic astrology, the path from the traditional ghost story to the modern weird tale has also endured a long, contradictory, and by no means continuous evolution in the centuries that followed the Baconian discovery of Nature, with inherited traditions and beliefs never fully winnowed out but, rather, were purified in order to create a supernatural tale as grounded in realism, reason, and science as possible: "Inconceivable events and conditions have a special handicap to overcome, and this can be accomplished only through the maintenance of a careful realism in every phase of the story *except* that touching on the one given marvel (Lovecraft, *CE* 2.177). This is also manifest when one compares the early Gothic narrative of Horace Walpole's *The Castle of Otranto* (1764), episodic and anticlimactic (Salomon 130), with the building tension of the innovative science fiction of Mary Shelley's *Frankenstein* (1817/1818):[9] the ultimate abomination, the eldritch supernatural event that defies the laws of nature and cannot *by any means* convince and be accepted by a modern reader typically comes forth considerably late in, if not at the very end of, the story—the final revelation that shatters the whole reality upon which the tale has been constructed.

---

9. From here on, dates are given for the time of writing, if known, and the date of publication.

The opposite scenario holds true as well. The genre of detective fiction, for instance, which can be traced back to Voltaire's philosophical tale *Zadig* (1747), only became established during the first half of the nineteenth century, with remarkable works such as E. T. A. Hoffmann's "Mademoiselle de Scudéri" (1819, tr. into English in 1826), E. A. Poe's "The Murders in the Rue Morgue" (1841), or the forgotten stories of the psychic detective Flaxman Low by Hesketh Hesketh-Prichard (1876–1922). Not only does the development and maturing of this rising genre run parallel to that of the weird tale, but authors engaged in detective fiction also employed similar devices to catch the new reader's attention and to ensure narrative continuity: The characters no longer suffer passively the dreadful apparition, but they actively interact through mechanical or scientific means with the unknown, fighting it, understanding it (or at least attempting to)—only to find out that the hitherto supernatural was in fact, simply and perfectly, natural (Thomas, *Detective* 41; Frank 21). Weird storytellers such as Algernon Blackwood and W. H. Hodgson paved the way for more popular detectives of the occult, from classical Sherlock Holmes to modern *Scooby-Doo, Where Are You!*

The "Spirit of the Age," as the influential philosopher John Stuart Mill called it in this homonymous essay, demanded a "departure from the modes of thinking of our ancestors" (12.231), which had become irrelevant and were no longer valid. Thenceforth, the supernatural could no longer be presented as an ontological category, but as an epistemological failure of our current, limited knowledge. This analysis seems to confirm S. T. Joshi's hypothesis that the weird tale, rather than a genre per se, is *"the consequence of a world view"* (*Weird Tale* 1; emphasis in original) that had everlasting impressions on a wide range of authors and genres and in the way these authors portrait *"a certain sort of human mood"* and *"half-formulated feelings"* (Lovecraft, *Letters to J. Vernon Shea* 75). In what follows, I shall try to portray the weird tale as a boundless, ongoing genre that, entangled as it is with the horrors of the Gothic tale and the rationalization of science fiction, supposes a compromise between them in an effort of distancing itself from all supernaturalism (successfully or not). As Robert Mighall explains, "horror fiction has a generic obligation to evoke fear," whereas science fiction "attempts to contain fear and offer a rational explanation" (xxiv). The weird tale transcends this dichotomy, making that rational explanation utterly dreadful in itself: from the creation of the modern Prometheus in *Frankenstein* (Derleth i) to the revelation of the feral nature of the Beast Folk in *The Island of Doctor Moreau*,[10] modern science has showed us that the horrors of materialism and rationalism may well surpass those of the immaterial (un)realities of our ancestors.

The first tale of interest to us that falls within the limitations imposed upon our definition of the weird tale is a very well-known work that needs no introduction: Mary Shelley's *Frankenstein; or, The Modern Prometheus* (1818, revised 1831).[11] This pioneering effort by an eighteen-year-old girl is so closely entangled with the science or natural philosophy of its time that little doubt can be entertained as to its interactions between science and literature. In the first place, Mary Shelley was the daughter of two important philosophers: her father William Godwin (1756–1836) was the founder of philosophical anarchism and a utopian rationalist who wished to "sweep away the whole fiction of an intelligent former world and a future state" and "to invalidate the doctrine of final causes" (4.417)

---

10. Despite contemporary reviewers' opinion concerning the "nauseating" effect of the novel (Wells, *Island* ix), my excuse for overlooking H. G. Wells's accomplished story in the pages that follow is that the author himself disregarded the horror element we usually see exaggerated in big screen adaptations: "The horror element [in *The Island of the Lost Souls* (1932)], for which I have never particularly aimed, prevailed throughout" (Katzman 20–21). Cf. his letter to Elisabeth Healey (late spring 1896): "I do hope that you don't think merely a festival of 'orrors" (Wells, *Island* x).

11. Pagination follows the 1818 first edition for the "Preface" and the main text, and the 1831 edition for the "Introduction," added therein for the first time but already published separately in *Court Journal* 3 (22 October 1831): 724, nine days before the new edition. For the superiority of the 1818 text and their differences see Mellor and Klinger.

(the teleological framework imposed by the religious belief in after-life and in the privileged position of man in the cosmos); her mother, Mary Wollstonecraft (1759–1797), although a lesser influence upon the young writer due to her premature death, was a celebrated feminist who authored the pioneering *A Vindication of the Rights of Woman* (1792). Most importantly, however, Mary Shelley conceived her *Frankenstein* when she was in a romantic relationship with Percy Bysshe Shelley (1792–1822), a renowned poet and philosopher, to whom she would soon be married. The idea for the story, as the author herself recollects in the "Introduction" to the 1831 edition, was the result of the philosophical discussions between Percy Shelley and Lord Byron and, therefore, it is safe to conclude that the weird tale in general and *Frankenstein* in particular were cradled within the bosom of philosophy:

> Many and long were the conversations between Lord Byron and [Percy] Shelley, to which I was a devout but nearly silent listener. During one of these, various philosophical doctrines were discussed [. . .]. They talk about of the experiments of Dr. Darwin [. . .] who preserved a piece of vermicelli in a glass case, till by some extraordinary means it began to move. (1831, ix–x)[12]

And perhaps, Shelley thought, "a corpse could be reanimated" or its parts "might be manufactured, brought together, and endued with vital warmth." Certainly, Shelley tried to establish the foundations of her story on solid ground, making explicit mention of "the physiological writers of Germany" as evidence for the possibility of manufacturing a sentient being (1818, viii),[13] and distancing herself

---

12. Shelley refers to vorticella, tiny protozoans, not "little worms" (vermicelli). For the reference to Erasmus Darwin's *The Temple of Nature* (1803), see Shelley (*Annotated* 341–42n18).
13. Probably referring to Johann Friedrich Blumenbach (1752–1840), whose work on comparative anatomy was translated by William Lawrence (1783–1867), Percy's physician, in 1809, as well as to Karl Rudolphi (1771–1832), Wilhelm Gottlieb Tilesius (1769–1857), Johann Baptist Ritter von Spix (1781–1826), and Friedrich Tiedemann (1781–1861), men-

expressly from any supernaturalism: "I have not considered myself as merely weaving a series of supernatural terrors. The event on which the interest of the story depends is exempt from the disadvantages of a mere tale of spectres or enchantment" (1818, viii). This conscious rationalization of the ghost tale can be seen in two of the central characters: Robert Walton, who serves as the frame narrator, is traveling to the North Pole to discover the cause of gravitation and planetary movements; Victor Frankenstein, on the other hand, starts as a follower of the sixteenth-century alchemists Cornelius Agrippa (1486–1535) and Paracelsus (1493?–1541), only to be confronted with the realities of modern science at the University of Ingolstadt, where he experiences a Baconian turn (1818, 3). After learning how alchemy relates to the development of modern chemistry, Victor eventually returns to the basics of the former, now enhanced by his knowledge of chemistry and anatomy, and it is from this purification of superstitious beliefs that the ultimate scientific horror arises (1818, 75).[14]

The Horrors Within: Psychological Monsters of the Victorian Age

As if following the equally slow and contradictory "purification" of science (Hendrix 104), this process of secularization of the Gothic story into the shape of the modern, scientific weird tale was by no means a continuous, lineal storyline unfolding sequentially forward. *Au contraire,* new scientific ideas lavishly blended and intertwined with superstitious beliefs, as writers still tried to clutch at the last straws of the spiritual and mysterious. In Edgar Allan Poe (1809–1849) we find precisely this transitional ethos of an age that is losing its faith, yet still dithers to embrace science in its entirety. Besides

tioned by Lawrence in his lectures (28–29). See Butler (12–14) and Brantlinger (129).

14. Shelley's reference to Paracelsus is paramount, for he is credited with the first mention of the homunculus, an artificially created little man. Victor, conversely, "resolved, contrary to my first intention, to make the being of a gigantic stature" (1818, 88).

the noticeable, recurrent motifs of premature burial and the death of a beautiful woman, Poe's works are caught between two conflicting themes. On the one hand, the *"literature of precise empirical science"* (Rabkin 134; italics in original) permeates important works, such as the early "Sonnet—To Science" (1829); the (almost) weird story "A Descent into the Maelström" (1841), which refers to Archimedes' *On Floating Bodies;* the long introductory paragraphs on analytical reasoning in "The Murders in the Rue Morgue" (1841); *Eureka: A Prose Poem* (1848), on the unity of the universe, dedicated to the German scientist Alexander von Humboldt (1769–1859); or the science fictional stories "The Unparalleled Adventure of One Hans Pfaall" (1835) and "Mellonta Tauta" (1849), which introduce, respectively, space and time travel (Fisher, "Poe" 84; Tresch; Poe, *Science*). On the other hand, Poe was also fascinated and absorbed by *"the literature of spiritual terror"* (Rabkin 134; italics in original), which he conveys through the portrayal of insanity and paranoia—linked but not restricted to feelings of guilt—in stories such as "The Fall of the House of Usher" (1839), "The Pit and the Pendulum" (1842), "The Tell-Tale Heart" (1843), "The Black Cat" (1843), and "The System of Dr. Tarr and Prof. Fether" (1845) (Fisher, *Cambridge* 22). It is in the first of these stories, however, that we find a particularly powerful communion between empirical science and spiritual terror, for whereas apparitions are disregarded skeptically as "merely electrical phenomena," the madness affecting Roderick Usher also infects the narrator until he experiences a "rapid increase of my superstition" (Poe, *Collected Works* 2.399, 411–13).

The pinnacle of the Poesque weird tale, however, appears in two well-known short stories: "The Mask of the Red Death" (1842) and "The Facts in the Case of M. Valdemar" (1845). In the former, the Gothic atmosphere of Walpole's *Castle of Otranto* is secularized by replacing the ghost with the physical manifestation of a terrible illness—a medical, scientific condition—in the shape of a disguised figure under whose garments and mask there is nothing but empty air.[15] As for the latter, it skillfully combines the (pseudo-)science of mesmerism with the strange continuity of the hypnotized conscience of a dying man within his already decayed body—a theme later used by Lovecraft in "Out of the Æons" (1933/1935).[16] Poe's remarkable legacy with respect to the development of the weird tale (and science fiction) is probably more important and pervasive than has been recognized hitherto.

The first heir of Poesque psychological nightmares to whom I wish to refer is Robert Louis Stevenson (1850–1894), an author who is usually (and surprisingly) disregarded in academic literary discussions (Duncan 11–12; Hammond 118–22). Such neglect stands in sharp contrast with the cornucopia of interpretations to which his most well-known work, *Strange Case of Dr. Jekyll and Mr. Hyde* (1886), has been subjected, and which are too numerous to be even mentioned herein with any thought of completeness. As is the case with other "urban gothic" (Fielding 5) tales of Stevenson, such as "Thrawn Janet" (1881), "The Body Snatcher" (1884), or "Markheim" (1884/1885), *Dr. Jekyll and Mr. Hyde*'s "uncannity" does not originate in any external conditions (ghosts, hallucinations, guilt, shame, or regret), but within our own psyche. Emotions may trigger the uncanny, but it has been there from the very beginning and, as we fight against the atavistic decadence of our personality resulting from a "sense of psychic fragmentation and conflict," we are meant to be eventually overcome and destroyed by it (Arata, "Stevenson" 55, 64; Arata, *Fictions* 33–53; Reid, *Science* 92–105; Reid, "Childhood" 47). Henry Jekyll's statement from the novel is also the author's purposeful voice: "that man will be ultimately known for a

---

15. The association between "mask" and the medieval Latin root mascus, masca, meaning both "spectre" and "nightmare," may have been known by Poe, but the sarcasm behind a personified illness respecting the rules of Prospero's masquerade ball is, it seems to me, particularly significant.

16. In collaboration with Hazel Heald (1896–1961), who provided the main idea of the living brain, although Lovecraft wrote the whole story (Lovecraft, *Medusa* 453; Lovecraft, *Fortunate* 255). Poe's influence on Lovecraft, has been discussed in Joshi and Schultz 207.

mere polity of multifarious, incongruous and independent denizens" (Stevenson, *Strange Case* 53).[17] The psychological horrors of Poe, now rationalized and explained through scientific (and pseudo-scientific) inquiry into the nascent branches of evolution, psychiatry, or psychology, are not a lurker at the threshold of our conscience, but our unawakened conscience itself.

Whereas scholarship on Stevenson is conspicuous by its absence, the opposite is true for his direct successor, the British author Rudyard Kipling (1865–1936), whose weird works, as was the case with Stevenson's, have also been subcategorized within the Gothic tradition—in this particular instance, as part of something called the "imperial Gothic" (Brantlinger, "Imperial"). Although popularly remembered for his appealing *The Jungle Book* (1894), Kipling's uncanny short stories constitute a by no means negligible part of his oeuvre, and one that is as much indebted to Poe as it is to Stevenson. Poe's influence, once superficially noted, has been firmly established since Burton R. Pollin's seminal study and the publication of a letter to Fred[erick] M. Hopkins regarding the preservation of Poe's cottage in Fordham, New York, for which Kipling offered $50 (about $1,500 today). In this letter Kipling, who had read Poe's works unceasingly when he was studying in Devon, explicitly recognized that "my own personal debt to Poe is a heavy one" (Pollin 13–14). Indeed, we can find traces of Poesque motives from his early tales and poems, such as "The Dream of Duncan Parrenness" (1884) or "Study of an Elevation, in Indian Ink" (1886), to the late science fiction novella "With the Night Mail: A Story of 2000 A.D." (1905), modeled after Poe's "Mellonta Tauta" (Pollin 22–23; Carrington 54, 70, and 274). Kipling was also a devoted and passionate admirer of Stevenson, who was likewise a great enthusiast of Kipling's works. Kipling had planned to visit Stevenson in Samoa in late 1891, following a brief epistolary exchange, but external circum-

---

17. Curiously enough, this was written when Freud had just started his career as a psychoanalyst in Vienna in 1886, years before he developed his well-known threefold division of the human mind.

stances dissuaded him from this enterprise. According to Kipling's wife, when Stevenson passed away three years later, he became so deeply devastated that he didn't work for a week (Stevenson, *Letters* 3.271–72; Gilmour 99, 105; Kipling, *Diaries* 19 December 1894).

This literary covenant between the Poesque and the Stevensonian in Kipling's work finds its most intense expression in his popular weird tale "The Phantom 'Rickshaw" (1885). Written a year prior to Stevenson's *Dr. Jekyll and Mr. Hyde,* it tells the story of one Jack Pansay who, after having an affair with the wife of an officer, disowns her and becomes engaged to a young woman. Soon the former lover dies of a broken heart, and Jack starts being haunted by her ghost, riding the eponymous rickshaw where he saw her for the last time. Hallucination and paranoia lead Jack to despair until he finally abandons himself to death, having lost both his fiancée and his friends. As in other weird tales authored by Kipling, the supernatural has been replaced by an explicit medical condition—Jack's "conceited brain, too little stomach, and thoroughly unhealthy eyes" (Kipling, *Phantom* 21).[18] That the compulsory insanity and delusion of the dying man are not the result of a "real" supernatural apparition, but the direct consequence of a moral transgression that consumed him with guilt, is something the reader is being told about a number of times: "My only anxiety was," recalls Jack at the end of the story, "to get the penance over as quietly as might be" (30). Also in line with other Poesque tales from which Kipling has drawn this and other elements of the story—a found manuscript, a self-confession, increasing paranoia—is the fact that only Jack can see the phantom (as it happened in Poe's "The Black Cat" and "The Tell-Tale Heart") (Carrington 54; Pollin 15), and that both his lover and her rickshaw appear just as they looked the last time the nar-

---

18. The story was first published in *Quartette: The Christmas Annual of the Civil & Military Gazette* (1885): 87–105), together with another Poesque tale, "The Strange Ride of Morrowbie Jukes, C.E." (50–70), probably based on "The Pit and the Pendulum," and where fever seems to be the catalyst of the weird.

rator saw them, and not as they were in the moment of the accident or her last breath. Just like Stevenson, Kipling's tales are permeated with the novel idea that not only can science explain the formerly supernatural world, but, more importantly, that those horrors that we thought to be from beyond the grave were in fact within ourselves, in the most recondite regions of our material brain. As it has been pointed out, the dichotomy between the respectable gentleman and the atavistic lust was commonplace among Victorian writers (Hammond 125),[19] and it was thus, consciously or not, also exploited by writers of the weird.

A similar example of this Victorian ethos, transformed into horror through the glass of science and reason, can be found in the works of the prolific novelist H. G. Wells (1866–1946). Trained in biology under Thomas Henry Huxley (1825–1895) and highly influenced by Darwinism (Haynes 12–17), Wells also embarked in weird literature, following the steps of Shelley, Stevenson, and Kipling.[20] His most notorious tale is "Pollock and the Porroh Man" (1895), which has been accurately described as a reworking of "Poe's 'The Black Cat' (1843) with a Kiplingesque [. . .] setting" (Williams 46). The direct influence from Kipling's ghostly rickshaw is evident: Pollock is cursed by a witch doctor, the Porroh Man, because of a moral transgression committed against the woman of the latter. Although the curse is by no means real, and Pollock knows this as well as Kipling's Jack Pansay, the paranoia resulting from Pollock's belief in the powers of the Porroh Man ultimately leads him to suicide. The very same theme reappears in "The Red Room" (1896), the tale of the skeptical visitor of a haunted room whose scientific

---

19. Other similar examples of horror from paranoia can be found in most of Robert W. Chambers's *The King in Yellow* (1895) and in Algernon Blackwood's "The Listener" (1907).

20. For instance, in his draft of *The Island of Doctor Moreau* (1896), Wells mentions both Frankenstein and Dr. Jekyll and Mr. Hyde. Wells's story can be considered an updated version of *Frankenstein*. Wells and Kipling exchanged a few letters in 1902, and he mentions the imperial Gothicist seven times in his novel *The New Machiavelli* (1910) (Haynes 24; Philmus 9nn2–3).

explanations give way, ultimately, to paranoia: "there is no ghost there at all, but worse, far worse, something impalpable," he concludes, "Fear!" (Wells, *Complete Short Stories* 197). Fear itself, of course, grows from within.

The Horrors Without: Cosmicism Unbound

Although psychiatric interpretations of supernatural phenomena pervade late nineteenth-century weird literature and may thus be linked to a preoccupation with the status of Victorian morality, now shaken by the anthropological discoveries of Darwinism regarding our evolutionary origins (Wells, *Island* xviii), notice should be taken as well of the role of other branches of science. Cosmicism, or the insignificance of human existence when the vastness of the cosmos is considered from an atheistic perspective, was an inevitable outcome of the historic process initiated by Bruno and Bacon, and it largely preceded the anthropological discoveries that resulted in the collapse of the Victorian ethos.

Ambrose Bierce (1842–1914?) was probably the first writer of weird fiction to take science into serious and conscious consideration. Even if Bierce cannot be regarded as a systematic philosopher per se (Joshi, *Weird Tale* 147), he was indeed a philosopher who wrote literature—the Curmudgeon Philosopher, he called himself in a number of essays, one of which opens with a recognition of Bacon's role in the formulation of "true science" against blind superstition (Bierce 10.77; 10.331; Bierce, "Town" 9). Bierce's philosophical views on the relation between science and horror, and how the weird should be treated in order to achieve the lost uncanny of the Gothic tale, anticipate Lovecraft in many ways. For instance, in "The Damned Thing" (1893) we are told that "We so rely upon the orderly operation of familiar natural laws that any seeming suspension of them is noted as a menace to our safety, a warning of unthinkable calamity" (3.287), and idea repeated again a number of times, for instance, in "The Boarded Window" (2.368) and "One of Twins" (3.12; cf.

Joshi, *Weird Tale* 153). But whereas "The Boarded Window" (1891) is still a Poesque tale of premature burial and "One of Twins" (1888) a Kiplingesque take on the classical Doppelgänger theme,[21] "The Damned Thing" presents an outward terror in the shape of an unseen presence whose invisibility is not the result of its supernatural constitution, but of scientific, chemical properties from actinic rays that produce a color that we cannot see.[22]

The invisible takes a new direction with Arthur Machen's (1863–1947) *The Great God Pan* (1894). Despite his metaphysical convictions, which place him in the antipodes of Bierce, and his firm belief that "all science is a lie"—a statement that appears, curiously enough, after a quotation from Sir Francis Bacon– (Machen and Evans 70),[23] Machen's conception of the weird tale goes beyond the ordinary ghost story, considered by him "commonplace and tedious" (Machen, *Great God Pan* 90). Science may be a (partial) lie, but it is at least useful, as long as it helps us restore that lost sense of wonder as an aide of the spiritual. In "The Inmost Light" (1894) a scientist incarcerates his wife's soul in a jewel, leaving an empty vessel that is promptly occupied by *something else*, whereas in *The Great God Pan* a surgeon amplifies human conscience through "a slight lesion in the grey matter" of a little girl, "a trifling rearrangement of certain cells" (11) that provokes a true vision from beyond. It is

---

21. Bierce mentions Kipling in numerous texts, for instance "On Literary Criticism" (10.46), "The S.P.W." (10.88–91, and 102), "A Poet and His Poem" (10.179), and "Some Disadvantages of Genius" (10.287). Both tales are significantly similar to W. C. Morrow's (1854–1923) "The Permanent Stiletto" (originally published one year after Bierce's tale as "A Peculiar Case of Surgery") and "The Resurrection of Little Wang Tai" (published on 14 September 1891 as "The Ape and the Idiot," five months after Bierce's), which were in all probability modeled after Bierce's.

22. Further developments of this idea include, of course, H. G. Wells's *The Invisible Man* (1897) and Lovecraft's "The Colour out of Space" (1927).

23. For Machen's dalliance with theosophy and the Golden Dawn, see Machen (*Decadent* 12–16) and Graf (57–77). For his dogmatic bias against science, see Joshi ("Arthur" 19–21).

worth noting that, just like the "Fear" in Wells's "The Red Room," the invisible here is not a direct threat. It is somehow always there, ontologically present among us as an exteriority, yet inoffensive unless seen and known. In some ways, these Victorian anxieties are the reflection of a nature that must be kept hidden, for the untamed essence of the uncivilized world and of our own bestial dispositions can be easily triggered by the mere suggestion of it (Joshi, "Arthur," 16).

Cosmicism and science are, *a fortiori,* more unambiguous and straightforward in the works of Algernon Blackwood (1869–1951), who was, like Machen, a member of the Hermetic Order of the Golden Dawn, as well as the Theosophical Society. Unlike him, however, Blackwood was certainly more open to spiritual and (pseudo-)scientific teachings, as he was sympathetic to the influence of the Eastern spiritualism of the order and of important mystics such as George Gurdjieff (d. 1949) and his follower P. D. Ouspensky (1878–1947) (Joshi, *Weird Tale* 89; Graf 79–101). Blackwood, nevertheless, expresses a similar disdain for science and materialism, which he considered "murderous superfluities and sordid vulgarity" (Joshi, "Introduction" xiv; *Centaur* 44).

An example of the impact of his spiritual practices and, in particular, of his experiments with drugs, can be seen in the first story of his famous "occult detective" John Silence, "A Psychical Invasion" (1908). The case concerns a client who, through consumption of hashish, has opened his mind to formerly unseen forces that are now haunting him. This weird tale is clearly reminiscent of the invisible presence in Machen's *The Great God Pan* and the invasive entity in his *The Inmost Light,* and it shows how both authors' religious beliefs in the spiritual do not necessarily come into conflict with their particular uses of scientific experimentation. The process runs parallel to the healthification of astrology, where scientists resorted to different interpretations of their Christian beliefs in order to purify it from its most fantastical and bizarre contents.

Among Blackwood's most effective examples of cosmicism are several important tales that have become classics in their own right.

In "The Willows" (1907), which recalls his own experiences down the Danube by canoe in 1900, the supernatural is transformed into unnamable horrors beyond description that, just like Machen's Great God Pan, can only be seen under certain conditions. The intangibility and uncanniness of the apparitions, which manifest themselves visually but most importantly audibly, are strengthen by the fact that they lie beyond the world to which our familiar natural laws apply: "I don't think a phonograph would show any record of that," states the narrator's companion, "it is a non-human sound; I mean a sound outside humanity" (*Listener* 180). This outwardness is expressed masterfully by the slow yet progressive disintegration of the mysterious island, which seems to anticipate Hodgson's *The House on the Borderland* (1908)—something inherently incompatible between both worlds results in the collapse of the reality surrounding the borderland.

Cosmicism and the relative position and importance of humanity are similarly treated in Blackwood's novella "The Wendigo" (1910) and in his underrated short story "The Man Who Found Out" (1912). In the former, contact with an unseen presence cause mental damage and physical disintegration among a hunting-party. The entity is "not evil perhaps [. . .], yet instinctively hostile to humanity as it exists" (*Lost Valley* 130). And yet, we are reminded by one of the hunters, Dr. Cathcart, who has authored a book on collective hallucination, that "The spell of these terrible solitudes [. . .] cannot leave any mind untouched" (112). The indifference of the phenomena in "The Willows" and "The Wendigo" is not yet Lovecraftian cosmicism. As S. T. Joshi has noted, "civilization has separated us from the natural world, and our alienation may have engendered in Nature an indifference that borders on hostility" (Joshi, "Introduction" xii–xiii). As for the second story, it concerns the discovery of an ancient text of forbidden lore, the Tablets of the Gods, which contain "something so terrible and yet so obvious" about mankind's role in the universe ("Man" 137; *Wolves* 212) that the narrator's soul—"a man of science and a mystic" ("Man" 129; *Wolves* 196)—is immediately casted into oblivion. What the text actually says, of course, is never revealed: it remains as invisible as other Machen's and Blackwood's creatures, or as hidden as Frankenstein's means of giving life to his creature. Only hidden can the uncanniness be retained within the boundaries of our modern materialistic reality.

A final word must be said about William Hope Hodgson (1877–1918), who started writing rather late in his life—his first short story, the supernatural "The Goddess of Death," appeared in April 1904. Science and the spiritual are equally combined in some of his works, with a tendency to see the forces of decay and physical corruption by malevolent forces operating through the hidden processes of nature, lurking behind the protective boundaries of consciousness (Stableford 49–50). For instance, in "The Baumoff Explosive" (1919), a Christian scientist obsessed with the crucifixion is convinced that a chemical compound is responsible for the phenomena surrounding the last moments of Christ—the darkening of the sky, which he explains as an interruption of the transmission of light. The scientist introduces the compound in his own body and, after experiencing the suffering of Christ on the cross and the darkening of the skies, his conscience ends up being displaced by a demonic entity. It is not by chance that this story echoes both Machen's "The Inmost Light" and Blackwood's "A Psychical Invasion": capitalizing on contemporary trends, Hodgson also developed a Blackwoodian "occult detective" named Thomas Carnacki, who combined esoteric lore and pseudobiblia with science and modern instruments (Joshi, "Things in the Weeds" 81–82). Only half of the six original Carnacki stories deal with actual supernatural entities, the remaining three being cases of trickery discovered through scientific reasoning. Carnacki, however, already deems classic magic as a "useless and foolish superstition" ("Gateway" 410, *Carnacki* 80), and employs (pseudo-)scientific devices such as the Electric Pentacle to conjure off whatever sinister presence haunted his client.

Hodgson's most powerful and celebrated work, however, and the one that has also granted him the title of "Literary Copernicus," is beyond any question *The House on the Borderland* (1908). Despite featuring Poesque scenarios, such as a found manuscript, a huge mansion, and a dead lover, as well as the Frankensteinian *topos* of the unmarried, fragile sister (also present in Poe's "The Fall of the House of Usher"), Hodgson departs here, more drastically than in any other of his stories, from any previous Gothic or "weird" story-line through the use of potent cosmic imagery. A diary, found by two travelers among the ruins of a house surrounding a pit and near a silent lake (once again Poe's "House of Usher" resonates here), narrates a recluse's long-lasting struggle against the swine-things, human-like swine creatures that threaten his physical and mental integrity through oneiric and tangible continuous attacks.

The whole set of these experiences can be placed within the realm of modern science fiction, and yet their distressfulness is such that raises a terrible sensation of life-threatening danger. To begin with, the narrator experiences a hideous dream-quest through time and space beyond the known, dark abysses of the universe, deep into the center of creation, where an impossible Green Star and a pandemonium of mute gods await the final end of our system (solar, but maybe also political system).[24] Furthermore, Hodgson no longer confronts us with Poesque (or Kiplingesque) guilt-hallucinations out of Victorian morality, or with Stevensonian personality decay, but with real horrors whose chimerical bodily strangeness recalls Frankenstein's composite creation: the man-eating plants, the giant cuttle-fish and the tentacled humanoids in *The Boats of the "Glen Carrig"* (1907), as well as the consuming fungi in *The House on the Borderland* and "The Voice in the Night" (1912). The scientific materiality and subjection to natural laws (albeit not our own) of these beings and phenomena are firmly attested, and the swine-things, just like any of the other Darwinian monsters peopling Hodgson's tales, are

---

24. A green star is an impossibility. The idea may have been inspired by Jules Verne's "green flash" in *The Green Ray* (1882), although given the feasible identification between the swine-things and Irish peasants (Jones 40), it may be a disturbing image of Ireland itself.

thoroughly material beings that can be injured and dealt with by materialistic means. There is an "uncannity" in the fact that these creatures do actually belong to our own material world, sharing matter and even ancestry or genetical kinship with our species.

A Literary Baconian: Lovecraft and the Purification of the Weird

From Shelley to Hodgson, these authors sought to reconcile the seeds of the scientific revolution in science with their inherited supernatural and philosophical *Weltanschauung* in literature, in a way analogous to the multiple attempts and failures of reconciliation that science and religion experienced during the fifteenth to seventeenth centuries. This was a slow process wherein an emerging conception of the supernatural tale started to come together in a more concrete systematization of a philosophy of cosmicism that denied absolutely any possibility of the supernatural as well as the absurdity of a doctrine of the final causes, finally displacing mankind from its traditionally privileged position in the cosmos. Whereas other writers of the weird considered herein held to some extent supernatural beliefs, Lovecraft's distinctiveness lies in the very fact that he was the first to maintain, at the same time, an interest in the weird and a convincing materialism. His shift of paradigm was not groundbreaking: it was the natural outcome of an age of abandonment of the supernatural in the interest of scientific inquiry.

Lovecraft, however, also experimented with themes closer to the Gothic tradition and the supernatural before achieving this Baconian shift of literary paradigm. For instance, in "The Rats in the Walls" (1923/1924) the phenomena surrounding the narrator seem to be at first a hallucination—only he and the cat notice the rats in the walls, and the incidents only happen when he is in the house. Supernatural Gothicism abounds in his early production, with examples such as "The Temple" (1920/1925) and "The Moon-Bog" (1921/1926), and supernatural revenge makes its appearance in a number of tales: "The Tree" (1920/1921), "The Cats of Ulthar" (1920), "The Hound" (1922/1924), "In the Vault" (1925), and the late "Winged Death" (1932; with Hazel Heald) (Lovecraft, *Medusa's Coil* 142), where there is no clear explanation of the apparently supernatural process of personality displacement. Likewise, the use of drugs, devices, or other forms of expansion of consciousness, always met with terrible consequences, are a common topic in writings from the same period, with examples such as "Beyond the Wall of Sleep" (1919), "From Beyond" (1920/1934), "The Music of Erich Zann" (1921/1922), and "Hypnos" (1922/1923). These themes evidence that Lovecraft's creations were not a singularity, but the necessary development of a *fin de siècle* worldview that preceded his final, literary departure from the Victorian ethos.

A distinct, all-embracing motif with precedents in H. G. Wells and Hodgson were the different forms of anthropological horror—the burden of evolution, miscegenation, and a taint in the line—that permeate Lovecraft's tales, from "Facts concerning the Late Arthur Jermyn and His Family" (1920/1921) to "The Shadow over Innsmouth" (1931/1936), a theme that has been widely studied elsewhere (Guarde-Paz; Joshi, "Time") and that Lovecraft himself acknowledged:

> Reversion to primitive forms always inspires terror, & the terror is double when the stock concerned is close at hand & related to one's own civilization. *Decadence* always holds a horror which mere *primitiveness* does not. An African tribe may be *repulsive*, but it is not *horrible* –but an American community lapsing from civilization to a state like that of an African tribe *is* infinitely horrible. (Lovecraft, *Letters to Robert Bloch* 32)

An interesting derivation of this motif reappears in a number of stories that reformulate, in different ways, the European legends about the "little people"—gnomes and fairies, believed to be a real race of European or Nordic dwarfs that fought against the new Aryan invaders and stole their progeny, replacing it with their own malformed children (*CE* 3.323–27; Joshi and Schultz 93). This idea was already introduced into literature by Arthur Machen ("Folklore" 272), who may have known the anthropological and scientific theories of Karl Ernst Jarcke as endorsed by some historians in the late nineteenth century, later popularized by Margaret A. Murray's book, *The Witch-Cult in Western Europe* (1921). In "The Nameless City" (1921) the little people has become a race of underground reptilian dwarfs, still inhabiting subterranean cavities in the remotest areas of the Arabian Desert, whereas in "The Lurking Fear" (1922/1923) the creatures, now half-ape, half-mole, pierce through the more familiar Catskill Mountains, in southeastern New York. The little people reappear in "The Festival" (1923/1925), now transformed into a subterranean race of reptilian, winged creatures, half-fungi, half-mole, worshipped by the waxen-masked human crossbred that inhabits the surface. These themes, despite the recurrent claim of anti-Victorianism advocated by Lovecraft through his life (Joshi, *I Am Providence* 1.471–72; Lovecraft, *Letters to Maurice W. Moe* 249–50, 275, 285, and 289), were in fact the result of late Victorian imagination and morality, with its obsession with the theological consequences of Darwinism, the anxiety of degeneration, and the subsequent analysis of the foreigner or savage in terms of their biological proximity to the feared Darwinian beast within us (Wells, *Island* xxix–xxi).[25]

But it is in "The Whisperer in Darkness" (1930/1931) that Lovecraft expresses a more mature elaboration of the theoretical devices behind "The Festival," embodied with a rich scientific imagery. The winged fungoids are now fantastic alien forms from an undis-

---

25. In his introduction to Wells's *The Island of Doctor Moreau,* Darryl Jones points to Sir James George Frazer's *The Golden Bough* (1890) as an embodiment of these factors (xxix), a work Lovecraft read and which was an influence in both his fiction and philosophical essays (Calenbergh 21–23). Lovecraft acknowledges the importance of the scientific developments of the Victorian period, but calls its architecture "an insane nightmare," its fiction "insincere, rambling, unlifelike, & unconvincing," and philosophically "superficial & dependent upon false premises" (Lovecraft, *Letters to J. Vernon Shea* 333–34).

covered planet whose physical and chemical constitution, it is said, goes beyond anything familiar to our known laws, "with electrons having a wholly different vibration-rate" (*CF* 2.502) that, just like Blackwood's mysterious sounds in "The Willows," prevents them from being registered. They use scientific means to remove (or kidnap) the brain of certain human beings, although the reasons for this act are never truly specified in the story: the final revelation of a waxen-masked figure replacing Akeley's persona may be, however, reminiscent of the activities of the little people, who replaced human babies with their own offspring.

The use of science in his stories served two main purposes beyond mere aesthetic credibility: it either modernized classical (Gothic) themes or provided a scientific (or rather a science fictional, but not supernatural) explanation to strange phenomena. For instance, "Herbert West—Reanimator" (1922) modernizes the undead, offering an actual explanation for Frankenstein's unknown procedures; "Cool Air" (1926/1928) does the same with immortality, and "The Man of Stone" (1932; with Hazel Heald) with alchemy; "The Dreams in the Witch House" (1932/1933) offers a scientific scenario for witchcraft; and "The Shadow out of Time" (1934–35/1936), which culminates this long process of scientification of the weird tale, renovates spiritual possession and astral travel. Contrary to some of the existing literature (Callaghan 72), Lovecraft was not trying to "shove" science fiction back into the weird tale, evidencing a regression of his creative work to former pulp themes, but to transcend the supernatural explanations that the weird tale, and himself, had provided hitherto.[26]

---

26. This was recognized by Donald A. Wollheim (Lovecraft, *Letters to Robert Bloch* 14–15), who included "The Shadow out of Time" in the Viking *Portable Novels of Science* (Wollheim 394–479) together with H. G. Wells's *The First Men in the Moon* (1901), John Taine's *Before the Dawn* (1934), and Olaf Stapledon's *Odd John* (1935): "Because he was remarkably erudite, a master of languages, well versed in sciences [. . .] he did not need to draw upon occultism for the background of his literary terrors. He drew upon science and its problematic possibilities for the skeletons upon which

Lovecraft firmly believed that it was only through the ancillary use of science that the weird could be finally excised from its traditional supernatural framework, enhancing hence the credibility of otherwise unexplained phenomena that "*supplement,* rather than *contradict,* reality" (*Letters to James F. Morton* 227)—a conception akin to Bacon's purification of astrological science through astronomy. Lovecraft discovered astronomy in 1902 and had been writing extensively on this topic for local newspapers ever since, keeping his fascination alive for half of his life (Lovecraft, *Letters to Maurice W. Moe* 38). His famous diatribe of 1914 with a local astrologer, Joachim Friedrich Hartmann (1848–1930), whose article "Astrology and the European War" displaced Lovecraft's usual column in the Providence *Evening News,* is a paramount example of the contempt and disgust with which astrological predictions and pseudo-scientific beliefs were regarded by Lovecraft (*CE* 3.334–48).

It is interesting that, despite his usually coherent use of science and his denunciation of astrology, Lovecraft actually used superstitious beliefs as a core element in a number of tales mainly written during and after 1926. In "The Call of Cthulhu" (1926/1928) astrology appears in a rather embarrassing way in one of the most celebrated lines of the story: "When the stars were right, They could plunge from world to world through the sky" (*CF* 2.39). As Lovecraft had stated in his essays against astrology, there could be no "right" position for the stars, since these are just apparent and relative to our own point in the cosmos (*CE* 3.263). In a similar way, the earthquake provoked by the rise of Cthulhu following the "right" position of the stars—the actual Charlevoix-Kamouraska earthquake (Lovecraft, *A Means to Freedom* 210)—also evokes ancient beliefs of such phenomena originating in the will of the gods. There is a concrete reason for Lovecraft's use of these two pieces of supernaturalism in this tale: he was then working with C. M. Eddy, Jr. (1896–1971) on a couple of essays for Harry Houdini (1874–1926), "The

---

he pegged Poesque tales of cosmic dread" (Wollheim 391–392; Lovecraft, *Letters to Robert Bloch* 468).

Cancer of Superstition" (Lovecraft, *Dark Brotherhood* 246–61) and "Witchcraft" (Lovecraft, *Letters to Wilfred B. Talman* 46), and it is from his numerous readings on these two topics when preparing the manuscripts that he extracted the bulk of information on astrology and sorcery introduced in some of the stories from this period.[27] It is then not strange that alchemy and sorcery reappear immediately, among others, in *The Case of Charles Dexter Ward* (1927/1941) and "The Dunwich Horror" (1928/1929). Certainly, a few specific elements of the latter could be perceived as an unsuccessful attempt to consummate Lovecraft's own definition of the weird tale as a suggestive uncannity (Lovecraft, *Supernatural* 28)—the unconvincing portrayal of good vs. evil, black magic vs. white magic and its intrinsic anthropocentric psychology, or the visual perceptibility of the chimerical nature of Wilbur's twin at the end of the story (Joshi, *I Am Providence* 2.717–718).[28] However, it should also be acknowledge that, whereas Cthulhu was described as a Frankensteinian chimera composed of more or less recognizable and familiar animals—a conception that, at some point, Lovecraft seems to have deemed "a little childish" (*Fortunate* 406)—Yog-Sothoth, first introduced in *The Case of Charles Dexter Ward* but only described indirectly through the resemblance of his progeny in "The Dunwich Horror," presents the first radical departure from any form of earthly familiarity, only achieved before with the Biercean entity (or entities) in "The Colour out of Space" (1927).

---

27. Earthquakes in relation with supernatural phenomena are mentioned in "The Cancer of Superstition" (Lovecraft, *Dark Brotherhood* 255), as well as fetishes or idols from the African tribes (259).

28. Of course, it could be imagined, as does Brian Lumley in *The Burrowers Beneath* (1974), that there is a non-supernatural justification for the incantations against otherworldly creatures, such as "a sort of psychiatric science" through which mental blocks were implanted into the psyches of the extraterrestrial "gods" to conjure them away through signs or spells (Leiber, "Cthulhu" 121). But the anticlimactic nature of an unimpressive *scientia ex machina* is hardly preferable to the honest ignorance of a traditional, unexplained *deus*.

Conclusion

In the preceding pages, I have attempted to offer a brief outline of the complex interactions between science and the supernatural and the variety and evolution of scientific themes within the weird tale genre during a decisive period of our intellectual history. This path was never a straight line, reflecting similar developments in different branches of science and philosophy, and characterized by an exemplary flexibility and tolerance toward new and different beliefs. Our own path of scientific discovery is mirrored at the surface of literature, from the anthropomorphic horrors in Homer's *Odyssey* to the cosmic invisibilities of the Lovecraftian anti-pantheon. It reveals the importance of myth for mankind and its continuing role and endless conflict with science.

Lovecraft, far from being a pioneer, was mainly a man of his time who harvested the rich fruits of an ongoing revolution in supernatural literature, shifting familiar themes through the acute eye of a materialistic philosophy and purifying a long, inherited tradition of weird storytellers that had been struggling to emancipate themselves from the clanking chains of the ghostly linen. He appears to have been aware of his indebtedness to the prevailing social and scientific transformations of the times:

> Regrets are absolutely futile. The change is inevitable, because the last century brought to light facts never suspected before; which not only upset all the old notions, but explain with considerable clearness the psychological and anthropological reasons those notions were held in the past. The suddenness of the change is not surprising—its seeds were sown in the splendour of the Renaissance, when thought was emancipated and scientific progress begun. New instruments, exciting new zeal and opening up new vistas, have appeared in logical succession; and minds formerly applied to other arts have joined in the quest for truth. The nineteenth and twentieth centuries mark the logical culmination of the advance of 500 years—the growth of philosophies on the new data—so that he who would order us back to superstition is like Canute commanding the waves. Unfortunately or not, the illusion of spirituality is dead among the thinking classes (*CE* 5.59).

The weird tale lies on the borderland between the supernatural horrors of the Gothic tradition and the fictionalized account of scientific events that explains away those ancestral horrors. It integrates them within a new framework that increases their threatening qualities: personality disorders, psychosis, and hallucination jeopardize our own mind's sanity and survival; anthropological decay and bodily strangeness endanger our physical condition and earthly continuity; the vastness of a boundless and timeless cosmos—without a divine origin or eschatological end—threatens to destroy our relevance as individuals and our own delusion of transcendental immortality. With the modernization of the weird tale, the new scientifically explained reality has become more terrifying than the usual specter, vampire, or werewolf, because there is no spell, no cross, and no silver bullet that can protect us against them. The famous opening lines of Lovecraft's "The Call of Cthulhu" about the "placid island of ignorance" whence "it was not meant that we should voyage far" (*CF* 2.21) resonate with Frankenstein's speech in chapter four of Shelley's novel: "learn from me, if not by my precept, at least by my example, how dangerous is the acquirement of knowledge, and how much happier that man is who believes his native town to be the world, than he who aspires to become greater than his nature will allow" (1818, 87). Rather than reflecting the author's attitude toward knowledge, these lines reveal the modern fear of discovering something that can no longer be conjured away with repeated prayers and ceremonial gesticulations, and foreshadows our ultimate, imminent loss of control over Nature and ourselves.

Works Cited

Arata, Stephen. *Fictions of Loss in the Victorian Fin de Siècle*. Cambridge: Cambridge University Press, 1996.

———. "Stevenson and *Fin-de-Siècle* Gothic." In Penny Fielding, ed. *The Edinburgh Companion to Robert Louis Stevenson*. Edinburgh: Edinburgh University Press, 2010. 53–69.

Bacon, Sir Francis. *The Works of Francis Bacon*. Ed. James Spedding et al. London: Longman, 1876–83. 15 vols.

Bierce, Ambrose. *The Collected Works of Ambrose Bierce*. New York: The Neale Publishing Company, 1909–1912, 12 vols.

———. "The Town Crier." *San Francisco News Letter and California Advertiser* 22 (9 March 1872): 9.

Blackwood, Algernon. *The Centaur*. London: MacMillan, 1911.

———. *The Listener and Other Stories*. London: Eveleigh Nash, 1907.

———. *The Lost Valley and Other Stories*. London: Eveleigh Nash, 1910.

———. "The Man Who Found Out." *Canadian Magazine* 40 (1912): 129–38.

———. *The Wolves of God and Other Fey Stories*. London: Cassell, 1921.

Bowden, Mary Ellen. *The Scientific Revolution in Astrology*. New Haven, CT: Yale University Press, 1974.

Boyer, Pascal. *Religion Explained: The Evolutionary Origins of Religious Thought*. New York: Basic Books, 2001.

Brahe, Tycho. "Inclytis utriusque Astrologiae alumnis." In *De Nova Stella*. Ed. Tycho Brahe. Copenhagen: Laurentius Benedicti, 1573. 31–47.

Brantlinger, Patrick. "Imperial Gothic: Atavism and the Occult in the British Adventure Novel, 1880–1914." *English Literature in Transition, 1880–1920* 28 (1985): 243–52.

———. "Race and *Frankenstein*." In Andrew Smith, ed. *The Cambridge Companion to Frankenstein*. Cambridge: Cambridge University Press, 2016. 128–42.

Bruno, Giordano. *De Rerum Principiis*. In *Opera Latine Conscripta*. Ed. Vittorio Imbriani et al. Naples: Morano, 1879–86, 3 vols.

———. *The Expulsion of the Triumphant Beast*. Tr. Arthur D. Imerti. New Brunswick, NJ: Rutgers University Press, 1964.

Butler, Marilyn. "The First *Frankenstein* and Radical Science." *Times Literary Supplement* No. 4697 (9 April 1993): 12–14.

Callaghan, Gavin. "A Reprehensible Habit: H. P. Lovecraft and the Munsey Magazines." In Robert H. Waugh, ed. *Lovecraft and Influence: His Predecessors and Successors*. Lanham, MD: Scarecrow Press, 2013. 69–82.

Carrington, Charles E. *The Life of Rudyard Kipling*. Garden City, NY: Doubleday, 1955.

Caspar, Max. *Kepler*. Tr. C. Doris Hellman. New York: Dover, 1993.

Clasen, Mathias. "The Evolution of Horror: A Neo-Lovecraftian Poetics." In Sean Moreland, ed. *New Directions in Supernatural Horror Literature: The Critical Influence of H. P. Lovecraft*. New York: Palgrave Macmillan, 2018. 43–60.

Derleth, August, ed. *Strange Ports of Call*. New York: Pellegrini & Cudahy, 1948.

Descartes, René. *A Discourse on the Method*. Tr. Ian Maclean. Oxford: Oxford University Press, 2006.

Duncan, Ian. "Stevenson and Fiction." In Penny Fielding, ed. *The Edinburgh Companion to Robert Louis Stevenson*. Edinburgh: Edinburgh University Press, 2010. 11–26.

Field, Judith Veronica. "Astrology in Kepler's Cosmology." In Patrick Curry, ed. *Astrology, Science, and Society*. Woodbridge, UK: Boydell Press, 1987. 143–70.

Fielding, Penny. "Introduction." In Penny Fielding, ed. *The Edinburgh Companion to Robert Louis Stevenson*. Edinburgh: Edinburgh University Press, 2010. 1–10.

Fisher, Benjamin F. "Poe and the Gothic Tradition." In Kevin J. Hayes, ed. *The Cambridge Companion to Edgar Allan Poe*. Cambridge: Cambridge University Press, 2002. 72–91.

———. *The Cambridge Introduction to Edgar Allan Poe*. Cambridge: Cambridge University Press, 2012.

Frank, Lawrence. *Victorian Detective Fiction and the Nature of Evidence: The Scientific Investigations of Poe, Dickens, and Doyle*. New York: Palgrave Macmillan, 2009.

Freud, Sigmund. *The Uncanny*. Tr. David McLintock. London: Penguin Classics, 2003.

Geneva, Ann. *Astrology and the Seventeenth Century Mind*. Manchester: Manchester University Press, 1995.

Gilmour, David. *The Long Recessional: The Imperial Life of Rudyard Kipling*. London: Penguin, 2019.

Godwin, William. *Political and Philosophical Writings of William Godwin*. Ed. Mark Philp. Brookfield, VT: Pickering & Chatto, 1993.

Graf, Susan Johnston. *Talking to the Gods: Occultism in the Work of W. B. Yeats, Arthur Machen, Algernon Blackwood, and Dion Fortune*. Albany: State University New York Press, 2005.

Guarde-Paz, César. "Race and War in the Lovecraft Mythos: A Philosophical Reflection." *Lovecraft Annual* 6 (2012): 3–35.

Hammond, J. R. *A Robert Louis Stevenson Companion*. London: Palgrave Macmillan, 1984.

Haynes, Roslynn D. *H. G. Wells: Discoverer of the Future*. London: Macmillan, 1980.

Hegel, G. W. F. *Aesthetics*. Tr. T. M. Knox. Oxford: Oxford Clarendon Press, 1975.

Hendrix, Scott E. "Superstition and Modernity. The Conflict Thesis, Secularization Thesis, and Anti-Catholicism." In Uchenna Okeja, ed. *Religion in the Era of Postsecularism*. New York: Routledge, 2020. 103–22.

Hill, Christopher. *Intellectual Origins of the English Revolution: Revisited*. Oxford: Oxford University Press, 2001.

Hodgson, William Hope. *Carnacki, the Ghost-Finder*. London: Eveleigh Nash, 1913.

———. "The Gateway of the Monster." *Idler* 88 (1910): 403–16.

James, M. R. *The Collected Ghost Stories of M. R. James*. London: Edward Arnold, 1931.

Jones, Darryl. "Borderlands: Spiritualism and the Occult in *Fin de Siècle* and Edwardian Welsh and Irish horror." *Irish Studies Review* 17 (2009): 31–44.

Joshi, S. T. "Arthur Machen: The Evils of Materialism." In *The Secret Ceremonies. Critical Essays on Arthur Machen*. Ed. by Mark

Valentine and Timothy J. Jarvis. New York: Hippocampus Press, 2019. 15–26.

———. *I Am Providence. The Life and Times of H. P. Lovecraft.* New York: Hippocampus Press, 2010. 2 vols.

———. "Introduction." In Algernon Blackwood. *Ancient Sorceries and Other Weird Stories.* London: Penguin Classics, 2002. vii–xxii.

———. "Time, Space, and Natural Law: Science and Pseudo-Science in Lovecraft." *Lovecraft Annual* 4 (2010): 177–80.

———. "Things in the Weeds: The Supernatural in Hodgson's Stories." In Massimo Berruti, S. T. Joshi, and Sam Gafford, ed. *William Hope Hodgson. Voices from the Borderland.* New York: Hippocampus Press, 2014. 73–83.

———. *The Weird Tale.* Austin: University of Texas Press, 1990.

———, and David E. Schultz. *An H. P. Lovecraft Encyclopedia.* Westport, CT: Greenwood Press, 2001.

Katzman, Pearl. "H. G. Wells Talks about the Movies." *Screenland* 21 (1931): 20–21, 70.

Kennington, Richard. *On Modern Origins: Essays in Early Modern Philosophy.* Lanham, MD: Lexington Books, 2004.

Kipling, Carrie. *The Rees and Carrington Extracts from the Diaries of Caroline Kipling,* www.kiplingsociety.co.uk/members/diaries_fra.htm. Accessed 8 June 2021.

Kipling, Rudyard. *The Phantom 'Rickshaw and Other [Eerie] Tales.* Allahabad, India: A. H. Wheeler, 1888.

Klinger, Leslie S. "A Note on the Text." In *The New Annotated Frankenstein.* Ed. Leslie S. Klinger. New York: Liveright, 2017. lxxiii–lxxix.

Kraus, Joseph H. *Houdini's Spirit Exposés from Houdini's Own Manuscripts, Records and Photographs.* New York: Experimenter Publishing Co., 1928.

Kuhn, Thomas. *The Copernican Revolution.* Cambridge, MA: Harvard University Press, 1957.

Lawrence, William. *Lectures on the Physiology, Zoology, and Natural History of Man.* London: J. Callow, 1819.

Lear, John. *Kepler's Dream, with the Full Text and Notes of "Somnium, sive Astronomia Lunaris, Joannis Kepleri."* Berkeley: University of California Press, 1965.

Leiber, Fritz. "The Cthulhu Mythos: Wondrous and Terrible." *Fantastic* 24 (1975): 118–21.

———. "A Literary Copernicus." In H P. Lovecraft et al. *Something about Cats and Other Pieces.* Ed. August Derleth. Sauk City, WI: Arkham House, 1949. 290–303.

Lovecraft, H. P. *The Annotated Supernatural Horror in Literature.* Ed. S. T. Joshi. 2nd ed. New York: Hippocampus Press, 2012.

———. *Collected Essays.* Ed. S. T. Joshi. New York: Hippocampus Press, 2004–06. 5 vols. [Abbreviated in the text as *CE.*]

———. *Collected Fiction: A Variorum Edition.* Ed. S. T. Joshi. New York: Hippocampus Press, 2015–17. 4 vols. [Abbreviated in the text as *CF.*]

———. *Letters to J. Vernon Shea, Carl F. Strauch, and Lee McBride White.* Ed. S. T. Joshi and David E. Schultz. New York: Hippocampus Press, 2016.

———. *Letters to James F. Morton.* Ed. David E. Schultz and S. T. Joshi. New York: Hippocampus Press, 2011.

———. *Letters to Maurice W. Moe and Others.* Ed. David E. Schultz and S. T. Joshi. New York: Hippocampus Press, 2018.

———. *Letters to Robert Bloch and Others.* Ed. David E. Schultz and S. T. Joshi. New York: Hippocampus Press, 2015.

———. *Letters to Wilfred B. Talman and Helen V. and Genevieve Sully.* Ed. David E. Schultz and S. T. Joshi. New York: Hippocampus Press, 2019.

———. *A Means to Freedom: The Letters of H. P. Lovecraft and Robert E. Howard.* Ed. S. T. Joshi, David E. Schultz, and Rusty Burke. New York: Hippocampus Press, 2009. 2 vols. (numbered consecutively).

———. *Medusa's Coil and Others.* Ed. S. T. Joshi. Welches, OR: Arcane Wisdom, 2012.

———. *O Fortunate Floridian: H. P. Lovecraft's Letters to R. H. Barlow*. Ed. S. T. Joshi and David E. Schultz. Tampa, FL: University of Tampa Press, 2008.

———, et al. *The Dark Brotherhood and Other Pieces*. Sauk City, WI: Arkham House, 1966.

Machen, Arthur. *Decadent and Occult Works*. Ed. by Dennis Denisoff. Cambridge, UK: Modern Humanities Research Association, 2018.

———. "Folklore and Legends of the North." *Literature* 3 (24 August 1898): 271–74.

———. *The Great God Pan and The Inmost Light*. Boston: Roberts Bros., 1894.

———, and Montgomery Evans, *Letters of a Literary Friendship, 1923–1947*. Ed. Sue Strong Hassler and Donald M. Hassler. Kent, OH: Kent State University Press, 1994.

Mellor, Anne K. "Choosing a Text of *Frankenstein* to Teach." In Stephen C. Behrendt, ed. *Approaches to Teaching Shelley's Frankenstein.* New York: Modern Language Association of America, 1990. 31–37.

Mighall, Robert. *A Geography of Victorian Gothic Fiction: Mapping History's Nightmares*. Oxford: Oxford University Press, 2003.

Mill, John Stuart. *The Collected Works of John Stuart Mill*. Ed. Ann P. Robson and John M. Robson. Toronto: University of Toronto Press, 1963–91. 33 vols.

Moreland, Sean. "The Birth of Cosmic Horror from the S(ub)lime of Lucretius." In Sean Moreland, ed. *New Directions in Supernatural Horror Literature: The Critical Influence of H. P. Lovecraft*. New York: Palgrave Macmillan, 2018. 13–42.

Nietzsche, Friedrich. *The Gay Science*. Trans. by Josefine Nauckhoff. Cambridge, UK: Cambridge University Press, 2001.

———. *Philosophy in the Tragic Age of the Greeks*. Trans. by Marianne Cowan. Chicago: Henry Regnery, 1971.

Pascal, Blaise. *Pensées and Other Writings*. Tr. Honor Levi. Oxford: Oxford University Press, 1995.

Philmus, Robert M. "The Satiric Ambivalence of *The Island of Doctor Moreau.*" *Science-Fiction Studies* 8 (1980): 2–11.

Poe, Edgar Allan. *Collected Works of Edgar Allan Poe.* Ed. Thomas Ollive Mabbott. Cambridge, MA: Belknap Press of Harvard University Press, 1978. 3 vols.

———. *The Science Fiction of Edgar Allan Poe.* Ed. Harold Beaver. London: Penguin, 1976.

Pollin, Burton R. "Poe and Kipling: A 'Heavy Debt' Acknowledged." *Kipling Journal* 47 (1980): 13–24.

Ptolemy. *Tetrabiblos.* Tr. F. E. Robbins. Cambridge, MA: Harvard University Press, 1940.

Rabkin, Eric S. *Science Fiction: A Historical Anthology.* Oxford: Oxford University Press, 1983.

Reid, Julia. *Robert Louis Stevenson, Science, and the* Fin de Siècle. New York: Palgrave Macmillan, 2008.

———. "Childhood and Psychology." In Penny Fielding, ed. *The Edinburgh Companion to Robert Louis Stevenson.* Edinburgh: Edinburgh University Press, 2010. 41–52.

Reventlow, Henning Graf. "The Eschatologization of the Prophetic Books: A Comparative Study." In Henning Graf Reventlow, ed. *Eschatology in the Bible and in Jewish and Christian Tradition.* Sheffield, UK: Sheffield Academy Press, 1997. 169–88.

Rossi, Paolo. "Bacon's Idea of Science." In Makku Peltonen, ed. *The Cambridge Companion to Bacon.* Cambridge: Cambridge University Press, 1996. 25–46.

Salomon, Roger B. *Mazes of the Serpent: An Anatomy of Horror Narrative.* Ithaca, NY: Cornell University Press, 2002.

Shelley, Mary. *The Annotated Frankenstein.* Ed. by Susan J. Wolfson and Ronald L. Levao. Cambridge, MA: Belknap Press of Harvard University Press, 2012.

———. *Frankenstein; or, The Modern Prometheus.* London: Lackington, Hughes, Harding, Mavor, & Jones, 1818. 3 vols.

———. *Frankenstein; or, The Modern Prometheus.* London: Henry Colburn & Richard Bentley, 1831.

Simon, Gérard. "Kepler's Astrology: The Direction of a Reform." In Arthur Beer and Peter Beer, ed. *Kepler: Four Hundred Years*. Oxford: Pergamon Press, 1975. 439–48.

Spruit, Leen. "Giordano Bruno and Astrology." In Hilary Gatti. *Giordano Bruno: Philosopher of the Renaissance*. London: Routledge, 2016. 228–49.

Stableford, Brian. "William Hope Hodgson." In Massimo Berruti, S. T. Joshi, and Sam Gafford, ed. *William Hope Hodgson. Voices from the Borderland*. New York: Hippocampus Press, 2014. 45–55.

Stevenson, Robert Louis. *The Letters of Robert Louis Stevenson*. Ed. Sidney Colvin, New York: Charles Scribner's Sons, 1911. 4 vols.

———. *Strange Case of Dr. Jekyll and Mr. Hyde and Other Tales*. Ed. Roger Luckhurst. Oxford: Oxford University Press, 2006.

Stewart, Susan. "The Epistemology of the Horror Story." *Journal of American Folklore* 95 (1982): 33–50.

Tessicini, Dario. "Cornelius Gemma and the New Star of 1572." In Patrick Bonner, ed. *Change and Continuity in Early Modern Cosmology* Dordrecht: Springer, 2011. 51–66.

Tester, S. Jim. *A History of Western Astrology*. Woodbridge, UK: Boydell Press, 1987.

Thomas, Keith. *Religion and the Decline of Magic*. London: Penguin, 1991.

Thomas, Ronald R. *Detective Fiction and the Rise of Forensic Science*. Cambridge: Cambridge University Press, 1999.

Thoren, Victor E. *The Lord of Uraniborg: A Biography of Tycho Brahe*. Cambridge: Cambridge University Press, 1990.

Tresch, John. "Extra! Extra! Poe Invents Science Fiction!" In Kevin J. Hayes, ed. *The Cambridge Companion to Edgar Allan Poe*. Cambridge: Cambridge University Press, 2002. 113–32.

Van Calenbergh, Hubert. "The Roots of Horror in *The Golden Bough*." *Lovecraft Studies* No. 26 (1992): 21–23.

Wagner, Corina. "Genealogies of Monstrosity: Darwin, the Biology of Crime and Nineteenth-Century British Gothic Literature." In Dale Townshend and Angela Wright, ed. *The Cambridge History of the Gothic: Volume 2, Gothic in the Nineteenth Century*. Cambridge: Cambridge University Press, 2020. 416–44.

Weinstein, Lee. "The First Literary Copernicus." *Nyctalops* 3, No. 1 (1980): 17–19.

Wells, H. G. *The Complete Short Stories of H. G. Wells*. Ed. John Hammond. London: Phoenix Press, 2000.

———. *The Island of Doctor Moreau*. Ed. Darryl Jones. Oxford: Oxford University Press, 2017.

Westman, Robert. *The Copernican Question: Prognostication, Skepticism, and Celestial Order*. Berkeley: University of California Press, 2011.

Williams, Keith. *H. G. Wells, Modernity and the Movies*. Liverpool: Liverpool University Press, 2007.

Wollheim, Donald A. *The Portable Novels of Science*. New York: Viking Press, 1945.

Side Effects May Include

Barry Yedvobnick

Maybe she wants to bury the hatchet. Nevertheless, it started the moment I drove up to Elena's home, and sitting in her study my uneasiness grows. Something in her body language and voice is not right. Twenty-five years ago we were students in the same research lab, and briefly lovers. The brevity was my fault.

"You've done well, Tyler," she says, without smiling.

"So have you," I reply, thankful to move the conversation to science. "I read your latest papers and the data are fascinating, especially the worm experiments. Total regeneration of their heads after decapitation, brain and all. Very cool stuff."

"Yes, that's what I want to talk about. I see more than head regeneration. There's also memory restoration."

"Really—what can a worm remember?" Looking around the study, I'm surprised to see bars on the windows.

"I trained them to avoid an electric shock, and they can remember that. But if I train and then decapitate them, they still remember the shock after their new heads form."

"That's interesting: they get back their old memories," I say, only half listening. The windows continue to distract me. I can't understand why Elena has bars out here, so far from the city. Is she really afraid of break-ins?

"Right, and I've identified the cells responsible," she says. "Those cells retain a copy of memories as they grow into a new brain."

That gets my attention. I have a reputation in science for never missing opportunities, and this sounds like a good one. The potential application of Elena's research to human brain disease intrigues me. But I'm puzzled. Why does she trust me? "That's amazing. You must be thinking about medical applications, like Alzheimer's and other dementias."

She gives me an unpleasant glance. "Of course I am. I already transplanted worm cells into a strain of mice showing memory loss. The cells stabilized their recall of maze runs."

Feeling the adrenaline rush, I lean closer to her. "Look, you've got to move this into clinical trials with patients fast. But your lab group is too small, so let me help. We should write up a research proposal together, and my team will pitch in immediately." Watching her closely for a reaction, I'm already thinking about parts of the project my lab can own.

"It's too early for human testing, Tyler: there are side effects. The mice developed some disturbing features." She walks over to a cabinet, removes two cages, and brings them to me. "Take a look. The mouse in this cage was transplanted with worm cells."

The mouse shows the strangest animal behavior I've ever seen. It moves quickly across the cage floor, crawling and undulating like a worm, while opening and closing its mouth continuously. The mouse without a transplant acts normally in its cage. "That's so bizarre. What's going on with its mouth?"

"Oh, it's close to feeding time," she says.

Despite my earlier enthusiasm, I realize the project cannot proceed. "You're right. It's way too early to try on people."

She touches my arm. "I need to tell you something. It's already been tried on somebody. My father's been suffering from dementia, and after I saw the memory rescue in mice I transplanted worm cells into him. The mice weren't showing behavioral problems yet when I did it."

I stare at her in disbelief. "Are you serious?"

"His memories stabilized, Tyler. The transplant worked."

"But the side effects. How is he?"

"See for yourself." She walks to the study door and pulls it open just a few inches. "Dad, five minutes till lunch, and I want you to meet Tyler. He's the guy I told you about. The one who stole my research fellowship, back in graduate school."

I groan loudly. "I knew it—the fellowship. That's what this is about. It's been decades, Elena."

"Did you think I could forget?"

I knew she couldn't. Elena was brilliant and pitched some innovative research ideas to me back then, while lying in my bed. I can barely admit to myself what happened the next day. I took her best ideas and wrote them up as my own fellowship proposal.

Fearing she will derail my career, I think fast. "I'm sorry, Elena, that was horrible, but I'm not that guy anymore. Let me help you work out the side effect problems. I won't take any credit. Please, don't go public with this." Her reaction to my plea is odd. She looks at me and laughs.

"I'm not going to tell anyone," she says.

Relieved, I take a deep breath. "How can I help?"

"I need to show you some other side effects," she says, putting the normal mouse into the cage with the wormlike one. The undulating mouse quickly attacks and devours its visitor.

"This is unbelievable," I say. "And why are you smiling?"

"They're carnivorous now, and they only eat what they hunt themselves."

Suddenly the door opens wide into the study, and I notice it has a deadbolt that appears polished and out of place against the old wood. I'm wondering why she put a new lock on the outside of the study door, when I remember the window bars. The answer hits me. The bars weren't put there to keep people out. My heart rate soars, and I jump out of my chair. "Where's your father?"

She looks toward the door and then down at the floor. "Dad," she says.

A naked man slithers rapidly into the room and stops next to Elena, blocking the only exit. I back away, as the man raises his head and stares at me with his mouth opening and closing. Saliva dribbles onto the floor.

Elena walks out of the study, and I hear her bolt the door.

"I Dream a Golden Dream": A Brief Dunsany Correspondence— and Friendship

Darrell Schweitzer

The privately printed volume *Selected Writings of Violet Sturgis Cosby* (1925) tells the tragic tale of what may well have been a genuine loss to literature. Cosby (1905–1925) was by all indications a child prodigy, as brilliant as Lovecraft. She had mastered the art of reading by age five. By the time she was six or seven she was writing surprisingly good (or at least coherent) verse, albeit showing a very different turn of mind from Lovecraft's:

> Dancing through the merry hours,
> Playing with the playful flowers . . .

Or:

> The pretty little crocus all in shining white
> Is a happy little maiden of hopefulness and light.

This sort of thing might seem thoroughly sappy if written by an adult, but coming from a child of less than ten, it is remarkable. Violet seems to have been a voracious reader, starting with children's fairy tales (Grimm and Andersen) and such, but very quickly turning to conventional adult literature. In an essay called "A Tour of My Library," written when she was twelve, she expresses a fondness for Charles Dickens, Sir Walter Scott, Robert Louis Stevenson, George Eliot, W. M. Thackeray, Charles Reade (whose *The Cloister and the Hearth* was regarded as a classic in those days), and, among the poets, Keats, Byron, and of course Shakespeare. She is also religious, apparently Catholic. Her Bible gets pride of place. We can see in her tastes in literature an interest that goes far beyond what would have been regarded as suitable reading for young girls in the early twentieth century. She likes romance and a degree of exoticism.

While it seems that the first decade of her life, spent in and around New York, was happy, in one somber moment at the age of eight she said to her mother, "You will have to write on my grave some day, 'Here lies one who loved beauty.'"

Then disaster struck and went on striking. In an "infantile paralysis" (i.e., polio) epidemic of 1916, Violet and both of her younger sisters were stricken. One of the sisters died. Violet never walked again without braces. Despite this she went on reading, and writing. Her ambition was to be a writer. She graduated from high school with high honors and took some college courses (at Columbia University) until some mysterious malady (possibly related to the polio) put a stop to that. She suffered paralytic spasms that caused her to have serious falls. To make matters worse, her family household was "broken." We are not told in the memoir by her mother included in her book whether her father died or if there was a divorce. In any case, her mother had to take on the financial responsibilities, and then the mother's health began to fail. It was found convenient to send Violet off to live with relatives in St. Paul, Minnesota. She was reluctant to go, because she thought it would upset her mother, but she went. There, her condition worsened, and shortly before her twentieth birthday she died. Her last letter was not about her own suffering, but offered words of comfort to her mother.

None of this would be of any especial interest to readers of *Penumbra* except that in the last year of her life Violet Sturgis Cosby corresponded with Lord Dunsany. The letters from both are reproduced in her memorial volume.

The first letter is undated. Sometime in the spring of 1925 she wrote to Dunsany what was in essence a fan letter, heaping praise on his work, mentioning how she had discovered *The Gods of Pegāna* in the library about two years earlier. She humbly wishes he were unknown, "so that this letter might give you pleasure . . . but now you will probably never even read it . . . and what matters my voice to the universal chorus of praise?" She has mostly read his prose at this time, but she heralds him as a true poet, akin to Coleridge or Blake.

Much to her surprise and delight, Dunsany replied, on February 4, 1925, from Bahr el Zeraf, Africa. Dunsany says that her letter was so welcome that he wanted to hold off replying until he had the leisure to do so properly. That leisure came while he was on a steamer, eight degrees above the equator, sailing up the White Nile on a big-game hunting expedition. As endless papyrus swamps slid by, he took quill pen in hand and wrote:

> I think that our poets in England are seldom or never neglected, but we have one almost absolute rule, that to be appreciated they must be dead. This is why the appreciation of my work which at different times has come to me from America has meant so very much to me, apart even from the pleasure one has in the sheer generosity of it, for without it I would have worked without any appreciation at all, and to work at an art without any answer whatever from mankind is to have with one always the feelings of one that pulls the bell-rope to which there is no bell . . . (145–46)

International postal service must have been more efficient in those days, because by April 10 Violet has replied, remarking on the Africa postmark. (Now she is writing to Dunsany in London.) This time she goes into more detail about herself, about her preoccupation with beauty, and about the beauty she finds in the soaring New York skyscrapers, which echo Lovecraft's first (albeit rapidly disillusioned) glimpse of Manhattan, or Dunsany's own prose sketch "A City of Wonder" in *Tales of Three Hemispheres* (1919). She talks about her reading and asks if Dunsany had read George Meredith's Arabian Nights fantasy, *The Shaving of Shagpat*. She mentions seeing James Elroy Flecker's play *Hassan,* with its famous line about "the Golden Journey to Samarkand" (which is echoed in one of her poems), and she concludes: ". . . I dream a golden dream—that perhaps again I may hear from you."

Dunsany replied on May 1, 1925, from Dunsany Castle in County Meath. He too has been reading *The Shaving of Shagpat* recently and declares it "one of the finest things in English prose." She had asked about his definition of a poet, which had been quoted in the program of a performance of the Philadelphia Orchestra. This comes from his speech/essay *Nowadays* (1918), which had been published as a small book by then. (Dunsany notes there are two words left out of the text of the Four Seas Company edition.) He is not all that fond of *Hassan*, but he does admire the poem "The Golden Journey to Samarkand," which he feels was "dragged rather roughly into the play." To Violet's remarks on the beauty of language, Dunsany responds, "Certainly the rhythm of syllables and the sound of vowels carry some message to our intellects which the simpler ones are well able to receive, but the cleverest are not subtle enough to analyze" (152).

Violet writes back on June 1, asking if the "hippogriff" on his seal (the envelope had a stamped, wax seal, which you would expect from somebody who used a quill pen) is one of those that fly to the City of Never. (She has clearly read *The Book of Wonder*. Actually the seal shows a Pegasus.) She expounds more about beauty vs. ugliness, and appreciates how Dunsany distinguishes between the two in his writing. She states that the "great men" are the poets and dreamers, making the observation that when Robert Fulton perfected the steamboat, he was merely successful in a material way, but the great man was Keats, dying wretchedly of consumption at the same time.

She continues her discussion of plays, saying that the New York production of *Hassan* was poor. She asks if Dunsany has seen Barrymore's *Hamlet*. (She must have seen these a year or so earlier, as she would have been almost entirely crippled by June 1925.) She complains about the realism that is taking hold of contemporary theater, citing, among others, Eugene O'Neill's *Desire under the Elms:* "Drabness and gloom seem to be the fashion . . ."

More intriguingly, she recommends that Dunsany read Nikolai Gogol's *Taras Bulba,* a novel about Cossacks, more what you'd expect to appeal to Robert E. Howard than to a genteel, sickly young lady who has been schooled by Catholic nuns. But Violet Sturgis Cosby was clearly an independent thinker.

She mentions that she has read the poems of Francis Ledwidge, a poet Dunsany had sponsored, who was killed in the First World War. At no point does she ask him to sponsor her, but she is bold enough to enclose one of her short stories, a fantasy called "The Lady Francesca" to ask his opinion of it.

Dunsany's last reply is dated December 13, 1925. He is "beyond excuses" in apologizing for his tardy reply, but it seems he was busy writing a novel, which he has now finished and sent to Putnam's. (He doesn't say which one. Probably *The Charwoman's Shadow*.) Yes, he has seen the Barrymore *Hamlet*. Rather surprisingly for one of Dunsany's conservative tastes, he also praises a modern-dress version of *Hamlet*, which "just brings the mighty mind of Shakespeare nearer to our own time."

He liked her short story very much, but says that it is as a critic (noting previous discussions of various works of literature) that she seems "to start right ahead of 'the field,'" expressing a true appreciation of various works rather than trivially picking at faults the way many professional critics do. He thanks her for recommending *Taras Bulba*, which he sought out and found to be, indeed, a "masterpiece."

Unfortunately, Violet Sturgis Cosby never received this letter. She had died on September 8. The epitaph she had composed for herself at the age of eight was indeed placed on her grave.

Despite her own afflictions, Violet's mother (remarried as Virginia Dousman Bigelow) survived Violet by some years and co-edited the book of her writings. The correspondence concludes with a note from Dunsany, dated February 18, 1944, with which he encloses a copy of Violet's first letter, commends the mother's intention to bring out a memorial volume, and repeats his gratitude to Violet for recommending *Taras Bulba* to him.

Was Violet any good as a writer? I would say, yes. The story she sent Dunsany, "The Lady Francesca," is quite promising, if a bit overwritten in an attempt to be exquisite. It bears some resemblance to Hawthorne's "Rappaccini's Daughter." (In correspondence with a childhood friend, Katherine Post, also in the memorial volume, she mentions a fondness for Hawthorne.) It's about a lady so beautiful that anyone who looks into her eyes will die. One day a ragged stranger appears before her. He gets out a lute and sings praises of her hands, her mouth, etc. She is entranced. She asks him to continue. He begs her to raise her veil and let him see her eyes. She warns him of the danger, but he says he seeks beauty, not death. When he sees her eyes, he sings exquisitely, inspired beyond endurance, then drops dead. As the body is carried away, she asks her attendants who he was and she is told, "A poet." Certainly this is considerably better than much of what was being published in *Weird Tales* at this time. Her other sketches are literate and often interesting. In one there is a lovely description of used bookstores, which any antiquarian book lover can still appreciate.

Yes, she had talent. If she had lived, she might have made a name for herself. Lord Dunsany's involvement in her life was minimal, but his letters to her brought her great encouragement and comfort in her last few months.

Works Cited

Cosby, Violet Sturgis. *Selected Writings of Violet Sturgis Cosby*. Ed. Virginia Dousman Bigelow and Paula Kurth. Privately printed, 1945, in an edition of 500 copies by the Webb Publishing Co., St. Paul, MN.

The Lady Francesca: A Fantasy

Violet Sturgis Cosby

She was more beautiful than night and day, than spring and autumn, than life and death; she was more beautiful than all things on earth; and she was called Francesca. Her voice was like the murmuring of the wind-stirred palace pool; her lips were red as the rowanberry; and her hands softer and whiter than the pearled samite gown she wore. At night when she sat upon her balcony, and combed her long black tresses, the roses furled their petals that they might breathe the sweeter fragrance of her hair. In the morning, when she went across the sloping lawn, the trees bowed before her, for she was more graceful than they. Yes, she was beautiful. Throughout the world minstrels sang her praises; and people said no more—"It is beautiful," but—"It is like the Lady Francesca."

Yet even as they spoke, a look of fear would steal over their faces, and they would cross themselves, and whisper low. For this was the doom of the Lady Francesca: that no man might gaze into her eyes, and live. Always she wore a thin dark veil. If her hands and her body and her brow were fair, yet fairer than these, more wondrous, were her eyes. In them, so men said, was mirrored the supreme beauty. Enough for a mortal to look on it, and die; but in all the land there was no man who durst give that look. "Beauty is good," they thought, "but shall we give our lives for it? The earth is comfortable, so shall we be content with the lesser loveliness."

Sometimes a youth would become venturesome, and knock upon the great carven palace gate, and cross the old high hallways, till he stood in the presence of that most gracious lady. Then, at the last, he would be afraid, and turning, flee through the long corridors until he reached the outer courts, safe from that marvelous and deadly beauty.

Thus the days passed: the maiden moon grew old, and died; then, Phoenix-like, arose again young and fair as before. And the Lady Francesca sat in her bower alone.

One morning, when the world seemed faint with sweetness, the Lady Francesca walked in the garden; walked along the gray gravel paths where the little stones scarce moved beneath her feet, she was so light. The sky was blue, that deep, clear blue that blind men picture in their dreams of nature; blue the tender, nameless blossoms scattered over the grass; blue the tiny bird that darted by like a winged sapphire. The peacocks strutted past, and when the sun flashed on their huge fan-like tails it was as if a hundred separate rainbows shone there resplendently. The boughs of the apple tree wove lace upon the ground. The scent of a thousand flowers filled the air with heady, wine-like perfumes. The small round pool was quiet and smooth, fathomless as the night, and full of dim half-formed shapes. So still, so still, the garden dreamed beneath the summer sun.

The Lady Francesca seated herself on a cool stone bench and looked about. A sudden joy came over her, a sense of exultation at being part of all that beauty. Then she sighed, remembering and sorrowing at her loneliness, and leaned her head against the tree trunk, and sat quite still. She wore a pale green gown; and her hands, as they lay in her lap, were like white water-lily buds. A butterfly drifted past. The leaves rustled faintly.

Suddenly there was a noise as of someone drawing near. The Lady Francesca sprang up. A man stood before her, tall and fair to look upon. His crimson cloak was tattered, and the plume of his cap a sorry sight, but he bore himself with a kingly air, and his brow was wide and high. In one hand he carried a lute.

"Sir," spoke the Lady Francesca, "what would you here?" Her voice fluttered like a wounded bird.

The man answered no word, but caught up his lute and sang. His song was in praise of her hands; her long, smooth snowy hands; her hands that caressed the rosebush with gentler touch than the dew; her hands that cooled the sick man's forehead with swift, sure fingers.

The Lady Francesca sank back on the bench, and listened as in a trance. As he ceased, she leaned forward, "Ah, that was beautiful!"

But the man shook his head, and, touching his lute, began to sing once more. This time he sang to her mouth; her small red mouth that murmured soft, kind words; her mouth, the well whence flowed that crystal stream—her voice; her mouth, full and curled and scarlet, languorous with sweetness.

When he stopped, the Lady Francesca whispered dreamily, "Oh! sing, sing on forever!"

Then the man knelt before her, and said: "O wondrous lady, I ask a boon of you. I pray you lift your veil, for I would look into your eyes."

"Ah," cried the Lady Francesca, and her moan shattered the peace of the garden. "You are mad! Do you seek death?"

"No, my lady," answered the youth, "only beauty."

She stared at him incredulously. He was so young, so goodly, but in his eyes she saw a great longing, a burning, starry flame, unsatisfied. So she stepped slowly back, and drew aside the veil. The man, lifting his head, gazed straight into her eyes. For a moment he reeled, as though drunk with their beauty. Then a smile came over his face, and, for the last time, he took up his lute and sang.

He sang of vast vine-draped forests where night reigns all the day, of purple-shrouded mountains that rise up unto the very gates of Paradise; of rivers rushing to the sea, and of the sea itself, infinite, eternal, that gathers them to her bosom. The shadow fled from the sundial, and still he sang. Not a flower stirred, nor blew the tiniest breeze. In the dread silence, naught was heard save that one great golden song. He sang of life, its sorrows and its joys; he sang of death, calm, chaste death, the last, most precious gift the gods gave unto man; he sang of love that cometh to all men, and maketh their days to be glad; and then the song grew clearer, nobler, purer, and lo! he sang of Beauty, and how wheresoever she but brusheth the hem of her garment there is glory and radiance forever.

Even as he sang, his voice broke with joy; the lute dropped from his hand, and he fell dead at the feet of the Lady Francesca. Very quietly she bent over him. On his face was a look of ineffable happiness, a smile perfect and blissful as if he had glimpsed the ultimate vision. Before it, the Lady Francesca was afraid. She turned away as if she had seen some too holy sight; and she summoned her men-at-arms.

When they came, she asked them wonderingly, "Who was this man?"

And they answered: "He was a poet."

Evolution of a Younger God

Melissa Ridley Elmes

Evolve or perish—that was the mandate,
the edict passed down from some Ur-god
no one even knows anymore.
So I evolved, I grew, my mouth enlarged
until I could swallow souls of gods, the
worlds they created, whole galaxies—
I ate them all, unrelenting, mad to survive.
Never full, never satiated,
I opened wide and wider,
tore a hole in the universe so vast even I
finally fell into myself, so deep
there was no returning, so far I
became no more than a distant star
for someone else to wish on.

The Last Halloween

A Cautionary Fable for Mary Lou

John C. Tibbetts

That was the night when a sudden rush of air and a darkening of the twilight sky ushered in The Last Halloween. That was the night when ten thousand grinning, scowling, shrieking pumpkins disappeared from the front porches, window-seats, and fields all across America.

It happened suddenly.

High above the world, cloaked in invisibility, the spaceship settled in its orbit. Kkak-Ak sat back from the console, satisfied. Each of his three eyes blinked, and the wrinkles of his high-domed forehead relaxed. He had been studying this curious pastime these Earth people observed every year. They called it "Halloween." The ritual of the pumpkins gave him the solution to the problem: how to enslave these Earthlings.

And so it was that in the blink of his three eyes all the world was thrown into Pumpkin Darkness. The sudden disappearance of the pumpkins threw a bewildered world into confusion, even panic. Not just the pumpkins on the porches and the windows were gone; but the vast pumpkin patches were swept clean. Only a few stalks trailed across the rusting fields.

When Kkak-Ak had been called before the Council three days ago, his plan was regarded dubiously at first. Why not simply bombard the cities and towns with their neutron bombs and force these people to their knees into submission? But no, he argued, this way was better. Earthlings would bow to the will of the invaders without damage to life and limb.

Kkak-Ak saluted his four comrades, one arm upraised for each of them. Plan A was a success. And now it was time for the next step. Plan B was ready. Although no word issued from their tiny mouths, their approval and encouragement resounded through his head. He had done his homework. He had pored over the ancient volumes of earthly lore and custom. And there it was, in the mythology of the Greeks, that he found his answer.

He threw a switch. Then he sat back.

Suddenly, as quickly as the pumpkins had disappeared, a new batch of orange spheres suddenly arrived and settled on every porch and every window. Every street was cast into an eerie glow. Every field and patch burst aflame with pumpkin fire. Only these new ones didn't look like any pumpkins seen before. Their pumpkin features wrinkled and snarled. Their grinning, scowling eyes shot fiery light through the darkness. The awful flares seemed to issue an invitation to every person in city, town, and field. No one could look away. No one could resist. Not Grandpa and Grandma on the porch, not the night watchman on his rounds, not the farmer in the south-forty, not the lovers strolling hand-in-hand on the streets. Together, they all walked, and ran, and stumbled toward the grinning pumpkins.

One look into those flaring eyes and they stopped, paralyzed.

One look and they turned to stone.

Kkak-Ak had done his homework well. The Greeks had led the way.

In his language, Kkak-Ak's Project is known as *"Tt-34%!"*

Earthlings would know it at their last gasp as—

PROJECT MEDUSA.

The Weird Work of Mary Howitt

David Haden

In my continuing search for little-known local authors and neglected folklore of the northern part of Staffordshire in the West Midlands of England, I found a reference to the author Mary Howitt (1799–1888). I soon learned that in her prime Howitt had been one of the leading writers of her period, and indeed the leading foreign poet in America by the 1850s, although today she appears to be very little known even among academics. What follows are some preliminary notes, which I hope may aid others in the future. I regret I have not been able to see her two biographies published in the early 1950s. Before I give a short biography, drawn largely from her autobiography, I should state that Mary Howitt's letters are at the University of Nottingham's Department of Manuscripts & Special Collections, having been purchased in the 1990s. The same university holds an East Midlands Collection containing many books by Mary and her writer husband William Howitt (1792–1879). These would be obvious starting points for those with the time and funds needed for a full pursuit of her more macabre and supernatural work, although I understand another half-dozen British archives also hold her voluminous material. Such a pursuit would be a costly and onerous task, and I doubt I will undertake it.

Howitt came of age in rural Uttoxeter and the surrounding district, a comparatively riverine and lowland part of the isolated moorland uplands of northern Staffordshire. Her short book *My Own Story; or, The Autobiography of a Child* (1845) was the work that initially informed me about her local origin. I found the book to be very vivid and readable today, though sadly the chapter on "Town Customs" is short and notes only three customs. Such things were fading away, even back in the early nineteenth century. One of these customs is, however, given as a vivid view of the town's annual bull-baiting run and a child's view of it and is very valuable historically. I was then even more pleased to discovered that Howitt was the author of the classic macabre poem "The Spider and the Fly" (1828), for which she is still remembered today and which is still the subject of adaptation and illustration. This spurred me to try to discover more such material by her.

I initially found no survey-essay online, nor any bibliography that itemized the whole of her vast output, although after this essay was complete I found a good modern bibliography by Jones (1991). I have noted that in the 1950s there had been an Oxford University Press biography titled *Laurels and Rosemary: The Life of William and Mary Howitt* (1955), and a University of Kansas Press volume *Victorian Samplers: William and Mary Howitt* (1952). Both were found to be long out-of-print and not available online. Judging by one review from 1953, the latter book is actually more of a biography than the "sampler" that the title suggests. This was confirmed for me by the recent book *Writing Home: A Quaker Immigrant on the Ohio Frontier*, which calls the 1952 book "the best biography" of the couple and their place in the staunch religious sect. My further search for introductory reading found only *Quaker to Catholic: Mary Howitt, Lost Author of the 19th Century* (2010) by a local historian who lives in Uttoxeter, assisted by a ghostwriter. This appears to have made much of her religious conversion to Catholicism late in life, and I cannot find a review of it. There is also the 2008 article, "The 'Airy Envelope of the Spirit': Empirical Eschatology, Astral Bodies and the Spiritualism of the Howitt Circle," in the journal *Intellectual History Review*. As the title suggests, much is made of her husband's strong mid-life interest in and strong promotion of a "Christian Spiritualism" in the 1850s and '60s.

Unable to acquire any of the above, I then went to the source and perused her multi-volume *Mary Howitt: An Autobiography* (1889), which is freely available online. Chapter II details her "Early Days at Uttoxeter" while adding little to the local lore found in her

My Own Story. After her marriage she and her equally literary-minded husband went to live in urban Hanley, in my own city of Stoke-on-Trent. There they took over—of all things—a dispensing chemist's shop. This unlikely venture for a literary couple opens Chapter V, which also includes her eyewitness account of a lecture by the notoriously wild Stoke preacher Mulock (Byron's "Muley Moloch") operating at his height and his native element. The couple lasted all of seven months of 1821 in the quickly "despised" center of the smoky pottery town of Stoke-on-Trent, before moving away and ending up in the only slightly less dismal textile town of Nottingham over in the East Midlands. This brief stay in Nottingham—where husband William had come of age—appears to be the reason why the local university there holds most of her letters and a large collection of her work.

By the 1830s her autobiography has the couple down in the leafy and far more pleasant environs of Surrey in the more prosperous south of England, so as to be nearer the London publishers and magazines. The railways were then extending out from London and making such rural/city arrangements possible for writers. Prompted by the publisher's success of her *The Book of the Seasons* (1828), which had deftly presented the English months and their natural signs, sights, and sounds, Howitt set about working up her rural childhood memories into saleable material. Staffordshire was the setting for her conventional and profitable breakthrough adult book *Wood Leighton: A Year in the Country* (1836), set in the once-vast Needwood Forest adjacent to her home town of Uttoxeter. As an imaginative and adventuresome child Mary had been familiar with the surviving parts of this ancient forest. Her other book, *Tales in Prose* (1836), contains a section giving a number of more or less fantastical "anecdotes" from her childhood—including one where she is in Needwood Forest...

> What a horror now fell upon us! The glade was like an enchanted forest: all at once the trees seemed to swell out to the most gigantic and appalling size; every twisted root seemed a writhing snake, and every old wreathed branch a down-bending adder ready to de-

vour us. The holly thickets seemed full of an increasing blackness, which, like a dreadful dream, appeared growing upon our imagination till it was too horrible to be borne. We felt as if hemmed in by a mighty wilderness of gloom that cut us off from our kindred . . .

Howitt's *Autobiography* notes that her child-self delighted in places like Chartley: "It and its surroundings were all wonderfully weird and hoary." Chartley was an enclosure of the ancient Needwood Forest, and about as close to the deep and ancient Midlands greenwood as one could get in the England of that period. It was still inhabited by a herd of ancient wild "white" cattle, today ushered out of the few remaining forest nooks and kept as a key British "rare breed." There are other small hints of the macabre in her childhood memories. For instance, in her early poem "May Fair," a vivid account of the May Fair day at Uttoxeter, there is the line "And these will go to see the Dwarf, and those the Giant yonder," which adds a small touch of the fantastical. Other poetry reaches out to surrounding places and has either a macabre or a fairy cast to it.

For instance, her early poem *The Desolation of Eyam* (1827) describes a deadly outbreak of the plague in the Peak District in 1665/66. Some 260 villagers died, a third of the population, after voluntarily sealing themselves off from the world. This poem was a well-known success in its day and widely admired. *Eyam* seems to have helped to established her poetic reputation in America.

Later Mary also wrote at least one fairy poem set in the Staffordshire Moorlands:

> And where have you been, my Mary?
>   And where have you been from me?
> I've been to the top of Cauldon Lowe,
>   The midsummer night to see.

The above lines are from "The Fairies of the Cauldon Low," found in the collection *Ballads and Other Poems* (1847). Cauldon Low (a.k.a. "Lowe") was quite the sort of ancient moorland place where one might justifiably hope to encounter the spectral, due to its high misty tableland with ancient barrow cemetery. The same book has other fairy poetry such as "Isles of the Sea Fairies" and "The Voyage with the Nautilus." These seem lively and well done, and there is also the macabre backwoods "The Tale of the Woods." Of course her "The Spider and Fly" is still famous. Two poems also evince a delight in the macabre nature of the sea and Arctic climes. "Delicia Maris" imagines a temple in the northern wastes:

> Great kings have piled up pyramids.
> And built them temples grand;
> But the sublimest temple far
> Is in yon northern land.
> Its pillars are of the adamant.
> By a thousand winters hew'd;
> Its priests are the awful silence,
> And the ancient solitude!

Her companion poem to this, "Delores Maris," revels in descriptions of monsters under the sea in "viewless caves" and imagines them accompanied by a "ghastly company" of "unburied men with fleshless limbs." There further appear to be at least two interesting items of natural history, such as the comic poem "True Story of Web-Spinner" and the doleful pre-Darwin poem "The Fossil Elephant," the latter a lament for the mammoths which also evokes other prehistoric creatures:

> And the hydra down in the ocean caves
> Abode, a creature grim:
> And the scaly serpents huge and strong
> Coiled in the waters dim.

Possibly many more such are to be found in her book collections *Songs of Animal Life* (1843) and *With the Birds* (1850). Her "The Stormy Petrel," for instance, has been hailed as an especially fine Romantic-era sea-bird poem, and her "The Sea-gull" has similar but less sweeping qualities. I also see that her "An Old Man's Story" is cited as weird in her entry by Alexander Hay Japp in the book *Wom-*

en Poets of the Nineteenth Century (1907): "several of her pieces are inspired by a fantastic imagination, by a nimble fancy, and an unexpected power over the weird and wonderful. Such pieces as 'The Voyage with the Nautilus' and 'An Old Man's Story' suffice to attest this."

This poem deals with a curse on a ship's captain. Another early writer notes her early Miltonic poem cycle *The Seven Temptations* (1834) as being an unsuccessful attempt to marry visions of "satanic temptations to sin" with a poetic form appealing to Victorian ladies. Yet, with all this said, the bulk of her poetry is mid-Victorian and thus unpalatable today. Her book collections of poetry can certainly appear off-putting, padded with cloying "religious sentiment poems" of the sort paid for by the annuals, replete with the ornate "thee and thou" style of the era. One can quite understand why Howitt was not much remembered for her mainstream poetry by the 1890s–1900s, which were the decades immediately after her death. There was no collection or even appreciation of her more macabre work and tastes. Her sentimental conversion to Catholicism in old age (1883), complete with a move of residence to Rome, probably did not help her poetic reputation to survive in Britain.

But I then found that Mary Howitt was also a translator. As I have said above, she and her husband moved from Surrey to London itself from 1843 onward. This and her obvious talents allowed her to become the first English translator of Hans Christian Andersen's stories as *Wonderful Stories for Children* (1846), this volume apparently being done on the basis of her having already successfully translated several of his novels such as *The Improvisatore* (1845). The story collection was followed a year later by her translation of Andersen's *The True Story of My Life* (1847), and then *Hans Andersen's Story Book: With a Memoir* (1853). Her first book of Andersen stories was said to have been done in a slightly toned-down form, acceptable to an English publisher and his purchasing public and to reviewers. Only one of the stories in *Wonderful Stories for Children* actually had its plot slightly tweaked, such that the storks are not seen to deliver *dead* new-born babies to doorsteps. A continental

Andersen scholar was much later made apoplectic on discovering *"zis sacrilege by ze philistine Englisherz,"* and in the 1950s he effectively destroyed her reputation as a translator by finding about forty errors. Her translations were the first, and they do seem to have been a little stiff, and may well have been slightly expurgated. But how else could she have seen Andersen published and read by children in England and America during the prim years of Queen Victoria's reign? Howitt also translated many volumes of the work of Frederika Bremer, and Icelandic sagas and Swedish folk-songs as *The Literature and Romance of Northern Europe* (1852). The latter was apparently the first such anthology in English, and thus a seminal contribution to the recovery of the Northern imagination.

Mary Howitt was also editor of a paid-for journal-magazine with her husband, *Howitt's Journal of Literature and Popular Progress. Howitt's Journal* lasted only two years (1847–48) and was perhaps blunted by an attempt to blend the contentious politics of the day—in support of free trade and against the death penalty for criminals—with literary work and fine sketches. But even a cursory glance at the history of this title reveals an evident tendency to the macabre. For instance, Howitt's journal published three tales by another which were much later included in the modern Penguin Classics collection of Elizabeth Gaskell's stories titled *Gothic Tales* (2000). These were supposedly by "Cotton Mather Mills," a pseudonym for Howitt's good friend Elizabeth Gaskell. Howitt had first met Gaskell on an 1841 tour of the Rhineland in Germany, where she is said—by a modern feminist biographer of Gaskell—to have aroused in Elizabeth an abiding interest in the macabre by telling her terrifying night-time stories and thus set Gaskell on the path to writing such stories herself. Gaskell's first Gothic tales were then published for the public in *Howitt's Journal.*

The same journal also published Eliza Meteyard, who had a connection to Howitt's native region of the Staffordshire Moorlands/Derbyshire Peak District and an interest in, if not the supernatural, then at least the antiquarian life in a high and wild place of ancient barrows and crumbling stone circles. For instance, see Meteyard's *Dora and Her Papa* (1869), a sentimental but vivid and still readable long children's novel of the work of a Peak District antiquarian as seen by his motherless young daughter. This usefully records the home, personal museum, and surroundings of the pioneering antiquarian and barrow-digger Thomas Bateman (1821–1861).

I should also note here that Howitt was editor of *Fisher's Drawing Room Scrap Book* for three years in the early 1840s, a slim oversized annual that appears to have mixed fine engravings with "poetic illustrations." Again, this may be a possible source for incidental material of a macabre nature.

As if to confirm Howitt's interest in the macabre, a few years later she and her husband—by then become a veritable London "writing-machine" duo—also produced a hefty two-volume translation from the German of *The History of Magic* (1851). Apparently her husband and a friend made the translation to occupy themselves on a long ship voyage. But note here that Howitt also took the opportunity to compile and add a wholly new appendix survey of true-life accounts of such things, which at that time must have taken quite some doing in terms of reading and research. She was well ensconced in London society by this time, so presumably she had the British Museum and possibly some private libraries at her disposal. This professional interest paralleled "the temporary immersion of both of them in the fashionable practice of mesmerism [i.e., early hypnotism] and spiritualism of the eighteen fifties" (from an old review of *Laurels and Rosemary: The Life of William and Mary Howitt*, 1955). The couple's previously staunch Quaker beliefs had by then given way to an interest in insidiously genteel cults like table-rapping spiritualism, albeit with a "Christian Spiritualism" religious gloss.

In 1863 her husband published his weighty *The History of the Supernatural* in two volumes, under his own name. One review terms this his period of "extravagant spiritualism," which suggests his interest deepened and not lessened as the 1850s passed into the 1860s. Mary is not credited for this work. *The History of the Super-*

natural had followed the sumptuously illustrated book of "weird and hoary" places, *Ruined Abbeys and Castles of Great Britain* (1862). This was one of many topographical books written with her husband, although a publisher or sponsor appears to have heavily shaped the end result and insisted on the unfortunate addition of the antiquated long-s throughout the weighty text. Even so, this project again confirms Mary's interest in Gothic places and their lore. The couple also published a topographical book surveying the cultural history of the then vanishing Victorian-era North London, *The Northern Heights of London* (1869), which may be of interest to contemporary psychogeographers.

Through my local work on the journals of the North Staffordshire Field Club I also discovered that Howitt wrote at least one remarkably vivid topographical/autobiographical article of local interest, beyond the recalling of her childhood in autobiography. The 1896 *Transactions* noted:

> . . . articles from Mrs Howitt's pen appeared in the *Eclectic Review*, 1859, called "Sun Pictures", a delightful account of a journey [three nights, on foot] through this country [into the high Moorlands], and giving a charming description of Alton, Ipstones, and the district. I remember the landlord of the Inn at Ipstones was very indignant at his portrayal, and breathed out threatenings and slaughter at the author of what everybody but himself thought a life-like picture."

I was then pleased to find the *Eclectic Review* scanned and was thus able to rescue, extract, and compile the many parts of her "Sun Pictures" (1859) in a single new PDF file. This apparently utterly forgotten 22,000-word work was then made free.[29] I found it well

---

29. Freely available at potbanks.files.wordpress.com/2017/12/sun-pictures-1859-howitt.pdf Most of the real names in "Sun Pictures" are omitted or obfuscated under fictional names. She and her daughter appear to have first taken the train from Alton to Biddulph. The ornamental gardens and organ player are obviously at Biddulph Grange, though the place is not named. Then they took the train from Biddulph to Cheddleton or perhaps

worth reading, and although certainly topographically "charming" in a great many places, the charm is deliciously and seamlessly counterpointed by her obvious taste for the macabre—depicting things like an encounter with a creepy changeling child on a railway platform, an obsessed organist, various lovingly describing many grotesque and curious rural personalities, and encounters with gypsies carrying a strange misshapen woman in their sideshow caravan. Howitt also recounts a gruesome *olde time* murder in the wind-swept Moorlands. "Sun Pictures" has its share of dark among the light. It is out of copyright and if abridged it might make a graphic novel or even an *Under Milk Wood*–style audio drama/reading.

In conclusion, what is Mary Howitt's contribution to weird and imaginative literature? This question remains to be fully answered. But based on my very initial survey I feel able to make some suggestions. Some of her contributions were possibly profound, and yet tangential. By which I mean that it came not from her own creative work, but from her translations and published collections of primary material. Her translation of Icelandic sagas and Swedish folk-songs, published as *The Literature and Romance of Northern Europe* (1852), was a timely and seminal popular contribution. It was the very first of many, on which others would later imaginatively build, and which at the time usefully complemented the then-emerging philological scholarship on the inherently weird Northern imagination. Similarly groundbreaking were her early popular and relatively faithful translations of Hans Christian Andersen, which one assumes must have

---

Leek; then walked up into the hills. After that presumably Waystones = Ipstones; Rams = Foxt; Foxholes = Swineholes; High Stone Edge = the Ipstone Edge; Wyver = Cauldon; then a walk across Wyver Lowe = Cauldon Lowe; across the unnamed Weaver Hills ("to the west . . . lie the great quarries"); Welstone = Ellastone; Sturton = Alton; they end the journey by entering The Dale = Rakes Dale adjacent to Alton Castle, and they arrive at their summer home base at what may have been the small village of Hansley Cross which is adjacent to Alton. Thornborough Hall may = Alton Towers or perhaps even the Castle, and terming it a "farm-house" may be some jest by the author or some allusion to a common local jest.

helped to shape the imaginations of the children and young people of the stolid mid-Victorian period. Later, her original appendix to her husband's *The History of Magic* offered the world a choice selection of original source texts on the matter. The full story of the influence of her letters and conversation on the weirder side of the imaginative life of the Victorians—on painters such as the Pre-Raphaelites as well as on writers—remains to be surveyed in a modern form and with reference to the wealth of detailed biographies now available.

Her novels aside, in her poetry there is of course the famous and reputation-securing poem "The Spider and the Fly." But there are also a number of other poems of interest such as: the long plague-poem *The Desolation of Eyam;* the fine local whimsy "The Fairies of the Cauldon Low"; the bright sea poems "Isles of the Sea Fairies" and "The Voyage with the Nautilus"; the sinister "The Tale of the Woods" and the sea-captain curse of "The Old Man's Story"; the sweeping Romanticism of "The Stormy Petrel" and "The Sea-gull"; the doleful paleo-horror in "The Fossil Elephant"; and the pair of sea-poems "Deliciae Maris" and "Dolores Maris" (lost arctic temples, sea monsters). There may well be more or less macabre creature poems yet to be found in her books *Songs of Animal Life* and *With the Birds,* or included among her juvenile stories collected in books such as *Peter Drake's Dream and Other Stories* (1868). There is also Lewis Carroll's parody of "The Spider and the Fly" to note, the poem "Lobster Quadrille," which appeared in one of the *Alice* books. Indeed, Howitt seems to have commented on her own famous creation with her comic poem "True Story of Web-Spinner." It thus seems to me that her modern reputation could be enhanced by a future illustrated or graphic novel "comics anthology" edition of the poems suggested above, perhaps with a title along the lines of *The Spider and the Fly, with Other Fantastical and Animal Poems.*

Further contemporary illustrated books, perhaps newly annotated, might be fashioned from her appendix to *The History of Magic,* or even from her newly rediscovered "Sun Pictures" (1859), which might be accompanied by a small selection of extracts from her letters and her childhood memoirs. Admittedly, the latter would only have flashes of the macabre and would be primarily topographical and localist.

Works Cited

Dunicliff, Joy. *Quaker to Catholic: Mary Howitt, Lost Author of the 19th Century.* McMinnville, TN: St. Clair Publications, 2010.

Howitt, Mary. *Mary Howitt: An Autobiography.* Edited by her daughter, Margaret Howitt. London: Isbister, 1889. 2 vols.

Japp, Alexander Hay. "Mary Howitt (1799–1888)." In Alfred H. Miles, ed. *The Women Poets of the Nineteenth Century.* London: Routledge, 1907.

Jones, Nicholas R. "William Howitt (1792–1879) and Mary Howitt (1799–1888)." In John R. Greenfield, ed. *British Romantic Prose Writers, 1789–1832: Second Series.* Detroit: Gale Research Co., 1992. (10-page bibliography and short biography, now freely online.)

Lee, Amice. *Laurels and Rosemary: The Life of William and Mary Howitt.* London: Oxford University Press, 1955. (By Mary Howitt's grand-niece, drawing mostly on the letters and connections to the famous.)

Ljungquist, Kent. "Howitt's 'Byronian Ramblers' and the Picturesque Setting of 'The Fall of the House of Usher.'" *ESQ: A Journal of the American Renaissance* 33, No. 4 (1987): 224–36.

Merie, Mioara. "The 'Airy Envelope of the Spirit': Empirical Eschatology, Astral Bodies and the Spiritualism of the Howitt Circle." *Intellectual History Review* 18, No. 2 (2008): 189–206.

Shattock, Joanne. "Mary Howitt and Howitt's *Journal* (1847–48)." *Journal of European Periodical Studies* 6, No.1 (July 2021): 42–55.

Uglow, Jenny. *Elizabeth Gaskell.* London: Faber & Faber, 1999.

Woodring, Carl Ray. *Victorian Samplers: William and Mary Howitt.* Lawrence: University of Kansas Press, 1952.

Wright, Elizabeth Cox. [Review of *Laurels and Rosemary: The Life of William and Mary Howitt.*] *Bulletin of Friends Historical Association* 44, No. 2 (Autumn 1955): 116–17.

The Ornamental Hermit

Kurt Newton

"Oh, he never spoke," said the Countess
  to the Inspector on the case.
"His eyes were always downcast
  and he moved quite slow of pace.
  What he thought of us was lost
  behind the hair upon his face."

The Countess pursed her lips
  and raised her brow as if amused.
"Did he have any enemies?
  Anyone he might have angered or abused?"
  The Inspector eyed the Countess
  for the slightest glimmer of a ruse.

"He was an ornamental hermit," said the Countess
  as if nothing more need be said.
  The Inspector knew full well
  the life an ornamental hermit led.
  Perhaps only the flowers in the garden
  missed him now that he was dead.

But it was the Inspector's job
  to solve the case no matter how sublime.
  He excused himself then to go revisit
  the scenery of the crime.
  It was such a lovely late spring day
  with just a hint of summertime.

The gardens were extensive,
  a veritable feast for the eyes and soul.

The Inspector retraced the steps
to where the hermit played his role.
The small yet fanciful structure
suited less a man and more a troll.

The hermit's possessions were minimal:
a pot for tea, a bed for sleep.
There were several books upon a shelf
that farmers and gardeners might keep.
There was nothing of value
a murderous thief might choose to reap.

If anything, the hermit's cottage
was a spartan refuge among the wild:
a simple place of solitude
like the playhouse of a child.
How this could be perceived a threat?
The Inspector was beguiled.

On the moss-covered walkway
was where the hermit's body was found.
A single blow to the hermit's head
had sent him to the ground.
If he'd yelled or cried for help,
no one had heard a sound.

The Inspector thought, How lonely
the ornamental hermit must have been;
isolated among the birds and bees
with no humans heard or seen.
No spoken word except to those
who bow their heads among the green.

And yet, there was something inviting
to living in the moment;
to spring up each morning vibrant and alive

from a night of lying dormant;
to be unaware of the world and its woes,
its tumult, its tears, its torment.

Such an idyllic existence,
the Inspector enviously concluded.
His own life was a hurrisome swirl
of strife upon which he brooded.
Was there a more fulfilling endeavor
to which he was better suited?

The Inspector took a moment
to rest beneath a nearby tree,
to allow his thoughts to process
what could and could not be.
Perhaps there was something obvious
he wasn't allowing his eyes to see.

The warm air was like a moist breath
upon his desiccated mind.
It lulled him to a place
where he left the world behind.
And there was where the Inspector
dreamed a dream of a curious kind.

He woke inside the tiny cottage
in which the hermit dwelled.
The morning air was the freshest,
sweetest air he'd ever smelled;
the birdsong more beautiful
than any church bells ever knelled.

He dressed and stepped outside
into a world unlike no other
where every drop of dew and ray of sun
and every shade of color

was a gift of life as if
to a child from its mother.

The gardens were a-buzz
with bejeweled flying things;
the trees and shrubs a susurration
of feet and fur and wings;
the ground a host to toadstools,
baby's breath and fairy rings.

This Eden called Nature
that surrounds us like a wreath,
that provides the food we eat,
the water we drink, the air we breathe:
it is Nature that decides to give us life
or steal it like a thief.

It is Nature who calls us home
after many years of toil.
It is Nature who calls us home
to the bosom of her soil.
It is Nature who calls us home
so our spirit can uncoil.

That's when the Inspector woke
and reality rushed in like a flood.
To his left a branch lay broken
as if fallen from high above.
Upon its bark the Inspector
noticed a single drop of blood.

"It was an accident," the Inspector told
the Countless in his report.
"There was no murder,

no foul play of any sort.
The hermit died at the hand
of the very Nature to which he held court."

"And what will you do now?"
asked the Countess before the Inspector left.
The Inspector recalled the sweet morning air
and heard a buzzing in his head.
"Why, I will follow my Nature
and do what I do best."

The Inspector tipped his hat
and left the Countess at the door.
He stepped outside into a world
more beautiful than before—
a world where death was just
another part of life and nothing more.

But one mystery solved did not
resolve all the mysteries of life.
The Inspector returned to the city
where criminals and their crimes were rife.
Back to the blood and suspicion
that he coveted in place of a wife.

Perhaps one day when he's old and gray
and all his seeds are sown,
he'll settle upon a plot of land
unburdened and alone.
And there he'll rest among the green
until Nature calls him home.

The Candidate

Carl E. Reed

> Is it that by its indefiniteness it shadows forth the heartless voids and immensities of the universe, and thus stabs us from behind with the thought of annihilation, when beholding the white depths of the milky way? Or is it, that as in essence whiteness is not so much a color as the visible absence of color; and at the same time the concrete of all colors; is it for these reasons that there is such a dumb blankness, full of meaning, in a wide landscape of snows—a colorless, all-color of atheism from which we shrink? And when we consider that other theory of the natural philosophers, that all other earthly hues—every stately or lovely emblazoning—the sweet tinges of sunset skies and woods; yea, and the gilded velvets of butterflies, and the butterfly cheeks of young girls; all these are but subtile deceits, not actually inherent in substances, but only laid on from without; so that all deified Nature absolutely paints like the harlot, whose allurements cover nothing but the charnel-house within . . .—Herman Melville, *Moby-Dick*

"Get up." Voice a commanding baritone.

Pain erupted in my side.

"I said *get up*."

My eyes opened. The guy was dressed in blinding white: sharply creased trousers, *Mafioso*-style ankle boots, and leather trenchcoat. His close-cropped hair and goatee, though—black as the hole in the business end of a gun. Breath steamed from his nostrils in the chill morning air.

I groaned and rolled over, autumnal leaves crunching under my lanky frame. I'd crawled partway under a park bush to sleep for the night. And this was one derelict who intended to stay in bed.

"Go away," I said. A sour taste of vomit and cheap whiskey at the back of my throat.

Again the boot dug into my side.

"Up," Snow White repeated.

Motherfucker. I scrambled to my feet and swung for his face.

Snow White gave a dismissive sniff and stepped back.

Head whirling, off-balance, I stumbled and went down on one knee. I watched my tormentor through lidded eyes, bracing for his counter-attack.

"Violence," he said. "Admirable."

I laughed. It came out a contemptuous grunt.

"You're hung over," Snow White observed. "Hardly a fair fight."

"Just wait till I get my hands on you." I stood up.

"Your name," he demanded.

"None of your goddamn business." I took a shaky step forward.

Snow White smiled a sly, fox-stole-your-dog's-chew-toy smile. "Your name," he demanded again.

"Get out of my face." I held my bomber jacket closed at the throat; the once beige garment now mottled piebald with stains. The zipper was broken—a defect in insulation partially compensated for by the logo-less sweatshirt I wore underneath. I poked him in the chest with my free hand. "What are you, park police? Advocate for the homeless? Cruising faggot?" I winced from the retina-scorching whiteness of his clothes. "From the North Pole?"

He stood hipshot before me, that mocking smile gone, measuring me with an insolent head-to-toe surveil. "It'll come to you."

Smug bastard. I'd forgotten my own name. But how could he know that?

"Get lost," I said and pushed past him, striding down the curving brick pathway of the park.

When I'd taken a good dozen paces away, I glanced back over my shoulder.

Snow White: still as a statue. Watching me.

"See you around," he called. Brought his index and middle fingers to his brow, snapped them away. Salute.

Noon found me in a bright yellow booth eating tacos of greasy meat, wilted lettuce, and oily cheese from corn shells that tasted like re-fried cardboard. Tepid water dispensed from a soda fountain a-swarm with buzzing gnats helped me choke down these sad mockeries of Mexican cuisine. Early twenty-first-century American fast food: cheap, ubiquitous, sickening. *USA! USA! USA!* A crudely lettered, comma-deficient sign taped to the soda fountain read: *Sorry ice machine broken sorry.* An elderly couple four booths distant sipped coffee from Styrofoam cups. Behind them, a teenaged trio perched atop stools carried on an expletive-laden conversation concerning school, their television-centered home lives, and the trials-and-travails of currently trending social media influencers.

It wasn't just my name that I'd forgotten. I couldn't remember where I lived. What I did for a living. Who might have been looking for me these past two weeks.

My jaws were busy working a mouthful of red-sauced gunk into a ball of congealment when Snow White sauntered up and slid into the facing booth seat.

"Has it come to you yet?" he asked.

"How much you irritate me?" I swiped my lips with a napkin, tossed the crumpled ball of sauce-stained paper onto the table between us.

"Your name," he said.

"This again. Seems to be an obsession with you. Why?" I studied his face. "I don't know you. Do I?" Classically sculpted features, high cheekbones. Predatory, hawk-like eyes close-set above a sharp dagger of a nose. Bit of an overbite and numerous pockmarks masked by that Ming-the-Merciless, tar-black goatee. "Nothing better to do? Cable out? Refugee from original-series Star Trek—that absurd *Mirror, Mirror* episode?"

"Cold, warm, warmer."

"Fuck off."

"You are the candidate of the new millennium."

"Well, why didn't you say so?" I shoveled the last bit of taco into my mouth, chewed, and swallowed. "That clears up everything."

"The first suicide of every new millennium is automatically considered a candidate for the office."

"Fascinating." I picked up the paper cup, sipped room-temperature water, set the cup back down. "One flaw in your supposition."

Snow White arched a brow.

"I'm not dead. And I've no intention of killing myself."

Slight head nod from Snow White, as if in sympathetic agreement. "You're alive—now. But I assure you, you'll die tomorrow. By your own hand. Once you realize what you've done."

"I know where you were. I had you followed—you were with him!*" Her eyes blazed with anger and hurt.*

A white-hot jolt of pain in my head. I doubled over in the booth and grimaced, hands to my temples. Waited till my galloping heart settled back down to a stately trot. Straightened up again.

"See you around." Snow White slid out of the booth, stood up and moved toward the exit.

I watched his retreating back. White leather coat bright as Arctic sun-prismed icicles.

I opened my mouth to call out something sharp and stinging, but the words died in my throat.

Snow White: gone.

I went back to the park after visiting a local liquor store where I picked up a pint of rotgut whiskey. The purchase left me dead broke save for a solitary crumpled dollar bill in my right front pants pocket. I'd lost my wallet somewhere, somehow during these past two weeks—or so I guessed.

You didn't lose your wallet; you tossed it away. Along with your car keys and cell phone. When you awoke the next day in the park. Hung over, hurting, amnesiac. You didn't want to know; couldn't bear to know. Who you were and what you had done.

Something tried to surface in my consciousness and I shoved it back down into the pincer-clawed, crawling depths where it could do me no harm. I pulled at the whiskey in a series of molten-fire gulps over the course of the next hour while I sat on the bench thinking as little as possible. A pleasant, depressive ennui hit along with the numbness. Perfect. Just what I wanted.

Children played in the park around me. Red-faced, screaming. Racing around. Whoop it up, spawnlings. Just wait till you see what's around the corner. A couple of barking dogs romped at the end of long leashes. Sharp looks from various people who passed as I sipped from the pint. Eyes to yourselves, assholes. A smartly dressed woman in pleated pants suit and pearl earrings halted in front of me when I was halfway through the bottle, face a rigidified mask of disapproval. She opened her mouth to say something.

I met her gaze and waited for the rebuke.

She walked away without uttering a word.

I finished the whiskey and tossed the bottle over my shoulder.

Fuck 'em. Fuck 'em all.

I'd dozed off on the bench when the wail of a police siren snapped my head up off my chest.

"Good pinch, Jack."

I looked up from the paperwork I was filling out on the desk.

Double gold bars on the collar of a starched white shirt. Bannerman: precinct captain. Watch Commander this night.

"I hear the guy was dealing some weight. Ten kilos of blow. Belmont Cragin, right?"

"That's a roger," I said. "Behind the Brickyard. Third-floor walk-up. Dale and I kicked in the door—"

Dale and I! Uniformed patrol officers of the C.P.D.

Again, the bolt of pain in my head. I threw my hands to my temples, thrashed and moaned.

When I straightened up again Snow White stood before me.

"Hello, Jack. Or should I say: Officer Evers."

I stared at him, breathing hard.

"Let's go."

Snow White had an apartment on the third floor of an old brownstone five blocks from the park. His domicile had a curiously unlived-in look. It was a space devoid of all domestic clutter—save for a couple of pieces of furniture low-slung and sleek as Ferraris, and hundreds of leatherbound volumes ranked upon bowed bookshelves along the shortest wall of the living room. The books were in numerous foreign languages. Though I couldn't translate the titles I recognized French, German, Spanish, Latin, and Greek—in addition to English—printed on the spines. The subjects covered—as far as I could make out amongst the English-language titles—leaned heavily toward history, religion, philosophy, and the occult. World literature was well represented in the mix. In addition to the aforementioned languages there were titles in dozens of other tongues, though what these particular languages were I couldn't tell. I was a cop, not a philologist or linguist.

"I like to read in my off hours," said Snow White with a shrug.

"Clearly."

"I have my favorites, of course: Dante, Milton, Melville. The Marquis de Sade. Nietzsche and Camus." His tongue darted out to moisten his upper lip. "The tragedies of Shakespeare. You?"

"I'm not much of a reader."

"Pity."

For some reason that stung. "When I do read I prefer the works of Mickey Spillane, Joseph Wambaugh, Don Pendleton. You know: The Greats."

Thin smile from Snow White. "May I take your coat?"

"No."

The door closed with an audible click behind us.

With a sinuous shake-and-shimmy Snow White removed his leather trenchcoat and slung it on a brass hook beside the door.

We moved deeper into the apartment.

The rest of Snow White's interior space was not so much apartment as stage set. And, as I might have suspected—the entire apartment was a blinding study in white: carpeting, ceiling, furniture. Facing walls of the living room were unrelieved expanses of polar opalescence, naked of any adornment save for 16′ × 8′ mirrors mounted in Baroque gold frames. The laws of optics and light being what they were, these giant mirrors opened the space up to impossible distances. The room doubled and redoubled again, in ever-diminishing size, out to infinity. Caught in that dizzying cycle of funhouse refraction, I was seized by a sense of vertigo. A thousand arms moved as I put a hand out to the wall to keep from falling.

"Take a seat," Snow White ordered.

I staggered to the couch and collapsed.

"I'll get you a drink."

He left the room accompanied by a myriad mirrored images.

"I know where you were. I had you followed—you were with him!" Her eyes blazed with anger and hurt. "I've suspected for a while. That's why I hired a private detective. He texted me pics from your escapades tonight. You went to a leather bar on Halsted—"

"Dale and I—"

"—then a hotel."

"—were working undercover."

"Liar! Faggot!"

"Watch your mouth."

"Watch yours! Where's it been? On his cock or ass—or both?"

She'd been drinking. As had I.

"Ellen!"

"Don't 'Ellen' me!" She whip-cracked me across the face with a stinging backhand. "Liar!" she repeated. "Cheater!" She raised her hand to strike again—

And I stiff-armed her—both hands into her breasts, hard. She fell straight back, knocked off balance, arms flying up into the air. Her head hit the baseboard with a sickening flesh-dampened snap of bone. She sprawled there, limbs akimbo, head crooked at an impossible angle. Eyes glazing over in a fixed stare. . . .

"Ellen?"

Snow White re-entered the room. He carried a diminutive cup and saucer with such fastidiousness and concentration it struck me as faintly ludicrous and theatrical. Which it was. He set cup and saucer down on a glass-topped coffee table—beside a .40-caliber automatic pistol. I recognized the gun: a seventeen-round Glock with green-glow front sight and black Parkerized finish. A pistol authorized by the city of Chicago for police use. The model of pistol I used. I leaned closer. My gun? Couldn't tell. . . .

"Triple shot of espresso." Snow White seated himself in a well-upholstered armchair opposite me.

"Pity." I mocked his snobbish, clipped vocal inflection. "I was hoping for whiskey."

"You've had enough whiskey. Drink the espresso. Sober up."

"Why?"

"We've things to discuss. Such as why you killed your wife."

"I don't know what the hell you're talking about." I shot to my feet. "If this is some kind of joke—"

Snow White scissored one trousered leg over the other with a sibilant hiss of fabric. He looked at me intently. His eyes were of the coldest aquamarine blue—flint-chipped bits of Antarctica set in a flawless, strong-jawed face. The high cheekbones and narrow, classical nose gave the man the arrogant beauty of a Renaissance prince; though that tar-black mustache and goatee ruined the effect, rendering his countenance comic-book sinister.

His mouth fell open and he imitated—perfectly—the vocal pitch and cadence of Ellen's voice: *"Watch yours! Where's it been? On his—"*

"Stop!" I cried, raising both hands, palms outward, in a warding-off gesture. The hair prickled at the nape of my neck.

"You killed her," Snow White stated flatly. "Though it must be noted: It was an accident."

"Yes," I whispered.

I knew who he was now. Had, in fact, suspected for some time.

"Sit down." Snow White gestured. "Drink the espresso."

Why not? Where could I go? Dead broke, buzzed, memory-impaired.

I sat back down, raised the tiny cup to my chapped lips, and sipped. The espresso was warm, not boiling hot. Watered down. Dissolved ice cube? I drained the cup; set it back into its saucer on the coffee table.

"After you killed your wife, you left the house."

I frowned. "Did I?"

"You did." Flat declarative statement.

The caffeine from the espresso hit my bloodstream, overcoming the depressive effect of the alcohol. My pulse sped up.

"I can't . . . I can't remember."

"Sure you can."

Another bolt of agony in the brain. I groaned, doubled over.

"Where could you go? To whom could you flee?"

I stood on the concrete porch of the brick ranch, repeatedly jabbing the doorbell button.

    It swung open.

    "Jack!" said Dale. "What—"

    "Let me in."

    "It's three in the morning, for god's sakes!"

    "I think I've killed my wife."

"He let you into his home. You argued."

"No." I shook my head in emphatic negative denial. I was weeping now, detesting myself for the show of weakness but unable to restrain my emotions. Or further repress my memory. "No . . . no."

"Dale wanted to call a patrol unit to your house to investigate. If your story was true you'd need a lawyer. If Ellen was merely injured and not dead she'd need urgent medical attention. Correct?"

I made no response.

"I said—isn't that correct?"

"Yes."

"You'd both been drinking—everyone had been drinking that night. In addition, you and Dale had done a couple lines of Peru's finest white-flake export product earlier—back in the hotel, before the gymnastics."

I was sobbing now—chest-heaving, stomach-convulsing paroxysms of horror, guilt, and shame.

"In Dale's house the argument grew heated. Physical."

I recalled—in strobe-like, nightmarish flashes of images and sound—what happened next. Curses, gagging, drumbeat of heels against hardwood floor. Bulged eyes, white-knuckled hands around neck, protruding tongue.

"You broke your wife's neck; you choked Dale to death."

Agony: sudden, searing, white-hot. All conscious thought ceased as if a light switch had been flicked off. Or I'd hit a brick wall at Mach ten.

"Not that anyone cares about your sordid little sex games." Snow White sounded mildly apologetic. "That business was between you, your wife, and your lover. No, it's the pattern of lies, duplicity, and self-loathing leading to double-murder that renders you a fit candidate."

A long, keening wail broke from my throat.

"Rage—it's the first word of the *Iliad* in the new Fagles translation. Did you know that?"

I curled up into a fetal position on the couch and jammed my palms against my ears. I would hear no more.

"What a perfect candidate you are. Congrats! You're hired. Can't wait till you meet the staff—they're very thorough and experienced, I assure you." He shifted position in the chair; stroked his goatee in thoughtful rumination. "They have centuries of experience. In fact, millennia. *Sit up!*"

I continued to wail, hands clasped over my ears.

Snow White came out of the chair, grabbed a fistful of my hair, and dragged me upright on the couch.

"Stop that infernal caterwauling! It's most unseemly." He punched me in the face.

I barely felt it. The blow stopped my wailing, however.

He put a hand—dense and cold as mausoleum marble—on my chin and forcibly tilted my head up until our gazes locked. "You murdered the two people you loved most in the world. In so doing, threw your career—your reputation—your life away."

I stared at him blearily, numb as a corpse.

"What will your police comrades say? The in-laws? Neighbors? Mother?"

Snow White removed his hand from my chin, stepped back around the coffee table, reseated himself in the chair. "You'll be hot news—for a while. Till the next homicidal sex scandal knocks you off the front pages."

I picked up the pistol—ten thousand identical arms in front and back of me synced to my movement. The gun was light as a bit of wind-blown thistle.

"I know who you are," I said. I placed the muzzle of the gun against my temple. It tickled. "Only . . ."

Sharp look. "What?"

"Back there in the park. Your breath."

He chuckled: the burbling rumble of some dark river of Avernus over antediluvian stone. "Immortal, yes—but flesh nonetheless. As you shall be. The better to embody sin."

"Dead but . . . fleshed."

"Precisely."

"Monster."

He demurred.

"Demon," I said.

"Warmer."

More cryptic taunts.

"Enough." I was weary of the game.

"Say it!" Snow White barked. "Utter the two syllable moniker that trembles on your tongue: the one beginning in a sibilant and ending in a phoneme that constitutes a voiced alveolar nasal. Acknowledge the reality of what is happening here."

I tried. My lips locked.

His studied the manicured fingernails of his left hand.

"You're—" I said.

He raised an admonishing finger of the right. "No, *you* are."

Yes. It was an office, not a proper name.

I pulled the trigger.

She's Walking Home

G. O. Clark

She's walking home
through a spectral forest
thick with fog, one slow step
at a time;

below the August sun,
along their favorite beach,
beside great waves of memory
crashing;

down empty sidewalks
past the closed doors of her life,
and shuttered windows
beyond reflecting;

into the bedroom
where he sleeps, they slept,
the exhalations from his lungs
fogging her knife's blade.

The Kannibaali
(A Finnish Horror Tale)

Frank Coffman

> *"In my mouth the words are melting,*
> *From my lips the tones are gliding,*
> *From my tongue they wish to hasten…"*
> —Elias Lönnrot, from the "Proem" of *The Kalavala*

"Brother join me in the rune song;
 Sister, clasp my hands in chanting;
 In our rocking back and forward,
 Paraphrase the truth I'm telling.
 You will feel it through your fingers.
 It is not some idle prattling.
 Listen to my tale of horror;
 Give an ear to what I utter.
 Brothers, sisters please believe me;
 It is not a myth I'll tell thee.
 In this cold and cruel country;
 On the poor soil of our Northland,
 There are beings dire and dreadful,
 Wights who roam who are *All Evil.*
 Such are cruel, undead *vampyrri*
 And the werewolf, *ihmissusi;*
 Of course the ghosts, the *fantomeja;*
 Many monsters, *hirviöitä.*
 But the tale I now will chant out,
 Singing song of sorrows countless—
 This my long-dead father sang me,
 Clasping both my hands in his hands.

Rocked we back and forth together
As this grim tale he related;
And the truth flowed through his fingers,
I could feel the Fear remembered,
As we moved like waves of ocean,
Lapping on the Shore of Sorrow,
Crashing on the sharp-rock shingle."

'List, my son, unto my story,
Hear, my boy, my tale of terror.
I was only thirteen winters,
Just your age when this horror happened!
I had gone out from the village,
Left the safety of our homestead,
I was out to prove my manhood,
Bring back game to quell our hunger.
But I strayed too far in hunting,
And I found myself benighted.
But I soon learned that the darkness,
Night itself was not the horror.
In the woodland deep I saw it!
Glow of greenish light approaching.
Hid I then among the bushes,
When a noise of footfalls coming
And a growling sound foreboding,
Uttered by whate'er approached me,
Filled me with a sudden terror,
And I tried to stop my breathing
Seeking then to be most silent
As the Thing *stopped close beside me.*
I dared not look, at first, upon it;
Dared not lift my face to see it.
For it paused and grunted deeply,
And it sniffed the breeze about it!

Thank the gods, it kept on walking;
But I sensed it dragging something!
To my horror, when I dared look up,
I saw that it dragged a dead man!
That green glow was all about it,
Seemed to come from deep within it.
Why I did not run I know not;
Something in my soul compelled me.
And I followed that foul being;
At first, I could not see its features,
As it walked the path before me,
But I saw its giant stature,
Taller than a man by half!
Soon it came into a clearing,
Dragging the poor corpse behind it.
Then it dropped its dreadful burden.
And I had to stop from screaming
When I first beheld its features!
When I saw the fiery eyeballs
And beheld the fangs and fingers
Tipped with claws like curving knifeblades!
Then it started in to eating
That poor man. A Kannibaali!
A Corpse-Eater—ruumissyöjä!
Was this Thing *I had encountered!*
With knife talons tore the torso,
Lifted out the gory entrails,
Gorged upon the poor man's organs,
Ripped the limbs from off the body,
Cracking bones made awful noises!
At that I sprang from where I'd hidden
Heard I the Thing arise and follow;
Necrovore *was coming for me!*
Never ran one any faster;

How I lived I cannot answer.
Winding through those forest pathways,
Growling on the wind diminished,
Then I came into my village.
Only one, an Elder, heard me,
Nodding 'Yes' at my grim story.
All the rest thought I was crazy.
But I swear my tale's a true one;
You, my son, you must believe me.
When you hunt the deepest forest,
Be wary of the weird around you.
Stray not, stay not past the nightfall!
Beings nowhere close to human
Share our world! You must beware!'

"This the tale my father told me;
This the chant that chills my blood.
Brothers, Sisters, please believe me.
There are Evils far more fearsome:
Things worse than your darkest nightmares;
Things beyond our comprehension.
They are not mere stuff of legend;
They are *real*—and mean our Ending!"

Author's Note: The Finnish practice of rune singing, done by pairs of chanters [*rune-laulajia*] who sit facing one another, clasp hands, and rock back and forth, the second voice paraphrasing the first is traditional. The meter used in this poem is the trochaic tetrameter, approximating the rhythm of the Finnish songs. Elias Lönnrot's collection of traditional material for *The Kalavala*, the epic of Finland, is in this meter.

Killing the Pale Man

Darrell Schweitzer

It was a night for telling stories, inevitably, if only because we two were the only guests at the inn, the TV in the lounge wasn't working, and it was the kind of place where as likely as not your phone wouldn't get any signal. North-central Pennsylvania, the flyover part of the state, as some had unkindly put it: the blank part of the map that you reach if you go up through the Poconos and turn left, into rolling hills, dark woods, and a great deal of nothing occasionally dotted with little towns with biblical names, like Chorazin and Bethsaida and Emmaus. You can hear odd stories in these parts, about the *Waldgänger* in the woods, and witches who can swim through the earth; but it fell upon my colleague and myself to tell our own stories.

The theme was to be coincidence. It was a coincidence that I had not been in this region in many years. In fact I had never expected to come here again, since at my age I could have retired, as I am in that interval in life where you're definitely a senior and people start opening doors for you, but you're still fit and able to do what you want, even if you know you may not have a lot of time left. So when the high-end booksellers I consulted for asked me to go and evaluate the library of the estate of Marcus Rottenberg, noted author, occultist, and eccentric millionaire, it sounded interesting enough that I overcame any reservations I might have had, and I went.

The house stuck out in the brown, wintry landscape like a Gothic castle, though I suppose it was more a Victorian pile, like something out of a Charles Addams cartoon; in any case totally incongruous after you'd driven past those little towns and Amish farms and long stretches of forests. Mr. Rottenberg had been very rich—how he got that way was the subject of much mystery and speculation—and he was a man with decidedly individualistic ideas. Very likely he had had the place built (or at least altered) to his specifications. But he'd also managed to alienate such family as he had and die an embittered recluse, alone and without servants, because, so it was said, no one would work for him regardless of how much he offered to pay them. The house was shut up after his death.

That was why when the other estate evaluator and I got there, the electricity was off and we had to make do with kerosene lanterns, and there was no question of staying in that place overnight. We were met at the door that morning by a lawyer, who had a key, and who came by early in the evening to see us out.

The book collection was indeed fabulous, not merely expensive, but astonishing and even, by its implications, terrifying. A real treasure-trove for collectors and scholars and perhaps even the occasional madman like Mr. Rottenberg. I took a lot of photos with my camera phone just in case my employers did not believe me.

But the books are not really central to the stories Jeremy Hodder and I told, so I will not go into detail. He was a younger man, in the employ of an auction house, who was there to catalogue the antique furniture, the paintings, crockery, and the like. I gather that he too was impressed by what he found.

As I drove back to the inn, a few miles distant, I noticed a band of children, maybe five or six of them, in flowing white sheets and masks of some sort, out in the middle of a field, amid the dead cornstalks.

Later, at the inn, as we settled down in the lounge by the fire, Hodder remarked on them. He'd come in his own car, but he'd seen them too.

"It's too late for Halloween," he said.

"Yes, it is," I said. "But it's an old custom."

"Some of the customs around here are pretty strange."

"Stranger than you think," I said.

Outside it had begun to storm. Sleet rattled against the windows. I hoped those children had gotten home safely.

The landlord had provided us with a bottle of wine. I poured both of us drinks and began my story, as if I were unburdening myself of a secret I had been carrying all my life. It was just the right time for it to come out. I can't explain more than that.

You see [I began], I *know* what those kids are up to, because once upon a time I was one of them. It was, obviously, very long ago, well before you were born, I should imagine. My parents collected antiques. Also, my mother was a painter of the would-be Brandywine school—the Wyeth tradition and all that—so she loved these landscapes with their subtle shadings of browns and grays and the occasional deep blues of winter evenings. Whereas the Wyeths had done much of their painting in southern Pennsylvania, she hoped to find fresh inspiration in the north. Between these two interests, we were out in this region quite often. No, we didn't know Mr. Rottenberg, though I suppose we heard a few things people said about him. My parents had made friends with another couple, antique dealers and farmers, and we stayed on their farm sometimes, usually over weekends or on school holidays. They had two children, with whom I became quite friendly. Adam, the boy, was a couple years older than me. His sister Judith was three years younger. So when I was twelve that made Adam fourteen and Judith nine. There were only a few other children around, from neighboring farms, so age differences between us did not matter for much, and when we got together we formed our own little gang, of which I became an honorary member of sorts. Adam, who was the oldest of them all, was the natural leader.

I will skip the unimportant details. We played games. I helped Adam and Judith with chores, which, to a city kid, were curiously fascinating. I had never been around a cow before, much less helped herd one into a barn. The barn was filled with cats, which were semi-feral, though people who knew them could treat them as pets.

Never mind that. What matters is that on a night rather like this one, cold and windy, though it wasn't rainy, Adam told me to put on my coat and come with him. Our parents were elsewhere in the house. We didn't tell them we were going out. I wasn't sure why we were going, but Judith knew to be quiet and Adam's manner made it clear that I should be quiet also, so we slipped away. He was carrying a large satchel, like an army duffel bag.

We hurried off into the empty fields. It was indeed late in the year, well past harvest, too late for Halloween, just mud and dead cornstalks beneath a darkening sky. Too late for Halloween, but when we met up with the other children—there were seven of us in all—Adam set down his satchel and got out costumes for everybody, white sheets, which each of the others put on without being told what to do, though someone had to show me how to adjust it over my head so I could see through the eyeholes. We were all garbed as ghosts, only we wore little metal crowns with horns on them, made of tin, I think.

By this point I was quite puzzled and maybe a little frightened. I wasn't sure if this was a game. Adam merely said to me, "It's what we do. You have to do it too."

"Do what?"

There was no answer. We trooped across the fields, and gradually the others began to sing. I couldn't make out most of the words. Some of them were just gibberish. Some of them were in another language. It might have been Latin or something that once was Latin. *Peetra partra perry dicentem.*

Then, as we approached a barren hilltop, the lyrics switched to English, a low chant, something like:

> *Comes the pale man,*
> *comes the moon,*
> *comes the pale man,*
> *very soon.*

It was all very much like a dream to me. I was swept along in something I didn't understand. But these were my friends. They wouldn't hurt me. It couldn't be bad. It had to be some kind of secret they were letting me in on.

I tried to convince myself of that as we filed up to the summit of the hill, chanting. I didn't like this place. I felt an impulse to run. I saw stones arranged in a circle. No, not like Stonehenge, and no sacrificial altar, just round boulders the size of mailboxes, half sunk into the ground and covered with moss, as if this place had been prepared very long ago.

For what? I wanted to ask, but didn't, as Adam reached into his bag again and started handing out clubs, some of them sticks, a couple pieces of metal pipe, and, for me, a baseball bat.

Now the others were singing:

> *Kill the pale man,*
> *kill him dead,*
> *break his bones*
> *and smash his head!*

We danced around and around, inside the circle of stones, singing more of the gibberish, more of the Latin scraps, and quite a bit of *Rise up moon* and *coming soon.* We whooped and did what I could only think of as a war dance, waving our clubs, closing in on a bare spot at the center of the stone circle.

Meanwhile the moon, a little past full, had risen over the fields.

And the Pale Man came to us. At first I thought there was a scrap of cloth on the ground, in the middle of the circle, but no, the earth was heaving up and something of a dirty white color was climbing out, something very thin and shriveled, more than a skeleton though less than a man. Its eyes were terrible, burning. They transfixed me. I faltered. I stopped singing and staggered back, and I would have turned and run if Adam hadn't caught me by the arm and hauled me back into my place. He and the other children sang all the louder, the Latin scraps, the gibberish that I was sure none of them understood but knew they had to repeat just then, just right. Even so, another of our number faltered, one of the youngest ones, a girl, and the pale man caught hold of her in his talon-claws and his teeth chattered, and he was hissing, and the little girl was screaming, while all the rest of us chanted very loud and did what we had come to do.

I hit the Pale Man on the shoulder with my baseball bat, and his arm snapped off and he let go of the little girl. Adam sank his pipe through the skull. We all did our bit, striking again and again until the Pale Man, who had not even fully emerged from the ground, was broken into bits. We had snapped him off a little below the knees. Just to be sure, Adam reached into the hole from which the Pale Man had emerged and yanked out the remains of two stick-like legs and two bony feet, and methodically beat them into powder. Then we scooped up the powder and the bits of bone and dropped them back into the hole and covered it over with dirt.

By now the moon was high overhead. We were out late. We had done what we had come to do.

The little girl whimpered. Adam and I and the rest of us looked at her and saw she was cut pretty badly. Adam tore some strips from one of the sheets and bandaged her legs as best he could. He lifted her into his arms, so her head rested on his shoulder, and he whispered to her, "Next year you will do better."

He glanced at me, as if to say the same thing. I had nearly fumbled. Next year I would do better.

And so we returned home. I never told my parents what had happened. I don't know what Adam and Judith told theirs. The girl who was hurt was carried home by her siblings. There were no repercussions. Nobody said anything. A few days later I was back in the Philadelphia suburbs and it all seemed remote and far away, like this story as I am telling it to you now.

It sounds crazy, doesn't it?

So I stopped telling my story.

Jeremy Hodder had lit a cigarette. "You don't mind . . . ?"

"Oh, no," I said.

He flicked some ashes into the fireplace.

The storm outside had become quite violent, the wind howling. I very much hoped those children had gotten back safely.

"Did you ever ask yourself why there had to be a next year?' he said.

"No," I said. "I suppose I could have made a fuss and demanded that we not come here anymore, but I would have been lying and, worse than that, I would be betraying my friends, who had let me in on their secret, as if I'd joined a secret society and now was fully initiated, and there was an inevitability to it. Every year, for five years, we smashed the Pale Man."

"And then what happened?"

"We grew up. For some reason this has to be done by children, and we weren't children anymore. Adam got drafted and went to Vietnam and got killed. I went to college."

"Oh," Hodder said, and we were both quiet for a while. The fire burned low. The storm outside raged.

"It surprises me, I must admit, that you seem to believe every word," I said. "I could be insane, you know, or pulling your leg just to give you the creeps on a night like this."

"But you're not," he said firmly. "I know you're not. Because I went through the same thing you did, only my experience was considerably worse."

Now *that* was astonishing. Talk about coincidences. Here was a stranger, at least twenty years my junior, met under circumstances which had nothing to do with the subject of our concern, and *he too* had been one of those children, years ago, but not as many years ago.

He told me his story.

This will surprise you [Jeremy Hodder said], because I'm the kind of guy who will wear a three-piece suit to a rummage sale, but I actually grew up in this county. My parents owned one of these farms. I was a farm boy. I did all the usual farm boy things, and like other children in the area, I learned from other children those odd songs that none of us understood but which we recited in secret among ourselves.

Those who lived within a certain short distance of that hill with the stones upon it knew all about the Pale Man.

In time I was taken there when I was ten, but we screwed it up. Our leader was a thirteen-year-old named Tommy. He wasn't a farm boy at all. His father owned the garage in the village. He was a bright kid. He was interested in a lot of things, not all of them helpful at this point. Ideas travel slowly in this part of the world, so for all that things like that were long since passé where you come from, Tommy had just discovered hippies, New Age stuff, Oriental mysticism, and all that. He was into psychedelic music and posters and what he thought was philosophy and flying saucers and Atlantis and reincarnation. He called himself a guru. He said he would lead us to enlightenment. Part of enlightenment, he told us, was disbelieving everything we'd been told about the world. Everything was "bourgeois," he would say. That was his favorite word. That meant something was to be dismissed from all consideration. Only he wasn't bourgeois.

Since the rest of us were younger than him and he was amazingly persuasive for a thirteen-year-old—he could have grown up to be a politician or the world's greatest car salesman or maybe Charles Manson—the rest of us did what he told us to. It so happened when that night came around, when you go out and smash the Pale Man, Tommy had other ideas. We put on our ghost-sheets all right, and he carried our clubs, and we sang our gibberish songs, but Tommy led us up quite another hill, where there was an old abandoned shed. On that hilltop we sang very different songs that he taught us, and did different dances, and made strange motions that he called "rites."

Then we all crowded into the shed by the light of a flashlight Tommy had, and he revealed what else he'd brought along for the occasion. He called them "sacraments," but they were really a more familiar and illegal form of enlightenment. He had a coffee tin of marijuana, several pipes, and even some magic mushrooms.

So we performed esoteric rituals that night, but they weren't the "bourgeois" ones. Tommy said this was a better way to banish evil from the world. A couple of the smaller kids got scared and one of them threw up, but Tommy wouldn't let any of them leave; and as for me, I can only tell you that, subjectively, the evening was . . . interesting. I might have seen a couple flying saucers. At one point I was absolutely convinced that Tommy was the Maitreya, the Buddha to come, and the world was ending because "everything is relative," and for a while I felt really good about that, but then I had a sense of utter emptiness as if the world *had* ended and I had been left behind. Once the shed filled with light and Tommy's face was burning with soft white fire, and then it wasn't there at all, just a black void where his face had been, which detail was terrifyingly prophetic, considering what happened afterwards.

I don't know how many hours passed, but ultimately the lot of us got up and staggered into out the night, coughing and reeking. It was very late. The moon was almost down. Without any ceremony our little company parted and made for home. I had my little brother, Charlie, with me. He was seven that year. He never got to be any older.

It was only after a while, as I led Charlie by the hand across one of the endless, empty fields, that my mind cleared to the extent that I could begin to realize the enormity of what we had all done—or failed to do. I was afraid then. I nearly yanked Charlie's arm out of its socket as I turned and ran and dragged a wailing, sobbing kid brother after me. We arrived breathless at *the hill,* the correct hill, the one with the circle of stones, and without any chant or songs or other ceremony we went straight to the middle of the circle and saw what was there.

"He got away," Charlie said.

There was just a hole in the ground, with dirt heaped around it, as if, indeed, something had unburied itself.

The Pale Man was loose.

Charlie and I could only go home, still wearing our sheets and our crowns and dragging our useless clubs. Our parents had discreetly left the back door unhooked, so the two of us could quietly make our way up the back to the bedroom we shared.

Charlie just flopped down on his bed the way he was, but I went into the bathroom, did my best to wash the pot odor off myself, changed into pajamas, and then just sat on the edge of my bed thinking about how things had turned out. There were no stories about what happens when the Pale Man gets loose, because no one would ever allow that. That was impossible. It couldn't be.

I was still trying to convince myself when I thought I saw the moon rising outside my window. But my window looked west, and I would see the moon setting that way, and the moon should have been nearly down by now anyway. Yet something softly glowing *rose*, and no, it wasn't the moon, but the face of the Pale Man, who shattered the glass and lunged into the room.

Charlie let out no more than a gasp or a grunt, and then the Pale Man was coming for me, and I stood up, backing away from him, into the adjoining bathroom, all the while sobbing softly and trying to form the words to the magic songs—they had to be magic, they had to mean something—but I only managed a few syllables until I was backed up against the bathroom mirror and the Pale Man reached out with his terrible, stick-like claw and ripped the front of my pajama top right off. He carved an X in blood right in the middle of the chest, and about the time I whispered, "I'm sorry, please don't hurt me," he hooked one taloned finger into my armpit and with a savage yank damn near tore me in half, which left me screaming and huddled on the tiled floor clutching my belly, desperately afraid that my guts were going to come out like steaming sausages.

At that instant my parents burst in. They only saw a faint flicker, apparently, and then they turned on the electric light and they found me in the bathroom, bleeding and badly hurt, though my guts hadn't fallen out. I suppose my ribcage had saved me. But Charlie was worse. He was dead. His head was missing.

* * *

When he had finished Jeremy Hodder said, "If this were a chess game I'd say check and checkmate. I win. Mine tops yours."

"Yes, it does," I said grimly.

"There's more too. Tommy, our would-be guru, never even made it home. He was discovered later the next afternoon, face down in a field, well away from the road, and he was only found because the buzzards had started to settle. There wasn't much left of him. It was a terrible winter. Most of the other children died, either bloodily or from some kind of disease that was going around. Animals died too, lots of them. Farmers were ruined. Billy Sanders, who had been with us that night, said he had seen the Pale Man dancing in the moonlight in the pasture behind his house, and then Billy disappeared. It went on and on until spring, when the Pale Man finally crawled back into his grave. But both of my parents were dead by then and I went to New York to live with relatives, and I did everything I could for the rest of my life to distance myself from the farm boy I had once been, to become sophisticated, a city-slicker, the kind of guy who wears three-piece suits to rummage sales and antique shows. But I've still got an impressive scar. No, I won't show it to you."

"You don't have to."

"I couldn't very well use all this as an excuse not to come out here, could I? So when my firm ordered me, I had to come. Who would believe me?"

Coincidentally, I would.

I merely nodded.

I should add that I actually had an excuse. As soon as I turned in my preliminary report I would say that I wasn't feeling well and was retiring, and someone else would have to come out and oversee the removal and sale of the late Mr. Rottenberg's library.

Neither my companion nor I went to bed at all that night. We just sat there till dawn, until the storm died down and the sleet stopped rattling against the windows.

My God, I desperately hoped those children we had seen had gotten back safely, and that they had fulfilled their role in immemorial tradition.

How can I explain any of it? I can't. The coincidence of my meeting a total stranger who happened to have a story that topped even mine? Was that the synchronicity of fate or the Pale Man's last revenge? Certainly my dreams have been uneasy of late. I cannot rest. I see the pale face rising outside my window. Sometimes I hear scratching on the glass. Sometimes I am not sure I am dreaming.

I don't know how Mr. Hodder is doing. I haven't heard from him. I hope he is well.

Is it possible that we two violated some ancient, terrible compact by confiding our stories, even to each other?

I hope for those children.

Why children? Was it because only children could actually *see* the Pale Man for some reason, and all adults could see was maybe a flicker of light before they found the bodies? Maybe children knew the answer, if no one else did, and they shared the secret with other children, as they first taught the younger ones the strange lyrics— *peetra partra perry dicentem* and all that—and then initiated them fully into the mystery. As they became adults, they might forget some of it or convince themselves it was all a dream, though they might still bear scars. Who could possibly confess such a thing and not be thought mad, except, coincidentally, to someone who had shared the same experience?

I don't think it had anything to do with the sinister Marcus Rottenberg, reputed wizard, who was said to call monsters out of the sky at night and converse with invisible presences in broad daylight in front of witnesses, and to play cards with the Devil on his front porch. Maybe Rottenberg was attracted to this place because it was already contaminated with evil; but I think the evil is much, much older, something the Indians had to deal with thousands of years before any white people ever arrived. It was they, after all, who set those stones in a circle. I could well imagine their young people smashing the Pale Man with tomahawks, once a year, as it had to be done.

I think the Pale Man was some kind of god of cold earth and the moon and winter, and he has been around forever, dead, resurrected, dying again.

I can assure you that neither Hodder nor I had any intention of hiking up there to make sure there wasn't an empty hole amid the stones.

We could only hope that the children we'd seen had gotten home all right.

I'm retired. I'm not going back.

Everything depends on the children.

The Dead Learn Nothing

Ann K. Schwader

The dead learn nothing in those shadow halls
that they inhabit. What they knew, they know
incessantly, indelibly in scrawls
across our dreams. *What was must still be so,*
or all is lost. We rise believing—go
like desperate Odysseus, sacrifice
our dearest blood for counsel. Those below
crowd mad with thirst. Yet even once their price
is met, this murmuration of advice
drifts dry as dust. No comfort here. No light
we did not bring to guide us back. Enticed
by ghosts, or history, or both, we might
have spared ourselves the voyage: echoes fade
without a living voice. We wake betrayed.

Everil Worrell: Women, Religion, and Weird Fiction

S. T. Joshi

Everil Worrell was born on November 3, 1893, in Loop City, Nebraska, the only child of Louis W. and Florence Ellen Manatt Worrell.[1] During the first decade of her life she was obliged to move frequently as a result of her father's occupation: he was a principal at schools in Nebraska, Montana, and Oregon. For two years he was in Guam, working as an auditor for the U.S. Navy, during which time Everil and her mother lived in Iowa. In 1916 the family moved to Washington, D.C., as Louis had become a patent examiner and now worked at the U.S. Patent Office; he rose to the rank of chief of the Classification Division. The Murphys lived either in Washington or in Arlington, Virginia.

Everil was educated at Central High School in Arlington and displayed an interest in music that is frequently reflected in her work. She became a talented singer, studying voice for more than fifteen years. She then attended George Washington University, receiving a B.A. in 1915. During her years there she was president of the Women's Glee Club for a year and also wrote a school song.[2] Everil did graduate work at the University of California at Berkeley and at George Washington University, but did not receive an advanced degree. On April 3, 1926, she married Joseph Charles Murphy, who was working in the Bureau of Chemistry in the U.S.

---

1. What little biographical information there is on Worrell comes from a memoir by her daughter, Jeanne Eileen Murphy, in the brief article "Everil Worrell," *Weird Tales Collector* No. 1 (1977): 13–15, from which I have drawn extensively.

2. One published song in which Worrell was associated is "Come to Me, Dear" (1919), words by Everil Worrell and music by Leo Friedman.

government. Two years later they moved to New York City, but in 1929 he died of a heart attack. Everil returned—with her infant daughter Jeanne—to her parents' home in Washington and resumed the secretarial job she had had prior to her marriage.

Everil Worrell was fascinated with *Weird Tales* from the moment it hit the stands in March 1923, and she yearned to appear in its pages. Her devotion to writing dated from her high school days, and she now sent many stories to Farnsworth Wright, the editor of the magazine. At last the story "Leonora" was accepted, but it appeared after another story that Wright accepted, "The Bird of Space" (September 1926), which constitutes her first appearance in the magazine. She went on to publish eighteen stories in *Weird Tales* as well as two others in *Ghost Stories*. This constitutes her entire known output of published fiction. Other stories by her published under pseudonyms may exist but have to date not been identified definitively as her work.[3]

After publishing twelve stories in *Weird Tales* (along with the two in *Ghost Stories*) from 1926 to 1931, Worrell went silent for nearly a decade—at least as far as published fiction is concerned. Her daughter reports that "During the 1930's she wrote when she could but most of her time was taken up with earning a living and being a mother." Worrell suffered further personal setbacks when her father died in 1930 and her mother in 1935. But she was heartened by her participation in a *Weird Tales* fan club in Washington, in which Seabury Quinn, Earl Peirce, Jr., and others made her acquaintance.

Worrell published only one story in 1939 and one in 1942 be-

---

3. Jeanne Eileen Murphy writes in her memoir: "According to my mother's notes, there may have been several others [i.e. stories], but she was not positive to names and dates." Robert Weinberg, editor of the *Weird Tales Collector*, conjectured that three stories published in *Weird Tales* as by "O. M. Cabral" might be by Worrell. But this author has now been identified as Olga M. Cabral (1909–1997). Jeanne Eileen Murphy also notes that Worrell completed two novels and was working on a third at the time of her death, but none of these—which seem to be crime/suspense novels—appear to have been published.

fore lapsing into silence again for another decade. She was now working at the U.S. Coast Guard Headquarters. Although she became a member of several writers' organizations, including the Writer's League of Washington, and won numerous contests sponsored by them, she published relatively little. A final burst of fiction occurred in 1951–54, when she published four stories in *Weird Tales*. She retired in 1957 and died on November 27, 1969.

In surveying Worrell's work of nearly three decades, several features strike us at once. Perhaps the most prominent is that they are the work of a woman writer. It is dangerous to characterize a given work as the product of a male or female creator, as it is easy to fall into essentialist or stereotyped views of what constitutes literary work by men or women; and it is not merely the prevalence of strong, distinctive female characters or the emphasis on human emotions or human relationships that typifies Worrell's work. But there is no denying that women are the focus of many of her weird tales.

The early "Leonora" (*Weird Tales*, January 1927) is representative. We are here presented with the narrative of a sixteen-year-old girl (although it gradually becomes evident that the narrator is an older woman looking back upon a crucial incident in her girlhood) experiencing a fascination with a man driving a car who expresses an interest in her. In this tale, there is an exquisite tension between terror of a natural sort (the terror of being kidnapped and—although this element is deeply buried in the text—of being sexually assaulted) and being swept away by a supernatural entity. When reference is made toward the end of "the legend of Leonora," we are led to understand that Leonora has become fixated on the celebrated Gothic ballad "Lenore," by Gottfried August Bürger, about a young woman whose fiancé returns from a war and rides away with her on a horse—but who turns out to be a corpse. But does this mean that the whole account is merely a hallucination in the mind of Leonora, and that the tale is devoid of supernaturalism? We never know.

From a very different perspective, the fusion of romance and death is at the heart of Worrell's most famous and best story, "The

Canal" (*Weird Tales*, December 1927). Here, a man becomes fixated on a young woman residing on a boat in a canal—a woman who for some reason seems unable to leave the boat. As the narrative progresses, we sense that the woman is a vampire—and that her lover may be compelled to destroy her and her redoubtable father, even at the risk of his own death. At this time, the use of a female vampire in fiction—although it was the focus of J. Sheridan Le Fanu's pioneering novella "Carmilla" (1871–72)—was still a rarity, and Worrell's haunting tale is a triumph of weird atmosphere.

"From Beyond" (*Weird Tales*, April 1928) is the brooding and evocative tale of the possible telepathic abilities of a young woman; the final confirmation of the scenario comes in the very last sentence—indeed, the very last word. "The Gray Killer" (*Weird Tales*, November 1929) exhibits a woman in the hospital attended by a mysterious doctor who, she becomes convinced, is some sort of supernatural entity. As with "Leonora," what begins as a kind of serial killer story—is the doctor injecting his patients with some lethal drug, or perhaps killing them in some other fashion?—suddenly (and, in all frankness, implausibly) turns into an amalgam of science fiction and horror.

Worrell's frequent displays of female characters does not mean that she was a feminist. There are indications that her outlook on male/female relations was a relatively conventional one for the period. In "The Elemental Law" (*Weird Tales*, June 1928), it is stated that "a woman . . . wouldn't intrude herself into the hard world of men's striving." While it is unwise to attribute the sentiments of a character or narrator to the author, a similar point of view is expressed in "Vulture Crag" (*Weird Tales*, August 1928), where a male character speaks condescendingly of a woman's gaining the "shallowest ripples of science [at] a finishing-school" and goes on to say: "Women were never meant to pioneer among new dangers and new horrors." Both of these stories present highly artificial scenarios typical of pulp writing: in "The Elemental Law," we are treated to a variant of the strangers-trapped-on-a-desert-island motif, along with a love triangle; in "Vulture Crag" there is another love triangle, where a prototypical mad scientist seeks to destroy his male rival to win the hand of the female protagonist. But the latter does play a significant role in foiling the scientist's plans.

"Norn" (*Weird Tales*, February 1936), written under the transparent pseudonym "Lireve Monett,"[4] is the intense tale of domestic conflict told largely from the point of view of a small child (although, as with "Leonora," the account was presumably written when the child had become an adult). Norn is the child's aunt, and it quickly becomes obvious that she wishes to possess the child—in every sense of the term. While it is true that the story articulates fairly orthodox gender roles for the child's husband and wife, the portrayal of the evilly seductive Norn is at the heart of the tale—a tale that ultimately proves to be one of lycanthropy, although here it is interpreted in a largely psychological manner without relinquishing touches of the supernatural.

A far from conventional husband-and-wife scenario is at the heart of "Hideaway" (*Weird Tales*, November 1951), where a government agent tasked with investigating a married couple as a possible espionage risk becomes involved in a tale full of lycanthropy, vampirism, and even the Philosopher's Stone. This is one of several late stories by Worrell that focus on female characters of an impressively foreboding sort. There is the seemingly helpless and delicate Jennifer of "Once There Was a Little Girl . . ." (*Weird Tales*, January 1953), who may or may not have killed her cousin merely through the powers of her mind. This tale features implications of reincarnation, which is very much the focus of "Call Not Their Names" (*Weird Tales*, March 1954), where all the relevant characters—but especially a woman named Shalimar—appear to be reincarnations of characters out of Indian mythology, including the dreaded goddess of death, Kali. In "I Loved Her with My Soul" (*Weird Tales*, December 1953), a man becomes the helpless devotee of a woman who

4. As her daughter explains, the first name is an anagram of "Everil," and the last name is taken from her mother's maiden name, Manatt.

might be a witch, but who is herself the pawn of an even more formidable creature, her mentor Madame Slavini.

Another interesting feature of Worrell's work is its open expression of religious faith—a relatively unusual quality in weird fiction, for all that much work in the field is based on such implicitly Christian conceptions as the ghost, the vampire, the witch, and so on. There is no doubt that Worrell was a devout Christian for the whole of her life. "As a girl she . . . was active in church affairs, singing in the choir," Jeanne Eileen Murphy writes; and she concludes her memoir by noting that "She was always an active, friendly, intelligent person, with a strong faith and a sense of humor."

The religious focus comes out in several narratives. "Vulture Crag" emphasizes the critical issue of the distinction between body and soul—and, like Arthur Machen's "The Inmost Light" (1894), suggests that a separation of the two can occur. "An Adventure in Anesthesia" (*Weird Tales*, February 1929) presents a curiously conventional vision of hell (complete with a horned Devil) and goes on to show how a morally corrupt man reforms himself by means of the glimpse of hell he has been afforded. "Light-Echoes" (*Weird Tales*, May 1930) attempts to use advanced science as a justification for the age-old religious conception of survival after death. The portrayal is full of moving and sensitive touches, and also displays a fascinating reversal of the idea in its suggestion of the possibility of a hideous death-in-life.

It is interesting that the two tales Worrell published in *Ghost Stories*—"The Key and the Child" (October 1930) and "None So Blind" (March 1931)—are among her more avowedly religious narratives. In the former a woman whose husband has died is reunited with him in death. In the latter a man's love/hate relationship with a "chorine" (i.e., a chorus girl) leads to dreams of Jesus. Interestingly, the man has Jesus utter his celebrated prophecy of his second coming: "This generation shall not pass, until these things have been fulfilled" (Mark 13:30)—one of the most notorious instances of a failed prophecy in the entire text of the Bible; and yet, Worrell's narrator makes no note of it. The passing mention of "God's mercy" in "The

Rays of the Moon" (*Weird Tales*, September 1928) points to the fundamentally religious orientation of a story that depicts the lamentable fate of a medical student who jilted a girl, only to encounter her again in a very different context.

Several stories by Worrell approach the genre of science fiction, but these tales do not show her to best advantage.[5] Even "The Hollow Moon" (*Weird Tales*, May 1939), as a horror/science fiction hybrid that may or may not have been inspired by Charles Fort (who is cited in the text), has its elements of implausibility in its portrayal of a boat that somehow becomes a spaceship and ventures to the moon. But Worrell concluded her fictional career with a masterful and touching short-short, "The White Gull" (*Mystic Magazine*, August 1955), a virtual prose-poem that poignantly exhibits the endurance of love beyond the grave.

The work of Everil Worrell is a distinctive contribution to weird fiction. As perhaps the leading female writer for *Weird Tales* during the 1920s and 1930s, she may have set the stage for such later authors as Mary Elizabeth Counselman and Margaret St. Clair. But it would be too limiting to categorize Worrell as merely a woman writer of talent: although her tales focus on personal relationships and the fluctuating emotions of female characters of notable complexity and fascination, she also utilized venerable weird scenarios in innovative ways to make them accessible to a contemporary audience. Her work—particularly "The Canal" and "Norn"—has substantial merit, ranging from their smooth-flowing prose to their delicacy of character development to their powerful supernatural climaxes—occupies a high place among the weird fiction of her time.

---

5. These are "The Bird of Space" (*Weird Tales*, September 1926), its sequel "The Castle of Furos" (*Weird Tales*, October 1926), "Deadlock" (*Weird Tales*, September 1931), and "The High Tower" (*Weird Tales*, July 1942).

Bibliography of Everil Worrell

"The Bird of Space." *Weird Tales* 8, No. 3 (September 1926): 292–306, 428–29.

"The Castle of Furos." *Weird Tales* 8, No. 4 (October 1926): 503–19.

"Leonora." *Weird Tales* 9, No. 1 (January 1927): 627–34.

"The Canal." *Weird Tales* 10, No. 5 (December 1927): 789–801.

"From Beyond." *Weird Tales* 11, No. 4 (April 1928): 525–34.

"The Elemental Law." *Weird Tales* 11, No. 6 (June 1928): 753–66, 859.

"Vulture Crag." *Weird Tales* 12, No. 2 (August 1928): 171–86, 285–87.

"The Rays of the Moon." *Weird Tales* 12, No. 3 (September 1928): 395–405.

"An Adventure in Anesthesia." *Weird Tales* 13, No. 2 (February 1929): 257–65.

"The Gray Killer." *Weird Tales* 14, No. 5 (November 1929): 584–99, 717–20.

"Light-Echoes." *Weird Tales* 15, No. 5 (May 1930): 671–81.

"The Key and the Child." *Ghost Stories* 9, No. 4 (October 1930): 42–51 (as by "Everil W. Murphy").

"None So Blind." *Ghost Stories* 10, No. 3 (March 1931): 73–82 (as by "Everil W. Murphy").

"Deadlock." *Weird Tales* 18, No. 2 (September 1931): 217–31.

"Norn." *Weird Tales* 27, No. 2 (February 1936): 211–27 (as by "Lireve Monet").

"The Hollow Moon." *Weird Tales* 33, No. 5 (May 1939): 5–22.

"The High Tower." *Weird Tales* 36, No. 6 (July 1942): 60–74.

"Hideaway." *Weird Tales* 44, No. 1 (November 1951): 6–23.

"Once There Was a Little Girl . . ." *Weird Tales* 44, No. 8 (January 1953): 11–30.

"I Loved Her with My Soul." *Weird Tales* 45, No. 4 (September 1953): 2–31.

"Call Not Their Names." *Weird Tales* 46, No. 1 (March 1954): 2–39.

"The White Gull." *Mystic Magazine* (August 1955): 30–33.

An Edwardian Quartet

Geoffrey Reiter

M. R. James: The Uncommon Scholar

For Simon

Look to the storm-eroded crypts, where moss
Grows green on stone containing the remains
Of dread aristocrats, or in the veins
Of vellum volumes, tome on tome, across
The shelves of mages' *curiositas*
In libraries and in cathedral fanes,
Where ancient leaves yet bear the sickly stains
Of age or blood that blots a scribal gloss.
That's where you'll find him and his hapless scholar
Who, lured by lore and antique time's temptations
And prey to secret, hidden knowledge, wants
To seize a truth but calls instead the choler
Of malice summoned by those incantations
From distant history down to present haunts.

William Hope Hodgson: "Hope That Can But Hark"

You feel the ocean shudder to your bone,
Its voice a silent roar, and underneath
The lightning-lit wild waves, as white as teeth
Lie hosts of spectres speaking in a groan
In ghastly chorus with the sea, whose moan
You cannot translate, though its ancient breath
Has whispered secrets, tales of life and death
And God and man, if these could but be known.
He is your guide across the dark terrain
Of sun-dead night, where ghastly monsters roam
In horrid hordes—for as with X you grope
Near blindly, trapped upon a darkling plain,
Across the blasted land of endless gloam,
You hear the light of his lone voice cry Hope.

Arthur Machen: "Man Is Made a Mystery"

At first, it seems, you're plunging to the deeps,
Caught in the green round of some darksome knoll,
Beneath which pallid human Things patrol
Unhallowed hoards of treasure, stored in heaps
Of grisly glistering gold, within which sleeps
A rousing primal force to seize your soul,
Perhaps to burn it to a cinder-coal,
Or call you to a past where chaos creeps.
But then, you catch a glimpse of other gold,
A chalice dipped in ancient vernal wells;
Celestial choristers proclaim in chants
A Love above the dark beneath the wold,
A draught of wine and wellspring that dispels
The night with light and fairy tale romance.

Algernon Blackwood: Listening in Silence

You think you've listened to the woods or caught
The current of the flowing river and
Known Nature, like a lover of the land
Who finds in fields and forests what he's sought,
Escape from all the havoc humans wrought
Upon the woods and water and the sand,
Far from man's strictured structures that have spanned
The globe to grasp each golden grove and grot.
In those seclusions, fleeing far from all
The traps of human trappings, is there peace?
In spaces where Dame Nature reigns, there violence
And tranquil love conjoin, beyond the wall
Between man and wild wilderness, he sees
The border, bidding you to hear the silence.

The Witch's Lover

Garrett Boatman

The Grand Ball is magnificent to behold. Dancers, elegantly dressed in velvet and satin array of many colors and richly adorned with gold and precious stones, weave a stately pavane as musicians, by their art, fill the vast room with enchanted airs. The Prince of the Realm, bedecked in royal raiment of purple satin embroidered with thread of gold, sendaline lace, black velvet pumps, and scarlet hose, treads lightly with a fair and noble lady as he leads the resplendent procession of dancers about the vasty floor of polished Alexandrine tile. The dancers wear masks. High in the lofty-ceilinged ballroom, hundreds of white candles burn in chandeliers of silver and faceted crystal, their light reflecting off mirrors inlaid into the ceiling and marble walls, lighting the masque with a luminosity that borders brilliance.

Amidst this phantasmagoria of pageantry and splendor, two figures, that of a man and a woman, walk hand in hand down one side of the ballroom, apart from the dancers. They pass through the merrymaking throng, the gay, sumptuous colors, the musicians' adagio measures. They also wear masks that cover the upper half of their face but not the lower. The man has a neatly trimmed beard, black and tightly curled. The casual observer can see that they are happy by the lightness of their step and the way they keep turning to gaze upon each other. They come to a great doorway, a towering lancet arch beset with marble statuary and columns, the capitals of which are done in vines and garlanded flowers in high relief. They pass out of the Grand Ballroom that forms one wing of the Imperial Palace. They descend the nine broad marble steps that flow from the great arch. And when they have descended the stair and stand at the beginning of the royal garden, they stop and look upon each other. They smile, and the man moves to embrace the woman, but she blushes and turns aside. The man takes her arm and leads her into the verdant garden.

The garden lies beneath the lapis lazuli sky like a shimmering nosegay of many-colored gems, for there are roses amidst the evergreens, ferns, rhododendrons, fragrant honeysuckle, marigolds, chrysanthemums, purple clematis, huge nodding peonies, and a profusion of other bright-hued flowers. Fountains of statuary spew crystalline water into marble basins; and pellucid pools, upon which float hosts of lilies in white array, are placed about the garden.

The enamored couple walk a flagstoned lane bordered with eyebrights. Above in the cloudless midsummer firmament of the western sky, the Lion stalks his celestial prey. A full moon brightens the couple's path. They pass down the lane, which is ramified into other lanes so as to form a latticework of walkways within the garden, so that a person strolling on one lane cannot be seen by someone strolling upon another, less they be viewed from a fork. But some lanes form an impasse, and at the end of these are pergolas, covered above and on three sides by trelliswork, upon which grows climbing roses and ivy and intertwining moonflowers; and within each pergola is a bench of polished marble with massive legs carven into the likeness of dolphins. It is to such a private rendezvous the man and woman arm-in-arm in silence walk; and when they reach their destination, they sit upon the marble bench, she upon the left and he on the right. Vague strains of the musicians' art, sifted through the climbing roses and ivy and intertwining moonflowers, wafts to them upon the zephyr that ruffles the garden foliage.

Holding her hands in his, the man smiles amorously upon the woman. Below her seed-pearl-bordered mask her cheeks are tinged the palest pink as if warmed by the summer sun. Black is her hair, like polished onyx, and fine and soft to touch. She wears it coiled and pinned, the pins set with faceted diamonds that twinkle and glint even in the shadowy recess of the pergola. A single ebony tendril dangles over her white forehead. Green are her glittering eyes wherein dwells a witchfire irresistible to man. Upon her bosom rests a shimmering ruby pendant suspended from a necklace of pearls. The flesh of her bosom is pale as moonbeams above the ornate lace décolletage of her gown. Her gown is of white samite: it falls loosely to the ground whence it is gathered below her breasts: the sleeves are puffed and slashed with bunches of lace where they end below her elbows.

The man speaks:

"Now wilt thou teach me thy name?" Long auburn hair enframes his face wherein are set eyes deep-brown, luminous and large. He is attired in an ornate scarlet coat with gold cuffs, gold brocade waistcoat, lace cravat, scarlet breeches, white stockings, and black pumps.

"Thou hast not yet taught me thine," she counters in a voice pleasant and soft.

"But I told thee my name, when I introduced myself to thee within."

"Ah, so you did: Raoul, heir apparent of Flavius, Count of Laspasia, was the title, was it not?"

"I did not tell thee the whole of my title. I told thee naught but Raoul," says the man, surprised.

"But I know well of thee." Her eyes glimmer jewel-like behind her mask. "I have admired thee for a time."

"But never have I laid eyes upon thee ere this night. How can it be that thou hast admired me?"

"Though thou hast not seen me, I have watched thee from afar."

"Why didst thou never make thyself known to me?"

"I desired to do so." She blushes prettily; her gaze darts away, returns. "But I did not wish thee to think me overbold."

Her words are pleasing to Raoul's ears. "Howsoever long thou hast known my title and watched the goings and comings of my person, I feel that I have known thee equally as long, and surely I have dreamt of thee. Perhaps there is an auspicious star betwixt us that has brought us together."

Her smile is like the sun breaking through clouds. Her teeth are even and white between carmined lips. "Perhaps," she says. "Or perhaps it was the ball."

"Perhaps," agrees Raoul, "but one thing I know."

"What might that be?"

"That I should ever mourn and rue this day had I seen thee and not spoken with thee."

"I am whelmed and joyed thou didst choose to do so."

"But wait—thou hast not yet taught me thy name."

"I know." Her eyes, grown puckish, twinkle in the grotto's shade. "I desired thou shouldst wait perforce, for if thou didst truly desire my name, my telling would be better-seeming for the want. But now I shall tell thee: I am hight Lucretia."

"And thy lineage?"

"Thou shalt get no more of me, for if I told thee all, no mystery would I have."

"And wouldst thou be mysterious?"

"Truly, I would have thee think so."

"Yea. I think thee more so with each breath thou breathest."

The maiden, Lucretia, blushes afresh.

"Art thou abashed?" says Raoul in a voice that begs pardon. "I did not mean to cause thee embarrassment."

She brightens. "I am not abashed but flattered."

"Neither was flattery my intent: flattery implies guile and my compliment is heartfelt."

"I am glad to hear it. Thou setteth my mind at ease." Then, like a gauzy cloud dimming the moonlight, her countenance, all smiles a moment before, waxes serious. "If I be not overbold, there is a question I would put to thee."

"Think not of being overbold," insists Raoul, "but give voiceful flight to every thought thy mind invents. The music of thy tongue is mead to my senses."

"I am glad thou thinkest so. Erstwhile, thou saidst thou felt thou hast known me ere this night, though thou didst not, and that thou hast dreamt dreams of me," she says in a voice like the whispering zephyr that bestirs the moonflowers nodding about the bower's frame. "Then is it sooth to believe that thou dost love me?"

Raoul's cheeks are tinged with red. "Thou mayest well believe so, for so I do."

"O, Raoul!" She leans toward him and places her hand upon his breast. "I had thought it too much to hope!"

He removes his mask. Above his beard, his face is tanned and vigorous from hunt and sport. Youth has not faded from his brow, though lines of responsibility—his family is encumbered with a great fortune and extensive lands which he must manage—have begun their slow etch into his forehead. He is handsome and her smile broadens as she traces a finger through his beard.

He lifts his hands beside her mask. "May I?"

She nods and he removes the silken guise. His breath stops, for it is indeed the face of his dreams. Noble without austerity. Sensual without indecency.

"Lucretia," whispers he, embracing her. Her dark-lashed lids close. A kiss, ardent and lingering, is wrought betwixt them. The bliss of it beclouds Raoul's mind, and Lucretia's bewitching face floats amidst the clouds. At length they withdraw; and imbibing Lucretia's beauty with his enraptured eyes, Raoul speaks: "If I did waver or possess any whit of uncertainty when I spoke erstwhile, I speak now with positive knowledge of my heart's mood and desire: I love thee and desire thee! I feel elated tonight—the ball, this night, this garden and thee; and I think I would feel just as elated without the ball, the night or the garden—with naught but thee."

"O, Raoul, that speech is honey-sweet from thy lips, but if thou verily hast love for me, then I would that thou wouldst promise me a thing."

Raoul takes her hands in his. "But name the thing, and it shall be promised."

Through lips like the blushes of rose petals, Lucretia speaks her desire: "Promise thy heart to me."

"It is thine already," answers he.

"But thou must promise."

"This thing I promise thee: my heart is thine; as the moon is the night's and the sun is the day's, my heart is thine."

He presses a kiss upon the single curl that lies upon her brow; Lucretia rests her head upon his breast.

But after a brief and silent interim, Lucretia draws away from him. "Swear it to me," she says, her voice a feline hiss.

"Prithee, what shall I swear?" queries Raoul, puzzled by the altered character of her voice.

"Swear thy heart be mine."

"Was my promise not binding enough?"

"Promises sit prettily upon the mind, but they may fall and be broken; an oath affects one's honor."

"Then I swear it."

"Nay, that is not enough!" Her eyes flicker with emerald fire. "Thou must swear thy oath upon things mighty and everlasting. Swear by the night and the daemons that rule it, swear by the moon, and the power she hath over men; by these things most inexorable must thou swear!"

A fire lit by desire and fanned by her words kindles in Raoul. "By these things do I swear: by the night and the daemons that rule her, by the moon and the power she hath over men, do I swear my heart to be wholly thine, Lucretia!"

"Yea, Raoul, now verily it is mine." Though her voice is soft as the zephyr stirring the moonflowers, the witch fires in her emerald eyes leap for joy. She yields to Raoul's embrace, and their lips meet in a fervent kiss. She unfastens a button of his waistcoat and, sliding her hand beneath, presses her palm against the muscular flesh above his heart.

Strains of the musicians' art wafts upon the zephyr. Somewhere in the garden, a nightjar purls and is answered by an owl.

Deep within the great upland forest of the Realm far from the haunts of mortal men, a lofty tower of polished white stone glimmers in the light of the full midsummer moon. Like a softly glowing

spear it rears above the silent woods and points its summit at Boö-
tes, who strides the zenith.

Within the tower a stair spirals upward into darkness, lighted
only by moonlight falling through narrow windows. The nude form
of a maiden ascends the stair. She carries a globe-shaped object
draped with a cloth of sable velvet. Before her bounds a swart,
dwarfish creature with a hairless, apish body, and a gargoyle head
nigh as large as its torso.

The pair come at length to a small oaken door at the head of the
stair. Upon their right, moonlight flows through a southeastern
window. The maiden nods and the grotesque creature reaches a
gnarled hand above its head and turns a golden knob. The door
swings creakingly open, suffering a wedge of moonlight to slice into
the darkness like a silver gouge in ebony wood. For an instant the
maiden stands poised in the doorway, pale and slender, a finger of
white flame crowned with a mane of darkest sable that cascades over
her bare shoulders like the fall of night and the gathering of shadows. Witch-fires dance in her emerald eyes. She steps into the room
whose walls are yet mantled in the darkness of the sepulcher. She
nods again to the goblin-headed dwarf. It shuts the door, and the
moonlight vanishes from the room, returning it wholly to darkness,
but the maiden yet glows in its irradiance. She whispers a cantrip in
a tongue alien and lyrical, and the room is litten by flames that leap
from the four-and-twenty flambeaux mounted in the four-and-
twenty sconces set against the marble wall. The smoke spirals up
and gathers below the lofty ceiling. The floor is of a smooth black
stone like jasper, but it has no sheen, nor does it reflect the light of
the flambeaux; and in the center of the floor, inlaid in silver, is a
pentagram graven about with strange glyphs. Tables are revealed in
the torchlight, long and low, ranged against the circular wall, of
carven teak with legs fashioned like the trunks of trees with serpents
twined about them. Upon the tables, mounted upon low marble
pedestals, are more of the velvet-covered globes like the one the
witch-maiden carries. A single row of six upon each table.

"Where shalt thou put it, Lucretia?" The familiar's wide mouth is filled with yellow fangs; its small black eyes glitter like onyx stars.

"There." Lucretia motions toward a table upon which only five pedestals are occupied. Her bare feet tread softly across the cold, black stone as she hums an eerie melody. Her ivory form halts before the table. The unoccupied pedestal is topped with a concave depression. Still humming, the witch places the globe upon the pedestal. She runs her hands excitedly down her sides, then taking a corner of the velvet cloth betwixt her fingers, she uncovers the globe. Like the passing of a dark cloud from before the full moon or of an eclipse from the face of the sun, a golden glow reveals itself as the cloth is drawn away.

Lucretia speaks: "Look, my pet. Look upon my prize!"

"I cannot see," pipes the familiar, straining upon tiptoes to view the globe.

Lucretia lifts the gruesome creature to sit upon the table beside the newly filled pedestal.

"It is beautiful," the creature coos, grinning hideously.

Its mistress laughs softly as she folds her supple arms beneath her breasts, her green glimmering eyes bent upon the globe. On the front of the marble pedestal is a small graven plaque of gold. It reads:

"Raoul, heir apparent of Flavius, Count of Laspasia. A.D. 1648–1676."

The crystal is filled with a golden ichor, and in the golden liquid floats the red and palpitating heart of the witch's lover.

Under the Sign of the Hourglass: Elderly Protagonists in Horror Fiction

Silke Brandt

Mortality and transience are central themes of horror fiction, where terror arises from our fear of pain, insanity, and violent death—all of which mean a loss of control. Likewise, we instinctively react to decay with disgust and revulsion. But even if the genre requires a certain body count, death and transience are very often about avoidance: positively connoted regarding vampires and artificial intelligence, negatively regarding zombies, Frankenstein's monster, and ghostly hauntings.

Narratives often deal with life after death or one beyond decay: the inevitable is postponed—but what if aged narrators are concerned? Not as antagonists or monsters, but as figures of identification? I consider this question all the more relevant because speculative horror fiction had its second heyday during the 1970s, and the core readership is now approaching retirement age. Also, our society is considered over-aged. Is the young adult segment of horror and postmodern Gothic fiction such a bestselling subgenre because we expect the youthful protagonists to survive? And although cultural production has been dominated by the demand for a representation of a wide range of identities, social roles, and physical or mental capabilities for more than twenty years, the demand for elderly protagonists has been more subdued. Are protagonists in the last phase of life perhaps too uncomfortably close to our reality when they are themselves victims, possessing no supernatural powers such as Tolkien's Saruman and Gandalf, *X-Men* Magneto and Xavier, or William Hartnell's Timelord in *Doctor Who?*

In this essay I focus on elderly protagonists facing not only supernatural terrors but also the fear of their natural death. The stories date from the Victorian era to the present day; my sections here deal with tangible ideas (guilt and atonement, pain, death) as well as increasingly abstract ones (memories, decay, and the concept of time). Two central questions are:

- How are elderly protagonists portrayed in horror fiction, and which fears and terrors can be better told through them instead of younger ones?
- Which subjects and motifs are told by means of elderly protagonists in general?

For a statement on whether these motifs and character concepts are representative or which developments might have taken place over time, a quantitative study of an immense number of texts would be necessary. The novels and stories presented here are thus selected examples.

Innocence, Guilt and Atonement

Guilt—whether repressed or consciously concealed—is a common motif in horror, especially in Victorian Gothic tales. In 1843, Edgar Allan Poe wrote "The Telltale Heart" and "The Black Cat," both of which feature a protagonist driven mad by guilt, who is convicting himself after experiencing hallucinations or paranormal events. The perpetrator's subconscious—his conscience—forces him to condemn and then to execute himself by suicide. Not all stories about guilt revolve around protagonists of advanced age, but, for example, J. Sheridan Le Fanu, Jean Ray, and more recently China Miéville show that lifelong guilt creates very powerful tragedies. The twist can be more effective when we learn that someone maintained an illusion throughout a long life, only to be discovered in old age. This illusion also creates tension in the reader because we had been going along with it.

Guilt and atonement are the themes of all four stories included in Le Fanu's *Green Tea and Other Ghost Stories* (Arkham House, 1945), and two of them feature aged protagonists. "Mr. Justice Harbottle" (1872) begins with an elderly gentleman's account of the ghostly apparition of a sixty-seven-year-old judge who treated his opponents with sadistic malice, bringing even innocent people to the gallows through rhetorical sophistry. Told in retrospect, the pensioner Harbottle experiences a paranormal lucid dream: now he is the accused, judged by his own antagonistic mirror image. Harbottle is found guilty of murder, sentenced to death by hanging—and on the following day is indeed found hanged. The story is reminiscent of Charles Dickens's moral tales, but Le Fanu sets it apart from such parables by introducing the topic of suicide, in his era a shocking, taboo subject. As with Dickens's Scrooge, however, a lifetime of guilt weighs more heavily than the transgressions of a younger person, who could even be excused on grounds of immaturity.

"Squire Toby's Will" (1868) is about an old landowner, Charles Marston, who lives in a country house he inherited from his father. All his life, Charles has been at odds with his misshapen brother Scroope, who pursues him with envious hatred. Scroope also claims to be the rightful heir, and is driven into poverty by his legal efforts to prove it. Many years later, Charles finds a will confirming his brother's claim—but since he has made the estate his home and plans to spend his retirement there, he decides to destroy the will after months of wrangling. Shortly afterwards, Scroope dies. Instead of being relieved, Charles is tormented by guilt and believes that his dog is possessed by his brother's revengeful spirit: the animal turns more and more into a paranormal entity and ultimately drives Charles to suicide.

Both stories achieve their effect by dealing with a heavy guilt that overshadows an entire life and makes ageing a torment that can only be alleviated by ending one's life.

Jean Ray presents similarly guilty entanglements of aged protagonists in his short story "House of the Stork." Ray's surrealist concepts are more abstract, and the protagonists only become guilty at an older age. Coincidences play a role: spontaneous ventures lead to unforeseeable consequences.

The story is about an old captain who "has dropped anchor here after a turbulent life on the seven seas" and "has achieved a tolerable existence" (7) on a remote, peaceful riverbank—all of which makes him instantly likeable. The narrator is visited by his former mate, Bill Cockspur. It becomes obvious that the two of them were involved in some crooked deals. Cockspur mentions an old guard who has a key to a magical house that spits out gold coins in exchange for payment with human victims—whom it devours. After murdering several shady characters, the two seamen plan to trick the house: they want to secure the money without giving anything in return. In the process, the captain accidently torches the house and sums up: "If I had been filled with a burning thirst for knowledge, I might have been able to penetrate the darkest secrets of the afterlife; but I had been guided only by my buccaneer spirit and assumed that with this act of revenge and justice, the adventure would have been over" (20). However, he is now haunted by the ancient guardian of the house. Thus, the captain has deprived himself of his peaceful retirement: he ends up comparing himself to cursed souls burning in hell for all eternity.

In "The Shadowy Street" ("La Ruelle ténébreuse," 1932), Ray tells a similarly complex, convoluted story: part of a town's district exists outside the laws of spacetime. There also stands an abandoned house that contains magical treasures, bringing disaster to all who steal from it. The story is told as a flashback, making the motif of aging less prominent than paranormal timelessness or multidimensional realities. In both narratives, however, tragedy arises from protagonists who had led long, contented lives without incurring enormous guilt, and then, in old age, needlessly take a gamble that ends in catastrophe and destroys all hope of reconciliation. Due to their advanced age, these protagonists cannot expect a positive development before their natural end. Thus, motifs such as unjust or criminal enrichment are much more effectively executed through aged protagonists than through younger ones.

China Miéville portrays the narrator of his horror story "Different Skies" (1999) in a sympathetic manner similar to Ray's initial presentation of his captain: with endearing self-lies and irony, a pensioner overplays how much increasing frailty and isolation limit him. He gives himself a leaded glass window for his birthday, but it soon offers a view into a parallel ghost world. Though he lives on the fifth floor, the window looks out onto a lonely alley from where a gang of children taunts him, issuing death threats. The first-person narrator realizes that physically he's no match for them and admits to himself what he repressed up to this point: as a child, he had bullied fellow pupils and tortured animals. Our sympathy is put to the test; the boundaries between victim and perpetrator become blurred. At the same time, the narrator's unacknowledged mental confusion suggests that the threat might be nothing paranormal, but the onset of dementia: "I thought at first of telling somebody: Charlie, or Sam, or someone. But then I hear the same story told to me by a seventy-one-year-old, and I know what I would think: Alzheimer's, old-timers'. Or madness. Or blindness. Or a simple lie" (154).

Of all the stories discussed in this essay, "Different Skies" is the one that shows the transition into old age in greatest detail. Miéville offers an identification figure through his first-person narrator, then unsettles us with a pessimistic ending: the deeds we might have committed unthinkingly in adolescence could catch up with us in old age. The youth gang's threats are also realistic: the elderly are increasingly becoming victims of violence, especially in care situations. The story thus offers a disturbing future vision of our own twilight years, when we might be neither physically nor mentally able to manage our daily lives autonomously, unable to distinguish reality from memory or hallucination. And the horror is that we'd be aware of what's happening to us: "I was huddled like some pathetic child in the armchair, in darkness. The bulb of the lamp must have blown, I remember thinking. I stood shakily and heard the book fall from my lap. I looked around, confused and shivering" (152).

In reference to this topic, my eighty-year-old mother—who introduced me to classic horror, Lovecraft, Lem, and the Strugatzkys when I was a teenager—added an interesting aspect: in old age, there is a more pronounced withdrawal into inner worlds, whereas the environment loses relevance. If elderly protagonists have to live with, for example, a lifelong guilt or are tormented by the question of whether paranormal phenomena are not perhaps visual disorders or signs of dementia, these impressions and fears will have a much more extreme effect than they would have on younger ones. This is precisely because the elderly live more extensively in their inner worlds and are also more often left alone with their fears and traumas.

The horror in these stories is not only evoked by our identification with the elderly protagonists—by our fear that one day the same fate could befall us—but also by observing the stories unfold. We are not disturbed when children or young adults lose their composure in the face of terror; but with older protagonists we tend to associate a certain serenity that has replaced innocent naïveté, and a conscious relativization of drastic experiences leading to less rash, spontaneous responses—all of which is regarded as wisdom. When elderly protagonists are shaken and openly show fear, the paranormal phenomena appear all the more gruesome, and the story gains an additional disturbing quality.

Guilt and remorse are aspects that make approaching death particularly agonizing. But many people find not only mental but also physical decay profoundly disturbing. The finality of death, the process of decay—alienating the deceased through our instinctive disgust—and mourning the uniqueness of a dead person are the topics of the following chapter.

Borderworlds: Mourning, Decay and Disgust

> Life is a constant struggle, and death means peace—not the other way round. Everything that lives struggles for existence until it dies. Then it sleeps for all eternity and does no more harm to anyone. Those who pray for peace on earth are actually praying for the end of the world.—Stefán Máni, *The Ship* (350)

Self-awareness means a knowledge of death, and its inevitability can be felt as either tragedy or relief. Acknowledging our mortality becomes increasingly difficult as we physically and mentally deteriorate, and many consider the paranormal as an illusory means of escape: life after death or reincarnation. (Also, as mentioned above, surmounting death is a prominent motif in horror fiction.) Not to deny death but to face the eradication of the self is to face the uncanny unknown. For, as Lovecraft famously wrote in his essay on supernatural horror: "The oldest and strongest emotion of mankind is fear, and the oldest and strongest kind of fear is fear of the unknown" (25). He cites death and outer space as the most obvious examples. Dying cannot be experienced in advance, and this uncertainty triggers an existential fear: to face death is to gaze into an abyss, or as Lovecraft's narrator in "Dagon" puts it: "I felt myself on the edge of the world; peering over the rim into a fathomless chaos of eternal night" (*Collected Fiction* 1.55).

Mortality, decay, madness, and death are also featured in horror stories involving younger protagonists, but if they survive these events, it is implied that they will later find ways to cope with or repress their traumas. However, aged main characters lead us to expect that—similar to the issue of guilt discussed above—they will not be granted a healing lifetime after these traumas or horrors.

Trauma and death can be closely connected: "The Music of Erich Zann" (1919) is one of Lovecraft's short stories that speaks of the uncanny unknown through cosmic horror, but doesn't grant alien gods a central role. The horror is told through two human protagonists: a student and an aged violinist, Erich Zann. The latter plays extremely dissonant pieces when he believes himself unobserved. Fascinated by these tunes, the student wins the musician's trust and is invited to his room, which is just as marked by decay as its occupant; but in company Zann only plays conventional music. After secretly observing Zann and noticing his panicky demeanor toward a curtained window, the student breaks cover, pulls back the curtain, and gains a view into the black chaos of deep space, from which cacophonous sounds as well as a dark, overpowering consciousness emerge. Zann plays a crescendo, but it becomes apparent that alien forces move his dead body like a puppet. The story not only relates cosmic horror, but might also signify the tragedy of isolation, physical decay, and the proximity of death when self-determination is no longer achievable.

The Polish author Stefan Grabiński became famous for his sinister, speculative railway stories, published in 1919 and 1922 under the title *Demon ruchu* (The Motion Demon). These deal with existential fears: isolation, strange obsessions, loss of loved ones, and expiration of lifelong—and thus irreplaceable—friendships.

"Ultima Thule" (1919) is told retrospectively by an aged former stationmaster, Romek, who is unable to forget a certain incident: His closest friend, Joszt, is on duty at the last station of a railway line, situated on the slope of a misty mountain range. He ironically calls himself *Charon* and his station *Ultima Thule*. The narrator's visits are his only social encounters with other people; their relationship is amicable and cordial. Joszt describes the melancholy place: "How I loved this hermitage in the mountains! For me it was a symbol of mysterious boundaries, a mystical liminal space of two worlds, a kind of no man's land between the realms of life and death" (96).

During one of their meetings, Joszt repeatedly steers the conversation toward the metaphysical, an afterlife, and a boundary between two worlds—a sphere of which he considers himself a guardian. He reveals a second sight that allows him to foresee the death of others. After Romek returns to his own station he receives confused, ominous Morse code messages late at night. His friend signals: ". . . how hard, how hard to break free . . . disgust . . . revulsion . . . grey mass . . . viscous, malodorous . . . at last . . . I have broken free . . . I AM . . ." (104).

Romek faints, and in the morning he boards a trolley and rushes to Joszt's station. Upon arrival, he learns that Joszt died hours before the strange message was sent. His last premonition had been of his own death, and he let his friend be a witness of his crossing of into the beyond.

In contrast to Grabiński with his melancholy netherworlds that allow for a simultaneity of life and death, Mark Samuels could be described as a more nihilistic author who began his career with social realist plays. His short story "The Other Tenant" (2011) is about redundancy in a capitalist world and symbolically deals with the worthlessness of people unable to participate in production due to their old age or illnesses. The narrator, Robert Zachary—a misanthropic early retiree and disillusioned communist—takes stock: he was respected by colleagues for his work, but not appreciated as an individual. The employer's prudence might just as well have been an attempt at exclusion:

> With his being only a few years shy of retirement age, the state-owned company had decided that it would be possible to grant him his pension early, and thus allow him to battle his undiagnosed organic illness without having the worry of considering when it would be possible for him to return to work. In truth, however, Zachary suspected they were relieved not to have him lingering in the news office. (24)

Static noise, curses and sounds of pain seep through the walls of his stark flat; but the unit next door has been unoccupied for months. When Zachary flies into a helpless rage and breaks into the adjacent flat, he discovers an old television showing torture videos—and the face of the last victim is his own. After a bizarre, ironic self-execution, the circle completes itself: a new tenant moves into Zachary's old flat, now hearing *his* screams through the wall. When Zachary is no longer a useful cog in the production gears, he is physically obliterated. Even if the bitter, grouchy narrator makes identification difficult, his isolation, fear, and ultimately his lonely death do allude very effectively to real-life terrors.

In Samuels's "My World Has No Memories" (2014), the first-person narrator wakes up from unconsciousness—on board his yacht, suffering from amnesia. The navigation devices don't work, his last position in the logbook is undetermined. A glance in the mirror reveals: "A drawn, unshaven face that I did not recognise stared back at me. My reflection. I guessed that it belonged to someone in their mid-fifties. Eyes blue. White hair shaven close to the scalp. Very thin" (55).

On a shelf he finds a jar containing some pale, diseased plant that, in a fever-like fit, he believes is communicating with him. He throws the jar into the sea, but later it is back on the same spot, except that the flower has grown. Lacking navigation, the narrator blindly sails across the ocean until his yacht is stopped by a gelatinous mass of corpses, all bearing his features. After an attempt to burn the pale flower, which is obviously connected to the drifting corpses, he sails into a surreal world under a multicolored sun and feels the same black liquid seeping from his eyes that earlier oozed from the crushed flower.

As different as Lovecraft, Grabiński, and Samuels are, they all set aging, death, and decay in borderworlds or surrealistic parallel universes where bodies decompose, but their consciousness is forced to live on. These concepts could be counter-designs to a transhumanism that strives for immortality through artificial intelligence or sentient machines. Memories, however, form what we regard as our personality; we even associate them with *Dasani* and life itself. Memories can be a frail person's reason to keep on living, but they can also be extinguished by dementia. Similarly, there is a devastating fear that we might realize in the hour of death that our life was meaningless, that all our efforts and fears were in vain. In such stories, horror and personal tragedy are finely balanced, and the following chapter is about these.

Isolation, Futility and Meaninglessness

> Death has always asked man more questions than he can answer.—Andrey Iskanov, *Philosophy of a Knife*[1]

In philosophy, psychology and modern ethnology, there are different approaches to what constitutes individuality, but a personality is

---

1. *Philosophy of a Knife* (Russia, 2008). Scriptwriter and director: Andrey Iskanov.

usually an older person, a distinctive individual shaped by experience and reflection. According to this interpretation, the older the person, the more tragic their death. The death of a child or a teenage protagonist may be upsetting due to the break of a taboo and the notion that the victim was unable to fulfill his or her potential; this is, however, an optimistic, theoretical mourning (we don't know how they would have lived their lives). But the world expiring with older personalities is infinitely complex and their individuality a fact, not a projected hope.

In his late work, the linguist and philosopher Jacques Derrida deals with the idea that the past haunts us like a ghost—and with the process of mourning: "'the other's death, not only, but especially if it is someone you love, does not announce an absence, a disappearance, the end of some other life, that is the end of the possibility for a world (which is always unique) to appear to some living person. Each time death declares the end of the world in totality, the end of any possible world, and each time the end of the world as a totality which is unique, therefore irreplaceable and therefore infinite.' The subject is a fragile, shattered survivor of total irrevocable destructions, its own death is in temporary abeyance though already at work within it, foreshadowed in the multiple losses occasioned by the death of others" (Davis 129, quoting Derrida's *La Voix et le phénomène* [1967]).

The fact that only we ourselves can give meaning to our lives creates fear of failure. If young protagonists are affected by trauma, we assume they have sufficient time to give their life a new meaning later. Failure and futility, however, become threatening when they are told via aged protagonists who, on the brink of death, may no longer have the opportunity to heal and change. The end of a character's life might just as well represent the conclusion of a dramatic, but ultimately pointless, struggle.

W. W. Jacobs's "The Monkey's Paw" (1902) is one of the most famous ghost stories, despite leaving open whether anything supernatural actually happens. It is about a sympathetic elderly couple whose stance is rationalist-modern; they are well-connected and live in affluence. With a couple of a similar age, they gather by the fireplace for a social evening. One of guests presents an enchanted monkey's paw supposed to grant three wishes, and the hosts jokingly go for it. Their wish—an arbitrary sum of money—comes true: however, it is paid out as reparation after the fatal work accident of their only beloved son. The old lady, torn apart by grief and guilt, now wishes on the paw for her son to return from the dead. Her husband warns that the body has been mauled by heavy machinery and she would no longer recognize him. There's a knock on the door downstairs, but while the mother struggles with the bolts, the father wishes the son back to the grave—and she opens the door to a deserted street. The hitherto carefree, well-established lives of the two seniors are shattered due to their curiosity; a seemingly harmless parlor game ends with the couple being torn apart by grief and pain. Even if they were not already too old to reproduce, their son—who was an adult leading his own life and had acquired a uniquely individual history—could not be replaced by the birth of a new child. Also, the ending suggests that a happy married life is destroyed by the controversial handling of the son's death (possibly also his return), and they might not have sufficient lifetime left for healing or reconciliation.

Robert Edric's novel *The Earth Made of Glass* (1994) also deals with futility: recent experiences lead the protagonist to question the beliefs and actions of his entire life. As a last assignment before retirement, an inquisitor is to appraise church property in a remote northern English village. It is 1691, the beginning of the Enlightenment, and the inquisitor soon to be an anachronism. Increasingly weak from influenza, he faces a wall of lies and secrets: he hears about the lynching of a 'witch' thirty years earlier, and comes to realize that she was innocent. His host, the fanatical pastor Jonas Webster, was the initiator of the crime and is now concealing the location of her body. The deeply disillusioned inquisitor has only one goal: to solve this murder, find the remains, and prosecute the guilty party. Based on a clue, he finds human bones in a well in the forest. After a bout of fever forces him back into the village, he discovers the next morning that the community has disposed of all the evidence. Far away from the settlement, utterly exhausted, sick and disillusioned, the inquisitor collapses, convinced that all his long-held worldview is false. The heavy rain in the last scene suggests that he will die alone in the forest. As is typical of Edric, a depressing atmosphere of hopelessness, futility, and bitterness pervades the entire novel.

Both examples show how the protagonists' advanced age highlights the tragedy of their fate and the drama of the plot. If the protagonists are forced to re-evaluate their entire life, it can suggest that their personalities will be shattered and their identities—even before physical death—will be erased. Symbolically, the fate of the inquisitor, helpless in the face of his church's crimes, could also be interpreted as a pessimistic take on history, whereby destructive anachronism triumphs over morality and progress.

In her short story "Waiting" (1942), the surrealist painter and writer Leonora Carrington ironically contrasts the concepts of *individuality* and *time:*

> "The past," said Elizabeth, unleashing the dogs. "The adorable living past. One must wallow, just wallow in it. How can anybody be a person of quality if they wash away their ghosts with common sense?" She turned on Margaret ferociously and laughed in her face. "Do you believe," she went on, "that the past dies?"
>
> "Yes," said Margaret. "Yes, if the present cuts its throat." (86)

Concepts of time play a subtle but essential role in horror fiction. Ghosts haunt us from the past, dragging the *then* into the *now;* omens or time machines provide glimpses into a future that often represents the uncanny unknown; parallel worlds or Doppelgängers suspend the laws of physics. However, there are not only aged protagonists who are subject to time, but also those who embody it themselves. The last section is about them.

Under the Sign of the Hourglass: The Construct of Time

> Leafing through the volume, Shterer discovered a note in his son's childish hand. Next to the saying "Time marches on" was the scrawled remark: "But I'll make it dance in a circle."—Sigizmund Krzhizhanovsky, *Memories of the Future* (138)

Traditionally, time is symbolized by humanoid figures representing decay or death, often a violent one: Christianity's skeleton carrying a scythe or an hourglass, the man-eating goddess Kali with her bloody tongue and necklace of severed heads, the cannibalistic Baba Yaga, her three sons (through whom she rules the times of day) and her ancient husband, the Immortal Koschei, who have counterparts all across Finno-Ugric cultures.

Personified death symbolizing time in horror fiction is usually the antagonist, e.g., Rictus and Hood in Clive Barker's *The Thief of Always* (1992) or revenant Selenna Izard in John Bellairs's *The House with a Clock in Its Walls* (1973). There are, however, elderly protagonists in more sinister, adult speculative fiction, where the conception is closely related to the concepts of time in the natural sciences: themes related to aging and decay are combined with ideas borrowed from current physics, and both are combined in a fictional character. Here, protagonists both are subjected to time and are themselves its personification. They are perpetrators and victims alike, not clearly assignable to conventional notions of *good* or *evil*. Narratives dealing with concepts of time are extremely complex and worthy of in-depth consideration.

Aging, decay, and movement in space are the only ways for us to perceive time. It appears to us as if time is linear: the moment that was just *now* is now the past. Death and decay, like entropy, are irreversible, or as theoretical physicist Lee Smolin states: "People, animals, and plants are born as infants, grow up, age, then die. This can be called the *biological arrow of time*. We experience time flowing from the past into the future. We remember the past but not the future. This is the *experiential arrow of time*" (183; emphasis in original). In spacetime concepts, mortality is thus perceived as a metaphysical movement, or as the anti-natalist philosopher and emeritus professor Julio Cabrera writes: "*Dasein* [i.e., experience] is fundamentally a being-towards-death" (53).

The problematic relationship between space and time in explanatory models of physics can also be found in horror fiction: "I belong to the chosen few who are allowed to cross over from one realm into the other with impunity. Thanks to my 'derangement' I stand on the border of two worlds. [. . .] the concept of time does not exist for me. And yet something of the inadequacies of this side has stayed with me: I cannot get rid of the limits of space" (Grabiński 153).

The aged narrator in Stefan Grabiński's short story "Saturnus Sektor" ("Saturnin Sector," 1920) is a natural scientist recently discharged from a mental institution. He had never published his extensive research on the subject of time. His consolidated self-image is that of a triumphant intellectual—until a certain S. S. publishes provocative, sarcastic counter-concepts in the daily newspapers. The narrator is thus deprived of his peace of mind and sees his lifelong scientific research mocked. Then an ancient man wearing a Roman toga pays him a visit. The guest carries a scythe and an hourglass, and is addressed by the narrator as "Saturn" and "Tempus." The two engage in a shrewd duel of words, during which personified Death announces a second meeting—not in this dreamlike state, but in reality. Days later, the narrator discovers a watchmaker's workshop, owned by one Saturnus Sektor. He notices a strange resemblance between himself and the old man. Also, the shop is located at the back of his own house. During their debate, it becomes apparent that the narrator is a representative of the pre-industrial concept of time, when it was viewed subjectively, in flux. Saturnus, however, represents—like Death in the previous meeting—modern time, which divides up units of work and forces people under its yoke:

> "Life flows as a broad, closed wave within all appearances, and they are so profoundly intertwined that their division into moments is ridiculous, a caricature of reality. You simply transfer your concept of time to the sphere of space!"

"Isn't that a marvellous idea? Have you read the famous novel The Time Machine?"

"Certainly. That's what I was talking about. It's the best example of where the fabrications of the human brain can lead. Doesn't the very idea of a time machine insult the innocent virginity of life, which is constantly full of surprises? These are the consequences of the vivisection you perform on it."

Suddenly the narrator feels some kind of metaphysical exchange, as if Saturnus were now speaking from within his own self.

"If I didn't have the impression," the old man continued in a subdued voice, "that your thoughts might be a young shoot grafted onto my trunk, if I wouldn't have the impression that they would blossom splendidly in the near future . . ."

"Then . . . ?"

"Then I would kill you," he replied coldly. "With this instrument here." (160f.)

Saturnus hands the confused narrator a dagger. The narrator returns home, but on the next day learns that the watchmaker, who had also recently been released from a psychiatric hospital, committed suicide with that very dagger. Here, Grabiński switches to an authorial perspective, stressing the fact that both characters are one and the same person: modern Time switched bodies, leaving Saturnus (Death) behind and living on in the narrator. Thus he escapes the spacetime plane and becomes immortal text. This short, partly humorous story is one of the most complex literary explorations of time, death and the relativity of our perception.

Still a theoretical point of contention in "Saturnus Sektor," an actual time machine is put to use in Sigizmund Krzhizhanovsky's "Memories of the Future" ("Воспоминания о будущем," 1929). Since childhood, Max Shterer has been obsessed with building a time cutter (i.e., a sailing vessel), but only succeeds late in life. The story, similar to Jean Ray's, is told from different perspectives, occasionally sounding like absurd echoes of current concepts in physics, such as those by Lee Smolin and Julian Barbour: "In the classic

Raum und Zeit,' Shterer would later report, 'I investigated the *und* and saw that time, since it appears as an annex to space, invariably lags behind and doesn't manage, owing to a sort of friction of seconds against inches, to harmoniously correspond, to be correlative to its space'" (162).

Shterer's time machine is made of colored light and interacts directly with the brain. During a test run—full throttle into the future—he approaches the outer limits of time:

> [. . .] and everything, as though it had hit a wall beyond the horizon, stopped and froze. The reel of seconds threading through my machine had jammed at a certain instant, a certain fraction of a second—it wouldn't go forward, it wouldn't go back. Somewhere below the horizon, the sun's orbit had intersected with eternity. The air was a cindery gray, the way it sometimes is before dawn. The machine was silent. The undawning dawn, stuck between night and day, would not budge. (199)

In the end, the time cutter is wrecked and disintegrates, but the traveler's perception has greatly changed: His childhood plan to travel into the past to save a dying school friend has failed, but now his fellow human beings appear to him as marked by death, as if he has brought the gray wasteland of infinity with him into the present:

> My sense of the people now surrounding me is that they are people without a now, people whose present has been left behind, people with projected wills, with words resembling the ticking of clocks wound long before, with lives faint as the impression under the tenth sheet of carbon. Then again, a third hypothesis is also possible: I, Maximilian Shterer, am a madman who's denied even in a straitjacket, and everything I've told you is nonsense, gibberish. (205)

As with "Saturnus Sektor," encounters with in/finity can have grave consequences, and likewise Krzhizhanovsky's main character is associated with madness.

Another Polish author, Bruno Schulz, wrote about the theme of aging via a father figure who appears in almost identical forms in a series of short stories possibly inspired by his own life. Several stories in the collection *The Street of Crocodiles* are about a cold, inaccessible mother and a cherished father who suffers from illness and deterioration, but is ignored by everyone—including the son who claims to be particularly close to him: "the misery of a creature fighting on the borders of nothingness and death" (9).

Successively, the father is pushed out of the confines of the family home: he lives in a cupboard, turns into a cockroach, or dissolves, entirely forgotten. No one mourns him, and in the end there isn't even a body left to bury. In his famous story "The Sanatorium under the Sign of the Hourglass" ("Sanatorium pod Klepsydrą," 1937), however, Schulz breaks this pattern, showing father and son in reversed positions of power. The first-person narrator visits his sick (actually undead) father in an eerie hospice that is both a house of the dead and an uncanny parallel world where various possible realities exist simultaneously.

Katy Shaw's definition of hauntology could just as aptly outline Schulz's story: "Hauntology is 'the science of ghosts, a science of what returns.' It destabilizes space as well as time, and encourages an 'existential orientation' in the haunted subject, making the living consider the precarious boundary between being and non-being" (2; quoting Mark Fisher, *Ghosts of My Life* [2014]).

When the narrator arrives at the sanatorium, the house is dark and appears deserted except for an obviously frightened nurse. He is assigned to his father's room, which doesn't contain an extra bed, so he must huddle up to the sleeping old man, shivering from freezing drafts. The next day, the narrator feels strangely listless, but his father explains that he has to attend to his optician's shop. Later, the son also drags himself into town, which is partly deserted and dilapidated, partly busy: there are neither waiters nor guests in the restaurants, but his father's shop is crowded. Just as the father becomes hectic and busy in tending to his customers, so the son becomes passive: drifting into a dozing state, he soon falls asleep in the middle of conversations and becomes disoriented. Both a city of the dead cast in gray half-light and a parallel world full of life, the town overwhelms the narrator, who barely finds his way back to the sanatorium. Once in the courtyard, he is pursued by a monstrous, semi-human guard dog and flees into the train he arrived on. He regards the idea of committing his father to a time-suspending sanatorium as a failure: "I'm beginning to regret this whole undertaking. Time put back—it sounded good, but what does it come to in reality? It is used-up time, worn out by other people, a shabby time full of holes, like a sieve." And he pleads, "Enough of this! Keep off time, time is untouchable, one must not provoke it. Isn't it enough for you to have space? Space is for human beings, but don't tamper with time!" (259).

The narrator will never leave the train again; soon dressed in a threadbare conductor's uniform, he simply keeps traveling from one station to the next. But although according to his plea he only utilizes space, time is suspended: he becomes a Flying Dutchman of the modern age, and thus—just like his father in his own world—undead.

"Sanatorium" evokes the uncanny through the impossibility of locating ourselves as readers. life and death are not mutually exclusive, reality is multidimensional, contradictory states merge into an inexplicable coexistence, the past can no longer be separated from the present or the future. The vertigo felt by the narrator might also be that of the readers, who might question their perceptions. Schulz—like Grabiński and Krzhizhanovsky—finds an echo in current physics: "the manner in which space-time holds together as a four-dimensional construct is most striking. It is highlighted by the fact that there is no sense in which the Nows follow one another in a unique sequence" (Barbour 178).

And the same ideas are found in philosophy, invoking the semantics of speculative fiction: "The past is always in the present through the form of haunting, yet the spectre is also necessarily 'an entity out of space in time' and 'as something from the past that merges into the present, the phantom calls into question the linearity of history'" (Shaw 14; quoting J. A. Weinstock, "Introduction to the Spectral Turn" in Blanco and Pereen, *The Spectralities Reader* [2013]).

The narratives presented in this section go beyond a mere portrayal of aged protagonists in horror fiction and treat time—thus death and transience themselves—as an uncanny motif. They shatter spacetime planes and disrupt the world we know. They don't offer easy answers, unlike the concepts of vampires or zombies, which simply circumvent or negate mortality.

These examples were meant to show how disturbing horror can be when it involves elderly protagonists. The supernatural horror merges with a real-life terror that we can repress, but not cast off: the fear of being alone, worthless, helpless, and weak in old age, no longer being able to distinguish hallucination from reality and knowing the only way out is death—the ultimate uncanny unknown. The fear of aging and decay is amplified by the fact that both have the ability to destroy our self-image, personality, and identity. Horror fiction concerned with aging is challenging us to risk an unembellished look into the abyss.

Works Cited

Barbour, Julian. *The End of Time: The Next Revolution in Physics*. Oxford: Oxford University Press, 1999.

Cabrera, Julio. *A Critique of Affirmative Morality: A Reflection of Death, Birth and the Value of Life*. Brasilia: Julio Cabrera Editions, 2014.

Carrington, Leonora. "Waiting." In *The Complete Stories of Leonora Carrington*. St. Louis: Estate of Leonora Carrington, 2017.

Davis, Colin. *Haunted Subjects: Deconstruction, Psychoanalysis, and the Return of the Dead*. Basingstoke, UK: Palgrave Macmillan, 2007.

Grabiński, Stefan. *Das graue Zimmer: Unheimliche Geschichten*. Berlin: Verlag Volk & Welt, 1985.

Krzhizhanovsky, Sigizmund. *Memories of the Future*. New York: New York Review Books, 2006.

Lovecraft, H. P. *The Annotated Supernatural Horror in Literature*. Ed. S. T. Joshi. 2nd ed. New York: Hippocampus Press, 2012.

————. *Collected Fiction: A Variorum Edition*. Ed. S. T. Joshi. New York: Hippocampus Press, 2015–17. 4 vols.

Mani, Stefán. *Das Schiff*. (Icelandic original: *Skipið*, 2006.) Berlin: Ullstein, 2009.

Miéville, China. "Different Views." In *Looking For Jake and Other Stories*. London: Macmillan, 2005. p. 154.

Ray, Jean. "Das Storchenhaus" ("House of the Stork"). In *Das Storchenhaus: Phantastische Geschichten*. Frankfurt am Main: Suhrkamp, 1986.

Samuels, Mark. *Written in Darkness*. UK: Chômu Press, 2017.

Schulz, Bruno. *The Street of Crocodiles and Other Stories*. Tr. Celina Wieniewska. London: Penguin, 2008.

Shaw, Katy. *Hauntology. The Presence of the Past in Twenty-First Century English Literature*. Basingstoke, UK: Palgrave Macmillan, 2018.

Smolin, Lee. *Time Reborn: From the Crisis in Physics to the Future of the Universe*. Boston: Houghton Mifflin Harcourt, 2013.

[Translations of German texts into English are by the author.]

The Hearse and the Highwaymen

Manuel Arenas

At nightfall, on a brisk autumnal evening in Styria, an ornate funerary carriage is barreling down a forest road en route from Graz to a remote schloss in the derelict village of Karnstein. The gaunt coachman, shivering in his somber livery, leans in to slap the reins of his team, urging the horses on, till he sees a young maid up ahead, sprawled in the middle of the road. He grimaces as he tries to pull back the reins and draw up the coach, but his team will not obey him. If anything, they press on toward the supine figure.

When the carriage is but three rods distant, a giant man bellows "Márta!" as he lunges into the road to pull the lass away ere she is trampled by the onrushing team. Consequently, the coach is soon pursued by a band of mounted brigands that give it chase into a coppice of copper beeches, as darkness proceeds to enshroud the densely wooded area. The men are emboldened upon reaching the coach to find it halted. Practically lost now in the adumbration of the gloaming, the team of black mares, sable plumes bobbing on their stately heads, stomp in place with trails of steamy breath exuding from their flared nostrils into the chill evening air.

Believing they have the upper hand, they surround the grim carriage. Two mustachioed betyárs dismount, then scale the trap to pull down the driver, now quaking in fear. The imposing highwaymen lambaste the coachman for not yielding to their feint, yet strangely he does not seem to mind them as much the funest load within the carriage, upon which his squinting gaze is fixed. The young woman, a dusky Romani with a lush mane of jetty hair, catches his glance and orders the men in Hungarian to assess what lies within.

The mountainous dreadnought, springing to action, breaches the lock on the carriage door and reaches inside to pull back the somber curtain, revealing the trapezoidal ebon coffin enclosed within the glass. "Perhaps there is something of value inside?" she says, then orders it removed to be searched for plunder. "Quickly! Before it becomes too dark to see!" The brawny fellow pulls off his black-brimmed hat and szűr coat, then rolls up his sleeves, revealing hirsute forearms as thick as the branches of the surrounding trees. Bending, he prepares to pull the coffin from the bed of the carriage.

As he sets it upright against a nearby tree and pops the latches the henchwoman cries, "No, Koppány, lay it down. If it is filled with loot, it will spill out all over the forest floor!" As the giant's head is still turned to regard her, the lid bursts open, striking him in the temple. Dazed, he staggers, only to be snatched back by a dainty ivory hand at the end of a rigid arm clad in black gossamer gauze that protrudes from within the tapering box, followed anon by an emergent figure, obscured by a black veil, that ensnares him in its chill clutch; their red painted fingernails, filed to a point, sink into his stubbled throat. All extraneous commotion ceases while the highwaymen gawk in disbelief as their gargantuan comrade is manhandled by a shrouded revenant that smites him into insensibility. With its free hand the retaliatory lich lifts its shadowy veil to reveal a petite pallid woman of striking symmetry, her glowering red gaze intent on her quarry. The men are shaken from their stupor as the fell fairy curls her fingers inward, then prises them and shreds the gullet in her grasp. The men cry out in horror as she rolls her ruddled eyes upward and latches her broadening mouth onto the throat of her prey, riven by her raptorial talons, to quaff his lifeblood, which spurts in a crimson font that spatters her albescent face in stark contrast. Her repast completed, she releases him from her grip, to crumple to the frozen ground like a rag doll as the dark donna turns her baleful gaze upon the others, who quail at her devastating countenance.

She advances like a harpy, arms outstretched, taloned fingers gyrating like spider legs, their pointed tips poised to ensnare whatever prey is unfortunate enough to fall within their clutch. She is attired for the fateful occasion, in a black mourning dress of crape and sarsnet. About her pallid throat hangs an upside-down cross of cinnabar, and her garnet earrings, like her ungual appendages, resemble crystallized droplets of blood. The Romani woman, in a flash of ill-suited thought in an unfathomable moment, marvels at how splendid the demoness looks despite her ensanguined mien, and wonders how she isn't freezing in such slight attire. However, by the absence of a nebulous trail emanating from without the lady's gory maw into the chill air, she infers that the vivifying breath of God has long since withdrawn from that frosty fair breast.

The men turn on their heels to flee, but only the ones still on their mounts escape, leaving the others to fall under the inexorable footfall of death. A straggler, a young buck with a wispy beard, piercing brown eyes, and dusack sword, gallantly steps in front of the young woman, to shield her from impending harm, but his chivalric gesture proves unavailing as the bloodthirsty beauty comes down on him like a biting avalanche of doom.

Terrified, the young woman shrinks back into a tree trunk while defiantly thrusting out her hand with which she brandishes a poniard, as she calls upon Saint Anne to save her from the *vámpír* that encroaches steadily upon the lass. Cloaked in the lustre of glamour, tanzanite irids home in on the sloe-eyed young woman, petrified with bated breath. In a preternaturally mellifluous voice she utters her name, "Márta," as she gingerly disarms her. Leaning in closely, she presses her marmoreal cheek against the unnerved woman's fear-blanched face and whispers something in her ear that immediately subdues her. Returning the dagger, the dark lady rises to her brief but fearsome stature, pausing momentarily to regard her captivated thrall as she wipes the gore from her alabastrine countenance with a crimson kerchief. Turning away, she glides across the gore-imbrued detritus of the forest floor to the carriage; then, with a wave of her gracile hand, the coach lamps flare up with a phantasmal glow. In a dainty gesture, incongruous with their recent implementation, the vampiress takes the funereal veil in her ensanguined fingertips and draws it down, enshrouding her solemn visage, ere repairing to repose in her narrow house.

Awed, the young woman touches the place on her cheek where she fleetingly brushed with death, then inspects the resultant ruddy smudge on her fingertips. Snapping out from her momentary reverie, she scrambles to her feet and motions to the coachman, cowering behind a tree, and in broken German solicits his help in replacing the coffin into the carriage. Haltingly he complies, and the task betimes completed, he nervously tips his crape-girded hat to the young woman and then turns to climb into his seat; but afore his foot touches the mounting step he feels the fatal sting of the poniard piercing his back.

Stepping over the expiring coachman, Márta climbs into the driver's seat and carefully guides the horses back to the road before spurring them on to make up for lost time. Her mistress, the Vampiress Morbidezza Vespertilio, must needs make Karnstein castle ere daylight to relay the mournful news of the untimely death of her consort, the Graff von Totenlaut, to his blood relations.

"O Thou Who Art; but Not by Man Described": Searching for God in the Dark Seas of William Hope Hodgson's Poetry

Geoffrey Reiter

If William Hope Hodgson is remembered today, it is as the author of some novels that hover on the borderline of science fiction, fantasy, and horror. He has received praise from many connoisseurs of such tales, though it is almost always equivocal praise. H. P. Lovecraft found Hodgson's writing "[o]f rather uneven stylistic quality, but vast occasional power in its suggestion of lurking worlds and beings behind the ordinary surface of life" (77). C. S. Lewis appreciated Hodgson's novel *The Night Land* for "the unforgettable sombre splendour of the images it presents," but derided it for "a sentimental and irrelevant erotic interest and . . . a foolish, and flat archaism of style" (71). James Cawthorn and Michael Moorcock include Hodgson's novels *The House on the Borderland* and *The Night Land* in their survey of *Fantasy: The 100 Best Books*. A similar volume, *Horror: The 100 Best Books,* includes an entry for *The House on the Borderland* but calls *The Night Land* "unreadable" (72). But whatever the judgment on Hodgson's work, whether it is being commended for its weird dark vision or dismissed for its sentiment and style, critics have focused exclusively on his four novels and some short stories, ignoring entirely his poetry. Yet Hodgson's poetry carries with it the themes and images associated with his prose fiction, but often in a raw, more deeply personal form. In William Hope Hodgson's poetry we can see the record of a soul buffeted by the theological challenges of the early twentieth century.

William Hope Hodgson was born in Essex in 1877, the second surviving child of the Reverend Samuel Hodgson and his wife Lizzie. Hodgson's family did not stay in Essex—or any other place—very long, however. His father, who was ordained an Anglican priest in late 1871, was transferred frequently; according to R. Alain Everts, this was "due more to his temper and his disagreements with his Bishop than to his religious zeal" (2). Sam Moskowitz likewise notes that Reverend Hodgson was a "superb speaker, capable of delivering a rousing inspiration sermon extemporaneously," but that he was "strong-minded, and he disagreed with many doctrinal matters of the church" (15). Moskowitz claims that Samuel Hodgson "loved the children and was unfailingly kind to them" (15). According to Everts, however, Hodgson could be an insubordinate youth and apparently caught the brunt of his father's temper at times. In turn, he grew up with a temper of his own.

His anger had some unpleasant manifestations, particularly directed against his sisters and mother (Everts 7); but it would serve him well when, after several previous attempts, he ran away from home at age fourteen and joined the Merchant Marine. Far from being the grand romantic adventure a young person might expect, Hodgson's service on the sea was a dismal experience, and he was tormented rather than mentored by his elders. But once his apprenticeship ended, Hodgson went back to sea prepared, and his fiery temper, coupled with his substantial physique, allowed him to defend himself quite adequately. According to Moskowitz, Hodgson's

> relatively short height and sensitive, almost beautiful face made him an irresistible target for bullying seamen. When they moved in to pulverize him, they would learn too late they had come to grips with easily one of the most powerful men, pound for pound, in all England. Additionally, he was an advanced student of Judo! There is strong evidence that throughout his life one of his most delightful diversions was to pound seamen to jelly at the slightest provocation. (18)

Even then, however, Hodgson loathed his experiences and later explained in the *Grand Magazine*,

I am not at sea because I object to bad treatment, poor food, poor wages, and worse prospects. I am not at sea because very early I discovered that it is a comfortless, wearyful, and thankless life—a life compact of hardness and solidness such as shore people can scarcely conceive. I am not at sea because *I dislike being a pawn with the sea for a board and the shipowners for players.* (*Wandering Soul* 155; my emphasis)

Yet for all Hodgson's dislike of his years on the high seas, the experience shaped him in several very important ways. First, as has already been noted, it prompted him into the turn-of-the-century world of physical culture. By 1899, Hodgson had developed his own physique so impressively that he had the credibility not only to write on bodybuilding but to open his own "School of Physical Culture" in the city of Blackburn. While the school did not last, Hodgson maintained his own impressive musculature throughout his life. When his fiction features imposingly powerful protagonists, he is not simply capitulating to the "manly-man" stereotypical hero; he is being autobiographical.

But beyond Hodgson's interest in the human body, his experiences at sea provided ample fodder for his writing. Two of his novels, many of his poems, and countless stories are all set on the high seas and, as I will examine in more detail, the ocean consistently takes on a symbolic role in his work. Because of his many years spent sailing, however, Hodgson's symbolic use of open water carries with it an authenticity that is lacking in the works of writers with less direct experience. It is a complex symbol, because Hodgson's own opinions of the sea were so complex.

It was good for Hodgson that he had the ocean to serve as a muse, because when his ambitions as a physical educator proved unsuccessful, he turned to writing. He had already penned some articles on physical culture and had been writing some fiction and poetry on the side, but his first story, "The Goddess of Death," was published in 1904. Living with his siblings and widowed mother, Hodgson began to write feverishly in his room, and he plunged actively into the professional writers' world, joining the Society of Authors (Moskowitz 28). He wrote frequently to the *Author*, proposing among other things a system of visual "totems" to identify famous writers. The editor of the *Strand* began to implement totems for several more famous authors, apparently after reading Hodgson's suggestions (Moskowitz 38).

Over the next several years Hodgson churned out poems, novels, and stories, though only the last gained him any money or popular recognition. Potboiler stories sold well, both in Britain and America, providing him with a solid source of income. He struggled, however, to find a ready market for his novel-length fiction. In the end he was able to find publishers for four complete novels: *The Boats of the "Glen Carrig"* (1907), *The House on the Borderland* (1908), *The Ghost Pirates* (1909), and *The Night Land* (1912). These publication dates are misleading. Sam Gafford's extensive research indicates that the four books may have been published practically in the reverse order of their actual writing, beginning with *The Night Land* around 1903 and culminating in *The Boats of the "Glen Carrig"* in 1905. For Gafford, this is significant in that it shows Hodgson's development as a writer, moving from a pseudo-archaic to a more modern style (14). It also illustrates the difficulty Hodgson had in finding publishers for his work, especially as his novels sold quite poorly. But if publishing fiction proved challenging for Hodgson, finding a print market for his poetry was virtually impossible. For the most part, Hodgson could only work his poetry into publication as epigraphs, dedications, or interpolations in prose work; he sold only two individual poems in his lifetime (Moskowitz 39). Two posthumous volumes finally appeared in 1920 and 1921, commissioned by his wife.

That wife was Bessie Gertrude Farnworth—known as Betty—whom Hodgson married in 1913, when Hodgson was thirty-five. He had always been popular with ladies and had many girlfriends, along with at least one other fiancée, though he apparently refused to marry until his financial situation stabilized (Everts 20). The Hodgsons moved to France for a time, but when World War I broke out they headed back to England. Betty stayed with Hodgson's family while he enlisted with the military, despite the fact that he was in his late thirties at the time. He returned home for a time due to a broken jaw, writing more short stories. But he convinced the military to let him return after a remarkable recovery. In 1917 he saw his first active duty in Ypres, a Belgian town that was site to some of the most quintessentially dreadful World War I battles. Sometime in mid-April 1918—probably the 19th—William Hope Hodgson was killed, apparently blown up by a German artillery shell.

Though he lived much of his life in the Victorian era, Hodgson's writing career is almost exclusively Edwardian, and his writing retains characteristics of both ages. As Jonathan Rose notes,

> Of all the philosophical problems that troubled the Edwardians, none disturbed so many people as deeply as the decline of Victorian religion. . . .
>
> Victorian politics, morality, art, literature, charity, and education had been saturated with religious principles and controversies, and the decline of religion left an enormous intellectual vacuum behind it. Without God, the universe lost all coherence and purpose in the minds of many late Victorians. . . .
>
> Once, Christianity had provided a sense of universal connectedness: all things were created, related, and rendered coherent by God. Without God the Edwardians were forced to reknit the fabric of the cosmos on their own, uniting worldly realities and otherworldly aspirations to form a harmonious system of belief. (1–3)

Rose, however, asserts that intellectual Edwardians ultimately tried too hard to resolve and unify complex contradictions and "purchased inner peace by glossing over difficult questions and only connecting everywhere" (212). In this regard, then, Hodgson's writing most frequently reflects the late Victorian mindset, including its religious and moral approach. This is true of his fictional output. Hodgson is often read as a master of the weird, thanks in part to an extensive commendation from Lovecraft in "Supernatural Horror in

Literature" (77–79), and his most famous novels, *The House on the Borderland* and *The Night Land,* are (at least superficially) fairly bleak. Yet even the latter of these takes surprisingly optimistic turn, as does *The Boats of the "Glen Carrig,"* and one can often find in his shorter tales suggestions of a relatively conventional moral or religious worldview, whether in the afterlife of "The Valley of Lost Children" or in his less supernatural works such as "Judge Barclay's Wife" and "My House Shall Be Called a House of Prayer," which Ross E. Lockhart calls his "most devout explorations of Christian mercy" (ix). Lovecraft himself gestures at Hodgson's occasional literary flirtation with a traditional Victorian worldview when he reluctantly acknowledges "a tendency toward conventionally sentimental conceptions of the universe, and of man's relation to it and to his fellows" (77).

What is evident in some of Hodgson's fiction is no less true of his poetry. Often expressed in a formal, Victorian meter that was all but unpublishable even in the early twentieth century, his poems also follow Victorian motifs, such as laments for the deaths of children or loved ones. But more substantially, it is not at all clear in Hodgson's verse that he has ever resolved to his satisfaction the spiritual conflicts about which he writes, conflicts that reflect the tumultuous spiritual state characteristic of so many nineteenth-century intellectuals—the so-called Victorian crisis of faith. Thus, even though the stanzas may appear old-fashioned at times, Hodgson's poetry contains some of his rawest, most intensely personal writing.

As noted earlier, Hodgson saw himself as more than a mere hack writer. In the introduction to one of the posthumous poetry collections, Arthur St. John Adcock writes of Hodgson, "He aimed high and, taking his art very seriously, had a frank, unaffected confidence in his powers which was partly the splendid arrogance of youth and partly the heritage of experience, for he had tested and proved them" (3). It comes as no surprise, then, that Hodgson had his own opinions about how his poetry ought to be published. According to Jane Frank, much of it was written between 1899 and

1906, before most of his fiction saw publication, though at about the same time he wrote his four published novels (vi). Yet, as Frank notes, "For a novice writer, Hodgson was remarkably attentive to editing" (ix), and he had gathered together many of his poems into three projected volumes of poetry, entitled *Through Enchantments and Other Poems, Mors Deorum and Other Poems,* and *Spume.* Some of those poems saw print in his wife's first commissioned volume, *The Calling of the Sea* (1920), but it was not until Jane Frank's 2005 volume *The Lost Poetry of William Hope Hodgson* that they were all printed exactly as he had envisioned.

Given the fact that Hodgson was so thoughtful about his approach to the literature he wrote and the way in which it was presented, he surely put great care in the thematic content and organization of his three projected books. It is therefore intriguing that each volume contains poems that appear to espouse incongruous, sometimes contradictory, worldviews. Take, for instance, "Mors Deorum." The title is Latin for "Death of the Gods," which would seem to square nicely with R. Alain Everts's assertion that Hodgson "was totally atheistic and quite contemptuous of the Church and religion in general" (7). The epigraph Hodgson wrote for the volume also supports such a view:

> And shall men chaunt my songs when I am dead,
>   They will not know the better part of me
> Is crying through their mouths, from Hideous Lands,
>   My terror and mine agony. (*LP* 23)

These brief, untitled lines underscore Hodgson's interest in literary posterity, hoping his verse will be read posthumously. But they also express a bleak outlook for his own state after death. Yet what are the "Hideous Lands"? Does he refer to his life at the time of the writing, or is he suggesting he will find himself in hell, in "Hideous Lands" after he is dead and only his words remain? Are his "terror" and his "agony" those of a man suffering eternal torment? Or are they the terror and agony of one who is tormented in the present by philosophical confusion?

Curiouser still, the first full poem in the volume is "Madre Mia," in which Hodgson's description of his own mother seems to blend into suggestions of the Virgin Mary. Lizzie Hodgson would only have been in her fifties at the time the poem was written, and she survived her son by fifteen years. There are no hints of terror and agony in the poem. He muses that she still retains her youth in his eyes. "No mark / Destroys" the "calm serenity" of her hair, and "Like gold / Of Evening light, when winds scarce stir, / The soul-light of thy face is pure as prayer" (*LP* 25). It seems an odd affectation for a "totally atheistic" man to describe his beloved mother's face as "pure as prayer." Hodgson would also use this poem to preface *The Boats of the "Glen Carrig,"* arguably the most upbeat of his four novels.

And yet, immediately following this piece, Hodgson would have printed the title poem, "Mors Deorum." This work, the most substantial in the collection, contains within it all the myriad ambivalences that so characterize Hodgson's poetry as a whole. Its narrator is a pagan warrior who wakes in his tomb to realize that a personified Death is about to destroy the ancient gods. The warrior implores the "God of gods" to give him the means of stopping Death's planned attack. God grants him a weapon and send him in a chariot, driven by Time, in pursuit of Death. The narrator overtakes Death at the last minute, but ultimately Death is victorious in their combat and succeeds in destroying the gods. Needless to say, "Mors Deorum" raises all sorts of questions. It is, of course, unlikely that Hodgson is suggesting Greek gods really existed and were literally vanquished by Death. Perhaps he means to show symbolically the history of religions—that despite the best efforts of devout pagan believers, the gods of Olympus were doomed. The narrator ends his tale with the assertion that the God of gods is above all death:

> . . . ere my breath has left me, I
> Have realized that none may cope with Death,

> Save the great God of all the gods, and He,
> In his own time, shall make an end of Death,
> As Death has ended me—
>
> . . .
>
> There is but one real God, and Him, foul Death
> Can no more harm than I can touch the stars. (*LP* 34)

But the narrator also questions God's sovereign plan, even as he acknowledges it:

> And still, in dying, comes the thought, why did
> The great one God of all the gods send me
> To my sad doom—He must have known the end,
> And yet, I know not; God perchance has erred
> In His great trust—I know not; still have I
> Done all that man may do, and so farewell. (*LP* 34)

The poem ends with the lament, "I am but mortal, and Death has prevailed. / And so I sleep—" (*LP* 34).

Thus, the poem that furnished the title of the volume *Mors Deorum* is not, as one might expect, explicitly atheistic, and indeed frequently affirms God's existence. Instead, it questions, however tentatively, God's goodness. This stands in sharp contrast to the "pure as prayer" imagery of "Madre Mia" or other poems in the collection, such as "The Morning Lands" or the final lines of "Old Time Hands," which depict an active and loving God:

> For deeply God understands
> The pathos of old hands,
> Those poor, tired, crinkled things
> Pulling at His heart-strings. (*LP* 67)

"Thou Who Art Jesu's Mother" likewise seems to affirm God's divine care, even if it is in the midst of trauma (a mother whose child has died). Yet it comes immediately after "The Cynic in Hell," which interrogates whether life is truly worth the gamble if eternal punishment actually exists: "'Twere better life's small joy to miss / Than risk the agony of Hell" (*LP* 52).

The *Mors Deorum* collection begins to raise these theological questions, using a variety of tropes, stories, and methods. In the third of Hodgson's collections, *Spume,* those same questions are tied more explicitly to the symbol that so fascinated and so troubled Hodgson throughout his life—the sea. All the poems in *Spume* are joined by their use of nautical imagery, but like *Mors Deorum,* they do not offer wholly consistent worldviews. The beauty of the sea for a conflicted soul like Hodgson lies precisely in the fact that it is variable and moody, and can literally or symbolically change form. It may be calm and tranquil, representing peace; it may be tempestuous and choppy, depicting conflict. For the committed sailor who drowns, it takes on the ultimate ironic intimacy with its killing embrace. Yet it is also vast, illimitable, unknowable, with an apparently infinite horizon to symbolize the afterlife. According to Emily Alder, the sea in Hodgson's fiction is a liminal space, and it "represents the edge of human experience; it is a fluid and permeable boundary, a fragile barrier between the physical world and a region of unspeakable terrors" (144).

Hodgson's complex relationship to the sea and his complex relationship to God are on full display in *Spume,* where the sea is omnipresent and always performs some symbolic function. But he can, and does, change its symbolic meaning depending on the poem in question. The first poem in the collection, "O Parent Sea!," resembles "How It Happened" in depicting God as a hostile power who may eventually be assuaged:

> O Sea! O Sea!
>> When I, thy child, have passed beyond the veil
> And looked upon God's awful mystery,
>>> And He, with some cold gesture of His hand,
>>>> Has beckoned me from Heaven's silent gates
>>> Into the wildness of an unknown land;
>> Then wilt thou, Parent Sea, encompass me,
>>> And let thine arms, encompassing avail
>>>> My shuddering soul until God's wrath abates. (*LP* 89)

Subverting biblical imagery, here the sea, not God, becomes the loving parent, sheltering the narrator from a capriciously wrathful God. Such an affectionate view of the sea seems curious in Hodgson, who so loathed his years at the sea, that chessboard upon which his soul was played. But Hodgson also could recognize the intense beauty of the sea; an avid photographer, he often captured this beauty in his pictures, even as he would also capture its potential horror. On the psychological level, one could read into such a poem Hodgson's possible hostility toward his own deceased father, the servant of God who by turns could be loving or harsh. In "O Parent Sea!," the figure of God resembles the stern clergyman, while the sea becomes a loving protector.

Elsewhere in *Spume*, however, the figure of the uncaring God is fused to the figure of the uncaring sea. "The Shore of Desolation" ends with the plea,

> Answer me, Sea, great Sea ere I pass hence.
> E'en though I land upon that awful shore
> Where Nothingness is all, and life is not.
> Answer me now, so aeons I may know
> Thou didst not *willingly* forsake me—dead! (*LP* 117; emphasis in original)

So here, the narrator feels the sea has betrayed him. Yet reading the poem's overall metaphor closely, the narrator's desire is not to escape the sea, but to die within it. He fears the sea will forsake him by sending him "unto that frightful shore / Whose stark and warmless silence frights my soul" (*LP* 116). Implicitly, then, the sea becomes a stand-in for the infinite God who might envelop the narrator within himself eternally, a comforting form of afterlife. The land becomes annihilation, a place "[w]here Nothingness is all."

In "The Shore of Desolation," death within the sea is "some calm state, / Of a prolongéd quietness" (*LP* 116). In the collection's next poem, the sea is anything but calm and quiet. "Thy Wandering Soul" depicts life as stormy and perilous:

> Thy spray-dewed soul o'er many a sea has ridden,
> > Borne unseen through the spume where tempests ever call;
> > > Where seas in shuddering mountains, tortured, driven,
> Heave smokily along . . . (*LP* 118)

In this poem, death beneath the sea is no comfort, but rather "that sad sleep far in the deeps below" (*LP* 119). This is the sea as we would expect it from Hodgson the dissatisfied sailor, a sea that is, as another poem puts it, "[p]regnant with terrors the dead only see" (*LP* 132). "The Place of Storms," the longest work in the collection, implicitly reverses the roles of "O Parent Sea!" Much of the poem consists of lengthy descriptions of frightening weather formations one might encounter while sailing; though natural phenomena, Hodgson's vivid imagery gives the formations an aura of preternatural terror, evoking other literary images of turbulent terror, such as the chaotic spaces of Milton's *Paradise Lost* or the grim supernatural nature in Coleridge's *Rime of the Ancient Mariner*. But the poem ends not with its narrator's hopeless, senseless death but with the coming of morning, when at last

> . . . across the failing waves, I saw,
> Lighting the far-off East, the coming dawn,
> Which grew and strengthened up, until at last
> The great white maw of day devoured the stars. (*LP* 100)

Unlike "O Parent Sea!," then, in "The Place of Storms," it is the sea that becomes the wrathful character, while God—implied in the "blazing light" (*LP* 101) which conquers the storm—is the one who protects the narrator.

Hodgson's fullest poetic use of the sea, however, is not found in *Spume*, but in his longest piece of verse, *The Voice of the Ocean*. While much of Hodgson's nautical poetry from *Spume* and other collections was published in 1920 with *The Calling of the Sea*, *The Voice of the Ocean* was substantial enough to warrant a book all to itself, published the following year. As in "Mors Deorum," the frame narrator in *The Voice of the Ocean* is dead, apparently buried beneath the waves rather than beneath a mountain. The poem is largely a theological dialogue overheard by the narrator, where some skeptic or doubter raises an objection to God's existence or his goodness, only to be answered by the Ocean. The Ocean claims special insight into the mysterious ways of God, because he is one of God's earliest creations,

> [a]nd so I came to know of God till we
> Talked many an age of years—He teaching me
> From the surrounding chaos of the world
> Dread lessons writ in storms and roaring fires . . . (10)

Perhaps there are some ironies present in the poem. Why would Hodgson, who so disliked life at sea, make the Ocean the all-wise spokesman for Almighty God? There may also be some ambivalence in the poem's final image, when the sea "poured its living foam upon the world / In cataracts of light" (46). After all, a cataract can be a cause of reduced vision, implying perhaps that the Ocean does not see things as clearly as he claims.

Yet such a reading is unlikely. More likely "cataracts" refer to the floodgates of heaven in Genesis 7, as well as the more generic use for any water disturbance like a waterfall or waterspout. Moreover, there are on the whole few indications within the poem that it is meant to be taken as anything but earnest. At times, the Ocean's responses to God's doubters seem overly simplistic, but they are often variants of genuine arguments from theistic apologetics. And the frame narrator's own journey through doubt, the climax of the poem, is more difficult and deeply felt than those dialogues which precede it. The theology espoused in *The Voice of the Ocean* departs substantially from church teaching in some regards, mixing in reincarnation and salvation by good works and eschewing most explicitly Christian references. Even so, the overt theism of the poem is a far cry from the "totally atheistic" Hodgson depicted by Everts. The overall variability of Hodgson's poetry suggests that he exhibited an instability like that of the sea, changing his mind and his mood frequently. But poems such as *The Voice of the Ocean* would appear to indicate that, at least at some points in his life, Hodgson found the evidence for God's existence compelling.

As I have elsewhere noted, some of William Hope Hodgson's "poems suggest a tragic nihilism, others a resigned agnosticism, others an unorthodox yet distinctly theistic perspective" (Reiter). Taken as a whole, then, his verse comes across as an unfinished dialectic, the writings of a man who was caught between the thesis of faith and the antithesis of doubt and was never able to resolve them within himself. Perhaps no poem of his manifests this tension so personally and so plaintively as the opener to his projected collection *Through Enchantments and Other Poems.* Entitled "To God," the poem's final stanza reads,

> O Thou Who Art; but not by man described—
> A Force all hidden to the eyes of Proof,
> Believed in dumbly, or with foolish word,
> By man whose thoughts are by emotion bribed,
> If Thou art there, so utter and aloof,
> Answer my heart that flutters here, absurd,
> Asking unguided questions of the Dark—
> Hope asking—hope that can but hark. (*LP* 1)

Hodgson's upbringing as a clergyman's son surely made him familiar with the traditional arguments for the existence of God, evident in *The Voice of the Ocean.* Yet in "To God" and elsewhere, he rejects these arguments of a God "hidden to the eyes of Proof." He rejects tradition or biblical revelation of a God "[b]elieved in dumbly, or with foolish word." He rejects feeling, for emotion is a corrupting force out to "bribe" his thoughts. And yet, for all these objections and rejections, Hodgson begins the stanza addressing "Thou Who Art," capitalizing each word for emphasis. Yet without scripture, tradition, reason, or experience, he has only a vague hope to build on. The final line is especially significant. While his first name was William, Hodgson was called "Hope" throughout his whole life. Thus, like Shakespeare in several of his sonnets (e.g. 135, 136, 143),

Hodgson in the poem is playing with the connotations of his name. On the literal level, it is only his hope in the possibility of God that sustains belief. Yet read personally, the final line becomes part of an intensely felt plea. He, Hope, is asking. And Hope wants more than hope as a basis for belief—he wants God to "answer my heart that flutters here, absurd." As the poem ends, he can only listen for these possible answers: he is the "Hope that can but hark."

Works Cited

Adcock, Arthur St. John. "Introduction." In Hodgson's *The Calling of the Sea*. London: Selwyn & Blount, 1920. 3–6.

Alder, Emily Ruth. "William Hope Hodgson's Borderlands: Monstrosity, Other Worlds, and the Future at the *Fin de Siècle*." Ph.D. thesis: Edinburgh Napier University, 2009.

Cawthorn, James, and Michael Moorcock. *Fantasy: The 100 Best Books*. New York: Carroll & Graf, 1988.

Everts, R. Alain. *William Hope Hodgson: Night Pirate, Volume Two: Some Facts in the Case of William Hope Hodgson: Master of Phantasy*. Toronto: Soft Books, 1987.

Frank, Jane. "The Lost Poetry Books." In *The Lost Poetry of William Hope Hodgson*. Ed. Jane Frank. Leyburn, UK: Tartarus Press, 2005. v–xi.

Gafford, Sam. "Writing Backwards: The Novels of William Hope Hodgson." *Studies in Weird Fiction* No. 11 (Spring 1992): 12–15.

Hodgson, William Hope. *The Lost Poetry of William Hope Hodgson*. Ed. Jane Frank. Leyburn, UK: Tartarus Press, 2005. [Abbreviated in the text as *LP*.]

———. *The Voice of the Ocean*. London: Selwyn & Blount, 1921.

———. *The Wandering Soul: Glimpses of a Life: A Compendium of Rare and Unpublished Works by William Hope Hodgson*. Ed. Jane Frank. Leyburn, UK: Tartarus Press, 2005.

Jones, Stephen, and Kim Newman, ed. *Horror: The 100 Best Books*. New York: Carroll & Graf, 1988.

Lewis, C. S. *Of Other Worlds: Essays and Stories.* 1966. Ed. Walter Hooper. San Diego: Harcourt, 1994.

Lockhart, Ross E. "Introduction: That Delicious Shiver." In *The Dream of X and Other Fantastic Visions.* The Collected Fiction of William Hope Hodgson, Volume 5. Ed. Douglas A. Anderson. San Francisco: Night Shade, 2009. ix–xi.

Lovecraft, H. P. *The Annotated Supernatural Horror in Literature.* Ed. S. T. Joshi. 2nd ed. New York: Hippocampus Press, 2012.

Moskowitz, Sam. "William Hope Hodgson." In *Out of the Storm: Uncollected Fantasies by William Hope Hodgson.* Ed. Sam Moskowitz. West Kingston, RI: Donald M. Grant, 1975. 9–117.

Reiter, Geoffrey. "William Hope Hodgson: A Light in the Night Land." *Christ and Pop Culture* (19 April 2018). christandpopculture.com/william-hope-hodgson-a-light-in-the-night-land/. Accessed 8 April 2022.

Rose, Jonathan. *The Edwardian Temperament: 1895–1919.* Athens: Ohio University Press, 1986.

Whispering Wires

W. H. Pugmire

[The following is the first published story by Pugmire (1951–2019), appearing in *Space & Time* (September 1973).—Ed.]

The evening will purvey an active imagination with numerous ideas, legions of swaying images one could almost smell: it can arouse fears, it can populate one single speculation into one million terrifying mysteries.

All it takes is a little imagination, and a wee bit of kava; aye, kava, that wonderful beverage Tina had come to love since her husband had introduced her to her first sip of the relaxing drink.

Now Alex was dead, had been dead for a week or there about. Alex just died, unexpectedly.

Obliquely, Tina lifted the corner of her lips, forming a grin. Alex enjoyed kava too, she laughed. His last glass hadn't agreed with him.

The drug made Tina silly; she giggled at the thought of committing murder. Alex was only the first. There would be others.

She switched on the stereo. Zeppelin III began, and Tina started dancing to the beat of "Gallows Pole." The rhythm was in tune with her active imagination.

Soon she tired, and slumped into a chair, but the music continued.

Robert was early, so Tina invited him inside while she finished fixing herself up for the evening. She spied the kava on its shelf as she passed through the kitchen. Not yet, she silently snickered.

The car moved quickly down the avenue. Tina saw that the cemetery was just ahead.

"Slow down, please . . ." Tina asked.

"What, here? C'mon, Tina, haven't you forgotten yet?"

"You were his good friend, have you forgotten him?" Tina knew just what to say and how to phrase it.

"That's not what I meant." Robert was uncomfortable. "It's a cloudy night, it may not be safe to stop and the parking isn't . . ."

"Park along here, just for a second. Oh, Robert, just for a second." She forced a tear from the corner of her eye.

"Oh, man, what a— Okay, darling, but only for a second."

They got out of the car. Approaching the car park, they encountered the long pole that prevented people from parking in the lot at night. They ducked under the pole and ventured towards Alex's grave, near the edge of the yard, off the avenue. It wasn't a night for driving, and the avenue was silent. Tina gazed at the tombstone. She shivered slightly, and Robert offered her his jacket.

"Why are we here, Tina? This isn't what I had in mind for tonight." Robert was disturbed by the area, understandably.

"I don't know . . . I don't know why I wanted to come here." Tina was lying. She had a purpose: she wasn't satisfied with torturing Alex when he was alive. Her methods lingered on after the grave was sealed. "Oh, Robert, hold me!"

Tina threw herself into Robert's arms. He was glad things were going as he desired them to, although embracing Tina in front of Alex's grave on a foggy night was the last thing he expected.

Tina, however, pressed her lips tightly against Robert's, and as she kissed him her thoughts spoke to Alex. "Look, Alex," she thought, "look at me and Robert making love in front of your cold body. Isn't that funny, hilarious? Oh, come on, Alex, I can't hear you laughing! Isn't this the perfect scandal? Laugh, Alex, say something, dear loved one! I can't hear you."

"It's a pretty picture, Tina-bird . . ."

Tina gasped, wild-eyed, pushing Robert savagely. Robert was stunned.

"What the hell's wrong with you?"

"You! You dirty . . . You scared me half to death. Only Alex called me Tina-bird!"

Robert was genuinely puzzled. "Hey, I don't think we're communicating. What are you talking about?"

"You! You talking like Alex!"

Robert smiled. "I wasn't able to speak a word, honey, not with you working on me like that." He took her arm. "You must have imagined you heard Alex. I knew this place wasn't healthy for you. Let's get out of here, huh?"

Tina stared at Robert. It wasn't him. She was making sure her kiss was tight and long. They were still in each other's arms when . . . She began to shudder, her eyes focused alarmingly on Alex's tombstone. "But . . ."

"It's the wind, Tina, the wind whispering through those telephone wires. Let's split, babe, okay?" Robert led Tina to the car. Try as he could, he could not get her attention back all evening. He was happy to take her home.

Tina took a few gulps of the kava. It worked slowly, but gradually she began to relax. She laughed at her actions of the previous few hours. She hoped Robert didn't suspect anything: she thought she had heard the voice, and was visibly shaken. Maybe Robert would dismiss it. Not that it mattered, not for long, what Robert thought, for he wouldn't be thinking for very long. But poisoned kava, no, it was old, she had used it before with Alex. Alex dug kava, maybe Robert would refuse to drink it, maybe he would get suspicious. No, not kava. There had to be a better way, a new thrill experience, a new method of murder.

Rain started hitting the window. Tina went to the patio, rubbing her hands along her arms. The house, the trees, everything he had belonged to her. That was the vow he had made. It was there, on the patio, that he knelt and made that promise the week before their marriage and the wonderful honeymoon in the Hawaiian Islands. Oh, how he kept that promise! Everything Alex had was hers, all belonged to her. But the joy she felt in murdering him had become a passion. She enjoyed murder. She would use the men that loved her for her own lustful desires, and then she would do them in. It might be boring after a while, thought Tina, but for now it was deadly fun.

The light rain moistened Tina's face. She watched the drops, shimmering in the light from the street lamp, as they fell from the wires and splashed on the ground. The wires glistened in damp splendor. The wind began to blow.

"Everything, Tina-bird . . ."

Tina gasped and ran for the door. A wild gust of wind reached it before her, slamming the door shut. Tina grasped the handle, but it wouldn't turn. She pulled desperately, and finally managed to open the door. Rainwater dripped from her drenched form. At least whoever was playing this foul joke was getting theirs. She went to the phone and picked up the receiver, but before she could ring the operator, a man's voice began speaking.

"Everything, this is my vow to you. I will not, I cannot, I *shall not* rest until all I have is yours. I vow to share everything that is mine with you, now and *forever!*"

Once, those words had sounded inviting. Now, they were terribly macabre.

"Get off this line . . . who are you?"

"Everything, Tina-bird . . ."

"Stop! Leave me alone! *I hate you!*"

The voice ceased, but she could still hear the man's faint breathing over the line. She slammed the receiver down and began sobbing.

The breathing continued to fill the room.

Looking down, Tina saw that the wire of the phone had been cut, just before it reached the wall. She hadn't been talking to anybody, at all.

"Everything . . . my love."

The voice came from behind her. Turning, she stared at the horror a few feet from her.

Alex, or what was left of Alex's flesh and bones, stood before her, arms outstretched, a skeleton grin on his now-misshapen face.

Robert received a phone call that morning, to report immediately to the police station. Tina's body had been discovered in her husband's grave, and Robert was wanted for questioning.

Alex, bless his heart, had kept his promise.

I Know There Are Giants under Our Hills

Darrell Schweitzer

I know there are giants under our hills.
Their corpses shape the landscape,
their limbs beneath the long, rolling ridge lines,
their gaping skulls weathered into caves,
their bones gleaming in the chalk cliffs.

I know there are giants under our hills,
their slow and sombrous dreams transpiring
through root and branch in the dark forests,
into a darker sky, until
we too are dreaming them.

I know there are giants under our hills,
eyes wide, staring into the darkness,
buried deep but filled with rage, waiting
until the trembling earth splits apart,
and they might rise for their revenge.

A Nice Day for a Red Wedding:
Repurposing Celebrations for Horror

Cecelia Hopkins-Drewer

"The Horror at Red Hook" by H. P. Lovecraft and "The Red Wedding" sequence in George R. R. Martin's *Game of Thrones* both introduce horror into marriage celebrations. The ritual and splendour of a wedding is subverted into an occult scheme in one tale, while a cunningly wrought revenge plot is executed in the other saga. Lovecraft's tale is characterized by the grime of gangland crime, whereas Martin's story involves kings and fantasy.

On February 11, 1929, Lovecraft wrote to Elizabeth Toldridge: "Doubtless I am the sort of shock-purveyor condemned by critics of the accepted urbane tradition as decadent or culturally immature" (*Letters to Elizabeth Toldridge* 27). Certainly, "The Horror at Red Hook" (*Collected Fiction* 1.480–505), purportedly narrated by the collected "gossips of Chepachet and Pascoag" (481), utilises a level of sensationalism that brings to mind another shocking "red wedding" with a following in popular culture.

"The Horror at Red Hook" begins by introducing the reader to Thomas F. Malone, a "New York detective" whose "sudden nervous attack" due to post-traumatic stress disturbed the village streets (480–81). The detective is the sturdy vehicle designed to encounter the thrills and terrors of Lovecraft's "film noir"–style Mafia story. The character is something of a paradox, with "the Celt's far vision" and also a "logician's quick eye" (482). This combination of strengths has "led him far afield . . . and set him in strange places" (482).

Malone looks below the surface of crime in his precinct, finding "a faint stench of secrets more terrible than any of the sins denounced by citizens" (485). He therefore concludes that the gangs must be worshipping the devil. At this point, the tale could benefit from more "show not tell," because Malone's reading of "Miss

[Margaret] Murray's 'Witch-Cult in Western Europe'" and speculating about the origins of primitive ceremonies seems superfluous (485).

The narrative, which is neatly structured into readable segments, now moves on to describe "the case of Robert Suydam." A recluse and descendent of the original Dutch settlers, Suydam had once possessed "independent means" (486). He is now poor and insignificant: "merely a queer, corpulent old fellow . . . and nothing more" (486). Suydam's relatives attempted to have him declared mentally incompetent, but he was lucid enough to prove his sanity at a hearing (487–88).

The police become interested in Suydam because his "associates" included the "most vicious criminals of Red Hook's devious lanes," and about a third of them were "known and repeated offenders" (488). Some of these criminals were people smugglers—a subject still topical today. Lovecraft's language—for example, "unclassified Asian dregs wisely turned back by Ellis Island" (488)—may be offensive, but the issue remains: for every illegal immigrant who enters a country, there are hundreds of legitimate refugees awaiting processing.

Malone is ordered to round up the illegal residents. These are rather unclassifiable: they "used the Arabic alphabet" but are not "Syrians." They have no "credentials" and attend a "nominally Catholic" church denied by the priests of the Diocese of Brooklyn (488–89). Malone discovers that these people "were indeed Kurds, but of a dialect obscure and puzzling to exact philology" and identifies them as "Yezidis" (489). Local "gangsters" tell Malone that "some god or great priesthood had promised them unheard-of powers and supernatural glories," so it sounds as though the "newcomers" are being exploited by the people smugglers (490).

Lovecraft's research was thorough, because the Yezidis or Yazidis are an obscure minority group with a unique religion. According to the Minority Rights Group International (2017), the Yezidis have been persecuted by both Ottomans and Kurds for centuries. After Iraq was founded, they remained a minority and the persecution continued. The Yezidis have been victimized by Saddam Hussein, Al Qaeda, and the Islamic State. The similarities end there, because the representation in this story is fictional entertainment, with a focus upon the grotesque, not the humanitarian.

Robert Suydam begins to undergo a transformation "as startling as it was absurd" (491). He starts to shave, loses weight, and dresses well. He is "frequently taken for less than his age" because of "an elasticity of step" and "curious darkening of the hair which somehow did not suggest dye" (491). Suydam appears to be getting younger, which in the horror genre often means that the character is sucking energy out of others, and there is a corresponding "wave of kidnappings and disappearances," which suggests he is acquiring victims (491).

Suddenly, Suydam announces his engagement to "Miss Cornelia Gerritsen of Bayside, a young woman of excellent position, and distantly related to the elderly bridegroom-elect" (492). In the build-up to the wedding there are raids upon the "dance hall church," where nothing was found but "crudely painted panels" depicting "hideous monsters of every shape and size," and ominous cabbalistic writing in red letters, together with "circles and pentagrams" (492–94). This all sets the scene for the most dramatic "red wedding" in popular culture before *Game of Thrones,* season 3, episode 9: "The Rains of Castamere" (see IMDb).

The wedding occurs in "June" (494), when "Flatbush was gay for the hour about high noon" and "pennanted motors thronged the streets," It seemed that "No local event ever surpassed the Suydam–Gerritsen nuptials in tone and scale." The farewell party represents "at least a solid page from the Social Register" and the happy couple ostensibly sets off on a honeymoon cruise to Europe (494). However, as the ocean liner pulls away from the pier, a "tramp steamer" arrives blowing its whistle, and a scream issues from the Suydam cabin (495).

The sailor who opens the door of the cabin goes mad. Investigators find the wife is dead, with a "claw-mark" blazoned on her throat (495). The husband seems to be dead too, and the culprit escapes through "the open porthole." The word "LILITH" is flickering on the wall in "fearsome Chaldee letters," and there are also hints of a cloudy "phosphorescence." The doctor hears a "hellish tittering" but does not see any creature (495). Uniformed Arabs emerge from the tramp steamer to demand possession of the body of Robert Suydam (495–96).

Meanwhile, Malone is conducting a raid on Parker Place in search of missing children. The raiders disperse a group of unidentified residents and find blood, instruments, and gold (497). Malone enters the cellar of Suydam's flat, where he seems to see a door open, followed by a vision of an occult wedding attended by ancient Babylonian and Canaanite beings and "misshapen fauns" (498–502). The Lilith myth is obscure, and like other obscure myths, a source of fascination whenever fleshed out in literature. Wilkinson (24) describes her as "a terrifying goddess of death" associated with Mesopotamian mythology, and a demoness who stole babies.

Malone rationalizes the horror by assuming it is a dream (502). The "realities of the case" include the collapse of "three old houses" that kills a number of police and captives. Malone only survives because he is deep underground, near the "night-black pool" at the end of the people-traffickers' canal (502). Other underground tunnels are discovered leading to crypts beneath the church. A horde of skeletons, "four mothers with infants," and other evidence of human abuse is uncovered (503).

The least satisfying part of the story occurs toward the end, where racism and patriarchy appear to dominate. The Yezidi, who ought to be considered victims, are confirmed unreservedly as "devil-worshippers" (503–4). Moreover, "Robert Suydam sleeps beside his bride in Greenwood Cemetery" (504), a return to conventionality that fails to recognize the consequences of spousal victimization. The conclusion—"As of old, more people enter Red Hook than leave it on the landward side" (505)—is clever, however.

Another writer who perceived the potential for horror at a wedding was George R. R. Martin—an admitted admirer of Lovecraft. In his online journal, "Not a Blog," Martin reports that he "fell in love with monsters and scary stories . . . thanks to a gentleman out of Providence who had died before I was born" ("A Horrifying Announcement"). The scene for horror is set in *Game of Thrones 3: A Storm of Swords: Part 1: Steel and Snow* (2001), where Robb Stark, who was declared "King in the North" by his banner-men (see flashbacks, 276, 280), has broken his promise to marry one of Walder Frey's progeny.

The "marriage contract" had brought around 3,000 knights and another 3,000 foot soldiers into the northern army (195). Unfortunately, Robb impulsively marries the Lady Jeyne Westerling (193), causing him to lose the Frey's alliance (195). This is considered a "grievous insult" (196), and the northerners "must win back the Freys" to have any chance of survival. Robb has decided to offer apologies, gold, land, and an alternative alliance (271).

A new match is arranged between Edmure Tully and Roslin Frey in a bid at appeasement (485–87). It is unlikely to be enough, as the breach of promise is represented in moral terms and not merely as an affair of the heart. Tyrion Lannister, who is the voice of practicality in the book, remarks: "He foreswore himself, shamed an ally, betrayed a solemn promise, where is the honor in that?" (271).

The story continues in *Game of Thrones 3: A Storm of Swords: Part 2: Blood and Gold* (2001), when the family set off to attend the wedding. Catelyn Stark warns Robb to "tread lightly" (53–54). She also suggests that he eat some food so as to acquire the protection of "guest right" (100). Upon arrival, Grey Wind, Robbs's dire-wolf, senses danger and has to be restrained. Robb makes his public apology, admitting: "All men should keep their word, kings most of all" (106). The visitors eat bread and cheese, which gives them a false sense of security and builds suspense (106–8).

As the wedding commences, the drums are pounding and Catelyn's head is aching (122). After the feast, Walder Frey orders the "bedding" ritual to progress (128). The drums are still beating, and Edwyn Frey rudely refuses a lady's invitation to dance. Suddenly, the band begins playing "The Rains of Castamere," an enemy theme song. Amicable members of the Frey family are missing, and Catelyn wonders why the bride cried. She touches Edwyn Frey and feels armor concealed under his clothing (131).

As Catelyn raises an outcry, Robb is shot with a "quarrel," and the Stark party are horrifically pierced with arrows amidst the remains of the banquet (131). The door opens and men with axes enter. Catelyn attempts to shield herself behind Walder Frey's intellectually disabled grandson. Then she cuts the youth's throat. Someone severs Catelyn's neck in return. The mother's point of view fades (132–33).

Outside, Arya Stark survives because Sandor Clegane, also known as "the hound," prevents her from entering the Frey compound (135–36). The pair see tents burning and battle-exiting Frey men. "The Rains of Castamere" continues to play like a screen direction as the pair bolt away on a horse (136–38).

In the following chapters, a coded message is delivered to the Lannisters, generating a reiteration of the horror from several new perspectives (142, 149). The signature appellative "The Red Wedding" is invoked when Salladhor Saan reports the incident to rival king Stannis Baratheon (151). The term "red wedding" will become a catch-phrase among fans.

Both tales present scenes of explicit and visceral horror, but Lovecraft and Martin work within different genre conventions. Lovecraft favors the tightly structured detective story, pioneering gangland motifs and a dark grimy atmosphere that would be adopted by the noir films of the 1940s. (See Doll and Faller for a definition of noir.) Martin's "A Song of Ice and Fire" series would be classified as high fantasy because it involves kings and battles, as well as dragons and necromancers. The story has no detective, only seekers after survival, yet the constant machinations create suspense, and its dark scenes are also somewhat noir.

The two tales have a number of motifs in common. For example, in both instances the wedding is a trap. Lovecraft has employed the traditional joining of husband and wife and expectations of cohabitation and patriarchal assumption of possession by the husband to enable Suydam to acquire an unsuspecting victim. Martin cleverly utilizes the obligation of attendance to bring a large number of the Stark allies into the Frey compound, and harnesses the expectations of courtesy to render them vulnerable to ambush.

The ritual desecration of bodies features in both tales. In "The Horror at Red Hook" privateers drain blood from the corpse of Mrs. Suydam and then ferry Suydam's body into the tunnels (495–96). In *A Storm of Swords: Part 2,* Robb's corpse is beheaded and the direwolf's head is sewn onto his body, while Catelyn's remains are dumped into the river (151).

The two tales both involve post-mortal animation. Suydam's letter appears to indicate that he expects to have agency after his death, referring to making explanations "later" (496), although the result appears transitory. The televised version of *Game of Thrones* abandoned Cately Stark's narrative at that point in season 3, episode 9, leaving her dead. However, the "Epilogue" of *A Storm of Swords: Part 2: Blood and Gold* introduces a more horrific element, an undead agent of death leading a band of "outlaws":

> . . . her face was even worse than he remembered. The flesh had gone pudding soft in the water and turned the colour of curdled milk. Half her hair was gone . . . her face was shredded skin and black blood. But her eyes were the most terrible thing. Her eyes saw him and they hated. (553)

Although sentient, the revenant Catelyn cannot speak, because the "bastards cut her throat too deep for that" (*Part 2,* 553–54). Motivated by grief, Lady Stark has undergone a descent into moral decay, including kidnapping an innocent Tyrion Lannister (*Part 1,* 481) and committing "treason" by countermanding Robb's arrangements (*Part 1,* 33–34). Moreover, one of the sources of resurrection in the book is the cult of R'hllor, a fire god also known as "the Lord of Light" (*Part 1,* 535) According to Chalakoski, Martin may have based his fantasy on ancient Persian mythology. These factors combine to make Catelyn a Lilith-like figure and represent a bold, post-Lovecraftian stroke.

Both stories appear to predicate a cycle of violence. The final paragraphs of "The Horror at Red Hook" make it clear that the gangland crime wave will continue, as Lovecraft aptly asks the rhetorical question, "Who are we" to think to change it? (505). *A Storm of Swords: Part 2* ends with Merrett Frey jerking at the end of a rope (554). Martin has made it clear that Merrett was an insignificant member of the Frey clan, a "*ninth* son" (*Part 2*, 545), and the horrific reprisal has just begun.

In conclusion, both "The Horror at Red Hook" by H. P. Lovecraft and "The Red Wedding" sequence in George R. R. Martin's *Game of Thrones* utilize a nuptial celebration in order to create graphic horror. Expectations of renewal and reconciliation effectively give way to perversions of blood and death. Both tales draw upon ancient Mesopotamian mythology and share the motifs of post-morbid vigor. Lovecraft's genre is the short story, while Martin writes a lengthy fantasy series, but both strive to maximize the elements of shock and sensationalism.

Works Cited

Chalakoski, Martin. "George R. R. Martin Hinted That the Lord of Light in 'Game of Thrones' Based on Ancient Zoroastrianism of Persia." *Vintage News*, 2017 (accessed 27 May 2021) from www.thevintagenews.com/2017/07/19/george-r-r-martin-hinted-that-the-lord-of-light-in-game-of-thrones-based-on-ancient-zoroastrianism-of-persia/.

Doll, S., and G. Faller. "*Blade Runner* and Genre: Film Noir and Science Fiction." Scraps from the Loft, reprinted from *Literature Film Quarterly* 14, No. 2 (1986): 89–100, accessed 26 May 2021 from scrapsfromtheloft.com/2018/02/14/blade-runner-and-genre-film-noir-and-science-fiction/.

IMDb. *Game of Thrones,* season 3, episode 9: "The Rains of Casta-mere." IMDb.com, accessed 24 May 2021 from www.imdb.com/title/tt2178784/

Lovecraft, H. P. *Collected Fiction: A Variorum Edition.* Ed. S. T. Joshi. New York: Hippocampus Press, 2015–17. 4 vols.

———. *Letters to Elizabeth Toldridge and Anne Tillery Renshaw,* ed. David E. Schultz and S. T. Joshi. New York: Hippocampus Press, 2014.

Martin, George R. R. *Game of Thrones 3: A Storm of Swords: Part 1: Steel and Snow.* 2001. Book Three Part One of *A Song of Ice and Fire.* London: Harper Voyager, 2013.

———. *Game of Thrones 3: A Storm of Swords: Part 2: Blood and Gold,* 2001. Book Three Part Two of *A Song of Ice and Fire.* London: Harper Voyager, 2011.

———. "A Horrifying Announcement." In "Not a Blog", Live Journal, accessed 25 May 2021 from grrm.livejournal.com/534795.html.

Minority Rights Group International. "Iraq—Yezidis." *World Directory of Minorities and Indigenous Peoples* (2017), accessed 25 May 2021 from minorityrights.org/minorities/yezidis/.

Wilkinson, Philip. *Illustrated Dictionary of Mythology: Heroes, Heroines, Gods and Goddesses from Around the World.* London: Dorling Kindersley, 1999.

China Miéville's "Säcken": Folk Horror, New Weird, and Gender Politics

Deborah Bridle

"Säcken" is a short story written by British writer China Miéville, published in his collection *Three Moments of an Explosion* in 2015. In that collection, "the formats range from classic short stories to fictional movie trailers, from reports and observations, to rules and manifestos, and finally flash fiction" (Scholz, "Three Moments"), while the genres cover fantasy, surrealism, SF, horror, and realism. China Miéville is usually categorised as an SF/F author—a wide spectrum that barely covers the bulk of his work, which tends to resist classification by always reinventing itself.

"Säcken" belongs to the realm of folk horror, with its eerie setting by the lake of a German forest and its haunting monster. It tells the story of a British lesbian couple, Mel and Joanna, who rent a house by the aforementioned lake so that Joanna, a scholar, can work on her research project on the history of Dresden. While Joanna works, Mel goes rowing on the lake every day, until she disturbs a presence deep down. That presence first takes the form of a large misshapen object that later attacks Mel in her room at night. This prompts her to go back to London, terrified, leaving Joanna behind. A few days later, when Joanna goes missing and the boat is found empty on the lake, Mel decides to go back to Germany to discover what the monster is and to prevent it from causing more harm. After some detective and research work, she understands the object is a large sack, the one that contained the last person to have ever been executed by *poena cullei*, a Roman type of death penalty. In 1734, a woman found guilty of infanticide was sewn up in a large sack along with three live animals and thrown into the lake. Mel then tries to understand what the woman in the sack wants after all those years, and the story focuses on her trial and error until one final encounter with the monster.

In this article, my point will be to show how Miéville uses folk horror as a means to explore womanhood in a story entirely focused on women, in which they play the roles of victim, killer, monster, hero, and detective. As is frequent in Miéville's work, "Säcken" is loaded with a political subtext, one that allows the author to explore social and political dynamics of gender in the context of fourth-wave feminism.

I. Woman as the Locus of Horror

A. The Poena Cullei—A Punishment against Womanhood

The first written accounts of the *poena cullei* date back to 100 B.C.E. It translates to "penalty of the sack" and consisted of sewing up victims in a large sack before throwing them into the river or the sea. There was no mention of any live animals at the time. The *Lex Pompeia de Parricidiis,* a Roman law promulgated around 55 B.C.E., establishes the *poena cullei* as the punishment for the crime of parricide and makes a clear distinction between the murder of the father and any other type of murder, the latter being seen as a private crime that needed to be punished privately by the family of the victim. According to historian Yan Thomas, "the murder of the father is a public crime which involves the city for prosecution and punishment because it endangers the essential foundation of the Roman legal order" (abstract; my translation). With time, the punishment itself became further refined, the animals being added one by one—a dog, a cock, a monkey, and a viper. The *poena cullei* then fell out of use until it was revived by the Emperor Constantine (r. 306–37 C.E.), and it was extended to cover infanticide. The Emperor Justinian (r. 527–65) then reinstituted the penalty two hundred years later. It remained the typical punishment for parricides (which included the murder of a son or daughter) for about four hundred years, before it was replaced with being burned alive. It then knew a final revival in late medieval and early modern Germany, especially in Saxony. The last documented instance of the *poena cullei* tells of a 1734 case in Saxony, when a woman was executed for having killed her child or children (see Radin 122, Grimm 696, and Meumann 113).

This historical case is Miéville's starting point for "Säcken." In an interview, the author talks about his interest in "questions of law and taboo" and the "internalization of . . . social mores," and the way people always find new ways of breaching taboos (Schmeink 5). The murder of one's parent or child is a powerful taboo, one that was regarded as deserving a punishment like the *poena cullei*. The striking element here is the fact that the penalty crossed over from pagan times to the Christian era. Scholars such as Ronald Hutton (17) and Tanya Krzywinska (58) have noted this phenomenon of assimilation and absorption regarding pagan rituals and festivities. But it might be argued that a highly ritualized and symbolism-heavy execution method is relatively different from the celebrations usually studied. Interestingly, the forests of Saxony lend a very rural tone to the story in which the emergence of the ancient *poena cullei* is reminiscent of the British folk horror films of the 1960s, where "the countryside is more than simply a pretty backdrop for the action, as it is linked to the evocation of pre-Christian agrarian religious practices" (Krzywinska 78). Therefore, making the last instance of the *poena cullei* the keystone of the story enables Miéville to explore the question of taboo in a context that blends together ancient and Christian law, while the ritualistic aspect of the punishment allows the tropes of folk horror to develop in an alien rural environment. When Mel reads about the *poena cullei* for the first time, the syntax that associates anaphora and hyperbaton strongly emphasizes the central role played by the punishment and its oppressive heaviness: "This punishment, she read in the dark. [. . .] This punishment, she slowly read. [. . .] This punishment, she read, was last imposed in Germany in the eighteenth century. The punishment, she read, of a woman for infanticide in Saxony" (161–62).

The very particular specifics of the *poena cullei* have puzzled historians over the centuries. According to Max Radin, it was "not an apparatus of horror intended to act as a deterrent influence, but a religious ritual." He further defines the punishment as a *"procuratio prodigii*—a disposal of a thing of evil portent" (120). As mentioned earlier, *parricidium* was no mere murder: it threatened the foundations of society by attacking a symbol of authority and founding element of the family. Therefore, "the perpetrator was not merely a criminal amenable to punishment, but a foul thing, unclean, causing the gods to withdraw their presence from a world he polluted, and requiring therefore hasty removal from the world in such a manner as to remove at the same time the miasma his body would inevitably spread" (Radin 120). For Yan Thomas, "parricide is a taint of which the city as a community purifies itself through a rite of expulsion which involves, actually and symbolically, the whole of the community" (704). Indeed, it was believed that separating the culprit from the fundamental elements in life *and* in death was a way to cut them off completely, as shown by this account written by Marcus Tullius Cicero:

> They would not expose his body to wild beasts, lest we should find them more savage for having touched such wickedness; they would not throw them, naked as they were, into the river, lest, when they were carried down to the sea, they should defile that element by which all else that is defiled is supposed to be cleansed; there is, in fact, nothing so worthless and common that they would leave them any share of it. For, what is there so common as air to the living, earth to the dead, the sea to what floats, the shore to what is washed up? They live, while they can, in such a way that they cannot draw breath from the air; they die under such conditions that the earth cannot come in contact with their bones; they are thrown about by the waves so that they never can be cleansed; they are so cast ashore, that they cannot, in death, find rest even on the rocks. (24)

The meaning of the animals and the reason for their inclusion in the ritual is not clear, all the more so as some of them may vary from time to time: sometimes fewer than four were used; sometimes the monkey, which would have been an expensive addition, was replaced by a cat; and sometimes a token was used to represent the animal that could not be procured. This is what presumably happened to the woman in "Säcken," since Mel finds a piece of wood bearing on one side the carving of a monkey. Max Radin, after offering suggestions as to the symbolic function of each individual animal, rather proposes for them all an expiatory and apotropaic purpose linked to a religious mindset, which seems to further the aforementioned ritual of expulsion and purification: "If a ritual function rather than a purely symbolic one is to be sought, . . . such a function is not hard to imagine. These animals may be a means of carrying off the pollution of the crime. It is a familiar belief that animals can do so, that they may be or may become the physical incarnations of sin. Thus by expelling the animal the sin is removed" (129). As if the imprisonment in the sack were not enough to make sure that the culprit would be truly cast off by separating them from the elements, the animals were added to allow for a transfer of the evil forces the victim carried in them. This understanding of ritual is what Barbara Creed develops in her analysis of horror films through the prism of Julia Kristeva's concept of the abject: "Ritual becomes a means by which societies both renew their initial contact with the abject element and then exclude that element. Through ritual, the demarcation lines between the human and non-human are drawn up anew and presumably made all the stronger for that process" (51).

In that sense, the *poena cullei* can be construed as more than a legal punishment: it is a sacrifice that the community makes for the sake of its surviving members. In Tanya Krzywinska's description of sacrifice—abduction/rescue vs. sacrifice/restitution—the *poena cullei* belongs to the second mode of representation, which entails the reestablishment of the natural or supernatural order. With the advent of Christianity, it was sin that needed to be driven out of the community, but the outrage to the gods that parricide represented for the Romans is not all that different from the taint of sin that corrupts a man's soul for the Christians. But what about a woman's soul? For Barbara Creed, the "definition of sin/abjection as something which comes from *within* opens up the way to position woman as deceptively treacherous. . . . It is this stereotype of feminine evil . . . that is so popular within patriarchal discourses about woman's evil nature" (166–67). For what could be more evil than a woman murdering her child?

B. The Woman as Witch—Seeing the Woman as Antagonist

In the story, women are constructed in opposition to men, not so much in terms of a conflictual mode as in terms of a fundamental difference. Similarly to what Carol Clover sees in the film *I Spit on Your Grave*, "Säcken" offers a transition from a city-vs.-countryside axis to a female-vs.-male axis (see Clover 121). Miéville plays with stereotypical assumptions on men and women, and at the same time embraces a complex picture of the latter. First of all, he toys with the common image of woman as an emotional and fragile creature, mostly as Mel is the only one who ever sees the monster, which prompts people around her to think she has been dreaming at best, or her sanity is impaired at worst.[1] Joanna even compares Mel to Alice in her boat, thereby increasing the shroud of doubt around the objective existence of what Mel sees. The fact that Mel is unable to describe her first encounter with the sack only heightens her unreliability in the eyes of others, and her adamant but impossible-to-justify wish that she and Joanna immediately return to London makes her sound on the verge of hysteria—a potent word that Miéville does not use but whose spectre he manages to convey around Mel.[2] In her various encounters with the monster, her reactions correspond to what Carol Clover defines as "gendered feminine" emotional displays: "angry displays of force may belong to the

---

1. See Clover 73: In horror films, female characters are in general more prone to believe in the supernatural than the male ones.
2. At various points in the story, Mel sounds crazy to Joanna because she is unable to explain what she saw and is seized with uncontrollable panic (156, 158, 166).

male, but crying, cowering, screaming, fainting, trembling, begging for mercy belong to the female" (51).

Until Mel's first meeting with the sack, which causes Mel's estrangement from Joanna, the two of them also stand apart from men because of their sexual orientation and their autonomy as individuals and as a couple without any need for men. This independence can take on the form of a statement—as when Mel tells Joanna that she should focus her research on Maria Aurora, King Augustus' mistress, rather than the monarch himself—or be the material of a shared form of humor between the two women—for instance when they joke about the double meaning of 'cock':

> "There's some chippy little cockerel around here," Mel said.
> "Das ist der countryside. Are you surprised?"
> "I don't know from cocks," Mel said. (150)

They stand outside of the common social structure that is expected of women, something of which they are aware. When they visit a small Saxon town, their social status as urban foreign unmarried gay couple is presented as alien from the one that defines local women:

> A middle-aged woman in a saggy dress nodded to the tall young Englishwoman.
> "Spying on the locals?" Joanna said.
> "Just greeting the polite Fräulein."
> "Frau, I feel certain," said Joanna. (144)

After Joanna's disappearance, Mel is even more isolated as she is confronted by traditional male figures of authority: the detective in charge of the investigation, the priest whom she calls to preside a ceremony by the lake for the executed woman, as well as the neighbor who has reported Joanna missing. The reader was introduced to him and his wife before during one of Mel's outings on the lake,[3] but as the person invested with power and authority in the structure

---

3. Only the woman waves back at Mel when they see her (149): could the man not approve of Mel and Joanna's relationship?

of the family, he is the one who goes to check inside the women's house when the boat is found empty in the middle of the lake.

As Phoenix Scholz writes in an analysis of the concept of queerversity in Miéville's fiction,

> Problems arise whenever power is consolidated as authority—with structural or institutionally legitimated hierarchies directing or blocking existing power dynamics—and whenever power relations are dominated by violence. . . . Symbolic or normative violence takes form in discrimination, in hierarchies of values, and in reactions of rejection based on the inability to acknowledge and/or understand certain experiences and ways of living. . . . Symbolic violence, for instance, often takes the form of classification and normative violence then assigns these classifications values such as 'normal'/'abnormal'—establishing boundaries of inclusion and exclusion and thus legitimising social practices of regulation, discipline, criminalisation or pathologisation. ("Queerversity")

In "Säcken," women are seen as subjected to those "legitimated hierarchies," whether it be through Mel's and Joanna's relationship, through the dismissal of what Mel saw, or through her having to resort to male figures of authority and apparent knowledge. However, Miéville subverts those socially established hierarchies by having Mel understand what the monster is on her own. Mel is able to do that through research, but also because of the way she feels and perceives the environment around her, the way she responds to the physicality of the water, its touch and its smell, and the sound of the wind. In his paper "Spiritual Embodiment and Sacred Rural Landscapes," Julian Holloway opposes this focus on "embodied and felt nature" to "ocularcentric theories of landscapes," which rest on "a disembodied eye viewing the world from a vantage point . . .—a visual framing which constitutes and confirms certain ideological and hegemonic positions (patriarchal and bourgeois for example)" (163). For Holloway, the body is a legitimate actor in the creation of thought and knowledge which, when turned toward perceiving the landscape, allows "a dialectical relation where . . . the landscape speaks back to or performs to the spiritual seekers" (168). Because she acts as a spiritual seeker who engages with the setting with her body and senses, Mel is able to understand the rural landscape and to unravel the mystery it hides.

This power also gives her a mystical aura that draws her closer to the figure of the witch, the ultimate female outcast. This link between Mel and the natural world around her makes her kin to the sorceresses of the past. Mel's mischievousness, especially when compared to Joanna's more down-to-earth and rational disposition, gives her an impish air and draws the picture of an unpredictable woman who does not wish to conform to the rules. Twice in the story, the narrator also describes an animal presence in her, as when she pretends to be a cat to amuse Joanna and she curls up in an armchair next to her (147), or when she hisses back at a real cat (168). Furthermore, according to Barbara Creed,

> the witch is defined as an abject figure in that she is represented within patriarchal discourses as an implacable enemy of the symbolic order. She is thought to be dangerous and wily, capable of drawing on her evil powers to wreak destruction on the community. The witch sets out to unsettle boundaries between the rational and the irrational, symbolic and imaginary. Her evil powers are seen as part of her 'feminine' nature; she is closer to nature than man and can control forces in nature such as tempests, hurricanes and storms. (283)

Mel's ability to perceive the natural world around her can therefore be seen as "evil powers" that are part of her "feminine nature," but the unnamed victim of the *poena cullei* is the one who causes the disruptions in the weather and the atmosphere, establishing her as the primal witch in the story. Her status as "enemy of the symbolic order" and "the community" can be linked to Tanya Krzywinska's observation: the figure of the witch is associated with fantasies that "enable sex to be wrested from the hegemonic constraints of seeing it as part of the heterosexual romance, an expression of romantic love and a means of making a family" (123). Mel is the embodiment of such a fantasy, but even more so she is the victim of the sack. Because she has murdered her child, she has tried to escape society's constraints on womanhood. The link between witchcraft and infanticide is noted by Krzywinska, who sees the sorceress Medea's murder of her children as a way to hurt patriarchy.[4] Mel has committed a sin against the family and against social order by choosing not to conform to the role that was expected of her. According to Krzywinska, the witch's narcissism goes against the ideal of motherhood, which demands that women sacrifice themselves for their children. When the unnamed woman of the story decides to go against what society expects of her, she constitutes herself as witch, as a threat to patriarchy that needs to be eradicated in a way that allows the community to cleanse itself from her taint.

II. Universalizing the Experience

A. Subverting the Genre

Miéville therefore manages to make the woman's traumatic fate in the sack universal. He does so by filling in, then subverting the reader's expectations of the genre, moving beyond the boundaries of horror. In his Introduction to *Folk Horror Revival: Field Studies*, Andy Paciorek uses Adam Scovell's "chain of elements that comprise a Folk Horror film." Even though we are dealing with literature, the same guidelines can be used for our understanding of folk horror in the written form. Those elements are "landscape, isolation, skewed moral beliefs, and happening/summoning" (13–14). Although folk horror may be found in an urban setting, its most frequent occurrences happen in a rural environment, corresponding to what David Bell names "anti-idyll" (94). "Säcken" immediately starts on foreign land, in the vicinity of Dresden, and German towns are soon left

---

4. See Krzywinska: "The act of infanticide is intended to hit the patriarchal order through its most sensitive point—patrilinearity—and is meant to cause deep and irrevocable anguish" (107).

behind and replaced with a wild landscape of forests. Tony Venezia notes that Miéville always establishes a special focus on space, whether it be through the creation of imaginary realms or the "doubling of contemporary London" (204). "Säcken" offers a different type of environment, but one that nonetheless furthers the author's "spatial focus." The place is characterized by its alterity from the city, as seen through the description of the women's trip in the first page of the story: "They left the city and drove on busy roads for more than an hour through diminishing satellite towns. Then through smaller towns still and a rolling damp landscape" (144). The gradation based on comparative forms establishes at the same time Scovell's second element of folk horror: isolation. As they drive, the landscape is "thick with trees" and "small rivers" (144), and as soon as the lake can be glimpsed, it clearly becomes the highlight of the setting, the jewel in the midst of a lush countryside. But when they arrive on the property they have rented, Mel ironically declares: "That can't go wrong, [...] a gate in the middle of the country. We'll be fine" (145), a tongue-in-cheek comment on the propensity of horror stories to take place in secluded and rural settings.

According to Dawn Keetley, the main source of conflict in folk horror is not religious but spatial: "the less overt yet actually *much more important* conflict involves humans and their natural environment." She sees the landscape as an active agent, which is something that clearly happens in "Säcken": the lake is invested with a strong *genius loci*, a spiritual presence that is first hinted at proleptically when Joanna compares Mel to Alice in her boat (145). The episode she refers to is the one from *Through the Looking Glass* when Alice keeps catching crabs with her oars, a nautical expression meaning that her oars get stuck in the water because of her improper method of rowing. Alice does not understand the meaning of the expression and wishes she had brought the crab to the surface to take home with her. This is exactly what Mel will unwittingly do after disturbing the presence in the lake: take it back home with her.

It does not take long for the lake to become the active agent of landscape referred to by Dawn Keetley, both figuratively and literally. For instance, when Mel plunges her hand in the dark water, the lexical field used by the narrator is one of willing aggression on the part of the water: "The lake was green and silty. Mel reached into it. Her skin disappeared. Even in the sunlight the dark water amputated her hand only a few centimetres down" (149). A more literal action on the part of the landscape is the repeated impression that the lake is surging, that something is coming up from below, coupled with the rising of the wind and of a damp smell. This idea that something is lurking deep down is a manifestation of Miéville's fascination with what he calls "exabyssalism" or "eruchtonousness" ("An A-Z of China Miéville"), two terms describing the moment a dweller from the depths of water or the earth emerges on the surface, a moment of breach that is often the vehicle for horror.

Scovell's third element of folk horror, skewed moral beliefs, is exemplified through the past practice of the *poena cullei*. For Carol Clover, many horror stories start with "the visit or move of (sub)urban people to the country," to places "where the rules of civilization do not obtain" (124). In "Säcken," this countryside/city axis exists,[5] but the civilizational shift plays on a time divide. This corresponds to the point made by Matilda Groves in her paper "Past Anxieties: Defining the Folk Horror Narrative," in which she argues that folk horror "takes the reader away from the modern world, either by setting the story in the past, or by unfolding the protagonist's tragic journey in a sub-reality based on archaic traditions, or morals out of place with the contemporary conscience." This is what happens to Mel when she discovers the *poena cullei*, a practice so

---

5. See for example how Mel tries to "win over the shopkeeper" in a small town by speaking a few words in German, with no success (144). The word "local," used by Joanna to refer to the inhabitants of the town, establishes a distinction between them and the two women. Mel is not wearing appropriate shoes for the countryside (145) and is often seen as urban and new to this kind of environment.

horrifying for our civilization's standards and mindset that she is convinced the woman had not deserved this punishment, no matter what she had done.

Finally, the happening/summoning element is central to "Säcken," where it takes the form of the return of the woman in the sack. She can be seen as ghost, monster, perhaps even invocation if we decide to believe that it is Mel who has stirred up the lake and called her. The first eerie manifestation takes place when Mel finds a piece of wood by the lake. She does not know yet that the wood token represents a monkey and that the law allowed one of the animals to be replaced by drawings or carvings for the *poena cullei*. As she picks it up, "Mel stood quickly and swayed, dizzy. She shook her head at a sudden smell, and then the wind came in and brought a much worse gust" (148). The wind and the smell, associated to the crowing of the cockerel, will from this point onward announce the presence from the lake, one that reveals itself gradually, adding to the slow mounting of horror through the atmosphere. Those elements gradually become stronger and closer until the first apparition of the sack in Mel and Joanna's room one night.[6] The vision is a textbook thing of horror, characterized by its alterity, its hybridity, its abnormality, and its menace; it is a picture of abnormal excess supported by the use of polysyndetons, asyndetons, alliterations, assonances, and consonances to mark its hyperbolic and horrific nature:

> Something was on the floor.
> A darkness. A gross misshape.
> Something huge *and* wrong *and* wet. It blocked her way. Mel's throat closed. The new thing in the room dripped.

---

6. The multiple references to the sound of the cockerel are a good example of this gradation (149, 150, 151, 153, the sound getting closer and closer each time). Sounds are a crucial vehicle of terror in the story—as when a hiss and a snarl are added to the ominous crowing sound in the women's bedroom (153)—but other senses are used in a similar way (in the same scene, the room is invaded by a pungent stench and an atmosphere of moistness, while liquid sounds are added to those of the animals (154).

A nightmare calf born without limbs *or* head *or* eyes but full of tumours. A mound of leather in polling water. It was a bag, a sack full of bad presents, of coal *or* earth *or* bl<u>oo</u>d cl<u>o</u>ts *or* ruined roots.

The bl<u>ack</u> <u>sack</u> moved.

It shoved from within with *a* <u>s</u>ucking <u>s</u>ound, *a* <u>s</u>lurping. It lurched heavily toward her, spattering the floorboards.

A fitful dark groping, hauling her way. Its weight and spasming motion shook the room. I<u>t</u> <u>s</u>trained as if <u>t</u>o <u>s</u>pli<u>t</u>.

The thing had voices. *A* cluck, *a* hiss, *a* predator's growl. It slopped closer still and Mel heard a woman.

Mel heard a woman vomit old water. She heard it <u>s</u>patter on the in<u>s</u>ide of the <u>s</u>kin. The <u>s</u>ack convul<u>s</u>ed in mud that should not have been brought up. Kikeriki, whispered the rooster inside the bag with its throat full of lake.

The thing came with a scratch of claws, pushed through its own hide into the floor. It whispered. . . . Cluck cluck the sack went *and* hiss *and* growl *and* nein *and* it came close *and* it reached for her, so <u>c</u>lose she <u>c</u>ould <u>s</u>ee i<u>ts</u> wounds, <u>c</u>riss<u>c</u>ross <u>s</u>u<u>t</u>ures <u>t</u>aut-ening as the leather <u>s</u>tre<u>tch</u>ed, as if the <u>s</u>ack would bur<u>st</u>.

She screamed. (154–55)[7]

However, Miéville uses but subverts at the same time certain of the tropes of horror and folk horror, which is a feature of the New Weird genre. Despite being a rather loose and hard-to-define category, the New Weird is, according to Simon Barton, "a clarion call against the codification of protocols" and clichés that have come to develop in science fiction and fantasy. Just like the weird, the New Weird "appears to exist in the liminal zones, occupying different generic territories simultaneously." China Miéville states that the "New Weird—like most literary categories—is a moment, a suggestion, a tease, an intervention, an attitude, and above all, an argument" (quoted in McCalmont). The New Weird label has been dismissed by many writers who had come to identify themselves as

---

7. Polysyndetons and asyndetons are marked in italics, while assonances, consonances and alliterations are marked as underlined characters (our addition).

representatives of the movement, including Miéville, the tag having become a marketing tool according to them. But it does not diminish the relevance of its definition, which supports our analysis of "Säcken" as a renewed vision of folk horror. Miéville himself has often spoken against an easy and clear-cut distinction of genres[8] and he likes to play with and subvert traditional genre-related codes because he likes to surprise and unsettle his readers.

This component of surprise and unexpectedness can be found in the treatment of landscape and the feeling of isolation mentioned above. Mel feels that she has to go back to Germany and to the lake in order to appease the ghost because the horror is clearly associated with the spirit of the place. However, after she thinks she has managed to banish or calm the monster back into dormancy or eternal rest, she moves back to London, where the sack finds its way to her flat in the final pages of the story. The horror is no longer associated with rurality, nor is it bound to secluded places. It is also a subversion of the basic assumptions of ghost stories in general, according to which a specter is supposed to haunt a significant place, mostly the place where it died or where it lived.

Secondly, we can be tempted to consider Mel an archetype of Carol Clover's Final Girl: her masculine name, her resourcefulness, her being incessantly chased by the killer and her apparent prevailing against it make her a strong representative of the victim/hero as Clover analyzes her.[9] However, her victory is short-lived and the story closes on her probably being devoured by the sack. All the detective work that Mel achieves and that seems to give her a progressive understanding of the killer also makes the reader believe that

---

8. As in an interview by Cheryl Morgan in which Miéville says, "I don't think it's a question of 'deliberately' setting out to confound boundaries, it's a question of these boundaries were never the boundaries they thought they were, and so it's not me that's doing anything, it's the boundaries that were never stable, I think."
9. See the following pages in Clover for more detail on the figure of the Final Girl: x, xi, 39, 40, 63.

she is going to be able to appease the monster. Miéville cleverly releases information sporadically, placing us in Mel's shoes, only mentioning the *poena cullei* rather late in the story, after Mel has seen the monster and Joanna has disappeared. As readers and film viewers, we are used to seeing detective work rewarded in the end with the arrest or killing of the villain, but this is not what happens here for a very simple and crucial reason: the sack's motive is impenetrable, and the sack is therefore unstoppable.

This is where the true force of the story resides and what makes it so striking. Throughout the second half of the story, Mel tries to understand what the sack wants so that she can provide it for it and stop its murderous haunting. From the very first time she has met the ghost, she has felt a lack coming from the being, something missing.[10] Because of that impression, Mel assumes that the ghost wants something: "What do you want? Mel asked in her head. Revenge. She imagined answers from the sack. Justice. Company. My child. A retrial. None of those was what the woman had whispered for" (163). Nonetheless, she tries to give her something, starting with a Christian ceremony performed by a priest, "a prayer for the convicted woman, a plea to let her rest" (165). The strong wind that rises then tells her this is not the answer, "as if the woman was telling her to fuck off with her priest" (166). Her thoughts race and she thinks of hiring a lawyer to declare a mistrial (166), before turning to the symbolism of the animals. As she tries to make sense of it, she remembers the wood token she has discarded: maybe this is what the woman wants, to retrieve what the sack has lost? "The poena did not want justice. It wanted completion" (168). Since she cannot find the token that she threw away, Mel decides to give something else as she still tries to understand this lack, its purpose: "Perhaps the image had always been inadequate, had not been lost but spat out

---

10. Fortunately, as Phoenix Scholz notes in their reading of the story, Miéville does not fall for the easy and tempting psychoanalytical interpretation of what that woman might be lacking, in spite of the cock jokes placed here and there ("Three Moments").

for her to find. The sack reaching not for that token but for the nearest primate. Considering her. . . . There has to be a life, Mel thought, to fill that lack. That's how ghosts are made" (168). Just like the reader, Mel relies on her assumptions of what a ghost is and what a ghost wants. Having read that animals could be substituted for others in the ancient times when the penalty was used, she captures a cat and offers it as a sacrifice to the lake, to the sack.

Because horror is a "convention-bound" genre that relies on repetition (Clover 212), Mel assumes she has succeeded in her mission because she repeats things she has seen and heard before. She is as guilty as certain feminist critics if we are to believe Donato Totaro, for whom

> Much auto-feminist criticism points to the fact that there is no pleasurable room for female spectatorship, or more directly, does not address how the horror film may speak to female empowerment. Most feminist recuperations of the horror genre entail shifting the emphasis from . . . a male/Oedipal sadistic position to a female/Pre-Oedipal masochistic position. But when this happens, as in Barbara Creed's the monstrous-feminine, the "vagina-dentata," is still only an externalized reflection of male anxiety and fear of the female. The deeper problem resides in the built-in patriarchy of depending on a Freudian psychoanalytical model, where an active or powerful woman is nothing but a "masculinized" woman (or a closet lesbian).

"Female empowerment" is precisely what "Säcken" is about and what Mel completely fails to acknowledge. As she tries to calm the woman down into silence, she is also, in her way, conforming to the patriarchal model that inflicted the exact same penalty on her. The model that Mel is repeating may not be the Freudian psychoanalytical one mentioned by Totaro, but she is still perpetuating the law of patriarchy.

B. Gender Politics

There is therefore a problem of repetition in the horrific trauma that is at the heart of "Säcken," one that is first and foremost linked to the question of time. As Julian Holloway notes, certain landscapes can be said to hold an "excess of history," and he terms this "mapping of multifold history and the temporal reach of some of these representations" *"deep time"* (162). The lake certainly belongs to those history-saturated locations, and the woman's execution exerts a temporal reach all the way to Mel's present. Matilda Groves sees this resurgence of the past as one of the key features of folk horror, in which "the threat remains near to our homes, where we believe we are safe. . . . Folk horror . . . encapsulate[s] our shared anxiety of history repeating itself."

Indeed, the sack's murderous behavior seems at first to be one of repetition—the woman was executed for having killed her child, and now she kills for revenge against her executioners. Even though she is the one who murdered first, she is one of those female killers who, in the tradition of horror, seem justified in their actions. As Carol Clover explains, the second wave of feminism allowed for the role of women to expand in the horror genre, making possible the figure of the victim-hero (the Final Girl), and even complex female killers. According to her, female killers in horror are different from the males because the motive for their killing is usually linked to a specific trauma in their lives, rather than the psychosexual motive that usually characterizes murders by men. Clover even states: "cause a girl enough pain, repress enough of her rage, and—no matter how fundamentally decent she may be—she perforce becomes a witch" (71). Aviva Briefel reaches the same conclusion on male vs. female killers (20).

The real culprit in "Säcken" is therefore patriarchy and the law it imposes on women. No matter what the woman did to her child, Mel feels that she did not deserve the punishment she received, and it becomes clear that the monster haunting the story has in fact been created by patriarchy. For Phoenix Scholz, "Miéville is at his very best [in "Säcken"], showing us how Law is the monster, that torture and murder in the name of justice is the monster" ("Three Moments"). Making the readers empathize with the monster is, of course, not new, and monsters have always been used for varying purposes by horror makers, including one of social and/or political criticism (see for instance Creed 230). When the monster is female, the possibilities are multiplied and there is still much debate around whether the horror genre perpetuates misogyny or promotes feminism.[11] For instance, witchcraft is commonly seen as a way to criticize patriarchy and male authority, and witches were usually associated to figures of the counter-culture in the 1960s, but they are frequently vanquished at the end of the story (see Harmes 73, Krzywinska 60, 65). This is where the New Weird can shed a new light on horror. Simon Barton highlights the New Weird's embrace of contemporary concerns as well as its disruptive potential: "a key characteristic of the New Weird is an engagement with the future and a protean urge to never be pinned down to a single explanation or definition" (4). Because the New Weird is this fluid and ever-changing form, it allows authors like Miéville to avoid the conventions and clichés that abound in genres like horror. For Miéville himself, it offers "a fiction born out of possibilities, its freeing-up mirroring the freeing-up. The radicalisation in the world" (Venezia 204). Miéville's political engagement is no secret, and his writings offer radical new perspectives in a variety of domains, including gender.[12] Scholz remarks that in his writing Miéville manages to "[level] hierarchies and [counter] stigma and discrimination" associated to gender by creating "integrative, diverse norms, including fac-

---

11. See Stamp: "Horror, more than any other film genre, deals openly with questions of gender, sexuality and the body ... Yes, femininity, female sexuality, and the female body are often presented as 'monstrous.' But that doesn't mean that women aren't interested in watching and thinking about these issues. In many ways horror films bring to the fore issues that are otherwise unspoken in patriarchal culture—which itself constructs female sexuality as monstrous" (quoted in Berlatsky).

12. See for instance Tranter (online article) and Scholz ("Queerversity").

tors such as a fluid gender concept, race, class, dis/ability, religion and spirituality" ("Queerversity"). However, this is not the case in "Säcken," whose anchoring in the real world does not allow for such inventive counter-propositions. The horror is right at home, and the gender models the story offers are steeped in realistic prejudice.

But this is precisely how Miéville manages to instill a powerful message on gender politics, by keeping the horror real and contemporary. In a short text analyzing the concept of the "exceptional zone" in SF/F, he states that "it might now be time for a renewed attention on the quotidian, for stories in which the exception is at best a distraction, if it exists at all, from what goes on in the home worlds, the metropole, right here" ("An A–Z"). Even though the sack monster is hardly something quotidian, it points to the domestic and current problems that women face in reality. This is what anchors "Säcken" in the era of fourth-wave feminism. This wave started around 2010 and is most famously associated with the #MeToo movement, while advocating a greater visibility of all women, including traditionally marginalized groups, and the empowerment of women through the fight against harassment and for bodily autonomy and equal opportunities. The strong part played by technology and social media in the rise of fourth-wave feminism emphasizes the role of any and all women, who get to have a voice if they want to. This is what ties "Säcken" to this movement. Indeed, Mel seems to understand that the law is guilty, but she fails to acknowledge the woman's need for attention. Mel may be the sole focalizer of the story, but it becomes clear that she has no clue what the woman wants, and while she holds on to her central narrative status, the real hero of the story is not Mel, but the woman in the sack.

As early as the third page, Joanna chides Mel for being a spoilt child when the latter criticizes the place for not having been cleaned up: "Honestly, you don't know you're alive" (146)—a moment of proleptic irony but also a comment that could be taken at face value, considering the plight of women around the world. More importantly, a recurring feeling Mel has when she is close to the sack, or facing it, is one of having been noticed: "it pinioned her with its notice" (154), "what Mel thought was that Joanna had been noticed" (160), "Up from the water came scorn and want and notice" (166). Even when the sack finds her in her London flat, Mel thinks, "There is nowhere beyond some attentions" (172). But what if Mel misunderstands that notice? What if what the woman is after, that missing thing that Mel cannot put her finger on, that is neither a re-trial, nor a prayer, nor a sacrificial cat, is actually for people to notice *her*? Not to forget what she has been through? And even when, in her blind rage, in the bottomless pit of her pain, she attacks other women, might it not be for the simple reason of becoming a strong-er presence, a more visible entity, a more universal female voice?

When the sack attacks Mel at the end of the story, it has be-come bigger and has new voices, that of the cat, and that of Joanna that Mel recognizes in the very last line of the story. That is when Mel realizes that "there are lacks that won't be filled" (173). The woman is not seeking reparation, nor will she be appeased, because she will not be silenced again. Her insatiable hunger, nourished by her rage, is described through words like "voracious" (167) and "glutton" (173), a "stomach" that "will have her, and everything" (173), as if it would only stop if it obtained "the end of the law" (167). It becomes the law too, a sort of reversed and twisted law that, instead of undoing what it went through, applies the same sen-tence to the world: "The seams are law's mouths. They open not to let out but to take in. The Säcken opens to feed, to make her poena" (173). In the sack, everything is reduced to the simple expression of pain and rage.

When Mel was still trying to understand the symbolism of the animals, she knew at the same time that her efforts were vain: "in the water all that would dissolve. Everything in the sack would mean itself. A thing that drowns and bites, that drowns and claws, that drowns and bites, that drowns and screams" (167). The repeti-tions and asyndeton emphasize the never-ending character of this pain. Similarly, in the very last apparition of the sack, victims and voices get confused, "as a cat barks and a rooster hisses [. . .] as the leather strains and the poena looms and reaches and a dog tries to speak and a long-dead woman meows like a cat and a snake makes words and the poena opens and rank water pours out and Mel sees through the shadows what is inside at last and screams and screams and still hears a faint last sound" (173). That long polysyndeton, which highlights once again the universality of the sack as well as its voraciousness, ends with that final sound, uttered in Joanna's voice, the German word for "cock-a-doodle-do": "Kikeriki."

The central figure of the story is undeniably the sack, the eponymous character. In the spectrum of classic horror archetypes, the unnamed woman, before and after her death, stands for monster, ghost, witch, killer, and victim. Each of those archetypes is further enriched and given significance by her being female: it is impossible to read "Säcken" without at the very least wondering about gender politics at play in society, in the past and in the present. As Tanya Krzywinska notes, it is significant that "20th-century interest in witchcraft is linked to the growth of feminism and gender politics" (73), and the current renewed interest in folk horror certainly matches a particularly fertile era for feminism.

While the 1960s and 1970s films could be ambiguous in their treatment of witchcraft because of the frequent demise of witches—something that Leon Hunt and Tanya Krzywinska analyze as a means of restoring the masculine order of patriarchy—there is a more blatant embrace of female power in today's visions of women in folk horror, as shown by Eggers's *The Witch* or the TV series *American Horror Story*. That newly acknowledged power is steeped in acts of violence because it seems to be the only way for a truly female power to emerge and to be heard by all. By using a millennia-old piece of history, Miéville binds together the plight of women through time and space and gives those women the chance to emerge from silence, just like the sack emerges from the depths of the lake to take on the world.

Works Cited

"An A–Z of China Miéville." 26 Jan. 2012, www.panmacmillan. com/blogs/science-fiction-and-fantasy/an-a-z-of-china-mieville. Accessed 31 March 2021.

Barton, Simon. "The New Weird and Contemporary Genre Fiction: New Approaches to Language and Futures in the 21st Century." Unpublished paper.

Bell, David. "Anti-Idyll: Rural Horror." In Paul Cloke and Jo Little, ed. *Contested Countryside Cultures.* London: Routledge, 1997. 91–104.

Berlatsky, Noah. "Carrie at 40: Why the Horror Genre Remains Important for Women." *Guardian,* 3 November 2016, www. theguardian.com/film/2016/nov/03/carrie-stephen-king-brian-de-palma-horror-films-feminism. Accessed 3 May 2021.

Briefel, Aviva. "Monster Pains." *Film Quarterly* 58, No. 3 (Spring 2005): 16–27.

Cicero, M. Tullius. *Cicero Pro Sexto Roscio Amerino.* Tr. T. J. Arnold. London: James Cornish & Sons, 1885.

Clover, Carol. *Men, Woman, and Chainsaws.* Princeton: Princeton University Press, 2015.

Creed, Barbara. *The Monstrous-Feminine.* Abingdon, UK: Routledge, 1993.

Grimm, Jacob. *Deutsche Rechtsalterthümer.* Göttingen: Dieterich, 1854.

Groves, Matilda. "Past Anxieties: Defining the Folk Horror Narrative." *Folklore Thursday,* 20 April 2017, folklorethursday.com/urban-folklore/past-anxieties-defining-folk-horror-narrative/#sthash. OfhQdCYL.dpbs. Accessed 9 May 2021.

Harmes, Marcus K. "The Seventeenth Century on Film: Patriarchy, Magistracy, and Witchcraft in British Horror Films, 1968–1971." *Canadian Journal of Film Studies* 22, No. 2 (2013): 64–80.

Holloway, Julian. "Spiritual Embodiment and Sacred Rural Landscapes." In Paul Cloke, ed. *Country Visions.* Harlow, UK: Pearson, 2003. 158–75.

Hunt, Leon. "Necromancy in the UK: Witchcraft and the Occult in British Horror." In Steve Chibnall and Julian Petley, ed. *British Horror Cinema*. London: Routledge, 2011. 82–98.

Hutton, Ronald. *The Triumph of the Moon*. Oxford: Oxford University Press, 1999.

Keetley, Dawn. "The Resurgence of Folk Horror." *Horror Homeroom*, 6 November 2015, www.horrorhomeroom.com/the-resurgence-of-folk-horror/. Accessed 11 May 2021.

Krzywinska, Tanya. *A Skin for Dancing In*. Trowbridge, UK: Flicks Books, 2000.

McCalmont, Jonathan. "Nothing Beside Remains: A History of the New Weird." *Big Echo*, www.bigecho.org/nothing-beside-remains. Accessed 31 March 2021.

Meumann, Markus. *Findelkinder, Waisenhäuser, Kindsmord in der Frühen Neuzeit*. Munich: Oldenbourg, 1995.

Miéville, China. "Säcken." In Miéville's *Three Moments of an Explosion*. London: Macmillan, 2015. 144–73.

Morgan, Cheryl. "Observation Deck—Interview with China Miéville." *Aural Delights* No. 133 (5 May 2010), www.starshipsofa.com/blog/2010/05/05/aural-delights-no-133-arthur-c-clarke-award-special-2/. Accessed 5 April 2021.

Paciorek, Andy. "Folk Horror: From the Forests, Fields and Furrows: An Introduction." In Andy Paciorek et al., ed. *Folk Horror Revival: Field Studies—Essays and Interviews—Various Authors*. Durham, UK: Wyrd Harvest Press, 2018.

Radin, Max. "The Lex Pompeia and the Poena Cullei." *Journal of Roman Studies* 10 (1920): 119–30.

Schmeink, Lars. "On the Look-out for a New Urban Uncanny." *Extrapolation* 55, No. 1 (2014): 25–32.

Scholz, Phoenix. "Queerversity: Desire and Sexuality in China Miéville's Fiction." *Alluvium*, 30 October 2015, www.alluvium-journal.org/2015/10/30/queerversity-desire-and-sexuality-in-china-mievilles-fiction/. Accessed 12 May 2021.

Scholz, Phoenix. "Three Moments of an Explosion by China Miéville." *Strange Horizons,* 26 October 2015, strangehorizons. com/non-fiction/reviews/three-moments-of-an-explosion-by-china-mieville/. Accessed 5 May 2021.

Thomas, Yan. "Parricidium." *Mélanges de l'Ecole Française de Rome. Antiquité* 93, No. 2 (1981): 643–715.

Totaro, Donato. "The Final Girl: A Few Thoughts on Feminism and Horror." *Off Screen* 6, No. 1 (January 2002), offscreen.com/view/ feminism_and_horror. Accessed 3 May 2021.

Tranter, Kirsten. "Refiguring Fiction." *Overland* (Spring 2011), overland.org.au/previous-issues/issue-204/feature-kirsten-tranter/. Accessed 12 May 2021.

Venezia, Tony. "China Miéville and the Limits of Psychogeography." In Bianca Leggett and Tony Venezia, ed. *Twenty-First Century British Fiction.* Canterbury, UK: Gylphi, 2015. 197–217.

Notes on Contributors

Manuel Arenas is a writer of verse and prose in the Gothic horror tradition. His work has appeared in *Spectral Realms* and *Penumbra* as well as in various genre anthologies, including (most recently) *Knock Knock: Wyrd Folks and Wives' Tales* from Frisson Comics. He currently resides in Phoenix, Arizona.

Garrett Boatman is the author of *Stage Fright*, originally published by Onyx (1988), reissued by Valancourt Books (2020) as Paperback from Hell #11, and *Floaters: A Victorian Zombie Adventure* (Crystal Lake Publishing, 2021). His story "Rain" appeared in the *Valancourt Book of Horror Stories, Volume Four*. His nonfiction retrospective of 1980s horror appeared in *Little Demon Digest*. Garrett is an active member of the Horror Writers Association and the Science Fiction Writers of America.

Silke Brandt, born in 1967 in Germany, studied Anglistics, Art History, and Political Sciences. Silke relocated to Finland in 2008. She has worked in marketing and cultural management, as a film festival director, journalist, and professional deckhand on Dutch sailing ships. She has had essays and short stories published by traditional genre presses and literary magazines, as well as by Faber & Faber. She is the editor of the speculative magazine *Alraune* and of horror anthologies.

Deborah Bridle Deborah Bridle has a PhD in English and teaches at Université Côte d'Azur, France. Her research focuses on fantastic literature, specifically on short fiction and the subgenres of the weird and supernatural horror. She is interested in the expression of philosophical views such as pessimism and nihilism in horror and weird fiction, and in the representations of mysticism and esotericism in Decadent fantastic literature. Her latest publications are devoted to Thomas Ligotti, China Miéville, and Arthur Machen.

Harley Carnell lives and writes in London. Although he enjoys a wide array of literature, he has long been a devotee of speculative/weird fiction, deriving particular influence from H. P. Lovecraft, Thomas Ligotti, and fellow British author Ramsey Campbell. His work has been published in *Riptide Journal*, *Confrontation*, and *Litro*, among other venues. He has an M.A. in Creative Writing from Royal Holloway, University of London.

G. O. Clark's writing has been published in *Asimov's*, *Analog*, *Space & Time*, *Midnight under the Big Top*, *Daily SF*, *HWA Poetry Showcase VII*, *Speculatief (BE)*, and many other publications over the last thirty years. He is the author of fifteen poetry collections, the most recent being *Easy Travel to the Stars* (2020). His third fiction collection, *Aliens and Others*, came out in 2021. He won the *Asimov's* Readers Award for poetry in 2001 and was Stoker Award Poetry finalist in 2011. He is retired and lives in Davis, California.

Frank Coffman is a retired professor of English and Creative Writing. He has published speculative poetry and fiction in a variety of magazines, anthologies, and collections. His three poetry collections are: *The Coven's Hornbook and Other Poems* (2019), *Black Flames and Gleaming Shadows* (2020), and *Eclipse of the Moon* (2021). His first fiction collection, *Three against the Dark: Collected Dr. Venn Occult Detective Mysteries*, was published in March 2022.

Scott J. Couturier is a Rhysling Award–nominated poet and prose writer of the weird, liminal, and darkly fantastic. His work has appeared in numerous venues, including *The Audient Void*, *Spectral Realms*, *Tales from the Magician's Skull*, *Cosmic Horror Monthly*, and *Weirdbook*. His first collection of weird fiction, *The Box*, is available from Hybrid Sequence Media; his collection of autumnal & folk horror verse, *I Awaken in October*, is forthcoming in the fall of 2022 from Jackanapes Press.

Melissa Ridley Elmes is a Virginia native living in Missouri in an apartment that delightfully approximates a hobbit hole. Her poetry and fiction have appeared in *Star*Line, Eye to the Telescope, In Parentheses, Gyroscope, Thimble, HeartWood,* and various other print and web venues, and her first collection of poems, *Arthurian Things,* was published by Dark Myth Publications in 2020.

Wade German is the author of the poetry collections *Psalms and Sorceries* and *Dreams from a Black Nebula* (both from Hippocampus Press), *The Ladies of the Everlasting Lichen and Other Relics* (Mount Abraxas Press), the verse drama *Children of Hypnos,* and three slim volumes of verse in Portuguese translation, *Incantations, Apparitions,* and *Phantasmagorias* (Raphus Press).

James Goho is a writer and researcher who lives in Winnipeg, Canada. His most recent short story, "Calls from Home," appeared in the literary magazine *Fiction* #64. His newest book, *Caitlín R. Kiernan: A Critical Study of Her Dark Fiction,* was published by McFarland in 2020.

César Guarde-Paz has worked as a Lecturer in Spanish Literature and Language at Nankai University (Tianjin), and as Associate Professor of European Studies at Sun Yat-sen University (Zhuhai). His research interests include comparative philosophy and literature, German philosophy, and the interactions between philosophy and *fin-de-siècle* horror. His research has been published in *Nietzsche Studien, Asia Major, Philosophy East and West,* and *Lovecraft Annual,* among others.

David Haden is a former lecturer at the School of Theoretical and Historical Studies, Birmingham, UK. He is the editor of the monthly magazines *Digital Art Live* and *VisNews.* He blogs at *Tentaclii* (jurn.link/tentaclii/) on H. P. Lovecraft's life, and curates the open-access search-engine JURN (jurn.link/). Recent books have been on Lovecraft, the *Gawain* poet, and the early H. G. Wells. He is completing a 100,000-word book on Tolkien and the Old English word *earendel*.

Cecelia Hopkins-Drewer lives in Adelaide, South Australia. She has written a Masters paper on H. P. Lovecraft and a dissertation on "Fairy Tale Motifs" in novels. Short stories and poetry have been published in anthologies, including the "Dark Drabbles" series (Black Hare Press), the "Scary Snippets" series (Nocturnal Sirens), and *Festival of Fear* by Black Ink Fiction. Literary criticism has been published in journals, including *Penumbra* and *Lovecraft Annual*.

S. T. Joshi is a widely published literary and cultural critic and the author of *The Weird Tale* (1990), *I Am Providence: The Life and Times of H. P. Lovecraft* (2010), *Unutterable Horror: A History of Supernatural Fiction* (2012), and many other volumes. He has edited the work of H. P. Lovecraft, Ambrose Bierce, Lord Dunsany, H. L. Mencken, Leslie Stephen, and other writers.

Katherine Kerestman is the author of *Creepy Cat's Macabre Travels* (WordCrafts Press, 2020), a nonfiction travel memoir to destinations associated with macabre stories in history, literature, and film, as well as numerous horrific short stories and nonfiction articles in anthologies and journals. She is a member of the Jane Austen Society of North America, Mensa, the Horror Writers Association, the H. P. Lovecraft Historical Society, and the Dracula Society. She is wild about *Dark Shadows* and *Twin Peaks* and is known to frolic in the graveyards of Salem on Halloween.

Kurt Newton's poetry has appeared in numerous magazines and anthologies. He is the author of eight collections of poetry. His ninth collection, *Songs of the Underland and Other Macabre Machinations*, was recently published by Ravens Quoth Press.

Ngo Binh Anh Khoa is a teacher of English in Ho Chi Minh City, Vietnam. In his free time he enjoys daydreaming, reading, and occasionally writing poetry for personal entertainment. His speculative poems have appeared in NewMyths.com, *Heroic Fantasy Quarterly*, *The Audient Void*, and other venues.

Carl E. Reed is employed as the showroom manager for a window, siding, and door company just outside Chicago. Former jobs include U.S. marine, long-haul trucker, improvisational actor, cab driver, security guard, bus driver, door-to-door encyclopedia salesman, construction worker, and art show MC. His poetry has been published in the *Iconoclast* and *Spectral Realms;* short stories in *Black Gate* and *newWitch* magazines.

Geoffrey Reiter is Associate Professor and Coordinator of Literature at Lancaster Bible College. He is also an Associate Editor at the website *Christ and Pop Culture*, where he frequently writes about weird horror and dark fantasy. As a scholar of weird fiction, Reiter has published academic articles on such authors as Arthur Machen, Bram Stoker, Clark Ashton Smith, and William Peter Blatty. His poetry and fiction have previously appeared in *Spectral Realms*, *Star*Line*, *Penumbra*, *ParABnormal*, and *The Mythic Circle*.

Ann K. Schwader lives and writes in Colorado. Her newest collection, *Unquiet Stars*, was published by Weird House Press in 2021. Two of her earlier collections, *Wild Hunt of the Stars* (Sam's Dot, 2010) and *Dark Energies* (P'rea Press, 2015), were Bram Stoker Award finalists. In 2018 she received the Science Fiction & Fantasy Poetry Association's Grand Master award. She is also a two-time Rhysling Award winner.

A career-retrospective of **Darrell Schweitzer**'s short fiction was published by PS Publishing in two volumes in 2020. A veritable flood of Schweitzeriana is soon to follow from various publishers in the next year or so, including a new Lovecraftian anthology, *Shadows out of Time* (PS Publishing), *The Best of Weird Tales: The 1920s* (Centipede Press), *The Best of Weird Tales: 1924* (with John Betancourt, Wildside

Press), a weird poetry collection, *Dancing Before Azathoth* (P'rea Press), a new story collection, *The Children of Chorazin* (Hippocampus Press), and two further volumes of author interviews (Wildside Press). He was co-editor of *Weird Tales* between 1988 and 2007.

John C. Tibbetts is Professor Emeritus at the University of Kansas in Film and Media Studies. His books include *The Furies of Marjorie Bowen* (McFarland, 2019), *The Gothic Worlds of Peter Straub* (McFarland, 2016), *Those Who Made It: Conversations with the Legends of Hollywood* (Palgrave Macmillan, 2015), *Peter Weir: Interviews* (University of Mississippi Press, 2014), and *The Gothic Imagination* (Palgrave Macmillan, 2012). John has researched, written, produced, and narrated two radio series, *The World of Robert Schumann* (broadcast worldwide on the WFMT Radio Network) and *Piano Portraits* (broadcast on Kansas Public Radio). He was awarded in 2008 the Kansas Governor's Arts in Education Award, presented by Governor Kathleen Sebelius.

Stephen Woodworth is the author of the Violet Series of paranormal thrillers, including the *New York Times* bestsellers *Through Violet Eyes* and *With Red Hands,* as well as the Gothic horror novel *Fraulein Frankenstein.* His work has also appeared in such publications as *Fantasy & Science Fiction,* the *Black Wings* series of Lovecraftian fiction anthologies, and *Year's Best Fantasy.* His collection of horror short fiction, *A Carnival of Chimeras,* is available from Hippocampus Press.

Barry Yedvobnick retired from Emory University as Emeritus Professor of Biology in 2019. He writes mostly science fiction and horror flash fiction, and his stories have appeared in *Tales to Terrify, Flash Fiction Magazine, Brilliant Flash Fiction, Kzine, Night to Dawn, Every Day Fiction, East of the Web, Altered Reality Magazine,* and several other sites.

www.ingramcontent.com/pod-product-compliance
Lightning Source LLC
Chambersburg PA
CBHW060949030726
47503CB00003B/797